NEVER DATE YOUR ENEMY

NEVER DATE YOUR ENEMY

USA TODAY BESTSELLING AUTHOR

JULES BARNARD

Chapter One

Hayden

That *shit*. He got the promotion?

I read the email again, leaning closer to the screen. Adam Cade has been at Blue Casino for only nine months, hired as an assistant to the hospitality manager. And now he's replacing her?

I take deep breaths, my face heating to bursting. Hiring Adam to run hospitality will enlarge his pretty-boy inflated ego to mass proportions. He was overqualified when he came on board as an assistant, but still. I sink my forehead to the desk and thump it a couple of times, puffs of breath fanning across the smooth surface. This means Adam and I are at the same level. *Expected to work together...*

A knock sounds at the door, and I quickly look up. What are the chances it's Adam?

Given his knack for infuriating me? High.

I shove my keyboard away and stand, gazing at the distant view outside my window. Lake Tahoe's mountains,

1

the deep blue water, they're what I turn to when things fall apart. And until recently, I had left it all behind.

Adam's promotion is just one small annoyance on top of the heap of crap I've encountered after returning to Lake Tahoe to work at Blue Casino. This new stuff I've run into is worse than what made me flee in the middle of the night with my family eleven years ago, because it affects more than just a few people.

I square my shoulders and take a deep breath. "Come in," I say, and look toward the door.

I'm a professional. I can handle this...

The snick of the doorknob sounds, followed by the swish of heavy wood gliding over piled carpet. An Armani-clad, gorgeous man stands in the doorway. My breathing grows shallow and my stomach flutters, like they always do when he enters a room, dammit.

Adam's mouth twitches, his intelligent blue gaze taking in my face, the set of my shoulders. I'm pretty sure he's aware of the physical effect he has on me, but I'll never admit to it.

Another employee walks past my door, stops, and shakes Adam's hand. "Congrats, man. About time. Now you're *in*."

At Blue Casino, being *in* means having knowledge of and access to the casino's illegal activities, and there's a good chance Adam is a part of that now. Even with his qualifications, no one rises this quickly unless they've got an inside connection.

Adam dips his chin in a friendly nod. "Thank you," he says, and the man continues on. Adam closes the door, sealing us inside. His gaze returns to me.

Adam Cade is exactly the kind of snobby, rich guy I despise. He's been given every luxury in life—wealth, the right connections—whereas I've busted my ass academically and professionally and earned everything. "No need to gloat." I turn back toward the window, hoping the view will make this encounter less painful. "I read the email."

I should have been informed of Adam's promotion *before* it was announced; I manage the human resources department. Adam was on my short list, but I'd been working day and night to recruit someone else, certain I could find a person more qualified. The fact that the CEO hired Adam behind my back proves the CEO is once again putting me in my place and keeping me out of the loop.

I look over my shoulder when he doesn't comment right away.

Adam's sexy mouth is slanted in a mock pout. "No congratulations, Hayden?" His large, masculine hand—rougher looking than it should appear, given his rich-boy upbringing—presses the space above his heart. "I'm wounded. I truly am."

I snort and stare back at the lake. It doesn't surprise me that Adam is in with the CEO. Joseph Blackwell, head of Blue Casino, hadn't *wanted* to hire me. His hands were tied after a member of his team was caught in an attempted rape of another employee. Blackwell plucked me from the pile of applicants to replace the fired HR director and keep up appearances. Hiring another female in management was good PR in light of the scandal.

Overeager to climb to the top and prove myself, I only realized his reason for hiring me *after* I'd taken the position.

I returned to Lake Tahoe to prove to myself that I am not weak. There is no way I'm running from Blue Casino and the shifty way the CEO runs things. Those in power at Blue have harmed employees in the past, and I strongly believe they're still doing it, though I have no concrete proof.

I sense Adam approach, and my skin heats beneath the fitted blouse I'm wearing.

"How should we celebrate?" His deep, rumbly voice is near my ear, forcing me to step to the side. He's too close. The scent of fine thread and light aftershave fills my senses, and it bothers me. I hate that I'm physically attracted to such a jerk. "I'll even let you buy me a drink and some hot wings."

I shake my head and glare at the side of his chiseled prep-school profile. There are so many things wrong with that statement, I don't know where to begin. I start with the most obvious. "Hot wings?"

His blue eyes capture mine, and my mouth tenses in counterpoint to the hitching going on in my stomach. When he looks at me—*really looks*—I forget who I am. "They're my favorite," he says innocently.

Adam isn't a man you can stare at for too long without ovulating, but the humor behind his eyes obliterates my hormone haze. When he jokes or snarks his way through a conversation, I'm reminded of the man he truly is. He's the type of entitled ass who wouldn't think twice about throwing someone under the bus. I should know.

"I didn't picture you for a hot wings kind of guy," I tell him.

Hot wings guys are men's men who like football on Sunday and girls in bikinis, not Armani-clad up-and-comers with connections to the wealthiest people in town.

I glance out of the corner of my eye. His perpetual smirk has fallen, the look that replaced it unguarded—something I've never seen on him before. For a moment, my mind races. Did I hurt his feelings?

And why would that bother me? I owe him nothing.

He peers over seductively, and I want to slap myself for questioning whether I hit a nerve. "Don't judge a book by its cover, Hayden. That's what you do, isn't it?" His gaze flickers to the textbooks, business journals, and myriad other tomes on bookshelves covering two-thirds of the wall space in my office.

The books and even my red abstract painting of a woman's silhouette as she clutches her torso clash glaringly with the Blue décor. I bought the painting the week I graduated from the MBA program. Everything I've filled my office with reminds me of my education and how far I've come. Just because I relied on books to get me where I am, it doesn't mean I'm incapable of seeing people for who they are.

Adam is exactly who I believe him to be—an entitled, pretty little rich boy. Very pretty, to be exact, in his taupe suit that stretches over broad shoulders. Being susceptible to the pretty things in life is my one major flaw. The Louboutins on my feet, this beautiful setting I call home—and even Adam.

Just like in high school when I trusted another handsome face, I find myself slipping down a well without a rope, scraping the sides in my designer shoes and the backbone I've earned. I thought Blue Casino was the fresh start I'd built for myself. I'm no longer sure of that. But I'm not wrong about Adam.

"I'm busy tonight." Adam drives me nuts, but my unwanted attraction to him isn't his fault. He was born beautiful; every woman is susceptible to his presence. It's not fair to take out *that* particular frustration on him. "Congratulations, though. On the promotion. Quite a coup.

Blackwell took a liking to you from the start. Next thing you know, he'll be grooming you for his Blue Stars."

I watch for signs of nervousness, but Adam's chiseled jaw doesn't flinch. Nothing shows except the light smile that replaced the flash of vulnerability I thought I'd caught.

Well, that's that. He must expect to become one of the Blue Stars, or he would have said otherwise when I suggested our CEO wanted to make him one.

The Blue Stars are a group of men who strut around Blue Casino with sapphire signet rings they've obtained for outstanding performance or—according to rumor—for being complete dicks and running a prostitution and drug outfit inside the casino.

Someone needs to stand up for the victims inside this place. As far as I can tell, no one is. I'm going to find out what's going on, despite the CEO's determination to keep me out of anything of importance, and take the information to the police. If I can turn this place around and make Blue the dream job I hoped it would be, that's all I could ever ask.

I turn toward my desk to get back to work, but Adam's large hand wraps around my upper arm, sending a frisson of awareness through me. My gaze slides over his broad chest, past his beautiful mouth and straight nose, and up to his eyes that give me mixed messages.

His gaze falters and his fingers release their light hold on me. "I may not have earned it, but I am qualified, Hayden."

There it is again, that spark of vulnerability—this time I hear it in his voice. And then it's gone.

He turns and swaggers toward the door. "Feel free to join us at Farley's after work. Hot wings are on me."

I stare as he leaves because I can't stop myself from

checking him out, especially when he can't see me doing it. "Don't count on it."

Why, after all these months, am I wondering if I've misjudged Adam? I don't need doubt affecting my decisions. Not when calling out the casino is the right thing to do. Blackwell and the men he has lapping at his heels are guilty of a whole slew of crimes—I just need to find hard evidence; rumors aren't enough. But Adam? I don't want to question Adam's guilt. This is about justice. For the women who work at Blue Casino and God knows who else the CEO and his Blue Stars have manipulated and hurt over the years.

And if Adam Cade is involved...I'll take him down too.

Adam

"Mr. Cade, let me get that for you." James, the valet, holds the driver's side door for me as I exit my Jaguar XKR—an MBA graduation gift a couple of years ago from my father.

I toss James the keys and enter Club Tahoe through the back door, striding down dark hardwood floors and plush area rugs, past a vase with red flowers on a polished stone table. Even in the business offices, Club Tahoe is a thing of beauty.

Esther, my father's sixty-five-year-old secretary, glimpses my approach from her desk near his office, and grins. She's wearing a light gray skirt suit, the ruffle of an amethyst blouse peeking above the lapels of the jacket. The combination accentuates her silver hair and presents a sophisticated older woman. Esther is as much a fixture at

Club Tahoe as the ten-foot glass-and-wrought-iron chandelier over the entrance.

"Adam." She stands and engulfs me in a warm hug.

What few know is that along with being put together and elegant, Esther is like a second mother to my brothers and me. Or a first mother, given our own died when I was a child and my youngest brother an infant.

My mother chose to give birth to Hunter rather than fight the breast cancer doctors discovered during her second trimester. I sometimes wonder if she would have made the decision to hold off treatment until after his birth if she'd known how Hunter would turn out. Hunter is one of my favorite brothers, but he is also an unrepentant hedonist.

"How's the old man's temper today?"

Esther returns to the desk I'm certain still houses the first-aid kit she used to patch up my brothers and me when we were kids. We went to Esther for comfort because our nanny was a royal bitch. "Mild. His masseuse paid him a visit an hour ago. It was good timing after his investors' meeting."

It never matters how well Club Tahoe performs, or that it is world-renowned, Father is never satisfied, his investors equally greedy. They want more. More publicity. More wealthy patrons, though the price for a standard room exceeds the cost of a cross-country plane ticket. Whatever my father has, it is never enough. Which is why my brothers and I stopped trying to impress him long ago. School and sports accolades meant nothing compared to the resort our father built.

After our mother died, Ethan Cade checked out emotionally. Oh, he made sure we were taken care of, but he paid people to deal with those details. He provided for us financially, but even that came at a price. I am the only Cade still willing to pay it.

I have standards, and I like the lifestyle the family money affords. So I play our father's game, and I live in luxury, while my four brothers flounder in a world of their own making.

I'm envious as hell of them.

After rapping twice on the rustic mahogany double door, I wait for my father's voice. His deep baritone calls out for me to enter, and I do, with all the Cade assurance born to me. If there's one thing I've learned as Ethan Cade's son, it's never to appear weak, never to doubt myself.

I stride into the room and take a seat across from the patriarch, who studies me raptly, searching for a crack in the exterior. He won't find it. He trained me well.

"Adam, what brings you in today?" He tosses a fountain pen on the desk. His gaze appears distracted. "I'm assuming all goes well at Blue Casino?"

"Better than well." I try to hold back my satisfaction. What I have to say won't impress him. I'm not sure why I drove here to share it when a phone call would have sufficed. The fact that I did proves I still desire to please him, which will likely result in the opposite effect. But I wanted to see his expression. To see if, for once, I've done something that makes him proud, even if it is never verbalized.

I tug at my slacks and cross my ankle over my knee, attempting to keep things cool. "I've been promoted to manager at Blue. Effective immediately."

My father's stony expression doesn't crack. When he fails to respond, I uncross my legs—and wish I hadn't. Wish I'd stayed the fuck still.

"This is a surprise."

I feign nonchalance. "Not really. I graduated at the top of my class from Cornell, if you recall." Which he probably does *not*. "The CEO has been generous from the start." A fact even Hayden noticed, and one that seemed to bother her. She's not the petty sort. I'm not sure what that was about. "I was overqualified for the position you *encouraged* me to take," I remind him. "The promotion is a no-brainer."

My father drops his gaze. He lets out a heavy sigh and spins his full-grain leather chair to the window and the infinity pool beyond, where pine trees dot the landscape for a natural appearance. The deep blue of the lake and its sandy shore lie just past the pool. "You've always been loyal. I never realized how that might have held you back."

For a moment, I'm struck mute.

My father doesn't back down, let alone admit wrongdoing. His entire world revolves around Club Tahoe. I would have bet my life he wanted my world to revolve around it too. In fact, he stated as much when he insisted I work at Blue Casino to broaden my experience before returning to Club Tahoe full-time.

Is this some sort of trick? Is he testing my loyalty? "I've enjoyed the work I've done at the club."

He doesn't look away from the view. "Yes. Your brothers never did."

Was that longing in his voice? *What the hell?*

It's not like my father hates my brothers, but he hasn't spoken to some of them in years. They never did what he wanted, and their presence tended to make his blood pressure rise and his face turn a mottled burnt red.

I strain my neck and look around, expecting someone to jump out and yell, "Gotcha."

When I turn back, my father's eyes are forlorn. I have the strangest urge to soothe him, which has never happened in my entire life. Ethan Cade isn't soft. He doesn't need comfort. He's a damn self-possessed man. What's gotten into him?

"My brothers took umbrage at your shoving the company down their throats," I remind him.

There. That's more like our typical conversations.

He looks me dead in the face. "That was my mistake. I should never have pushed so hard. Should have given you and your brothers more freedom to pursue other careers."

Who is this man? To hear my father even suggest he'd be open to us working anywhere other than Club Tahoe sounds foreign. And why is he saying it now? "Dad: Levi, Wes, Bran, and even Hunt—they've made lives for themselves, regardless of the past. You don't need to...to worry."

He nods tightly. "You think they'll visit?"

I chuckle without humor. "Since when did you want us to visit? Work here, sure, but—"

He looks at the family photo of the six of us taken a year after my mother's death. In the picture, my father is standing behind us near the front gates of Club Tahoe. My brothers and I are wearing identical blue polo shirts and slacks we weren't permitted to so much as touch with our fingers, let alone get dirty. What's not revealed in the picture is that my brothers and I waited for over an hour for our father to show up. He'd been too busy with work to make the shoot on time. Which left four boys and an eighteen-month-old restless and confused.

"I've not been there for you," he says, shocking me further. "I shouldn't have put Club Tahoe first. I plan to change that."

Something is wrong here, or this is a setup. He's lost his damn mind. I'm twenty-seven; my brothers range in age from twenty-two to twenty-nine. We're adults. Even if this weren't a joke, it's a little late. "Look, Dad. I don't know where this is coming from or what you have planned, but don't push the others. They're happy."

I nearly wince at the intensity behind the gaze my father sends me. "Are they?"

"Happy?" I ask, just to be sure I'm following. Because this entire conversation is surreal.

He nods.

I'd like to say, yes, of course they're happy, but the truth is, I don't know. Sometimes I suspect my brothers are as lost as I am.

I sit forward. "They're grown men. They make their own choices."

He studies me for a long moment before his gaze flickers away. "Congratulations. On the promotion. You like it there?" He looks over at this last question as if my answer is important, when my happiness has never been important to him. In my entire life, my father has never asked what I wanted.

"I enjoy the work." Better to agree and get this uncomfortable conversation over with, but as soon as the words leave my mouth, I realize they're true. Working at Blue has felt right from the beginning. Or at least, from the moment I set eyes on Hayden Tate.

Hayden is...different. She doesn't cower. For some twisted reason, I like that. She's refreshing in a lifestyle that grows stale. Or maybe it's the way her curvy hips swish back and forth after I've pissed her off and she's storming away from me—I haven't decided. Either way, she's made Blue bearable, and now I've been promoted. It can only get better from here.

From what I've heard, management bonuses, coupled with the increased income I'll be receiving, will keep me in comfort. I won't need my father's money to stay flush. And I'd give anything to prove to my brothers that I can make it on my own.

I lost my brothers' respect when I started cashing in on the trust fund payments our father dangled while they walked away to live their own lives. My brothers have my back, but they've never understood why I put up with our father's crap.

I thought the job my father ordered me to take at Blue Casino was to ensure he still had me as his lackey, just more experienced. Some part of me still believes it. But if his words are true, and he's open to me working somewhere else, I'd just as soon never work at Club Tahoe again. I'd like to become my own man, the way my brothers have. Which means I can't screw up the opportunity Blue has given me.

I stand and reach across the desk, shaking my father's hand with a firm grip, the way he taught me to when I was four years old. "I'd better get back. I'm meeting with friends to celebrate."

"Don't be a stranger, Adam." He squeezes my palm, the look in his eyes sincere.

"No," I stammer. "Of course not." But I have no idea what he's talking about. My brothers and I are all strangers to him. It just so happens I'm a closer stranger than the rest of them.

I exit his office and stop in the reception area, staring blindly at the opposite wall. Whatever is going on with him, it can't be important, or I'd have heard about it in the local news. He'll be back to his overbearing, ornery self in no time.

"Everything all right?" Esther is sitting at her desk, her eyebrows pinched in concern.

"Fine." I grin and pull a butterscotch candy from my

pocket, placing it in front of her. My brothers and I used to leave Esther her favorite candy whenever we visited. Now, I'm the only one who sets foot in this place.

I walk toward the exit, and Esther's soft voice drifts toward me. "He's proud of you, you know."

My back stiffens and I freeze, a prickle of unease floating across my neck. The atmosphere in here is off. I'm not used to heart-to-hearts with my father. Or with Esther, as kind as she's been over the years.

I thought I wanted my father's pride in me. Now that I have it, I'm too disturbed by his behavior to feel anything but confusion.

I offer a confident smile that I don't feel over my shoulder, and exit Club Tahoe.

Chapter Two

Hayden

The receptionist informs Blackwell that I'm here and receives verbal approval for me to enter, but my boss is an all-around scary man, and he's never liked me.

I hesitate at the door, pray he's in a good mood, then step inside. "Do you have a moment?"

He doesn't look up from his computer. "Make it quick. I'm expecting a call."

I close the door behind me and put on my best game face. "I wanted to talk to you about the hospitality manager position."

"It's been filled," he says, clicking through a document on the screen.

"Yes...that's why I'm here. You asked me to hire someone."

Blackwell looks over, his beady brown eyes even smaller behind the wire-rimmed glasses he wears. "And? Do you have a problem with the person I selected?" His curt voice indicates I had better not have a problem. "Mary!" he calls.

His receptionist scrambles in, and he hands her a file. "Deliver this. You know where. Do it now."

Scary. Ass. Boss.

"No, of course there's no problem," I say once his receptionist has left. "I just thought you'd want to consult with me about the candidates I've been interviewing before you made a decision. And announced it to the entire company."

"Ahh." He shifts so that he's fully facing me. I have the urge to step back, but I don't. "Is that the issue? That I didn't ask for your opinion, Hayden?"

He hasn't invited me to sit, so I stand near the door in my designer heels that give me a sense of confidence. Because I earned them through hard work, just like I earned the degrees that got me a job in a luxury casino like Blue. "I'm concerned about how the team perceives my position," I say. "I worry that perhaps your disregard for the work I've done to fill the executive slot gives more ammunition to managers who have the wrong impression about my role here."

"And what impression would that be?" His smile is menacingly saccharine.

I inadvertently step back. "That I am a figurehead for HR."

Did I say that out loud?

"And here I thought we didn't understand each other." The receptionist comes over the intercom, telling him he has a call. He picks up the receiver on his desk. "Now, if you'll excuse me?" He presses the red light that's flashing. "Ed, thank you for waiting." He turns away in his chair, effectively shutting me out.

Blackwell *wants* people to believe I'm a figurehead? It's what I suspected, but I still thought he chose me because I'm capable. What is the point of my being here?

Right, for PR purposes. If Blue gets rid of me and hires someone else, it won't look good. Blackwell couldn't care less if I do my job, so long as I stay out of his way.

I reach for the door, and he calls my name. I slowly turn, my gaze unwavering. "Adam will be hiring several employees for a new venture." His hand is over the base of the receiver, preventing whomever he's talking to from hearing. "Stay out of his way and don't question whom he hires. If you don't, you won't like the consequences. Do you understand?"

Oh my God. What did I get myself into when I took this job? I knew things were bad once I figured out Blue's history of harassment, but it's getting worse.

"Yes." I exit his office before I throw up, nearly running into Eve in my rush out. Eve is one of two women I suspect brown-nose Blackwell so often she could diagram his colon.

"Pardon me, Hayden." She shifts the files in her arms and overtly lowers her knit blouse. Blackwell glances at the open door with the phone to his ear. He waves Eve inside, and she gives me an insincere grin that barely flexes her lips, as she shimmies past me.

I walk down the hall, disgusted, and so damned angry at myself for not asking around before I jumped at the position at Blue. Unlike Adam, *I* was underqualified. Or at least, a borderline fit for the human resources director. I had the degrees, but not the length of experience when Blue hired me. The applicant list for my job had to have been long. I'd thought they'd seen something special in me...

The only thing they saw was an easy target.

* * *

Adam

I ENTER Farley's and spot two guys I work with. I wouldn't call Paul and William *friends,* but they're close work associates. We catch up in the break room, and they've made certain I'm comped the few times I've entered Blue's nightclub.

Paul and William roll around Blue Casino like celebrities, and I can't say I mind it. As a Cade, I'm accustomed to deference in Lake Tahoe.

"Congrats, man." Paul grips my palm with a firm hand pump, his brown eyes sparkling. I watch as he gestures to the bartender and points to the Gran Patrón Platinum. Farley's is a hole in the wall, but they keep the good stuff around for execs who drop by after work, looking to blow off steam.

The bartender places three shots in front of us, and Paul holds up his. "To the new venture."

I pick up a glass and flick my wrist back, downing the clear liquid. The top-shelf tequila is about as smooth as it gets.

I slide the empty glass to the bartender, and it's bussed and quickly replaced with a bottle of Corona. Almost as if Paul or William requested it beforehand. Farley's is good, but they're not *that* good.

I raise my eyebrow and glance at the guys. "I get that we're celebrating, but what else is this get-together about? Does it have anything to do with the venture you've been working on but won't discuss? Blackwell didn't go into specifics this afternoon, but he mentioned that hospitality will handle the front face, and you two are to head up the back end." Which is an odd way of putting it, but hey— Blackwell's words, not mine.

Paul and William have remained tight-lipped about this

new project, and I'm anxious as hell to know what all of the secrecy is about.

Paul takes a sip of his beer, his head dipped low as if he's trying to hide his expression. He scratches the side of his brown hair. "In due time. Don't worry, you'll be filled in soon enough."

I gulp my beer. This is ridiculous. I've kept my mouth shut, not asking questions when I was nothing but the lowly assistant to the hospitality manager, but now I'm running the department. It's time someone filled me in.

I don't respond, giving them my best Cade glare.

William clears his throat, shooting Paul a conspiratorial look. "Blackwell told us you're hiring new people. Just make sure you hire the *right* people. The best you can find, and make sure they're discreet. If you have something on them, even better."

"Are you talking blackmail?"

William's black winged eyebrows vee upward. He holds up his hands, a douchey grin on his face. "You said it, not me."

I set down my beer. I understand the competitive nature of tourism, and casinos in particular. I've been surrounded by it my entire life, but Paul and William have my full attention now. "What else?"

William looks at Paul, who tucks his pointy chin, hiding a wide grin. "Hot chicks," they say at the same time. "With low morals," Paul adds.

I shove my hand in my pocket, my exterior cool, but inside I'm wondering what the fuck this venture is all about. Can't be illegal. It wasn't that long ago that Blue Casino was in the news for something an executive had done. Cost the casino a small fortune in PR to put out the fire, from what I'm told. Blackwell wouldn't risk it.

Paul leans forward and places a hand on my shoulder. "Find the hottest chicks with the lowest morals who won't say a thing."

I pull back and narrow my eyes. To be honest, I never liked girls with low morals. It's often coupled with low self-esteem, and that's a turnoff. "If this venture is some new revenue builder, why not scrape a few employees off the top? Grab the best performers and move them up."

"No, man." William shakes his head. "Can't be anyone from the inside. We tried that before and it backfired. Has to be new recruits who understand the discretion element."

Who do they think they are, the CIA? "It would help if I understood the venture."

"It's basically right in your wheelhouse. Hospitality," William says. "We're being *very* hospitable to our patrons. The new employees will provide everything our customers could ever want in a luxury resort, with the focus on risk-taking and pleasure—exactly why they come to the casino."

Paul taps his Blue sapphire signet ring on the side of his beer bottle. "Look at it this way—you can begin by hiring an assistant. Make sure she's hot and not a prude. In fact, look for her in the strip clubs. Any of those chicks would pine for a job at Blue. Bump up the pay, and make sure she signs the confidentiality agreement we send you tomorrow. Blackwell has contacts for bodyguards. Guys he knows through his connections prior to running the casino. They'll make sure everything runs smoothly."

Suddenly, my quick promotion and the guys insisting we head out to Farley's have my suspicions firing. "Tell me something." I grab my beer and take a long drag. "Are we working right now?"

"Business and pleasure." The sides of Paul's narrow chin pull in with his grin. "They go hand in hand. You play it right—find the right people, help us get these suites crowded with wealthy, pleasure-seeking patrons—and you'll be seeing seven-figure bonuses before you know it."

That'll do. I study both of their faces to make sure I heard right.

Seven figures, along with my regular salary, and I'll be sailing through without help from the Cade coffers. I could distance myself from the entire enterprise, and my brothers couldn't say anything about my holding on to Daddy's purse strings because I wouldn't need them. I won't cut off all contact with my father the way my brothers have. I've always been able to compartmentalize his behavior, and because of that, we have something of a relationship, even if it's mostly a working one. But with this new venture, I won't need to be dependent on my father financially.

I order another round of shots. So this thing has shady elements—the strippers, to name one. Can't be that bad, or they wouldn't be able to get away with it. And I'm no saint. I don't typically go for the low morals, easy lay, but I never said I haven't. Who am I to judge? "Just tell me how many employees we need, and when, and I'll take care of it."

"Yeah!" William slaps me on the back. "We knew you were one of us."

I grimace. I don't mind working with William and Paul, but they're not friends. I like to think I have better taste.

"Just make sure you keep that Hayden chick out of it," Paul says, and my back stiffens. "Use her for access cards—that kind of stuff—but tell her nothing. Matter of fact, probably best to keep the new employee files locked in your office."

I don't like hearing Hayden's name come out of Paul's mouth, let alone the disgruntled look on his face when he says it. I wonder how many times she's turned him down to put that scowl there. "Nope, won't involve her at all." Because I fucking don't want Hayden around these jackasses.

Hayden may despise me, but that's because I'm an asshole and she's smart. I need this venture and the cash I'll earn, but I also sense a seediness to it, and I don't want Hayden anywhere near that. "When do we begin?"

Paul and William explain the number of employees we need and the general job descriptions, the rest to be filled in later. For now, they want attractive, pliable candidates. High pay, low profile, and if I can find dirt on them, even better. Jesus Christ.

It turns out the celebration for my new promotion was an induction of sorts. But I'm game. Just as long as this job provides a future that doesn't involve the family business.

Chapter Three

Hayden

W hen I first left the CEO's office yesterday, I wanted to get as far from Blue as possible. But that's my natural reaction to bullies. Given a few hours of perspective, the fight in me returned. I came back to Lake Tahoe to build a life here because I love the area. I won't back down and run like I did before.

I stare at the pile of work in front of me. My initial thought was that Blackwell didn't care what I did at Blue, but that was foolish. He'll have my ass fired and replaced with a more pliant female manager if I don't do my job.

Blackwell isn't opposed to working me to the bone. He simply won't give me credit for it. Bonuses are reserved for his Blue Stars—the group I'd bet my right arm Adam is rubbing noses with. Those two jackasses, William and Paul, have been in and out of Adam's office all day. My little spies tell me so.

Mira, my assistant, and Nessa, who works in marketing, sit across from me. Both Mira and Nessa have long, dark hair, but Mira's hair is slightly wavy, and their faces look totally different. Nessa is petite, with a heart-shaped face and classical features, and Mira has stunning, high cheekbones, and rosy, bow-shaped lips. She's also slightly more tanned than Nessa, thanks to her Washoe heritage.

Mira's caramel-colored eyes flash with interest. "Rumor has it that Adam is looking for an assistant."

I grind my black pointy heels into the plush carpet of my office and let out a growl. "Dammit."

Mira places a document on my desk with an arrow pointing to a signature line. I glance at the form and scribble my name. It's for *Adam*'s new promotion.

I drop my pen. "How can he hire people without going through us?" As the head of HR, I'm aware this isn't protocol. I just want to hear it said, because it's crap.

Mira shrugs. "Blackwell's orders."

I sweep my long, thick bangs to the side and huff out a breath. "Fine. It's fine. Let Adam hire whomever he wants. It's on his shoulders if he doesn't do the proper security checks, and ends up hiring a serial killer." I glance at Mira. "You sure Tyler won't return as a Blue security guard? We could use him to protect us from Adam's new hires."

Mira glances up as though considering my absurd suggestion. "Pretty sure. His book is in its third printing, and the community college just made him tenure track."

"Fine." I roll my eyes dramatically. "I guess the world needs a brilliant biologist more than Blue needs a bodyguard with morals. Though it's debatable."

I rest my head on my hand, my elbow propped on my desk. Mira's smile fades as she takes in my face. "How much sleep did you get last night?"

I stretch my neck, not bothering to lift it off my hand.

Too much effort. "An hour. Maybe two. I couldn't sleep. Too disturbed after my meeting with Blackwell."

Nessa takes in a sharp breath. "Asshole." Mira and I both look at her. "What? He is."

Nessa is the sweet one in our group, but I'm not surprised at her outburst. These girls are loyal, and Blackwell's on our shit list.

"Come be with us tonight. How many times have Zach and I invited you over? Five, six? You always have work. Forget about this place for one night and have margaritas with us."

"Seriously, Hayden," Mira urges. "Knock off early. Put on some comfortable clothes, and bring an empty stomach. Zach and Nessa will take care of you."

Zach is a dealer at Blue, but he's also Nessa's live-in boyfriend, and from what I hear, an excellent cook. He hosts a taco dinner every week for their friends.

The deep rumble of a familiar voice has me grimacing. I glance over the girls' heads and catch Eve passing my office nearly attached to Adam's side. They're speaking in low tones, as though they don't want anyone to hear.

I grind my heels deeper into the carpet. "You know what? I will go. I could use a margarita."

Mira grins. "Tyler and I will pick you up. That way you can drink without worrying about moderation."

"Sounds perfect. I'm tired of moderation."

As MUCH AS I love my high-fashion heels, sometimes a girl wants to dress down. I do as Mira suggests and slip on white sneakers with jeans rolled at the bottom and pair them with a simple blouse. The early summer weather has been unseasonably warm, so I don't bother with a jacket. I comb my shoulder-length dirty-blond hair and sweep my bangs behind my ear, feeling ready for a night of unwinding with friends and comfort food. But just as I'm getting used to the idea of a night off, I realize that relaxing might not be in the cards.

Mira, Tyler, and I arrive at Zach and Nessa's house, and I see a ghost from my past standing on the other side of the room. I stare at the tall, handsome guy, his hair darker and shorter than the last time I saw him—when he showed up on my doorstep to apologize. He's changed since then, but I recognize him. He's someone I wouldn't easily forget.

"Jaeger?" My voice comes out sounding choked.

Jaeger glances up and cuts off a gulp of beer. *"Beth?"*

He sets his beer on the counter, and a pretty girl with golden-red hair walks over and touches his arm. Jaeger tucks her close to his side and says something in her ear. She gives him a sad smile.

Mira lowers her voice. "Why did Jaeger call you Beth?"

Before I can answer, Jaeger walks over with the pretty girl I'm assuming is his girlfriend. "Cali, this is Beth—"

"Hayden," I say. "I go by Hayden now. Elizabeth is my middle name."

"Hayden," Jaeger corrects, sounding somewhat surprised. "This is my girlfriend, Cali." He peers at the others in the room, who all seem to be paying attention. "Hayden and I went to high school together."

I say hello and shake his girlfriend's hand, then glance at Mira and Nessa. "This is the Cali you've been talking about?" They both nod. "Wow." I smile and shake my head. "I figured I might run into Jaeger when I returned to Lake Tahoe, but I never thought I'd be hanging out with his friends."

Mira and Nessa have talked about Cali and her boyfriend, but they never mentioned his name.

Jaeger glances at Mira and Nessa's questioning expressions. Even Zach and Tyler, whom I've known through their girlfriends and the casino, are staring. "Hayden and I dated for a short time," he explains. "I was a dick to her."

Cali squeezes Jaeger's waist and he hugs her back. At least he's with a nice girl now.

"The circumstances were crappy," I say.

Jaeger isn't a bad guy, and I don't blame him for what happened. He played a part in everything that went down, but his part was minor, all things considered.

He shakes his head. "I had no idea you were back in town."

"Blue hired me."

"Oh Jesus," Cali says, and throws up her hands, just as another couple enters behind us.

Mira, Tyler, and I step out of the way to let the new couple in.

"Why 'oh Jesus'?" the tall brunette with beautiful greenish eyes who just entered asks. "Hi." She smiles and holds out her hand to me. "I'm Gen. This is Lewis." She gestures to the dark-haired guy behind her, who rivals Jaeger in height.

I shake her hand. "We were discussing my job at Blue Casino."

"*Ohhh.* I'm sorry?"

Gen has more reason than anyone to be sympathetic to a woman who works at Blue. Soon after I hired Mira, she explained how her friend Gen had been assaulted and nearly raped by a manager. "I heard about your experience working at the casino. I'm really sorry. I'm trying to make sure nothing like that ever happens again."

"Not sure how safe you'll be working at Blue, but it sounds like it will be good for the employees that you're there," she says. "That place could use a few more people with a conscience."

Nessa sees me shift my purse and reaches for it. "I'll put this in one of the bedrooms." She disappears down the hall. When she returns, she heads into the kitchen toward a giant blender, with what I'm assuming contains the infamous margarita mix. Which I wouldn't mind a glass of right about now.

Running into Jaeger has always been a possibility. I just didn't think it would happen among my new friends. I wasn't expecting to confront my past tonight.

"Wait," Mira says suddenly, as thought she's finally put something together. "Most of us went to high school together. How come I never knew you then?"

Mira and I have gotten along since I hired her, but it's only been recently that we've grown close. I've never told her about my sordid past in Lake Tahoe—have yet to mention it to any of my new friends.

After a rapid-fire exchange of ages, years attended at the local high school, and friendship affiliations, we determine why I wouldn't have known them. Mira was a couple of years younger than me, and Tyler and Zach spent most of their time with their sports teams. Not to mention, I only attended my first two years of high school in Lake Tahoe.

"We were ships passing in the night," Mira says, and grins.

I laugh. "Something like that."

We move into the dining area and Cali places some kind of contraption around Gen's neck. She reaches for two more, and places them on Nessa and Mira as well. She turns to me.

"Mira mentioned her boss was coming," she says, and shakes another neck thingy. "I made sure to bring extras." Her voice is low, and a bit devilish.

The mischievous glint in Cali's eyes, coupled with Jaeger's head shake, has me worried. But I appreciate Cali making me feel welcome. Despite my past with her boyfriend, she isn't holding it against me.

Playing along, I feign wariness and glance at Mira while Cali slides the stretchy neck gear over my head. She pours margarita mix into a giant wineglass, then slides the glass inside the neck thing that magically holds it without toppling my drink.

She plops a fat straw in the glass. "There, now you look like us."

I peer at Mira and Nessa, who are holding back smiles, wearing the same ridiculous neck contraption I am. "I know I said I didn't want moderation tonight, but I'd like to be standing by the end of the evening."

I glance around the room. Jaeger is silently laughing, and Tyler and Zach are leaning against the counter with their arms crossed, smiles playing on their faces. Lewis leans over and takes a sip of Gen's margarita—right above her breasts. He winks, and she smacks him on the arm.

I take a long drag from my straw. "Okay, I like it. I mean, I look ridiculous, but come on, this thing is handy."

Cali claps excitedly. "I knew you would be game! I got these babies online. Just let me know, and I'll order you one."

I hold up my hand. "No, no—I'm good."

Cali pouts, and Jaeger puts his long, muscular arm around her shoulders. "Come on, babe. This is her first time. Let her get used to the gang before you ply her with drink paraphernalia." He turns to me, shaking his head. "Still can't believe we're running into each other like this."

I smile ruefully. "Small world."

Cali crosses her arms. "Fine, I won't order another one, but don't be surprised if you get it for Christmas."

I take another sip of the margarita dangling from my neck. "I've been forewarned, and I'm not afraid."

If my job depression wasn't occupying so much of my brain energy, I might feel slightly uncomfortable drinking a margarita out of neck gear and spending time with Jaeger Lang, who once betrayed me—as sweet as he may be now. I've come full circle, yet it doesn't feel as bad as I thought it would.

A warm sensation settles over my belly and limbs as the alcohol works its magic. I grab a handful of chips and dip them in the homemade salsa Mira brought, chatting as I eat and sip from my neck hanger. Mira tries to reach her straw without using her hands. She bumps it with her chin, and Nessa and I giggle as she chases the straw with her tongue. This is exactly what I needed. Good food, good people, and a reason to be silly.

I shove another chip overloaded with salsa in my mouth, and a knock at the door rises above the chatter and low hum of music.

Jaeger strides to the front from the kitchen, where he's been talking with the guys. He opens the door—to Adam standing on the other side.

What the hell?

First Jaeger, now Adam?

Jaeger and Adam were good friends in high school. Crap.

Adam steps inside and slaps Jaeger on the shoulder.

"How's it goin'?" Adam is tall, but even he had to reach up to slap Jaeger, who reaches nearly six and a half feet.

"Just getting started." Jaeger shuts the door behind Adam, who is casual in dark denim and a black button-down, the sleeves rolled to his elbows.

I've never seen Adam in anything but a suit and tie, and he is so handsome my chest aches. I'm in a room of good-looking men. This place is mancandy heaven between Jaeger, Lewis, Tyler, and Zach. But for some reason, Adam knocks normal standards of attractiveness out the window. As though he's the new gold standard and no one else compares. I hate that I like the way he looks. It's superficial; it shouldn't affect me, especially knowing what I know about him. But despite beauty that has no bearing on what's inside, I'm drawn to him.

My hands shake, my breath coming out choppy. It annoys me to no end that I lose myself around this guy. It's worse in this moment than when we're at work, where I feel a semblance of control. Ironic, given how messed up my work environment is. But when I'm working long hours using my mind to solve problems, there's an order to things. Ever since Adam stepped into Blue Casino, my foundation has shifted and I haven't managed to get back my equilibrium. Having him infiltrate my private life too? Unacceptable.

Adam enters the living room and our eyes connect. His forehead furrows—and then his gaze drops to the drink dangling from my neck.

Goddammit.

I pull my shoulders back, challenging him with my eyes to say anything about the neck gear—*anything at all*—and I will punch him between his perfectly masculine eyebrows.

His mouth quirks at the corner, but he follows Jaeger

into the kitchen and takes the beer offered to him. Not a second later, his gaze returns to me, and I promptly ignore it.

Attempting to calm the heck down, I glare daggers at Mira and Nessa, who are wearing twin looks of guilt.

"Shit," Mira mumbles. "I forgot he comes sometimes."

"Sometimes?" I hiss.

"He's friends with Jaeger," Nessa explains.

But I already knew that. I didn't think I'd be running into Jaeger, let alone Adam.

"Adam hasn't been here in a while," Nessa continues. "He started coming shortly after Cali and Jaeger hooked up a couple of years ago. Honestly, he's only been here a handful of times, and it's been months since his last visit. We had no idea he was coming tonight."

Cali returns from refilling her drink. "What's wrong? Why don't you want Adam here?"

Awesome. She must have overheard.

I pound my margarita through the straw, scrunching my face as brainfreeze takes hold.

"Adam works at Blue now," Mira says to Cali. "But I'm sure Jaeger said something about that. Anyway, Adam sort of works with us—and Hayden. And he is..."

"Hot?" Cali supplies, while taking a swig of her drink, her gaze lazily scanning Adam's body.

I do not blame her one bit. Ogling should be perfectly legal where Adam is concerned.

Mira twists her mouth. "That, yes. But he's also..."

Cali taps her chin and licks her lips, as if Adam is a piece of bacon she wants to take a bite out of. "Sexy in a preppy, athletic sort of way?" she suggests.

She *is* in love with Jaeger, right?

"Well, yes," Mira says. "But Adam is—"

I ball my fists, my short nails digging into my palms. "Infuriating. Superior. Spoiled." Mira, Nessa, and Cali look over, and I gulp back the rest of my margarita until the straw makes a loud vacuum sound. "No offense. I know he's your friend." I hold my drink away from my chest. "Is there any more of this?"

"Yeah." Nessa snaps out of her daze and hurries to the half-filled pitcher on the counter. I follow her, avoiding eye contact with Adam, but he doesn't get the memo. He steps around Jaeger, right in my path.

"So, Hayden, nice cocktail yoke you got there." His eyes are smiling, even if his mouth isn't.

Cocktail yoke? He knows the technical term?

It's funny. And that alone pisses me off. How dare he disarm me when I want to be armed and ready to fire back?

I finger the contraption. "It's convenient." I'm so pissed at this guy, and angry at my boss at work, but I'm wearing a cocktail yoke, and even I see the humor in the situation. I press my lips together to hide my thoughts, but the smile must leak through, because Adam smiles too.

I've seen Adam smirk, flirt, and swagger, but I have yet to witness a genuine smile. He devastated my equilibrium *without* it. With it, the effect hits much deeper.

I let out a slow breath and allow the grin to overtake my face, but only for a moment. "Don't think this means we're friends."

The smirk returns. "Oh, I wouldn't dream of it, Hayden."

I hate the way he says my name. Condescending and sexy at the same time. I was just having fun with Mira and the others. But I can't return to Zach and Nessa's if Adam is a part of the package. There's no way I want to be friends with him. "Nessa and Mira invited me tonight. I didn't realize you were a regular."

Adam runs his hand through his dark brown hair, longer at the top than on the sides. He glances at the others. "Zach's a good guy. I started hanging out with him more these last couple of years. Now we work together at Blue..." He shrugs one shoulder. "What can I say? Tahoe is a small world."

He's mimicking my thoughts now? "Small world indeed."

Adam lifts his eyebrow. "Are you agreeing with me? Because I wouldn't mind you agreeing with me for once." He grins, and thankfully, this one is all swagger.

I shake my head and gesture to Jaeger. "We used to know each other. Way back when."

I always wondered if Adam recognized me when he first started at Blue. Based on his blank expression, that would be a no.

When will I learn? Guys like Adam don't remember girls like me, let alone defend them.

His face goes still, his eyes delving a bit. He shoves a hand in his pocket and swirls the beer in his other hand. "Way back?"

I roll my eyes, appreciating the light buzz that's allowing this conversation to take place with minimal discomfort. I returned to Lake Tahoe to confront my past; there's no point in running from it now. My new friends should know about my past. And Adam should know his part...

"Jaeger was my boyfriend in high school—when I was a sophomore and accused of sleeping with a teacher. I'm the girl you told him to dump."

Chapter Four

O kay, that was blunt, but I'm tired of hiding my past. I ran from Lake Tahoe to get away from the rumors. They made me feel weak and helpless. I'm not that helpless sixteen-year-old anymore. And Adam should know what he did.

He chokes on his beer, the room suddenly going quiet.

Mira walks over, her voice gentle. "Hayden, you were *that* Beth? Beth Tate..." Her voice trails off as though she's putting two and two together.

Of course Mira heard the rumor about the teacher and me, even if I didn't know her in high school. Most people had heard it. "Yes."

"She didn't do it." Jaeger's expression is stern. He's stepped closer, obviously having picked up the conversation.

Somehow, Jaeger's public support of me, even in an informal setting, has the waterworks building behind my eyes. I push them back and move on. "No one believed me. And neither did Jaeger at the time. Though I've forgiven him for it." Jaeger glances away, as if ashamed, and Adam has a strange look on his face.

"Long story short," I say to everyone, because they're all listening now, and I don't want there to be secrets, "the teacher resigned, I fled Lake Tahoe, and now I'm back. Eleven years later. All's well." I grab a handful of chips and pop one in my mouth, focusing on the bite of the salt on my lips.

Adam's face is frozen, his eyes burning with...something. "Let me get this straight. You were Jaeger's girlfriend —*that* girlfriend? Beth..." His gaze scans my face and body, as though he's calculating all the changes and adding them up.

"For a short time, yeah. He broke up with me when he heard about the teacher. I understand you were instrumental in making that happen." I chomp into another chip and watch the tic in his jaw.

"And that made you leave Lake Tahoe." He swallows, as if even *he* can't stomach the truth.

"Well, not the Jaeger part, but yes, the other stuff. I was harassed by students—pretty much the entire town. Chip?" I hand him one, no longer having a taste for it myself.

He doesn't look at the food in my hand. Adam grabs the back of his neck. "I need another beer," he mumbles, and pounds the last of his.

Cali walks over and refills the margarita resting against my breasts in the cocktail yoke. Jaeger joins her. "I'm really sorry about that, Hayden," he says. "I knew it was rough on you. I didn't realize how bad."

"You apologized years ago. Water under the bridge."

Not that those waters didn't crash rocks against the shore, leaving deep gashes. But the scars that formed had less to do with Jaeger, and more to do with the entire town turning on me. Not having a single person I could rely on, besides my parents, left me feeling empty. Even Adam, who didn't know me, caused damage.

"Dump her," Adam said, as I stood around the corner from Jaeger's school locker, waiting for Jaeger to finish talking to his friend. I'd paused when I caught sight of them together, unsure if I should interrupt.

Jaeger switched out his books, and looked up, absently lifting a hand to a guy passing, whom I recognized as an athlete on the football team. Jaeger knew all the athletes. He was popular. Yet he'd chosen to date me, a mousy bookworm.

He closed the locker and leaned against the metal frame. "You think she did it?"

Adam snorted. "Don't be stupid. Get out while you can. You don't need to stand beside her just because you've dated her for a couple of weeks. No one will blame you for dumping her." Adam notched his head up and flashed a grin at a beautiful girl walking by. I'd seen the girl in my economics class. Not bright, but she'd been nice the few times I'd interacted with her.

She smiled sweetly at Adam, and walked on with her friend.

Jaeger's expression went pensive. "You're right."

Adam hitched his backpack higher, his gaze darting away. "Course I'm right."

That same day, when I was leaving school, Jaeger caught up to me. He broke up with me at the foot of the stairs to the parking lot. Thanks to Adam Cade pounding the last nail in the coffin, my boyfriend turned his back on me during one of the darkest moments of my life, along with the rest of the town. I couldn't walk into a grocery store without someone pointing a finger.

Small towns are a bitch.

Mira puts her arm around my shoulders, and Gen joins us. "That was messed up," Mira says. This coming from the girl who recently lost her mother to drug abuse.

What happened sucked. It was brutal at the time, and I'll never forgive Adam for being a jerk during everything, but I've returned because I'm ready to move on. "As long as you don't mind my sordid past, I'm over it."

She smiles. "Your sordid past has nothing on mine."

"Or mine," Gen chimes in. "Most of my life I never knew who my father was. This is small potatoes. And the rumor wasn't even true. Though, if you *had* hooked up with a hot teacher, that would be a good story to tell."

"I don't have a sordid past," Nessa admits. "But now I think you're even more badass for coming back and kicking ass in this town." She does a flashy karate chop in the air, and kicks up her platform heel.

Zach leans over and kisses Nessa on the top of the head. "Cutie." He smiles down at her.

The next hour goes smoothly. No more discussions about nasty rumors. And Adam keeps his distance. We eat, and it's not until we're outside, sitting around Zach and Nessa's new built-in fire pit, that Adam approaches me again. He lowers himself onto the camp chair beside mine and stretches out his long legs. "I was friends with Jaeg in high school."

I glare at him. "Yeah, I remember. You were *such* a good friend." I let out a breath and stare back at the campfire. I didn't return to town to hold grudges. "Look, I know you convinced Jaeger to break up with me. Maybe he would have anyway. Regardless, you didn't know me."

"Hayden—"

"Even so, that was a long time ago. We were young, and people make mistakes. I can't say it didn't affect me, but I've moved on."

He's silent for a long moment, his handsome face more serious than I've ever seen it. "You're right, I didn't know you, but that's no excuse for what I did. And you do judge me for the past, if the way you've treated me at Blue is any indication. You have every right. I'm sorry for what I said to Jaeg back then. It was a crap thing to do."

I can't take the look in his eyes. It's one of his rare sincere expressions, and it jumbles up everything. Confuses me. And his confession...I never thought I'd hear an apology like that from Adam.

A stretch of silence follows as I process his words. He turns away and stares at the fire pit. "In any case," he says, his voice soft and low, "I wish I *had* known you."

That grabs my attention, because apology or not, Adam gave every indication back then that I was dirt beneath his feet.

I glance at him out of the corner of my eye, shaking my head. "No one wanted to know me after the scandal. If you recall, I wasn't anything special before it."

"Special enough for Jaeg to snatch you up." An enigmatic look flashes across his face.

"You have some sort of competition going on with Jaeger?"

Adam huffs out a chuckle. "Jaeg's one of my best friends. We'd never poach from each other."

A sharp choking sound escapes my throat. "Are we talking about women or stealing chickens?" This is a serious conversation, but that poaching comment cannot go unchallenged.

His gaze slides to me. "Women. Always women."

Damn.

Suddenly I'm locked; I can't turn away. He's doing it again, staring deeply. Why would Adam say any of this? He didn't even realize I was the same Beth from high school until now.

"We were friends," I stammer. I don't know why I feel the need to explain. "I helped him with an English project. We became more than friends for a little while."

Adam's wide palm squeezes his leg above his knee. "Do you—do you still have feelings for him?"

"What?" I whisper loudly, and glance over to where Jaeger and Cali are sitting several feet away. "No. Of course not."

The last thing I want is for people to wonder if I have a flame burning for Jaeger. Whatever romantic feelings I had for him ended soon after he dumped me. He's a good guy, but that's all.

This conversation has grown too personal. I reach down and pick up a pine needle from the dirt. "How was your celebration at Farley's? Did you eat your weight in hot wings?"

Adam's expression lightens, and he rubs the corner of his mouth. "Not exactly. But this might interest you. I'll be hiring new employees."

I bring the pine needle to my nose, taking in the brisk, woody scent. "Which is to be expected, since your promotion has left a void for the assistant position. I'm happy to list a posting on Monday."

"No," he says sharply. "That's not necessary. Blackwell wants me to handle the new hires on my own."

I turn in my camp chair to face him, which isn't easy, as there's a dip in the middle of the canvas, and I wobble more than shift. "What are the positions? And why wouldn't you use human resources? We've had our disagreements, but we get along well enough to do our jobs."

Adam glances across the campfire. Mira is looking over with a worried expression, my elevated voice likely the cause. "Walk with me for a minute." He stands and heads toward the deck.

I rise from the camp chair and slowly follow, watching as Adam hoists himself up on the closed lid of the hot tub.

He reaches down. "Give me your hand."

My need to discover why he's hiring new employees without the human resources department outweighs my desire to avoid his touch. I do as he says, his large palm engulfing mine, warming me from the inside out. He helps me up, and I inch away, dangling my feet over the edge of the hot tub cover and creating space between us.

There's only one thing I want from Adam, and the imprint of his warm hand on my body isn't it. "What's going on at Blue? I know there's something, so don't feign ignorance."

I've asked around. Rumors indicate that Paul, one of Blackwell's Blue Stars, used to be just like Drake Peterson, the man who hurt Gen and the reason Blue hired me. A couple of admins said Paul was handsy with female coworkers and often propositioned the cocktail waitresses. Not that I trust rumors a hundred percent. I know better than anyone how wrong rumors can be, but with all the secrecy among management, I can't help wondering what Blackwell is hiding about his Blue Stars. And since I'm not a part of his inner circle, I have no problem pumping Adam for information.

He leans back on his elbow. "Nothing I can talk about. Some things are...exclusive."

My blood boils. I turn, bending the side of my leg over the cover in order to face him. "What kind of crap is that?" I glance at our friends and take a deep breath, lowering my voice. "Have you any idea how awful those guys you're chumming around with are?"

Adam frowns and sits up, his face inches from mine. "Why? What have they done?"

"Jaeger must have told you what they did to Gen and Cali?"

"Yeah, of course. It was terrible, but that was one guy, not the casino. And that guy is in prison. You have nothing to worry about."

"Oh really?" My sarcastic tone makes it clear I disagree.

His eyes narrow. "What's up, Hayden? What do you know?"

"Some things are *exclusive*." It's an immature comment, but forget him. Adam's turning into one of the Blue Stars; he probably knows all about Gen and a lot of other things, like the drug suite Mira and Tyler found around the time Drake was fired. But now he knows that I *know*—well, at least some of it—and I'm not going to ignore what's going on behind the scenes the way he's willing to do.

He studies me a moment longer. "Why do you hate me? Is this all because of what I did years ago?"

"Hate you?" I gasp. "Because I don't throw myself at your feet like every other woman?"

He glances up, as though considering. "Women throw themselves at my feet? If they do, I've missed a few. And I'm rather observant where women are concerned."

I ignore the taunt. "You traipse into Blue without a clue, and suddenly wind up as a manager, hiring people for a secret project that puts you in Blackwell's pocket? I don't know, Adam, why wouldn't I trust you?"

He leans closer. Probably because my voice is getting louder and louder the longer we talk. "I don't know, *Hayden*. If you're being honest and you've gotten over the past, then what do you have against me?"

Against him. His words echo in my head, and suddenly all that heat is back—the heat radiating off his body, the warmth building inside me from his nearness.

His blue gaze, nearly black in this light, dips to my mouth, and I suck in a breath.

"Screw you." I jump off the hot tub cover and walk toward the group, but Mira is already on her way over.

"What's going on?" she says, looking past me to Adam, who's leaning on his elbow again. But this time he's staring down and frowning.

"Nothing. I think I'll take an Uber home. I'm tired."

"Let's leave." She looks over my shoulder toward him. "Especially if Adam's being a ass."

I swallow and realize it's not Adam. It's Blue. "He isn't."

I don't know with certainty that Adam is in cahoots with the Blue Stars. Having suspicions about Blue Casino and not knowing for sure is driving me crazy. "I'm just frustrated with work," I tell her.

We return to the group, and Mira makes an excuse for us to leave. We say our goodbyes, and a few minutes later Mira, Tyler, and I make our way to Tyler's Land Cruiser parked in the driveway.

I hear my name called and I turn.

Adam is jogging toward us. "Hold up," he says.

Mira raises her eyebrow in question, but she and Tyler climb into the truck, while I stand outside with Adam.

He tucks a hand in the front pocket of his designer jeans. "I know it's awkward—me hiring people without your say. It's not normal, I get that. But it's how Blackwell wants things."

It should be cooler out here, away from the fire, but it isn't. It's hot and edgy. "I understand. You have to follow Blackwell's orders. But hiring the right people isn't as easy as it looks."

He smirks. "How hard can it be to hire an assistant?"

There we go. There's the Adam that infuriates me at work.

Instead of a sharp set-down to fire back, an idea springs to mind... Maybe it was the tequila tonight, or maybe it was unloading my disreputable past on my new friends, but I'm feeling the need to kick a little ass. "How do you feel about a bet?"

"We're betting now?" He chuckles. "Is this how far our relationship has degraded? I didn't take you for the gambling sort."

"When I'm certain of my odds, I'm willing to gamble."

He leans in, resting his arm on the side of the truck. "What did you have in mind?"

A whiff of soap and man hits me, and my mind blanks.

My body tips against the truck, and I blink hard. "Whoever you hire for the assistant position...I bet you'll let them go soon after." I glance up, mentally calculating. "I give it two weeks."

He looks into my eyes. Something crosses his face—curiosity? Respect? "I'll take you up on that bet. How about, if I win, you stay away from my new hires. No snooping in their files, or keeping tabs on them."

Interesting choice of criteria. And damning, if he's involved with the Blue Stars. "And if I win?"

He shrugs. "Whatever you want. I'm pretty good with my hands." He grins suggestively, and I roll my eyes. "You're a single girl. I'm sure there's something you need help with around the house."

"That's the best you can do? I'm not sure replacing a lightbulb is equal to me ignoring suspect activities at work. But putting that aside, how do you know I'm single? Just because I'm not interested in you, doesn't mean I'm not interested in another man."

His jaw shifts. "Are you single?"

I ignore that one. Won't give him the satisfaction of knowing my private life. "More to the point, how do you know *I'm* not handy?"

There's a moment of silence as Adam stares at me, his jaw still tensed from the first question. "Are you good with your hands, Hayden?"

That sounded like a double entendre. One that just made my chest flutter, damn him. And no, I'm not good at fixing things. "Fine. If I win, forget repairs—you can *build* me something. Since you're so good with your hands."

Oooh, I'd just love to see this pretty boy try to build something—*anything*. I bet he'd hammer a nail in his thumb, cuss a few times, and pay someone to take over. That in and of itself would give me ammunition to use against him for months. Besides, there is no way he's winning this bet.

He raises an eyebrow. "No hints as to what you need built?"

"You'll see. After I win." I glare at his arm beside my head, caging me in and causing ripples of heat to spiral down my body.

He drops his arm and I open the car door. I slide in the

backseat, ready to get away from Adam's scent, which is doing funny things to my head.

Tyler waves to Adam, who's rounding the front of the truck, and puts the car in reverse.

"Everything okay?" Mira asks.

"Yup. Just a little friendly bet I plan to win."

Chapter Five

Adam

I return to Zach and Nessa's living room, my chest puffed up, hands clenched and tingling from adrenaline. The only reason I agreed to Hayden's bet is because there's no way I'll lose. And I need her to stay out of this business Blackwell has me on.

There's nothing wrong with hiring a few people, but Paul and William have been acting shifty about this venture for months, and I don't trust them. That's not enough reason for me to back out—it would take a hell of lot more for me to pass up the opportunity to sever myself from the Cade money—but I will keep Hayden out of it just to be safe.

Jaeger stares at me like I've lost my mind. "What the hell was that?"

Did he overhear my conversation with Hayden? Because I've gotta say, I enjoyed our mental tussle. Always gets my blood firing, but I don't want Jaeg to know about that. He might get the wrong idea. I shrug it off. "What are you talking about?"

"You. And Hayden. What's going on?"

"Nothing. We argue. That's typical for us."

Jaeg's head tilts. "I've never seen you chase after a woman."

I scratch my neck. "I wouldn't say I *chased* her."

"*Chased.*" Jaeg enunciates the word very deliberately.

When I wasn't working for my father, I taught snowboarding with Jaeg and a couple of buddies at Heavenly during winter breaks. We were inseparable then and have been close ever since. The guy knows me, which, in this case, is inconvenient.

"Fine. She drives me crazy, but I work with her. I don't want there to be tension tomorrow. I went out to smooth things over." Sort of. I also might have antagonized her, but that's her fault. She brings out the animal in me.

Everyone is silent—Jaeg, Cali, Zach, Lewis. And they're staring. "What?"

Jaeg looks to Zach, who purses his lips and shakes his head, as if he doesn't believe me either, or can't believe what he's seeing. He turns toward the stove and collects pans, placing them in the sink. Lewis wraps a long arm around Gen's shoulders and continues to stare like he's never seen me before.

Jesus, can't a guy have a chat with a woman without his entire gang labeling it?

I walk over to Zach's dining table. It's new, and a vast improvement on the previous garage sale piece of crap. I've come to Zach's taco dinner a few times now. Typically, I don't care about what furniture people have. I know how lucky I am to afford what I do. But Zach's old furniture defied human decency. It had to be sixty years old, and gaudy as hell. Thankfully, his girlfriend, Nessa, has good taste. I've noticed a distinct upgrade in a few key pieces since she's moved in. As far as I'm concerned, she's a keeper. He's also all gooey over her, just like Jaeg is with Cali. That part I could do without, but them's the breaks.

Cali plops into the chair next to me. "So, Adam. Hayden?"

Here we go. I shuffle a stack of cards I snatched from the bookshelf near the table. "I thought we were finished with that conversation."

"We were, we were. But I thought you might want to—you know, *confide.* Because I'm a girl. We're intuitive, us girls. Just ask Gen. I'm a genius at dissecting the female mind and helping couples come together."

Gen chokes spastically a couple of feet away, and Lewis pats her back. "Cali!" she says.

Cali waves Gen off, her gaze intent on me, and me alone. "I got this, Gen. Why don't you and Lewis take a walk, or something?"

Gen rubs her temples, and Lewis hugs her with a grin.

I sense a history here. As long as Cali and Gen duke it out, with any luck, Cali will forget about Hayden and me. I deal out a game of solitaire and wait for Zach to finish the dishes so he can whip us up some dessert. The last time I was here he made ice cream sundaes. I saw that someone brought brownies. I could use some double-chocolate brownie with a pound of vanilla on top.

Cali folds her hands and eyes me. "Jaeger's right, Adam. You are different. I remember how you were a couple of summers ago with your last girlfriend. I don't want to say you were a jerk, but..."

I count three cards from the deck in my hand, and flip. "But you thought I was a jerk?"

"Maybe a little."

My last girlfriend was like all of my girlfriends. Beautiful. Entitled. And never happy with the amount of attention I gave her. I can't blame her, or any of the women I've dated. I *was* an ass. But they also had high expectations—expensive trips, nice gifts. I could afford it, but I got tired of ulterior motives. Even the rich women hanging around Club Tahoe and tucking their key cards in my khakis were using me for something.

By the end of my last relationship, my ex thought I had a wandering eye. I wouldn't say it *wandered,* so much as I could see when the writing was on the wall. If I thought a relationship was nearing its end, I moved on immediately and made sure I was the one who got out first. And Jaeg's right. I don't pine for the ones I've left behind. Once they're out of my life, they're out of my mind too. Which, now that I think about it, is incredibly fucked up.

I've always been a moody bastard after a breakup, but it's never for the reasons people think. I wasn't upset because the relationship ended, but because I felt nothing. Not one damn thing. And when you feel nothing, sometimes—occasionally—it seems like there's nothing to live for. I've never been suicidal, but I can relate to the desolate, dark places people mentally go to when life sucks.

I've flown solo these last couple of years because why get tangled up when it leads to frustration on both sides? I've been taking a page out of my younger brother's book. Hook up and make no promises. Easy.

So if Jaeg's right, why was I chasing Hayden?

I think about her more than I should. She's beautiful, smart—but there is no way I am going near that. I enjoy the banter, because she dishes out as good as she gets, and she puts me in my place the way my brothers do. But Jaeg is right about one thing: I feel too much around her. And that's not good. I've got to keep things under control. Keep a cool distance.

Cali stares at me as this shit flies through my mind—one disturbing realization after another leading too close to a bull's-eye I didn't see coming.

Do I like Hayden?

I shake off the chill that runs down my spine. *Not happening.*

Just when I think Cali might probe further into my *feelings,* she switches directions like a flame-haired samurai, knocking the breath from my lungs. "I like her, Adam. Don't hurt this one."

My mind works as I try to respond to that curveball. "Hayden isn't a *this one*. She's a work associate."

But I'm not making a good argument for myself when I do stupid things like run after her into the driveway. Cali's right—I don't want to hurt Hayden. I did that before, and dick that I am, I didn't even realize it. The woman who drives me nuts at work is the same girl whom I subconsciously noticed in high school. And who was dating my best friend.

This Hayden—the confident, sharply dressed power executive at Blue—is nothing like the Beth that Jaeg dated. But she has the same effect on my instincts.

I left a text message for one of my soccer teammates and waited for Jaeg by his red pickup in the high school parking lot. My brother scored tickets to a band in town, and I wanted to give Jaeg his ticket before I went to the mandatory employee meeting at Club Tahoe. I was working as a cabana boy, serving poolside, while discreetly getting patted down and padded up with tips by the frisky women who could afford to vacation at my father's resort. My job kicked ass.

My dad wanted me to gain experience in the business. Little did he know I was gaining experience in how to pleasure bored housewives while their husbands played eighteen holes. If I timed my afternoon right, I could use both of my breaks to score. Sixteen and six foot one, and women noticed. And I had lots of energy to entertain them.

Mentally mapping which discreet storage closets were located poolside for the leggy brunette who had been giving me the eye yesterday, and whom I expected a return visit from today, I finally caught sight of Jaeg loping down the concrete steps toward the parking lot. His mouth was spread in a wide smile as he veered toward the girl in jeans and a baggy T-shirt standing near a metal bench.

I'd noticed her, of course, and had quickly labeled her a shy nerd with no curves under that baggy shirt. Not my usual type. Her backpack was nearly as big as she was, the glasses she wore overpowering her features. But her long, sandy blond hair was thick and silky in the ponytail she wore, and I could tell she had nice legs through her jeans. Despite her not being my type, I'd kept track of her while I waited for Jaeg.

She smiled and ducked her head as Jaeg approached. He stopped in front of her and reached for her hand. A strange twinge pinched my chest, which I chalked up to the double-double cheeseburger I'd eaten for lunch. They talked for a moment, then Jaeg gave her a hug and walked away. The girl turned and watched him leave, this beautiful smile—like a fucking ray of sunshine—beaming from her face.

I'd never seen a woman smile like that. The smiles I received were licentious, calculating—just the way I liked them. There was too much to lose in a smile and a face that split you in two and left you vulnerable.

Despite my disinterest in the shy girl, and Jaeg's obvious claim on her, I found myself searching for her on campus. And that was as far as it went. I never asked who she was, or who her friends were. Never asked Jaeg about his interest in her. Even if Jaeg hadn't been spending time with her, I would have never gone near a girl like that. She was different from the girls I spent time with back then. She was the real deal. And at sixteen, that scared the hell out of me.

It still does.

A small part of me is happy things didn't work out between Hayden and Jaeg. Not that I wouldn't take away the events that had her fleeing town if I could. But even back then, when I was an extremely selfish prick, I would have spared Hayden the pain of dating me. I would have hurt her in the end, and Hayden endured enough crap in high school. She didn't deserve my brand of emotional baggage on top of it.

Things are different now. I'm older. Smarter, I hope. But that just means I know better than to even consider a relationship with her. Like Jaeg pointed out. I feel too much around her. That doesn't mean I like the idea of her with someone else. Damn her for avoiding my question about whom she's dating. That ate at me, but I let it go. I have no claim on her. Not then, and not now.

I set the cards down and stare at Cali. "Are you finished grilling me?"

"Yup," she says cheerily. "Just wanted to make it clear

that you need to watch yourself around Hayden, or experience my wrath."

That was obvious. And not because I'm afraid of a pint-sized Cali, though she is a formidable fireball I don't wish to piss off. I could never hook up with Hayden. Even I draw the line at going into something, knowing I might hurt someone. I have a history of leaving women behind, and Hayden is the last person I want to cause pain.

Chapter Six

Hayden

I load up my tray with a salad, chicken fingers, and a cookie. Some women forgo desserts, but that's madness. If my sweet tooth doesn't get quenched once a day, I'm cranky. I accommodate by eating my delectables at noon instead of right before bed. Gives me plenty of time to work it off while running around this crazy casino.

Mira plops a tray in front of mine on one of the cafeteria tables. Her meal is about as sensible as the one I have, minus the salad. Our metabolisms, however, are not the same. Mira has a supermodel's figure, while I've got what some might call an hourglass. Or a pear shape when I'm hard-core PMSing. "What have you found on Blackwell?"

"Nothing," I grumble.

Mira pauses mid-chew, her cookie dangling from her hand. She eats her desserts first, which I've got to admire. "Nothing? It's been months since Drake was convicted." She sets her cookie down. "He's already serving time for the assault and the money-laundering thing the casino pinned on him. Drake was a bully, but no one gets caught that spectacularly unless they're a pawn. Someone else is in charge."

"I know." I dismiss the healthy food and eye my cookie. Maybe Mira's got the right of it. Dessert first.

I've tried to find something on Blue Casino to take to the police. I've scoured every database and file I have access to, which has taken weeks in between working. I've even spent my personal time at functions the casino holds, thinking I might catch something. But nothing. Not one darn thing has gone down lately that I could label as suspicious, unless you consider Adam's promotion. Which I do.

Unfortunately, it's not illegal to promote someone, just like it isn't illegal to fire someone for poor performance. Adam's boss was fired after the file that held information on the suite Mira and Tyler found landed in my hands while the woman was out sick. It's clear the old hospitality manager got fired for inadvertently leaking information—information that went mysteriously missing from my desk.

On paper, Blue Casino is as clear as the lake it's named after. But dig deep enough, and there's a murky center. I just know it.

Like Mira said, it's hard to believe Drake was the only criminal in this place. Maybe I'm allowing past bullies to tarnish my relationship with the CEO. There are bad bosses out there who aren't involved in illegal activities. And I might believe that—if Blackwell wasn't so adamant about keeping me out of the business he has going on with his Blue Stars, and if Mira and Tyler hadn't found the suite filled with drugs the casino seemed to be supplying.

"I can't pin anything on him, and believe me, I've tried." I bite into my cookie. I don't believe for a minute that the Blue Stars quit what they were doing in that suite just because it was suddenly stripped. And there's something about these guys getting away with it that really pisses me off. Maybe it's because I was on the receiving end of people ruining lives—different bullies, same town—but there's no way I can walk away from this.

I set my half-eaten cookie down. "I can't find a paper trail. Blackwell and his Blue Star assholes have been extra cautious since Drake Peterson was jailed."

Mira winces. "I'm glad, in a way. Maybe they've cleaned things up?"

I shake my head. "I've considered that, but you said they were clearing things out when you and Tyler found the suite, not closing up shop. I'm happy there haven't been recent reports of assaults and that we haven't found another suite with drugs, but the casino is hiding something. Why else would Blackwell keep me out of the hiring of new employees? It's like he's setting something up he doesn't want me involved in."

"You're right. That is strange."

"I've given up looking internally. Blackwell keeps everything buttoned up around me. I can't get into his little Blue Star crew, so I've started researching his background. Maybe I'll find something there."

"Can't hurt." Mira takes a bite of her main dish, now that she's eaten her cookie. She studies my face as if deciding something. "There is one person among Blackwell's sapphire ring boys you could get close to."

I take a bite of the chicken finger. Okay, maybe grease is just as good as sugar for a pick-me-up. I swallow the bite in my mouth. "Pretty sure there isn't. I've tried, and not without a good deal of humiliation. Those jackasses who kiss Blackwell's ass taunt me. They let me know I'm not welcome, all while flirting shamelessly. I'm sure one or more would be game to sleep with me, but I wouldn't be getting any information out of it. Not that I would ever consider doing something so disgusting." I shiver at the thought of sleeping with Paul, or any of the men who walk around the casino wearing Blue Star rings.

"I wasn't referring to *those* guys." She smiles knowingly.

"Oh no." The sparkle in her eye should have warning signs. "Don't even go where I think you're going."

"Come on, Hayden. What do you have against Adam? I know you want him."

I choke on that last bite of chicken. "*Want him?* I'd rather have my eyebrows shaved than get close to that oily bastard. He's all charm and good looks, but you can't trust him."

Mira takes a sip of her lemonade. "Your eyebrows, really? I'm just saying, you should try. Does he push you away like the others?"

"Not exactly," I say warily.

"Right. He doesn't. You even said last night that it wasn't him you were angry with, but some of the things you've had to put up with at Blue. From what I've seen, Adam has tried to be your friend. Granted, he pushes your buttons, which I think he does intentionally to get a rise out of you. He's not a bad guy."

"He harasses me."

Mira's face scrunches in disbelief.

"He argues with me nonstop," I add.

"That's not harassment," she points out.

"It makes me want to throw a stapler at his head, so I consider it pretty darn harassing."

Mira balls up her napkin and spins her legs over the metal picnic-style bench, which causes every male head to swivel in her direction. "I'm just saying, in addition to your background check on Blackwell, be...a little more open to a friendship with Adam. He's a resource you've yet to tap."

"Tap?" What exactly does she want me to do with him?

She rolls her eyes. "Poor choice of words. You know what I mean."

I dab the corners of my mouth with my napkin and stand. "I'll try. But I make no promises. If he bugs me enough to consider strangling his handsome neck, I will not be held accountable for murder."

She chuckles. "You two. You should have gotten a room months ago."

Get a room? Is she crazy? "I don't care how good-looking Adam is; he drives me nuts. I'll remind you when disaster strikes that this was *your* suggestion."

She grins. "This should be interesting."

After parting ways with Mira in the Blue cafeteria, I head to my office, speed-walking past Adam's door, just in case he's out loitering. I said I would try. I didn't say it would begin today.

I'm a few steps past his office when I hear my name called. My shoulders slump. I groan quietly and turn around.

"Do you have a moment?" Adam asks, his hands tucked into his suit pants, coat opened to a dress shirt stretched over an athletic chest and trim waist.

I am strong. I can do this.

Maybe Mira is right. Maybe now is the perfect time to start being more civil toward Adam. I plaster a smile on my face. "Sure, what's up?"

Adam's eyes widen marginally. Okay, so maybe that was a little too cheery compared to my normal demeanor around him.

"I thought you might want to know that I found an assistant. I hired her this morning. She's *ideal*."

The glint in his eyes can't be a good sign. I saw Adam last night. How the hell did he find and hire someone in a few hours? "She?"

"She."

"How did you recruit her?"

"Let's just say she's a customer service professional. She'll be perfect in hospitality."

Civil, friendly, I remind myself. "Well, congratulations. I look forward to meeting her." My civility has its limits. "But you know, you haven't won the bet yet. We agreed on two weeks. If she's still here after that, then we can talk."

He grins, but his eyes narrow. "You can't fire her, Hayden. That would nullify our deal."

I turn and continue walking down the hall, saying over my shoulder, "Oh no, that's your job."

Chapter Seven

Adam

All is going according to plan. I hired an assistant faster than I thought I would, and the girl's perfect— exactly as Paul and William indicated. A perfect ten for sure, but she's also mercenary as hell. She grilled me on salary before I'd even offered her the position. She's got to be good if she negotiates like that.

I rinse the pasta I started after I got home from work, and turn off the burner that's heating the sauce. Most of the time, I grab takeout, but sometimes even that's a pain in the ass. Over the years, I've taught myself to cook the basics. A particular skill my brothers, as self-sufficient as they claim to be, enjoy taking advantage of by stopping by unannounced around dinnertime.

I put out a place setting and crank up *SportsCenter*, preparing to dive into a mountain of pasta and sports highlights, when the doorbell rings.

Jesus, how do my brothers always know? Their sense of timing is uncanny.

I mute the TV and cross the great room to the front door. Only, it's not one of my brothers.

"Are you Adam?" The woman standing on my porch is wearing heavy makeup and so many sparkles near her ears, breasts, and shoes that I'm momentarily blinded.

I glance at her friend—a brunette with a black choker and painted red lips. Both women are in mile-high heels and dresses that delve just below the sweet spot of their thighs. I'm pretty sure I could guess cup sizes as well, with the view I have.

"Sure, I'm Adam. What can I do for you?"

"Paul sent us." Blondie rattles off Paul's last name and description. "He told us to show you a good time tonight. Of course, if the cops ask, his name wasn't Paul and he was a tall Viking-looking guy." She grins in a kittenish manner and pulls out a velvet drawstring pouch. "He wanted me to give you this. Said you'd love it."

I take the pouch and peer inside—at a sealed bag of white powder.

Fuck. Leave it to the jackasses I work with to send over prostitutes and cocaine.

I get it that Paul and William are happy I'm on board, but this is going above and beyond. In fact, it screams of some kind of test.

If this were a true celebration of my promotion, Paul and William would be here. This is something else. I'm not exactly sure what it is, but turning these girls away would be a bad move. Knowing Paul, he'll take it as a personal insult. And if this is a test, I can't fail. I need their confidence if I want bonuses that will cover the income I receive from the family fortune.

I grin and step aside. "Come on in, ladies. Make yourselves at home." I pull out my phone and shoot off a quick text message.

The women walk in, and they do make themselves at home. And I mean *really* at home. They take off their dresses and bare themselves down to sequined bras and G-strings.

I pour glasses of wine, discreetly checking the time. I keep my expression bland and friendly.

The brunette with the black choker walks over. I reach to hand her a glass, but instead of taking the wine, she palms me. A spark of life that can't be helped occurs below. I've been celibate for I don't know how long. Months? *Too long.*

My smile is confident. "Why don't you have a seat at the table? You can join me for dinner."

Blondie eyes the bulge in my pants from across the island. "I see my serving right here."

"Me too," says Choker Girl, inching closer.

"Ladies, what kind of gentleman would I be if I took you straight to bed?"

"A normal one." Choker Girl giggles, which comes out warped, given she's painted up like a naughty Elvira.

Checking my phone beneath the counter, I grab one of the plates of pasta. "Well, call me old-fashioned. Besides, you'll need the energy." I wink and hand the plate to Blondie before grabbing the other one and checking my cell again, even though I just did two seconds ago. I pass the food to Choker Girl, who's sitting now.

This time, she reaches around and palms my ass. "Maybe we don't want old-fashioned."

I gotta give her props for assertiveness.

Holding the plate between us, I don't budge. She pouts and finally takes it.

I move to my end of the table, and just as I drop into my

seat, the door swings open. Well, *bursts* is more like it. My wayward youngest brother throws it open so hard it crashes into the opposite wall.

I sigh and shake my head. Hunt's chest is rising and falling, his breaths heavy. By the disheveled look of his hair and half-tucked shirt, I'm guessing he didn't waste time looking in the mirror before he headed over.

Hunt's gaze homes in on the half-naked women at my table, and he fingers his hair back. "Well, hello there, ladies."

Hunt lives up to his name, and aren't I happy he does? I'm not interested in entertaining these women, though I can't very well send them on their way and fail Paul's test. But my slut of a brother would be happy to oblige.

"Right on time. Ladies, this is my brother, Hunter. He's very friendly, and he enjoys spending time with beautiful women."

Blondie licks her lips and strips my baby brother bare with her gaze. "Yummy." If I didn't know Hunt ate women like her for lunch, I might worry about him.

Hunt kicks off his shoes, because he knows I don't like dirty shit in my house, and saunters over. "Tell me your names."

Choker Girl uses her trademark gesture and palms him, which my slutty baby brother leans into, cupping the breast she's blatantly shoved beneath his nose. Blondie stands and rubs on him from behind. Hunt reaches back and grabs her bare ass cheek... And this is my cue to leave.

I pound my red, grab a small box from the junk drawer, and exit the dining room, heading for the bathroom. Once inside, I pull out the velvet pouch and dump the white powder into the toilet. I flush three times to make sure it's all gone, then pull out a match from the small box and burn the plastic bag over the toilet, flushing that next.

I collapse onto the covered toilet seat and wait until I can't hear talking. But even then, I wait. No talking means other things, and I'm hoping my slut of a brother has the common sense to take it into the spare bedroom. I give him another minute or two.

Hunter is the brother with no shame. Not that the others haven't whored themselves out, myself included, come to think of it—I was a Club Tahoe cabana boy, after all. Hunt just took our errant ways to a new level of depravity.

I texted him as soon as the girls arrived, but he surpassed my expectations and arrived within a few minutes. Must have driven like the wind.

I lean forward, forearms on my knees. This better not be a mistake, passing off the women on Hunt. Oh, I'm not worried about my brother. He'll be thanking me tomorrow. I'm more concerned about what Paul will think. Sleeping with the women he sent holds no interest for me. I'm not a cabana boy anymore. My tastes have refined since then.

After a few minutes, I peek out the bathroom door to an empty living room. This is ridiculous, hiding in my own house... And yet I walk out silently, and sneak past the kitchen.

The fact that I can't see my brother or the women doesn't mean they aren't still here. In fact, the closer I get to the living room, the louder the thumping sounds come from down the hall. At least Hunt didn't use the master bedroom. I would have to kill him slowly when I saw him next.

With the women occupied and the coke disposed of, I grab my keys and escape the hell out of my house. The night air is warm as I jog down the stairs to the dock. The place

I've been renting over the last year costs me an arm and a leg, but being able to take out the Chaparral whenever I want is worth it. And now seems like a good time, with my brother and two prostitutes defiling my home.

I unhitch the boat from the dock and climb on board, reaching for a windbreaker inside the bow storage. I start the motor and cruise past the no-wake zone.

My home is on the eastern shore, slightly north of the California/Nevada border. I steer south, the blocky neon outlines of the casinos coming into view against the night mountain backdrop.

Paul never struck me as an upstanding citizen, but I'm redefining my opinion of him by the minute. The guy is bad news, but bad news or not, I need him. And I need Blue Casino.

As long as no one gets hurt, how wrong can all of this be? So Blackwell wants me to hire a few less-than-discerning individuals to fill positions for the new venture. Who am I to judge?

I can do this.

I glance up at the patchwork of stars. Out here, I am no one and anyone I want to be. Out here, away from the world, the pressure drains. I can separate myself from my family, from my work, from everything.

And for the first time, it's not enough. I want more, and that scares the hell out of me.

* * *

I ROLL out of bed the next morning and throw on a T-shirt and jeans. The women and Hunt were still here after I returned from my boat ride, but glancing out the front window, I only see the girls' sports convertible. A nice sports convertible. Paul wasn't playing around. He paid good money for these women.

Shaking my head, I make it into the kitchen. Better scramble some eggs. The disappointment will go over easier if the women have been fed.

Minutes later, the ladies roll out, their faces less made up than the night before, hair a bit worse for the wear. I've never heard of a prostitute staying the night. Which goes to show the effect Hunt has on women. Bastard.

Blondie looks around. "Where's your brother?"

I dish eggs onto two plates. "Gone. You take your coffee with milk?"

The women glance at each other. "Gone?" Choker Girl asks, minus the choker this morning, a desolate look on her face. "He left without saying goodbye?"

Perfect. Hunter breaks even call girls' hearts. "Were you hoping for his number?" I ask dryly.

The women reluctantly sit at the bar and pick at the breakfast I've set out.

"Just so we're clear," I say as I refill their coffee, "you had an excellent time last night, correct?"

"Oh yes." Blondie's eyes are dreamy. "Your brother is a god in bed."

I cringe. "Yeah, I don't need to hear that." I pull out the stack of bills I grabbed from my nightstand before I came out. "If anyone asks, your services were utilized and most welcome. Are we clear?"

Blondie's eyes narrow. "You don't want Paul to know you didn't sleep with us."

I smile. "Smart girl."

"Are you gay?" Choker Girl asks, taking a bite of her food, eyes curious but without judgment.

I chuckle. "Uh, that would be a no." In fact, there's one

woman who's speared her pointy heels into my chest and is becoming a pain in my ass.

I should have taken these women up on their offer last night, considering I'm not interested in strings, especially strings with strong emotions. And anything with Hayden would be intense. I don't need or want that.

The women finish their breakfast, and fortunately, there's no need for me to usher them out. They grab their purses and head for the door.

Blondie turns back. "Next time Hunter wants to party, tell him to call Celia. I left my number in the back pocket of his jeans."

I raise my eyebrow. "You knew he wouldn't be here in the morning?"

She shrugs with a light smile. "Guys like him don't stick around. But they do come back for seconds." And with that, she and her friend leave.

Chapter Eight

Hayden

I jam a handful of chocolate-covered peanuts in my mouth and eat through my stress. I've found jack after searching the casino, but scrolling through the online news releases on my laptop, my feet nestled in fuzzy socks, I've come across articles on Blackwell's past that paint an interesting story.

*Joseph Blackwell, heir to the Blackwell real estate fortune, uses his San Francisco connections to make a name for himself in Lake Tahoe real estate.—**The Lake Tahoe Merchant***

*Joseph Blackwell, heir and owner of the Season Hotel in San Francisco, has lunch with his godfather and Mexican businessman Jose De la Cruz. De la Cruz has been linked to drug trafficking, but never convicted.—**The San Francisco Tribune***

Right, *linked*. That's the media's way of saying, *We're pretty sure he's a psychotic drug lord, but since he's so clever at not being caught, we have no hard evidence.* It's not a direct hit, but then again, I didn't think I'd find one, or Blackwell wouldn't be our CEO. Mira and the others are on their way over to talk about where to go from here, and this gives me something to show them.

Maybe Blackwell isn't running some kind of drug and prostitute ring at Blue. Maybe it's this De la Cruz guy? As I ponder the connection, a face appears on the other side of the window right next to my head.

"Helloooo," Mira says through the screen, cackling.

I jump back, nearly falling off the couch. "Holy shit." I hold my laptop precariously with the tips of my fingers as I brace myself between the couch and the coffee table, catching my breath.

I carefully set the computer on the table and scramble to open the front door. Mira is bent over laughing and clinging to a large paper bag. "Not funny," I say. "You could have given me a heart attack. I should fire you for that." There's absolutely no truth to my words, but dammit, she gets me every time!

She straightens, a look of innocence on her face. "Hayden, you love me. You'd never fire me."

Mira enters the house, followed by Gen, Lewis, and Tyler. "You do make life easier at Blue," I agree. And she's right; I love her like a sister.

When I returned to Lake Tahoe, the house I grew up in felt smaller, but with the guys filing in, it's bursting at the seams. Lewis's head is only a few inches below the low-beamed wood ceiling, and standing shoulder to shoulder, Lewis and Tyler might actually be able to touch the walls on either side.

My parents originally bought this place as a starter house. After a few years, they loved it so much we stayed. And with only one child, two bedrooms never became a problem. But that's not the case with two overgrown men and their girlfriends inside. Any minute now, we're going to be bouncing into each other like pinballs if I don't put these guys somewhere.

"Have a seat." I gesture to the small L-shaped sectional next to the wood-burning stove my dad installed when I was five.

Lewis and Tyler take up the couches, and Mira, who's been here before, heads for the galley kitchen I remodeled six months ago. I hear her clanking around in the refrigerator. When she returns, she's juggling cans of beer and handing them out. I take a seat in the rocking chair across from the guys.

Gen pops the top of her can and sits on the arm of the couch Lewis's large body is taking up. "I spoke to my dad today." Gen's famous ex-quarterback dad was instrumental in getting Drake Peterson behind bars after her attack. "His lawyers say that unless we have more evidence against the casino or Blackwell, we can't do anything. Which is pretty much what we already knew. I can't believe Blackwell has managed to keep the relocation of those suites a secret. It's been weeks since Drake's conviction." She nudges Lewis with her elbow. "Can't you tap into the security cameras while you're working on electrical or something?"

Lewis and his father own Sallee Construction and are often hired by the casino for construction jobs.

He frowns. "Illegal. I could lose my license, and you might not be able to use the footage. Pretty sure you need a warrant to get that sort of thing."

Mira squeezes between Tyler's legs on the other couch.

"We could try to get in with the security guys who work the surveillance system. Like, oops, we just stumbled upon this here footage of an old guy paying the casino for drugs and kinky sex with a beautiful woman."

"Already looked into that," I say. "The surveillance guys signed confidentiality agreements. They could serve prison time for stealing surveillance footage. And like Lewis said, I don't think it would count in court."

"And they need a strong reason to order a warrant." Gen sighs and slides down the arm of the couch until she's sitting on one of Lewis's legs. He absently pulls her higher on his lap. "According to my dad, as far as the police are concerned, Drake Peterson was the cause of the casino's illegal activities, and he's been taken care of."

"So we have nothing." I tip my head back and stare at the planked wood ceiling. I love this ceiling, but right now I barely see it. "I work as a manager. It should be easy to find something to take to the police, if there's really something going on."

Have we been wrong?

Mira snarls. "Those sapphire ring guys are such bitches. How the hell are they hiding everything?"

I shake my head. "I wish I knew."

"What about the background search? Did you find anything on Blackwell?"

Remembering the articles I found, I rock forward and stand. "I did, actually."

I head into the spare bedroom and grab the print-outs I made. I hand one to Tyler and Mira, and the other to Gen and Lewis. "Blackwell comes from money. And he has serious connections. His family started out in San Francisco real estate, made a fortune, then bought and ran several successful hotels.

Check out the connection between him and a Mexican drug guy."

Mira scans the article. "The suspected drug trafficker? There's nothing to confirm it." She pulls out her iPhone and starts searching.

"No proof, but come on, a major drug dealer? We know Blue stockpiled illegal drugs in the suite you and Tyler found. That can't be a coincidence."

Mira shakes her head as she reads from her phone. "One or two articles suggest a connection between him and that guy, but there's not much."

"I know," I say, "but don't you think it's possible he's Blackwell's supplier?"

Tyler shifts behind Mira. "Kind of a stretch. Plenty of drugs in this town. If Blackwell wants connections to dealers, all he has to do is step outside his door."

I bite the corner of my lip. "Am I the only one who thinks the link is suspicious?"

Mira sets down her phone. "We're just playing devil's advocate, Hayden. You could be right, but that's not the point. We need evidence. Regardless of whether or not Blackwell is getting help from De la Cruz, everything is behind closed doors. We've got nothing to go on."

Blackwell wouldn't be able to get away with selling drugs and prostitution at one of his hotels in San Francisco. But here? Nevada promotes gambling and sin. It's the perfect setup. On the other hand, Blue Casino isn't some legal brothel off the beaten path. If Blackwell is hiding illegal drugs, and what we suspect is a prostitution ring, it would be inside a conventional establishment.

"What about Adam?" Mira asks. "Did you take my suggestion?"

I roll my eyes. "I thought about it, and you'll be proud. I

actually smiled at him after we parted the other day after lunch."

Mira shakes her head. "That's a start, but you had better be prepared to make an about-face and kiss his ass."

"Mira."

"What? Work on that, will you? He's our best lead."

Lewis inches over, giving Gen more room to sit. He stares at Mira. "What does Adam have to do with this?"

Tyler tosses a chocolate-covered peanut in his mouth from the bowl of snacks I left out during my Blackwell research. "Mira and Hayden think Adam's getting involved with the Blue Stars." He chomps on the food and scratches his head. "Adam and I were on the soccer team together in high school. He can be a jackass, but he's a decent guy. I don't think he'd do that."

"That doesn't sound like Adam," Lewis agrees.

Tyler raises his brow at Mira as if to say, *I told you so.*

She crosses her arms. "Tyler, you saw the same thing I did." She glares at Lewis. "And what happened to family loyalty?" Mira is like a little sister to Lewis. She's clearly pulling the family card. "Something's going on. We can't just ignore this."

"No," Lewis says, "but I don't think Adam is involved. Not to mention, his family is richer than this entire town. What would he get out of it?"

I scrunch my nose. I'd forgotten about Adam's family. I mean, he walks around like a runway model for Armani. Even with his management salary, it's nothing compared to the cash he must earn just by being a Cade.

So why *would* Adam risk everything to get involved with Blackwell? Lewis is right. It doesn't make sense.

Have I been wrong about Adam working with the CEO? The guy is an opportunist, but maybe not as bad as I originally thought. He seemed sincerely upset when I told him I was the girl he'd told Jaeger to dump.

Tyler grabs another handful of candy. "I'll talk to Adam. See how things are at work."

Mira twists around and steals a chocolate-covered nut from him. "Would he tell you what they're doing at Blue?"

Tyler shrugs. "Can't hurt to ask."

She looks back at me. "You need to try talking to him too. You work side by side with him now."

I press my fingers to my forehead. "Don't remind me."

I forgive Adam for the past, but that doesn't mean I trust him. Mira's right, though. We need inside information, and I'm the best person to get close to him at work and check things out. And for the first time, I hope Lewis is correct and Adam isn't involved in anything illegal.

Chapter Nine

Adam

B ridget shows up for her first day of work, and she cometh bearing coffee.

Entering my office, she sets down a to-go cup on my desk. "No cream or sugar. You don't seem like a sweets sort of guy." She winks, and right away my day is off to a good start.

Bridget is wearing a light tweed pantsuit with a tasteful amount of cleavage in the form of a cream blouse with the top two buttons left open. A woman with forethought and a keen sense of aesthetics—what more could I ask for? As far as I'm concerned, I am a genius. I've hired the perfect assistant.

Hayden will be furious.

I rise from behind my desk, buttoning my suit jacket. "Why, thank you, Bridget. Let me show you where your office is." I pick up the coffee and take a whiff. It's a nutty, herbal scent. Gourmet.

Everything about my second encounter with Bridget is

different. The day I hired her, I tracked her down at Club Desire. She'd been recommended by Paul, and was wearing a lot less. Despite her lack of clothing during the interview, she carried herself with a professional air and seemed eager for a change of environment.

I guide Bridget out of my office and to the right, where another room resides—this one small, but efficient. "IT set up your computer and connected your phone line. Most of our correspondence will be over email. You said you're proficient with office software?"

"Oh yes. The girls and I needed to be." She runs a finger along the edge of her desk, her expression shielded. "You'd be surprised how much extra business is done over the computer."

Do I want to know what she's referring to? I have a very good imagination.

"Why don't you log in and get the lay of the land? A default password is posted on your monitor, along with instructions on how to change it. I've linked my calendar to yours. I'd like you to attend and take notes at all of the meetings highlighted in green, so please check the dates and times."

"Of course." Bridget sets her bag beside the chair at her desk and boots up her computer. She looks over, smiling. "I'll just get settled."

"Excellent." And what a fine time to gloat it is. Hayden has accused me of it before; no need to disappoint her now. "I'll be back in a few minutes to talk about the first meeting we have this afternoon."

I head down the hall with a spring in my step. I rap on the door that is as familiar to me as my own.

"Come in," Hayden calls.

I enter her office and notice her desk, which is, as

usual, cluttered. And then there's Hayden across the room, perfectly groomed in a snug, lightweight belted cardigan over a navy pencil skirt that hugs her shapely hips as she reaches to tuck a folder on the top shelf of a bookcase.

One of the first things I noticed about Hayden was her incredible figure, and I'm not talking skinny waif, but curves in all the right places and a small waist.

Her honey-brown hair and golden eyes flash as she glances over. "Oh, it's you," she says, as though she already knew it would be.

Am I that predictable? Hmm, somehow that doesn't bother me.

I walk over and reach above her head, gently slipping the folder from her hand and putting it in place.

"Thank you," she mumbles, and tugs in her bottom lip with her top. It plumps back out, wet and inviting. A thrill more potent than Blondie grabbing my junk last night bolts through me.

I clear my throat and glance at her desk. "You should straighten that up so the cleaning crew can do their job."

She squints at me, sparks firing from those beautiful eyes. "Did you come here for a reason?" She returns to her desk, shoulders tense as she drops briskly into her chair.

I can't hold back my smile. God, I love my job.

I follow her over and run a finger along the surface. Her gaze tracks the motion as I rub my thumb and forefinger together, as if there's dust. "Just wanted to know if you've had a chance to meet my new assistant?"

Bridget walked into the building only ten minutes ago, so I know Hayden hasn't. All the more reason to let Hayden know that my assistant is here, and that the bet is *on*.

"She's busy familiarizing herself with my calendar." I

raise the large to-go container in my hand. "Even brought me coffee. Bridget's thoughtful like that."

Hayden frowns and crosses her arms.

I turn and walk to the door. "Prepare to lose that bet, Hayden."

"It's not over yet," she calls as I exit the room, beaming. A soft *thump* sounds on the other side of the wall and my grin widens.

I whistle as I make my way to my excellent new assistant.

Okay, so *excellent* was a poor choice of words. Bridget has only been at Blue a couple of hours. Of course it will take her time to adjust.

"I'm so sorry, Adam. I didn't realize I'd be deleting the appointments from your calendar as well." Bridget smiles sweetly, a chagrined look on her face as she stands in my office.

Everyone makes mistakes now and then, right? "It's your first day. I don't expect perfection. Just make sure you connect with Blackwell's secretary and fill in the meetings that were deleted. I'll need that by the end of the day. Stay late if you have to."

"Oh, absolutely. I'll take care of it." Bridget hurries toward the door, right as Paul enters. He steps aside for her, winking and checking out her ass as she departs.

Paul hooks his thumb over his shoulder. "I told you she was the one, didn't I?"

"She'll do once she learns the ropes." I pull on my glasses and look over the floor plan Paul's secretary walked over before lunch. "So what is this?"

Paul closes the door. "*That* is what you've been asking about. It's the new venture. As head of hospitality, your services are integral in setting up Bliss. We started with two suites, but four brand new ones are under construction."

"So what are they for, exactly? In-room gambling, personal masseuse? I see the full bar in the schematics."

He grins, his jaw shifting as though he's attempting to hold back his amusement. "Those things, sure. And more."

I set the plans on my desk and let out a deep breath. "Explain *more*."

Paul drops into one of the chairs across from me and crosses his legs at the knee. "For one, there will be women— let's call them professional dancers."

"You're hiring strippers?"

"*Exotic dancers*. And they'll be under contract, and not actual employees of the casino."

"So strippers. What else?" I glance at the plans again. There are four bedrooms per suite, and what looks to be a large, elaborate communal dining area, a desk area—which is more of a reception inside the suite—and no balcony. All of Blue's suites have balconies. "According to these plans, the Bliss suites are larger than anything we have at the casino. Why wouldn't they have balconies?"

"You know how the rich and famous bring in drugs, and there's nothing we can do about it?" I nod. "We're going to" —he wags his head, as if attempting to come up with the right words—"continue to turn a blind eye. Balconies and low windows are too convenient for prying eyes. We want to protect our most ardent clientele."

"So women and drugs," I say, making sure I've nailed the finer points.

Paul nods with a shrug. "Basically."

I pull off my glasses and rub my temples. Paul's leaving

stuff out, and he's not one to hold back. He has a tendency to share *too* much information, particularly when it comes to female conquests. "Do I want to know what you aren't telling me?"

"Don't know what you're talking about," he says straight-faced. "What you see is basically it. And your job," he says slowly, as if I'm a toddler, "is to help us hire the strippers, bodyguards, and get that Bridget trained so she can support the suite concierges."

With four brothers, I've learned to control my temper. But whatever Paul's not saying about Bliss and, most especially, the condescending manner in which he's speaking to me, have my blood rising.

I stand and face the window and the view of the lake. My view is different than Hayden's, facing northwest toward my home and Club Tahoe instead of Heavenly and South Shore. A different shade of beautiful.

This job is my chance at freedom from the family funds. I could find another job, but one where the financial gain means no change in lifestyle? Not likely, with or without the Ivy League degree. Which means I need to put up with Paul's condescending mouth. Can't be worse than what I put up with working for my father.

I turn my back to the window and lean my hip against the ledge, crossing my arms. "As I said when you first proposed this venture, give me a list of employees and the attributes you want in them—since I'm sure you have something in mind if you're hiring strippers—and I'll take care of it."

Paul stands and tilts his head toward Bridget's office. "More like her. I'll make a list of exactly what we're looking for and have it to you first thing tomorrow." He strides to the door and pulls it open. "Tonight, I'm going to see what plans your assistant has."

"Paul," I say before he's gone. "Keep your hands off Bridget. You remember the last executive who thought he could touch?"

Paul's face turns stony. "You weren't here then, so I suggest you mind your own damn business."

He exits, leaving the door open, and heads in Bridget's direction.

I have no doubt she can handle herself against guys like Paul. Probably had to deal with them every day at her old job. But she works for me now, and I'll keep an eye on her just the same.

I sink into my chair and stare at the schematics. "What are you, Bliss? A luxury suite built for pleasure, and what else?"

Chapter Ten

I pull up to my eldest brother's place. Levi lives in a log cabin off State Route 207. This eastern part of the Tahoe Basin looks different than the west side, the land here filled with brush and evergreen bushes. When glaciers scoured out the western side thousands of years ago, it skimmed off the topsoil, but these soils were left intact. The mountains where my brother lives are almost lush compared to the craggy granite and pine of Emerald Bay.

Grace, Levi's dog, darts out the screen door and launches herself at my legs, her strong little body butting up against me. "Hey there, Gracie. You been a good girl?" I scratch behind her ears with one hand and close the door with my other, leaning into her body so she doesn't get caught between the door and the side of the car in her wiggle frenzy.

Grace licks my pant leg and marks up my polished shoes with her tongue, taking a moment to sniff one. "Just me, girl. Haven't traded you for another lady."

The screen door opens again, and Levi hobbles out, his ankle in a cast, a nearly full-grown beard on his face. I've never seen a black eye as bad as the one Levi's been sporting these last couple of weeks. It covers his face, going from the middle of his forehead across the slope of his nose and halfway down his cheekbone, and looks nasty as hell.

"When was the last time you saw a razor?" Beards are popular again, but Levi is a clean-cut guy. He grew whiskers younger than the rest of us, and has been fighting the battle ever since.

He scratches his beard. At least the T-shirt he's wearing appears clean. "Can't remember." Levi gives Grace a pat, since she's tossed me over and turned her attentions to him. "What brings your sorry ass around?"

He moves to the side of the porch and props his walking cast on a bench, dropping onto the porch swing.

I climb the steps and glance pointedly at the Italian suit I'm wearing, then back at his cast. "My sorry ass? My sorry ass is in fine form, or so the ladies tell me." I grin cockily.

"Is that what you tell them to get laid?" he says absently, rubbing the top of his leg above the cast that stretches up to the bottom of his knee.

"No need, brother. They flock." Of course, I won't mention to Levi how long I've been without a woman. He'd give me crap for it.

Women in town are either looking to settle down, or searching for someone with deep pockets, and both types are transparent as hell. There is one exception...Hayden is feisty, but she keeps me on my toes. I'm not sure what I would do if she changed her mind and took me up on my flirtation. I'd like to think I'd be smart enough to stay away from the disaster that would be any relationship we attempted, but I'm not sure my large brain is in command anymore where she's concerned.

I fold my suit jacket on the bench opposite Levi and sit,

tugging my pant leg to cross my ankle neatly over my knee. I shake my head. "Levi, we gotta get you out. You look like a lumberjack, and not a healthy one at that." That's not entirely true. Levi is a fireman. He's always been physically fit, but the patches of his skin that aren't black and blue are pale now with a grayish tinge.

Levi pats his thigh and Grace hurries over, licking the crap out of his hand. That dog is easy. "I'm doing fine right here. I figure by staying in the house for a while I'm saving the mothers out there a conversation about the bogeyman."

"Who cares what you look like? The cement that fell on your stubborn skull could have killed you. You're lucky you made it out with all of your limbs and your brain intact. When did the doctor say you could return to work?" If anything will snap Levi out of his funk, getting back to the fire station will. He loves his job more than his own brothers.

Levi scratches Grace's side and stares at her fur coat, his voice barely audible as he murmurs. "No more jobs."

I take a moment to decipher his meaning. "Your ankle's busted up, but once it heals, you'll work again."

"I said *jobs*—fires. There's no going back. They wanted to reclassify me to a desk. So I quit."

I drop my foot and lean forward. "Why would they do that? You're set to make captain in a couple of years." I glance at his cast. "You said it was a clean break."

He absently touches the left side of his forehead, right above the angry red scar he sustained after a partial roof collapse during his last fire. "The ankle was a clean break. The knock to the head...I lost some vision. Nothing I can't live without, but enough that the fire department wants me on desk duty."

I take in the desolate look on his face, the tension in his

wide shoulders. Levi carried the weight of the family—was the responsible one, while I catered to our father and the others ran wild. He knocked our skulls together when we fought, told us to get up when we fell down, and went up against our father when he was being pigheaded about who our friends were, our plans after high school—pretty much everything. And right now Levi is trying not to fall apart; the brother who's always had it together.

I swallow the dry ball that's lodged in my throat. This can't be happening. Cade men are tall and athletic, but Levi is built like the houses he protects. He's a brick of a man, and to see him weakened mentally or physically is unnatural.

I rub my face. "Jesus Christ." Being a firefighter is the one thing he's ever wanted. Desk duty would be like a death knell for him. No wonder he's been holed up these last two weeks, not wanting to see my brothers or me. The only reason I'm here is because I'm a pushy bastard who never listens to what my brothers say.

I was the conformer in the family, accepting the sports cars our father gave me whenever I did something he liked. I dressed the part of a Cade, wore designer clothes, lived lavishly, while the rest of my brothers did whatever the fuck they wanted. They pursued careers outside of Club Tahoe, lived month to month on their working-class paychecks as waiters, tour guides—firemen—while I danced to my father's tune, doing whatever Ethan Cade told me to do. Just as long as I got my monthly trust fund check.

I stare blindly at the pile of logs off to the side. I came here today to lean on Levi and ask what he thought about this Bliss venture, but he's the one who needs someone to lean on. And I'm no good at being dependable.

I stand and unbutton my dress shirt. I drop it on top of

my jacket. "Wood needs chopping." I tug my undershirt from my pants and stride across the yard to the ax.

I don't know if Levi needs more wood in the bin, but he's getting some, because I need to hack things up.

My older brother can't be a mess. If he is, that leaves me, as the second eldest, in charge. Not a single one of my brothers respects me. Loves me? Sure, as much as brothers who've harassed and argued all their lives can love one another. But their respect was something I lost years ago when I gave in to our father's demands.

Chapter Eleven

Hayden

I sort the paperwork for the auction and burlesque event. I've spent countless hours researching companies to find the right talent for the project that Blackwell put William in charge of. William is one of Blackwell's Blue Stars, but he's given me a surprising amount of freedom in helping him. He even handed over things he probably should have managed, like selecting party-staging companies. I can't complain. I would have had my hand in the formal paperwork no matter what, as head of HR. This way I got to have fun selecting the décor for the party, even if it was extra work.

I stare at the contracts in front of me. My documentation is thorough; the amount of work I've put in obvious. There's no way Blackwell can ignore my efforts. I've gone above and beyond what I was asked to do. I don't expect praise, but appreciation would be nice.

Nessa walks in and pauses near the door. "You busy?" She's wearing dark slacks and a white blouse, but her height is average today, so I know she's got her platforms on under those long pants, or she'd be four inches shorter.

Nessa normally comes to my armpit. She is tiny in every way, and beautiful. She probably has no problem finding the right fit when shopping, while I have to buy everything bigger, and either deal with poor fit, or take in the waist. Sucks.

"I have a minute, but I'm about to head to a management meeting." I stack my folders and check my hair and makeup in the mirror I keep in the desk drawer. No stray locks sticking up. Lipstick on—*check*. I'm ready to make a good impression.

"I won't keep you," she says. "I just wanted to find out if you've seen the new girl?"

Ugh, again? Why does everyone want me to meet the woman Adam hired? "I haven't met Adam's new assistant."

"That was fast," she stage-whispers. "Did he pick her up off the street?"

I walk around my desk and meet Nessa at the door. "No idea, but I've already got a bet running with him that she won't last."

Nessa's eyes widen. "Really, a bet? So Mira got to you? She told me how she wants you to get close to him and find out what he knows."

I snort sardonically. "She's living in dreamland if she thinks we'll become close, but I've been harsh on him. He's annoying as hell, but not a bad guy." I straighten my sweater. "And as far as the bet goes, I'm doing that to prove a point."

"Which is?"

"That my job isn't as easy as everyone believes."

Her brow furrows. "Who thinks your job is easy? You're one of the hardest-working employees here."

And just like that, I want to cry. I love Nessa and Mira. They know how much time and effort I put into Blue. And that I care about making the casino the best it can be, despite what Blackwell believes. I swallow and take a deep breath. "Thank you."

She makes a sound of disbelief at the back of her throat. "It's the truth. Well, look, I won't keep you. I've got to meet with Deborah about the burlesque show." Her eyes widen with excitement. "Wait until you see our promo plan. It's going to blow your mind. You bring in the celebs and dancers, and marketing will do the rest."

* * *

Adam

WITH A TINTED glass dome that overlooks the heart of the gaming floor, the executive conference room of Blue Casino is in a class of its own. And I have Club Tahoe for comparison—a thirty-thousand-square-foot casino-hotel situated on the shores of Lake Tahoe and designed to feel like an elegant log cabin. There is nothing like Club Tahoe, with its indoor lazy river, the center of which boasts secluded fire pits for roasting s'mores. But Blue Casino has a vibe Club Tahoe can't surpass. The patrons come to Blue Casino for high-stakes gaming, a glitzy atmosphere, and the best-looking cocktail waitresses this side of the state line.

I grab the report off the top of the stack at the entrance, and make my way to the U-shaped meeting table. Blackwell typically runs our meetings with strict efficiency, but you never know. My father's meetings often ran into lunch. I'm still waiting for that one long-winded coworker to put us to sleep with his meticulous housekeeping of cocktail umbrellas and vending-machine supplies. And thus, I find a spot for optimal people-watching down below in case the meeting drags.

Scanning the agenda, I note the two upcoming events. Blue Casino is one of the premier entertainment providers in Lake Tahoe. Because of the scope of our next events, it will be all hands on deck today. Which means Hayden will be here. Speaking of whom...

Hayden stops in the doorway, her figure accentuated in a gray tailored short-sleeved fitted dress. Some chunky gold necklace drapes her throat, cream stilettos pushing her calves into soft swells, and damn if I'm not entranced. I love a put-together woman. Though even if Hayden were in sweats, she'd draw my eye. Despite her prickly nature—or because of it—Hayden has that effect on me.

A lock of caramel silk hair covers one eye as she rifles through a stack of manila file folders. William—damn his roaming hands—touches her shoulder, alerting her she's blocking the entrance. She bustles to the side and grabs the agenda. Glancing around the room, she spots me and frowns. She dashes to the opposite end of the table, only to be blocked by Eve, who steals the seat next to Blackwell.

That's right, Hayden, only two empty seats left.

Hayden darts for the second seat, across the table, but William snags it first.

The universe has it in for her. I cannot contain the joy that fills my heart knowing Hayden is forced to sit next to me. We often get stuck next to each other. Not that I'm complaining. The view works out just right for me, but I think she might object. If I were a different man, I might feel bad, but since I enjoy riling her up, it's a perk of the job.

"Are we all here?" Blackwell asks, though the question is rhetorical. He's already gestured for Eve to close the door.

"Let's make this quick. I have a meeting in thirty minutes." Blackwell rattles off a few details about the concert coming up, and checks in with the man in charge. When he gets to the celebrity auction and burlesque show, he turns to Hayden. "You've worked with William on contracts for outsourcing décor? We're spending a small fortune to transform the club that weekend."

"Yes." Hayden pushes around her manila file folders. "There are two contracts that support our company policy. These two places are by far the best available. And the burlesque dancers—"

Blackwell holds up his hand. "Those will go to William. William?"

William rises and walks around the table. Hayden hands him the folders, her expression one of stunned confusion. "I just received the contract proposals. Three out of the four burlesque companies are in conflict with our policies. I'd hoped to discuss it with you before we moved forward."

"That won't be necessary. William will take over from here. This event must be a success. We'll arrange for the contracts to go through a special account."

Hayden's jaw drops, and to be honest, I'm stunned as well. "I don't understand," she says. "Any time we hire, even for temporary positions, contractors and new employees must be prescreened."

Blackwell folds his fingers and sits back. "And they will be. As I said, William will handle it."

"But—" I squeeze her knee under the table and a squeak erupts from her throat, but she doesn't say any more. She stares straight ahead, her lips clamped.

After a moment, she cuts me a look, and I hold her stare. Blackwell pulled her off a project. One she should be involved with, but to speak out against the CEO is career suicide.

Blackwell turns to Eve. "Next up on the agenda?"

Eve outlines a few new policies the casino enacted to keep the employees safe—all lies, since Blackwell is working around his own system, which in effect nullifies the policies if no one polices them.

A secretary enters the room. "Your next appointment is here, Mr. Blackwell."

Blackwell presses his palms to the table and stands. "That'll be all for today."

Hayden stares as the management team files out. "Why'd you do it?" She looks over once they've left, her eyes furious.

I stand and close the top button of my suit jacket. "Because you were about to piss off our boss, and I couldn't watch you go down like that. From what I've witnessed these last few months, you're on shaky ground with him."

Every time Hayden stood up to our illustrious CEO, she had just cause, but working at Blue is a political game. One Hayden seems hellbent on not playing. Selfish of me, but I enjoy having her around. I don't want to see her get fired.

She stands and lifts her chest—the effect drawing my attention down instead of in the vicinity of her eyes. "Why the hell do you think you can tell me how to do my job?"

"Hayden." My voice is deep, a warning. This is to protect her, and I'm not sure how much longer I can allow her to think she has a say in it. It's about more than her getting fired. The more I learn about Blackwell and Paul, and the rest of the power management at Blue, the more unscrupulous I find them. I fully intend to win my bet with Hayden, but even if the world falls off its axis and I don't, I'm not letting her stoke the temper of our dubious CEO.

She crosses her arms. "Have you any idea how much time I spent curating the companies for this event? We've never hosted a burlesque show, and a celebrity auction on top of that? I've spent months—*months,* Adam—reaching out to contacts and meeting with people. And Blackwell hands it off to William, as if William has any idea what he's doing? It's ridiculous!"

"Don't take it personally."

"Don't take it—Have *you* ever worked your ass off and had your efforts ignored?" She flings out a hand and looks away. "Of course not. You're the prince of Lake Tahoe, Adam Cade, who can do no wrong."

I lean forward, her fiery temper and that chest she's thrusting in my face making me want to toss her on the table and show her how bad I can be. "I've been in your place before."

She glares back. "I don't believe you."

I've worked at Club Tahoe every summer since I was sixteen, in every facet of the business, and not once have my efforts been acknowledged, not even after I made Club Tahoe's golf course a stop on the PGA Tour. I've had my work handed off to others more senior than me, my ideas disregarded, or used and not acknowledged. I know what Hayden is going through, but no matter what I tell her, she wants to believe I'm still that insensitive asshole who convinced her boyfriend to break up with her.

"It doesn't matter what I've been through," I tell her. "What matters is that you can't show your emotions when your boss pisses you off. You're like one of those books you pad your office with, Hayden. We read every emotion that plays out on your face."

She steps forward, her chest nearly butting mine. "And that's worse than being an iceberg?" Her eyes narrow. "Do you enjoy hiding in your icy cave, Adam? Does it keep you warm at night? Is that why they like you? Because you're so cold, just like them?"

I breathe deeply, the muscles along my arms bunching. I grab her waist and pull her those last precious inches to my chest. She's wrong. About everything. "I didn't tell Jaeger to dump you because I was thinking about *him*."

She winces and her chest rises and falls. Hayden's eyes dart to my lips and she swallows. Before I can regain my senses and figure out what the hell I think I'm doing, she pulls away.

"Go back to your ice cave, Adam."

Chapter Twelve

Hayden

Hands shaking, I close the door to my office and lean against it. When Adam grabbed me, my overwhelming instinct wasn't to slap him, or run away. It was to grab his head and kiss him.

What is *wrong* with me?

If the meeting this afternoon proved anything, it confirmed Adam's complicity in Blackwell's plans for the casino, whatever they are. Adam supports the Blue Stars. He wouldn't have told me to keep quiet if he didn't. Sure, he said that business about not wanting to see me get fired, but what does he care?

And if he's involved in Blue's background activities, why in the world would I ever let him get close to me?

He's attractive, but I've always been able to distance my emotions from physical qualities. Until now. Unless it's not just the surface I'm attracted to.

"God." I slink across the room and drop into my chair, pressing my forehead to the desk. "What's wrong with me?"

Adam loves to bother me, but he wouldn't cross the line, would he? Because if he did...I'm not sure I'd refuse him. I'd like to think I would, because I need an unscrupulous jerk in my life like I need a coronary. But with Adam's sexy mouth hovering above mine, his strong arm locked around my waist, I'm afraid I might kiss him back—at least until I came to my senses.

Mira storms in, and I jump, my knee hitting the bottom of my desk. "Stop sneaking up on me like that."

She raises her hand. "Sorry. Didn't know you were having a moment."

"I'm not. I'm just—The meeting didn't go well."

Her eyebrows pull together in concern. "Your face is flushed." She walks forward and sits, absently setting paperwork on my desk. "What happened? Blackwell again?"

I rub my temples. "Among other things."

To say my brain is muddled would be an understatement. There's Blackwell and my job, but somehow it's taking a backseat to Adam's lips.

How much of the tension I've felt these last few months at work is because of Blackwell and the way he treats me, and how much of it comes from working with Adam? I thought I hated Adam because of our shared past. But maybe I never wanted to read into my feelings.

Do I want him?

I groan in frustration and Mira cocks her eyebrow.

I can't want Adam. He's not as bad as I thought when he first started working at Blue, but he has no qualms about giving in to Blackwell and the Blue Stars. Which means I don't really know Adam at all, because my suspicions about the Blue Stars aren't good.

"What am I going to do?" I mumble. Despite my awful boss, I actually like my job. I might not have appreciated the way he went about stopping me, but Adam was right. I'm going to get myself fired if I can't keep my cool around Blackwell.

Mira leans forward and crosses her arms on the desk. "We have a plan, Hayden. We've got dirt on Blackwell, or, at least, we will. You're not the only person who's suffered because of the way he runs Blue, and I'm not talking about our CEO being a prick to his employees. Gen's near-rape, the suites we think he's using to issue drugs and possibly conduct other illegal activities in-house—these are things that shouldn't be going on anywhere, let alone be sanctioned by a mainstream casino. Blackwell is using the Blue as a front, and we'll stop him."

Mira thinks my distress is entirely because of the CEO, when it's more complicated than that. But she's right about one thing. I need to remain focused on what we're doing to clean up Blue. I'm not the only person who loves their job. Mira and Nessa have found their callings at Blue too. There's no reason we can't make this place safe for everyone.

"You're right. We've got our plan and we'll push forward." I give her a weak smile and scan the documents she brought in. "Was there something you wanted me to look at?"

She sorts the paperwork. "These came in this afternoon. They're the last two contracts you were expecting. They're from All Out Burlesque and Bags o' Fun." She grins. "Bags o' Fun, get it? The burlesque companies are hilarious."

I shake my head. "Yes, well, you can pass those along to William. Blackwell pulled me off the event."

She sighs. "Great. He has you do all the legwork, then hands it off to someone else? What's his reasoning now?"

"Apparently, he's hiring the talent through a special account. It's a loophole so he can bypass our department before they sign anything."

"Why would he do that?"

"I don't know. But I have a feeling that if I figure it out, I'll be one step closer to finding the suites."

* * *

Adam

I STARE at Paul and William in confusion. "I thought you wanted strippers."

Paul glances at William, who shrugs. "We do. And these are upscale strippers—some of the best chests in the business. Burlesque showcases sexy, high-style talent. They're not simply performing striptease; they're seducing. It's classier. Blackwell believes they'll make a nice addition to the suites. They'll be here for the show anyway, and we want to look into recruiting a few of them."

William hands me a brochure of the burlesque dancers. "Make sure you're at the meeting next week. Charm the ladies. If any of the dancers brings down the house, we want to make them an offer they can't refuse."

I toss the pamphlet on my desk. "Throwing around a lot of money, aren't you? The bonuses, paying my assistant what most low-level executives make. I want the success as much as anyone, but is it worth the expense?"

Paul smiles devilishly. "Extremely. Based on the figures from phase one of the venture, we'll more than make up for it in revenue earned." He glances at William and nods toward the door.

William stands and walks across the room. He closes the door, silencing the sound of voices and office activity on the other side.

Paul crosses his legs. "Blackwell wouldn't sanction the suites unless they were lucrative. And Bridget isn't just an assistant. She's going to be much more as soon as the Bliss suites are up and running. So stop with the pushback. It's getting old. Or have you changed your mind about making a mint in bonuses by keeping your mouth shut? Did the ladies I sent you not treat you right? They said you showed them a good time. I assumed you were game for all that's involved in Bliss. Was I wrong?"

Paul and William watch me in silence. The last thing I want is to screw up the one thing capable of providing me quick financial freedom.

"Of course not. I'll attend the meetings with William— when I'm not interviewing the dozens of strippers and bodyguards you've sent my way. Because that's my job, right? Hiring? Oh wait, I'm hospitality, not HR."

Paul gives me a tight-lipped smile. "Watch yourself, Cade. We need you to be a go-to man."

Not fifteen minutes ago I was lecturing Hayden about keeping her cool, and here I am blowing a golden opportunity. "Count me in. I'll take care of it."

Paul and William leave, and I proceed to get my priorities straight. Seducing Hayden is not one of them. Though that didn't seem to stop me in the boardroom. I don't know what that was...too much abstinence. Jaeger is right; I'm not myself around her, which means I need to stay away from her.

I've played a dangerous game where Hayden is concerned, which I'm only just beginning to realize. She's not like other women, and neither is my reaction to her. I need to remember I'm at Blue Casino for one reason only. Originally, it was to please my father. Now, it's to free myself from Cade Enterprises and the money I've depended on for too long.

I check my calendar and the interviews Bridget scheduled for next week. There's a conflict with the meeting Paul and William arranged with the burlesque dancers. Instead of emailing Bridget, I walk next door to talk about the conflict and see how she's holding up in her new position.

Only when I get there, I can't see her through the swarm of men crowding her office.

I knock loudly on the open door. "Is there a problem?" I ask, my patience in short supply this afternoon.

Between losing my head and nearly kissing Hayden—at work, no less—and receiving a drilldown from my douchebag colleagues, I'm not in the mood for whatever this is.

Bridget's head pops up above the men leaning over her desk writing down what appear to be notes on business cards. "No, Adam. Everything's fine." She smiles, a touch of nervousness in her eyes.

I enter, glaring at one of the men in my way, who gets the message and scurries out. "What's going on?" Several others notice the look on my face, and quickly tuck their cards into Bridget's outstretched hand.

"Oh, this is nothing. I just wanted to make sure I have everyone's information."

Bridget didn't come from a corporate environment, but I figured she knew the basics about how an office runs. "You have their information. Contacts are located in the company directory and in your work email account."

She steps around her desk and the last of the men, except for one, file out of the room. "Oh, right, but these are their cell numbers. Just in case of an emergency."

"That's right." Paul hovers near her desk. He must have left my office and come straight here. "Anything comes up, particularly in regard to the special venture we have going on, we want everyone within reach. Bridget is seeing to it that she can get hold of us no matter where we are. Isn't that right, Bridget?"

She grins and lowers her eyes. "Yes, absolutely."

"Even the engineers?" I ask skeptically.

"Especially the engineers. The Bliss suites are high-tech." Paul slaps me on the shoulder and saunters out of Bridget's office.

I watch him leave, then turn back to Bridget, who's moved behind her computer. "Are they bothering you? Because if they are—"

"Oh no." Bridget looks up quickly, her expression sincere. "Everything's fine. Really. They've been support-ive." She smiles and stacks the cards the men handed her, tucking them in a plastic box.

Maybe I'm overreacting. I can't say my actions have been the smartest this afternoon. But that's just it. They've been primitive, instinctual. "Let me know if that ever changes."

"I'm sure it won't. Everyone's been very welcoming."

Too welcoming. It's almost as if the entire male work-force knows Bridget is a former stripper.

What do I care if they do?

I make my way back to my office and stop in the door-way. It's half past four, but I turn and move down the hallway for the exit. I'm not in my right mind. Better to leave early and come back tomorrow with a clear head.

My pace slows as I near Hayden's office. I consider apologizing for what happened earlier.

But I've never been one to look back. No need to start now.

Chapter Thirteen

The following day, Bridget, Paul, William, and I make our way up to the infamous Bliss suites under construction.

The hallway is filled with workers applying finishing touches, the emblems on their T-shirts unfamiliar. "We're not using Sallee Construction?" I say. "I thought we had an agreement with them."

Paul pushes open a wide double door. "They were unavailable."

That doesn't sound right. Lewis's construction company has a long-standing relationship with Blue Casino. I make a mental note to give Lewis a call.

The first thing that strikes me as we enter the suite is the sheer size of the space. Just seeing the floor plan didn't prepare me. The main living area is at least three times the normal size of a luxury suite at Blue.

Modern burnt-red sofas and chairs covered in thick plastic provide seating. The floors are a deep ebony hardwood with plush white area rugs that have been rolled off to the side. A ten-person oblong onyx glass dining table with a white base and acrylic chairs presides over the back of the room. The glass and chrome fixtures are also covered in plastic, the walls made of the same ebony hardwood as the flooring, creating a den-like feel.

There was nothing like Bliss previously at Blue Casino. Only one suite at my father's Club Tahoe resort comes close in terms of size and luxury, but the presidential room fails where Bliss succeeds in extravagance. And the presidential room at Club Tahoe runs several thousand dollars per night.

There's something wrong with the Bliss venture. For one, why the secrecy? The Bliss suites are nearly complete, and the casino hasn't made a single mention of them to the public. The amount of money that went into their construction has to be astronomical. Any company footing that kind of bill would be gearing up promotion.

"What are the suites for?" I say quietly, but Paul's eyes dart my way, confirming he heard me.

"Bridget," he says. "Go see Eve. She'll fill you in on the supplies we'll need for the bedrooms."

Bridget nods and walks over to where Eve is talking to a contractor. After a brief greeting, Eve leads Bridget into one of the bedrooms.

"Well?" I say, once the women are out of earshot.

Paul glances at William and tilts his head to the construction manager. William walks over and takes up where Eve left off.

"The Bliss suites are exclusive," Paul finally says.

I watch the workers, but my attention is on the slick manager who's been dishing out crumbs of information on a venture I'm beginning to question. "Define exclusive. The suites are massive and well appointed. How do you expect to keep them filled?"

"Each patron that wants in pays a premium for part

ownership of the Bliss line of suites. Your family owns Club Tahoe. Think of it as a golf resort membership."

"Our members pay over a quarter of a million dollars for club and golf access, and then an annual fee on top of that."

Paul looks over, his gaze sharp. "Precisely."

I glance around the room. "Why would someone pay a quarter of a million for a penthouse they can rent for a few thousand a night?"

"Bliss isn't just a suite, it's an experience. A seductive, top-of-the line experience for the pleasure-seeking connoisseur. There will be women, like those in the burlesque show, who will provide our members with...well, a taste of bliss, for lack of a better term. Whatever a member desires, we want to provide. At a premium cost, of course. Everyone who enters Bliss must be eighteen or over, and consenting. It's in the contract members sign."

I think about this town: the gaming, the drugs, and the rich, debauched bastards I grew up around at Club Tahoe. I lost my virginity to the thirty-five-year-old wife of a billionaire. There's a wide range of debauchery, the least of which includes drugs.

I peer around. "What else besides access to prostitutes and gaming?"

"That's roughly it. Don't worry. Everyone will be kept safe, partly because everything is in-house. That's the beauty of Bliss. Membership is by invitation only and confidential, which was a requirement by the charter members." He nods toward the tall windows that, at six foot two, I'd have to jump to see out of. "The celebrities don't want paparazzi discovering their hideout. We'll have bodyguards, which I'm assuming you have under control."

"I've spoken to two men on the list you sent me. Neither of them graduated from high school, but they have quite the background in private bodyguard service. One of the candidates is an ex-Marine."

Paul nods. "The bodyguards are a necessary precaution. One of many we put into place." He points to the side of the room, past workers and covered furniture. "One of these doors leads to a password-protected elevator that will take people to a regular floor, as well as the ground level in case of an emergency. A member had a heart attack with the first luxury suites we designed. It was a challenge to get the guy to a regular room before the ambulance arrived."

I blink. "You're joking. You risked some poor bastard's life to hide his mistress?"

Paul shrugs. "He paid for privacy. The guy survived. Barely. And in case you're wondering, he was the first to enroll in Bliss 2.0. If we hadn't handled the situation as well as we did, he wouldn't have come back."

"Some people are masochists; that doesn't make them the best judge of what's good for them."

Paul tips his chin toward one of the bedrooms. I walk into the room and he closes the door behind us. "The casino isn't in the business of worrying about what's good for its patrons. I thought you were in, Cade? Which is it—bonuses and prestige, or are you looking for another job? And if you think you're going to talk about the Bliss venture, you can think again. Blue Casino will nail your ass to the wall for slander." My jaw tightens at the blatant threat. He thrusts his hands in the slacks of his suit, his shoulders taut. "Look, don't try to go up against Blackwell. You don't understand the connections he has. He'll ruin you, and that's if he's feeling generous. Do you get my meaning?"

"I don't think I do. Are you threatening my life?" The glare I level at him has him flinching.

He holds up a hand and the false smile returns. "Not

me. And it doesn't have to come to that, as long as you keep your mouth shut. But I need to know you're all in." He lets out a sigh. "Come on, Adam, we chose you because you're smooth under pressure. No one knows who you are behind the cool façade you've got going. That kind of discretion is what we were looking for. You have the right temperament for the Bliss project."

I finally take in the bedroom. Few furnishings fill the space, but there's a stripper pole at the foot of an oval mattress. The view into the bathroom reveals a six-person hot tub and mirrors on every wall. "It's a hundred percent consensual? No one gets hurt?"

"Not unless they want to." Paul crosses his hand over his chest. "Scout's honor. And no one underage."

I heard him the first time. It doesn't fill me with confidence that Paul felt the need to give me that reassurance.

I tip my head back and stare at the ceiling. Another mirror up there as well, this one branded with the Bliss logo.

Sex, gaming, drinking, and who knows what else. But what do I care? At least in this environment there's someone monitoring to make sure people don't get out of hand.

Anyone who pays a quarter of a million for membership knows what he or she is getting into. I have to assume Blackwell's found some loophole to keep everything on the up-and-up.

I may live to regret the decision, but for now...

"I'm in."

* * *

I RUB my eyes under my reading glasses, the words on the computer blurring, but not because I'm tired. I can't stop thinking about the blatant threat Paul made when he thought I might back out of the Bliss venture. I'd beat the hell out of him if he ever tried anything, and he knows that. This wasn't about him. He was warning me about Blackwell and his connections.

A feminine throat clears, and I look up. Hayden is standing in the doorway to my office, and just like that, my concern evaporates and a new tension builds.

I rise and walk around my desk, leaning a hip against it and crossing my arms. "To what do I owe this pleasure?" Usually, I'm the one tracking Hayden down. Purely for work purposes. And to gloat. Or goad. But hey, I'm keeping her alert. Wouldn't want her to fall asleep on the job.

Her eyes are fixed on my glasses. "I was just...When did you get glasses?"

I pull off the black-rimmed reading glasses and toss them on my desk. "I've always had them. I don't wear them all the time."

She huffs out a breath. "That's just great," she mumbles.

"Excuse me?" This time, I didn't intentionally frustrate her, so I'm interested in how I accomplished it so easily.

She plasters on a tight smile. "It's nothing. I came because I wanted to know if you've heard anything about the burlesque dancers. Did William decide on subcontractors?"

I take in the unaffected expression she's trying to pull off. Then, because I can't help myself, my gaze dips. She's wearing a navy skirt with small white polka dots and a sheer blouse that I'd be able to see through if it weren't for that unfortunate camisole. Hayden isn't short, and in her nude heels, the top of her pretty head hits me at eye level. The heels, I note, have a sexy strap across the ankle, sending images of binding her flashing through my mind, though I'm not normally into that.

109

With Hayden, all bets are off on what is normal for me. I can see myself doing a lot of things I wouldn't normally do, just to rouse her, or—make her happy.

Where did that come from?

I clear my throat. "Hayden, are you trying to probe for inside information?"

She steps the rest of the way into my office and closes the door.

My heart rate increases at the thought of being alone with her, visions of her naked still close to the surface. I raise an eyebrow. "Do we need privacy?"

"Stop being difficult. It's a simple question. I just want to know what company William settled on." She moves next to me, tilting her sloped hip against my desk in a similar pose to mine, only her figure is a work of art. She reaches out and absently fingers my glasses.

I glance down. "You have a thing for glasses? I'd be happy to put them back on."

She quickly withdraws her hand. "What? No!"

A knock sounds at the door, and Bridget's head peeks around the corner. She looks from Hayden's blushing face to me. "Oh, sorry. I didn't know you were in a meeting. Should I come back?"

"It's fine, Bridget," I say. "What can I do for you?"

She pushes the door open all the way, carrying her purse and a sheet of paper. "I'm off to go shopping. There are some things from...my previous place of employment that Eve wants me to pick up. In the gift shop," she says carefully.

Given Bridget was a stripper before I hired her, I pinch the bridge of my nose, imagining exactly what Eve has in mind.

"Oh! Don't worry," Bridget adds quickly. "Eve ordered

most of the items she needs online. There are just a few things my old work sort of...specialized in. A few products I recommended."

I glance quickly to Hayden, whose brow is furrowed. "Yes. Fine," I say. "You'll be reimbursed."

Bridget leaves and Hayden's eyes narrow. "What was that about?"

"Nothing."

Her delicate jaw shifts. "Why must you be so difficult? I'm trying to be civil here."

"Civil," I say, rolling the word over my tongue and studying her pert expression.

"Yes. Civil. We're work friends, right?" Her look is almost eager now, which is new. Hayden has never expressed an interest in friendship, for business purposes or otherwise.

"Are we? I didn't realize."

"Forget it." She turns to leave, but I grab her hand. She barely budges, keeping her distance, which is predictable. She wants something, and it's not friendship.

I let go of her hand. "I apologize. Arguing with you is a bad habit." I reach back and grab the edge of the desk I'm leaning against to keep from touching her again. "Yes, we're work friends. And no, I haven't heard anything about whom William wants to hire for the burlesque, but I have a meeting with him next week. I'm assuming the decision-making will take place then."

She smiles, but I don't trust it. Hayden's smiles are few and far between, and never aimed at me with any sort of honesty. "Was that so difficult?"

I tap my finger on the desk. "Is that all, or would you like me to put my glasses back on?"

Her face flushes and she swallows. "No. I should go."

She scurries out the door, and I stare at her hips swishing back and forth in agitation.

Sweet Hayden has a nerd fetish. I shouldn't be surprised, given her bookish tendencies.

I return to my computer. It's late, but I've got a busy week ahead. I'd like these dozen or so interviews to go smoothly. I enjoy interviewing about as much as I enjoy dinner with my father, which is to say, not at all. The sooner the bodyguards and burlesque dancers are hired, the sooner I can keep Hayden from snooping and expressing undue interest in my business at Blue.

Bridget's two-week anniversary and the day I win the bet with Hayden can't come quickly enough.

Chapter Fourteen

Hayden

My little birdies (a.k.a. Mira and Nessa) tell me Adam has had interviews lined up over the last two days. The interviews have all taken place in the large conference room, which is completely soundproof, dammit. Not that I haven't walked past several times to test the theory.

Time to pay a visit to Adam's new assistant. I'm a manager. She can't refuse my inquiries. Unless Blackwell warned her off the way he has the Blue Star managers... Fingers crossed he's done what he always does, and left the secretaries and assistants to their own devices.

Pain in the ass though he is, Adam doesn't cater to Blackwell's every wish like the rest of the managerial herd. It must explain why he still talks to me. I don't think Adam would have told Bridget to stay away from me.

I drink the last of my twenty-ounce super espresso latte, type out one final email to the data manager who's updating our HR system, and shake out my pleated skirt. It's an icebox in the casino with all of the indoor air conditioning, but between the hot drink and the hyped-up energy I have over conducting sneaky reconnaissance while Adam is tied up in meetings, my face is flushed.

Grabbing a notepad, I hurry out the door before I lose my nerve—and Mira barrels into me.

"Back, back—*go back!*" She shoves me inside. "You can't snoop."

"Why not? You just texted me that the coast is clear."

"It was, but your dad showed up." Her eyes are wide and harried.

"What? Why?" I say, mostly to myself. My family moved to Reno after the high school incident. They come down to visit, but never unannounced.

She holds up her hands in exasperation. "You're asking me? And never mind that. He's talking to Adam."

"I thought you said Adam was in an interview."

"Well, he's not. He's talking to your dad."

Anxiety fills my chest. "That needs to stop, like, right now. I don't want Adam getting friendly with my dad. What does he think he's doing?"

Mira twists my shoulders around, opens the door, and shoves me out. "You should go ask him, because he's looking a little too comfortable with your father and you might want to put an end to that."

Thin as she is, Mira has a hell of a heave. I catch myself before I trip in my heels and face-plant.

I peer down the hallway, and just as Mira said, my dad and Adam are talking several doors away. My father is even laughing at something Adam said.

Adam looks up and catches sight of me first, a knowing expression crossing his face.

What is that? This is my reconnaissance mission, not Adam's day to infiltrate my personal life. I sweep down the hallway, and Adam's gaze drops to my hips, his mouth turning up at the corners. I stop in front of him and glare.

My dad looks from Adam to me, appearing confused. I'm usually more polite than this, but my dad has no idea how much Adam presses on my every last nerve.

"Hayden," Adam says. "I didn't realize your dad was a Warriors fan."

I stare at him. Who cares if my dad is a Warriors fan?

Apparently, men do, because my dad grins, as though those are all the credentials he needs, and says, "Go Dubs."

I blow out a frustrated breath. "Dad, what are you doing here? Were we supposed to meet? I don't have it on my calendar."

"Well, no. I was in town and thought I'd drop by."

"Oh." I sound disappointed. Crap, of course I want to see my dad. The problem is I'd just psyched myself up for this information-gathering mission while Adam was supposedly preoccupied.

I turn my shoulder to inch Adam out of the conversation. For some reason he's still standing here. "That's great, Dad. Do you want to grab dinner? I'll be off in a couple of hours."

"Actually, honey, Adam here just offered to give me a tour."

I cast an irritated glance at Adam, who's smiling. "But Dad, I gave you a tour at the last casino where I worked. Don't you remember?"

"Sure, honey, but this is Blue Casino. I've always wanted to check this place out. See how they run the fancy ones." He grins cheekily.

Well then, Adam's the perfect person to give my dad a

tour. He's behind everything, along with the rest of Blackwell's Blue Stars. "Sorry, Dad. I didn't realize. I'd be happy to take you around."

He squeezes my arm and plants a kiss on my cheek. "No, no—you go back to work. I'll make a quick sweep with Adam here, and return later to pick you up. How does five thirty sound?"

I can't hide the hostility rolling off me in waves as I stare daggers at Adam. Why is he befriending my father? And how did he wrap my shrewd father around his rich-boy finger so quickly?

"Can you give us a quick sec, Dad?" Not waiting for my father's reply, I pull Adam into the nearest empty room, which happens to be the facility manager's office.

I shut the door and whirl around on him. "What do you think you're doing?"

"Taking your father for a tour?" the jackass says, all innocence.

"I don't think so."

"No?" He chuckles as if he's getting some sort of pleasure out of this.

"You're up to something. Do you think this will somehow get you out of our bet?"

He steps toward me. "Why would I want that? I'm looking forward to winning."

For a split second I'm ruffled by his suggestive tone and nearness—which I consider progress, considering how much his presence disarms me. "Leave my father out of this."

Adam's face grows serious and his voice softens. "Hayden, he was lost and I was giving him directions. When he explained he was your father, we started talking. That's all. I offered to give him a tour, because he said he'd never been here before. Honestly, I can't believe you've worked at Blue nearly a year and you haven't offered him one."

Okay, fine. I'm a bad daughter. But in my defense, I had no idea my dad was interested in Blue. He's never mentioned it before. "A tour and that's all?"

"I promise to have him back in plenty of time for your dinner date." He inches back, giving me space to walk past him and leave, but I suddenly realize the importance of where we are. This is the facility manager's office—the guy with access to every room in this entire building.

Adam follows my gaze. "I don't like that scheming look in your eye. What are you thinking?"

Why didn't I consider it before? Adam and his assistant aren't who I should focus my reconnaissance on. There are people with information at their fingertips that could be more helpful. And they're not even a part of the Blue Stars.

"Hayden, did you hear me?"

I walk toward the door. "Better hurry up, Adam. My dad's waiting."

He opens the door, still frowning, and I pass him, but I can feel his heated gaze on my back.

I smile at my father. "All set, Dad. Adam will give you the tour."

My dad's eyes narrow with suspicion. "Will he? Well, I'm glad *you've* decided."

I give my dad a hug goodbye. So it looks suspicious that I dragged Adam into a room to talk in private. But my father hasn't a clue about the things going on at Blue, and it's best that way. He'd worry, and the point of returning to Lake Tahoe wasn't to give my parents another reason to worry. It was to show them and the world that I'd risen above what happened in the past.

I shoot Adam a glare. "Take care of him."

Adam responds to my warning with a charming grin that has probably persuaded hundreds of unsuspecting parents to hand their precious daughters into his safekeeping. I'd be concerned, except that my father can take care of himself.

I head off toward my office. Oh, not for long. I fully intend to return to the facility manager's room. Just as soon as I confirm with Mira that the space will be empty for at least half an hour.

* * *

I PEER down the hall to make sure no one sees me, and quickly enter the facility manager's office, closing the door behind me. Mira says I have forty-five minutes until the manager returns.

I rush to the desk rimmed in every bobblehead ever created, and carefully look through the paperwork on top. Just a hint of where the secret suite is located—some sort of building site plan—that's all I need.

The paperwork on the desk is for a vendor lease, another stack for an energy efficiency plan—none of it what I'm looking for.

Opening the desk drawers, I sift through files on security services, parking services... *Come on, buddy, where do you keep information on secret suites?*

There's no way the facility manager isn't in on the suite Mira and Tyler found. He has access to everything going on in the building. I slam the drawer shut, and all the bobbleheads nod their agreement. It's got to be here somewhere.

Scanning the rest of the room, my gaze stops on a tall file cabinet in the corner. One of the drawers is locked, but the others aren't. I head over and open them one by one. And strike gold. The manager keeps site plans for the building as well as work repair documents in the file cabinet. I'm definitely getting warmer.

Riffling through the papers, I find nothing out of the ordinary. Which coincides with the other digging I've done. I've searched every hotel floor at Blue Casino and have yet to find a suite that doesn't look like all the others. One of the floors has been under construction for months, but it was the first place I looked. The completed portions check out. These documents do too.

I shut the bottom drawer of the cabinet and stare at the top, locked drawer. If someone wanted to hide something, it would be under lock and key.

I hurry back to the desk and search for keys. I'm running out of time, and the facility manager has about two hundred keys in his desk to choose from. Only a few are small enough and look like they might fit. Grabbing the small keys, I scramble back to the cabinet and I try each in the locked drawer. None of them work.

Crap. I look around once more. The office is simple: a desk and chair, the cabinet, and a crap ton of bobbleheads. Most of the bobbleheads are sports themed, but a few are interesting, including a jaunty little skeleton pirate with a square treasure chest...

A treasure chest that looks like it opens.

I return the keys to the desk drawer and stare at Mr. Pirate's treasure chest. I reach over and flip the lid.

And see a small key inside.

I grab the key and carry it to the drawer, my hands shaking. I slide the key in the lock and it turns, the cabinet opening for me.

Locked cabinet drawers are suspicious, but that's not

why my heart is blasting through my eardrums—the row of files labeled *Bliss* inside the drawer is why. Everything I've found so far I could identify as something I've seen or heard of before at the casino, but not Bliss. I've never heard of this project, and as a manager, I should have.

Pulling out a handful of folders, I cross to the desk and lay them out.

The penthouse wing has been under construction for months. Blackwell told us a while ago that it was being renovated, and it was the first place I searched after Mira and Tyler found the suspicious guest room. The penthouse suites checked out, but according to the Bliss files, one half of the penthouse level—a portion separated by an outdoor veranda—is entirely different from the other half. And this portion of the floor has been blocked off from employee access these last few months while under construction.

According to these documents, there are four suites, each with the same layout. And they are so large as to be ludicrous. We have wealthy patrons who stay in our regular penthouse suites, which cost a couple of grand. Those rooms are booked for special events, at the most, and I've never heard of anyone leaving disappointed. The only reason the casino updates them is to keep current with trends. But maybe there was another purpose for the timing of the remodel.

The four Bliss suites that take up the second half of the penthouse floor are insanely extravagant, with a bar, an elaborate living area, their own elevator, and almost no windows—which is odd. The penthouse suites are known for their sweeping decks and views of the mountains and lake.

This whole time, I thought Blackwell switched rooms

for his illicit activities. But what if instead of sneaking them in with the scenery, he's created a new space for them? One so conspicuous it blends with the existing high standard of the penthouse floor?

Technically, no one has been allowed to look at that section of the penthouse floor. Sending unauthorized employees to a construction zone is a liability for the casino. The noise alone forced us to block off the floor beneath in order to maintain a standard of quality for hotel guests. But when I consider it, not allowing people onto those top floors has also provided a buffer and a level of privacy for whatever they want to do up there.

The Bliss suites are huge, their layouts strange, and based on the floor plan, there's no reason they couldn't serve the same role as the suite Mira and Tyler stumbled upon. This has to be it.

Male voices sound outside the facility manager's door.

I look up, then glance at the files spread haphazardly across the desk, my eyes flaring wide as panic fills my chest.

I slap the files closed and race to the cabinet, shoving them back inside the drawer and locking it. I could pretend I was leaving a note for the facility manager. Which means I need to create one, dammit.

I scurry back to the desk and jot a quick note for the manager to come see me. I'll think of a reason later. Lunging for the door, I freeze midway.

The key.

Spinning around, I run back to return the key to the pirate bobblehead's treasure chest, but my heel catches on the carpet. I fly forward, and the key launches from my palm. I catch myself on the edge of the desk before I take a nosedive, but the key is nowhere in sight.

Shit, *shit.*

I drop to the ground and crawl, searching beneath the desk. After a moment of frantic patting of the carpet and not having much luck at finding the key, cold prickles race down my spine.

The sound of the door closing comes from behind and I suck in a breath, holding it.

"Hayden? What are you doing?"

Only Adam. I can talk my way out of this.

I let out my breath and scoot back from under the desk. As I do, I spot the key leaning against the leg post. I look over my shoulder and capture his gaze. "How did you know it was me?" I reach for the key while he's staring at my face.

He looks pointedly at my ass and grins lazily.

"That's sexual harassment, you know." I hobble to my feet in my four-inch spiked heels—wishing I'd chosen a more practical pair for today—the key snugly in my palm.

He walks over and peers around the desk, and I slide the key back into Mr. Pirate's treasure chest when he's not looking. "Oh please. It's not sexual harassment to recognize someone from...behind." His gaze flickers suggestively.

My mouth twists. "Very funny."

He tips his head at the floor. "What were you doing down there? And don't tell me you dropped something. That look of guilt you're sporting tells me everything I need to know."

"Fine, I won't tell you I dropped something." I move to walk away. "Goodbye, Adam."

He grabs my hand and tugs me toward him, my shoulder lightly bumping his chest. "Don't do this." His eyes are sincere, for once.

My smug grin fades. "Do what?"

"Don't get involved, Hayden."

"Why would an iceman like you care?" There's only one reason I can think of, and it must be because he doesn't want to get caught, along with the rest of the casino execs, after I figure out what they're up to.

"I prefer caveman." He tucks a lock of hair behind my ear and his eyes drop to my mouth, his expression filled with concern that slowly shifts into something more...heated. Lots of heat behind those eyes.

My head swims. His hand is warm and wrapped around mine, his chest large and protective, brushing my left breast. Suddenly his actions don't seem selfish.

I exhale on a shaky breath. I hate the physical effect he has on me. It's screwing with my head. Adam is guilty. He's in with Blackwell and the others. I know it, but I can't look away from his mouth.

His lips are a shade darker than his lightly tanned skin, the bottom one fuller than the top. I want him to press his mouth to mine and hold me—tell me it's going to be okay. Because Adam *is* the ice king. Nothing gets to him. And even though he's working with the enemy, I could stand to have his strength. You'd have to be a rock to keep it together and never show weakness. I wish I were that strong. I'm not sure whether to admire him or despise him, but my body says admire. Definitely admire.

He swallows and takes a step back. His eyes have changed, the intensity burning behind them no longer filled with desire. "Dammit, Hayden, stop getting involved." He brushes past me, and strides out the door.

My chest slumps, whatever string he was holding that kept me suspended in place snapped.

I don't want Adam to be anything other than what I

pegged him for on his first day of work when he didn't remember me. He's supposed to be shallow and self-serving.

But shallow, self-serving assholes don't bother to warn girls of danger. And right now, I can't tell if he's more worried about his own skin, or mine.

Chapter Fifteen

M y dad ladles jasmine rice on his plate, followed a moment later by yellow chicken curry and pad Thai noodles. We decided on our favorite Thai restaurant after he picked me up from work for our dinner date.

"So my tour with Adam was short." He gives me a disgruntled look, as though it's my fault.

"I'm sure he was busy," I say distractedly. I haven't gotten over the anger on Adam's face when he left me this afternoon. It should bother me that for a moment he looked like he was going to kiss me, but nope. It was the angry part I didn't like.

My dad passes the noodles. "I got the impression there was tension between you two."

Understatement. "Adam and I are always at each other's throats. We don't get along." No need for him to know every source of my and Adam's frustrations.

Dad shovels in a forkful of food, his forehead scrunched in thought. He chews for a moment. "That's not what I picked up. During the tour it seemed like he wanted to get back to you. Just be careful. Workplace relationships can get complicated."

"Dad, there's no relationship." How do I explain Adam to my father? "If Adam wanted to get back to me, it was to give me a hard time."

"Did he? Go back and give you a lecture?"

Adam caught me snooping and warned me off, so... "Yes."

My dad pours tea into the tiny restaurant teacup. "He's not your boss, is he?"

"No." I swallow the food in my mouth. "Though I'm sure he wishes he were, so he could control me."

He sets his cup down. "I don't like the sound of that. He came across as a good guy when we spoke in the hallway and during the tour. I must have read him wrong."

I could allow my father to believe that, and a few weeks ago, I would have. But I can't ignore the glimpses of Adam that have me thinking differently. "You read him fine. He's not a bad guy. We just...disagree."

My father takes another bite and studies my face. "And that's it? Nothing else is bothering you? You seemed distracted the last time you called home. Your mother sent me down to make sure everything was all right. You're making friends in town?"

Doesn't matter how old I am. My parents will always worry.

"Yes. I'm fine. It's just work stuff."

"Anything you want to talk about?"

My father would freak out if I told him what I suspected went on behind closed doors at Blue Casino. Which is why I won't. "Nope." The look in his eyes tells me he's still concerned. "Dad, I'm twenty-seven. I can take care of myself."

He tries for a smile and pats my hand. "Age doesn't change anything. You're still my daughter."

"Got it. Once a parent, always a parent. Now eat your food. We wouldn't want Mom to have to wait too long to find out how our dinner date went."

Ever since my mom became vice principal at a junior high school in Reno, she's been working long hours. She doesn't get down here as often as my father, but it doesn't mean she's out of the loop.

He grins. "Good point. I'm sure she'll call me on the way home. So I had better get some information, or I'll never hear the end of it." He takes a sip of hot tea. "So, about this Adam fellow. Why don't you guys get along?"

"Dad, really?" He raises his eyebrow, challenging me to deny there's anything unusual about my relationship with Adam. "It's complicated."

"Adam appears to be a professional, good-looking guy, and he seems interested. Still not sure it's a wise choice to date a coworker, but if you say he's a decent person, then..." He shrugs, a questioning look on his face.

"What? *No*. That's not going to happen." I shake my head. "Adam—" I'm about to say *hates me*, when I catch myself. Because that's not true. I've learned enough these last couple of weeks to know he doesn't hate me. He drives me crazy, but he doesn't hate me.

"He isn't interested in anything serious," I finally say. Not that Adam has expressed interest in me, but at least that will put my father off without me having to explain the complicated past I share with Adam.

"Hmm," my father says, his mouth twisted.

I don't like the pensive look on his face. "What does *hmm* mean?"

"Well, it's just that most of us guys aren't the settling-down types—until we do."

"Is that some kind of crazy man-logic? What's that supposed to mean?"

He tosses me a mint and pulls the bill to his side of the table. "Only that we never know which one of you is going to knock us off our game. Permanently."

"So, you're saying there aren't nice guys out there. Every guy is a player until he finds the right girl?"

"There are nice guys. But even they'll get the daylights knocked out of them when they find *the one*."

My face heats. "Good talk, Dad. Glad to know you were a player before you met Mom. I'll have to scour that image out of my head later. For now, you think you can come to the house and clean out the gutters?"

Chapter Sixteen

Adam has avoided me this entire week. How do I know? Because I haven't seen him. Which just goes to show all those times we ran into each other or were forced into close proximity in conference rooms were orchestrated for maximum *annoying Hayden* purposes. But I don't like the alternative. Because I need to be close to Adam. The facility manager's office was a huge step in the right direction. I know where I'm looking now. But if I want to learn more about Bliss, I still need someone on the inside.

I tried to return to the facility manager's office, armed with my phone to gain photo evidence, but the office was locked. Which wasn't a complete deterrent. However, by the time I got the door unlocked with the help of my trusty assistant Mira the locksmith, I discovered the cabinet that housed those interesting Bliss files was gone. Completely removed from the dang office.

It's all Adam's fault. He's on to me, and he must have given the facility manager the order to remove the cabinet. But I'm not letting that stop me. I know about Bliss now—

know where it's located. And would bet money that's where Blackwell moved his illegal suite.

Bridget packs up her folder after the marketing meeting we just finished for the burlesque show. "Do you have a minute?" I ask her.

"Sure." She smiles, then bites the corner of her lip. "Do you mind following me back to my office, though? I've got a quick email to shoot off."

I tell her that's fine, and we make our way down the hall. Adam and Blackwell may have warned me away from Adam's new assistant as the HR director, but that doesn't mean I can't talk to her as a coworker, right?

Bridget and I chat about the meeting, and Mark from IT scuffles by, his face shiny and a tad red. "Hi, Bridget," he says quietly.

I'm impressed. Mark usually avoids eye contact.

Bridget greets him and I nod hello, and we resume our discussion about the promo for the big event.

Not two seconds later, another employee passes, an equally smitten look on his face.

"Good afternoon, Bridget." This time, it's one of the building engineers. An insanely shy man. The only reason he's said two words to me is because I sign his paychecks.

What the hell? I do a double take. "Looks like you've got fans." I smile. If Bridget is pulling people out of their shells, that's great.

"Oh yes. Everyone has been so nice." Her expression is unassuming, and I realize I actually like Bridget. She's pretty, so I can see why the guys like her, but she's just as friendly with the women, from what I've witnessed. And Adam hasn't said a single bad thing about her performance. I'm going to assume that's because he's happy with her and not because he's hiding something just to win our bet.

Damn. I can't believe Adam is going to win. I was certain he wouldn't be able to hire a suitable candidate. This is going to make learning about the other people he's hiring more complicated. I promised to keep my nose out of things if he wins. Of course, I'll still stick my nose in his business, but now I'll have to be stealthier about it.

We enter Bridget's office, and I close the door. "We haven't had an opportunity to sit and talk, and I wanted to make sure you've settled in okay. See if you need anything from human resources?"

I'm totally breaking the rule about not talking to Bridget on official human resources business, but I need an excuse to talk to her, and it's a silly rule anyway. Bridget may need something from my department, and how's she supposed to get help if we're banned from speaking to one another? Besides, I need a reason to ask probing questions about Adam. He's avoiding me. Desperate times and all that.

She shrugs happily. "All settled. Though I do have a question about health benefits. Can you wait one sec while I shoot off that message I mentioned?"

"Of course. Unless you'd rather come to my office when you're finished?"

"Oh no. This will just take me a moment." Bridget pulls up her email and clicks quickly through the screens.

She glances over and smiles nervously. I realize I'm staring, so I glance around the room to give her privacy.

"There," she says, and minimizes the screen. "All set."

Bridget asks me a few questions about company health benefits. All things Mira and I would have gone over had Adam let me brief Bridget when she started, but I'm happy to help her now.

"Thank you so much for the information," she says. "That really cleared things up."

"Oh, good." I stand to leave. Maybe I shouldn't say it, but I want to be available to every employee—screw Adam and Blackwell. "Come by anytime if you have more questions."

Bridget smiles broadly, and I know meeting with her was the right move. Yes, I had ulterior motives, but she's still an employee and deserves what her human resources department has to offer.

It's going to suck once Bridget's two weeks are up. Adam and I will need to establish boundaries around this no-questioning-my-new-hires rule, because it's obvious the employees he hires will have questions he can't answer. At least, I think they will, unless Blackwell contracts them out. Bridget isn't a contract employee, but I don't know what Blackwell has planned for the others.

I stop near the door. "Before I go, how is Adam? I haven't seen him at the meetings lately." Hopefully my light probing isn't too obvious, but darn it, Adam's been MIA, and I'm so close to figuring out this Bliss thing.

"He's been busy with the new suites. Blackwell has him working late to make sure everything is up and running in time for the burlesque show. It's all hush-hush, but just to reassure you, everything is going *really* well. You should see what I bought for the rooms. Those suites are going to be amazing."

I haven't heard anything special about the suite remodel, other than that it was taking place. Nor did I realize Blackwell wanted them ready for the burlesque show. Bridget's comments confirm that the suites under construction are more than the casino is letting on to the public and the rest of the employees, and that both she and Adam are involved. No wonder he doesn't want me near her.

"What sorts of things did you buy—"

"Interrogating my employees?"

I spin around, my heart hammering. Adam is standing in the doorway, and he looks pissed. "Just getting to know your new assistant." No way am I letting him intimidate me. "She had a few questions about benefits." I glance back. "Bridget, I'll let you return to work. Remember what I said about coming to see me anytime."

She smiles, and I walk toward Adam, stopping in front of him. "Can I talk to you in my office?"

He steps aside and I pass him. Once we're out of the office, and out of earshot of Bridget, he catches up to me. "Blackwell gave you specific orders not to interfere with the hiring of my assistant." His voice is not his normal elegant cadence, but hard with a steely edge.

True, I'm guilty, because I asked Bridget questions I knew Adam wouldn't want me knowing the answers to, but there's something going on in this place and I'm going to find out what it is.

I shoot him a look. "Blackwell didn't say anything about not talking to new people once they're hired. Your employee had specific questions about her benefits. I highly doubt you would have been able to answer them without coming to me."

"You were asking her about my work."

I walk into my office, and Adam closes the door behind us. "That's not a crime. Whatever projects hospitality has going on should be known to every member of management," I say sweetly.

He lets out a breath of frustration. "Hayden, there's what, one—two days left until Bridget's been here two weeks? Our bet is nearly up. And I didn't take you for someone who reneges on a bet. Admit you lost, so that we can move on from this."

"No. But even if I lose the bet, we need to establish terms. The deal was for me to stay out of the hiring process. You can't expect me to never talk to new employees. I'll need to be accessible to them for benefits and other HR needs."

Instead of sitting in the guest chair, Adam walks to the side of my desk, hand tucked in his pant pocket. He stares out the window. "The others are being hired as contractors. No benefits. They can come to me with any questions they have."

Blackwell said in our last meeting that the burlesque dancers would be hired as subcontractors through a special account. I'm not surprised Adam is hiring employees through a similar process. But it pisses me off. This is wrong. Human resources is designed to protect the company and its employees. But we can't do that if they don't use us—if they go outside the walls of our jurisdiction.

And I don't know how to stop them.

I cross my arms over my chest. "That is a ridiculous waste of everyone's time. You seriously want to be the go-between?"

He looks at me as though frustrated. "If I must."

Okay, I'm not making things easy, but it's for a good reason.

I study the hard edges of his handsome face. "Why is everything here so secretive?" My voice is filled with judgment. I want Mr. Iceberg to admit what we both know. That Blue Casino is doing something illegal.

His gaze narrows. He parts his lips to say something, and my cell phone buzzes. A half a second later Adam's cell phone buzzes too.

He breaks eye contact and reaches in his pocket. I grab my purse and reach for my phone, because if we're both receiving messages, it's probably something important.

The text is from Bridget, along with a series of images. For a moment, I don't know what I'm looking at. "Is that a cucumber...in her...? Oh. *Ohhh!*"

"Son. Of. A. Bitch." Adam shoves his cell in his pocket and storms from my office.

Bridget said she had an important email to get out. She'd seemed nervous when she realized I was looking over her shoulder. But it's been half an hour since then. Maybe what she was doing is related to this?

I rest my hands on the desk, blinking in disbelief. Why would she...? Doesn't matter. It's done.

I check the text message again. She sent it to everyone. All upper management. But no clients, thank God. We can contain this.

I pick up my desk phone and dial IT. "Remove it from the server. Now!"

"Already on it," the support guy says, his voice sounding anxious.

My next call is to security. "This is Hayden Tate in human resources. I need you to escort an employee out. Yes, she's being fired."

Or at least she will be. I'm assuming that's where Adam was headed.

What Bridget did—even if it was a mistake—no, just *no.* Beyond inappropriate. And a serious case of sexual misconduct. This is no slap-on-the-wrist situation. Particularly so soon after the assault charges brought on by an ex-employee on company property. Bridget's actions are cause for immediate dismissal.

I head for her office and hear Adam's voice from down the hall.

"What were you thinking?" His tone is calm. Chilled. Not the hard-edged voice he used on me earlier, which I interpreted as pure Hayden frustration. This voice is scarier in its iciness.

Adam would never hurt Bridget, but I rush down the hallway anyway.

"I'm sorry." Bridget's voice quavers as I round the corner to her office. "It was an accident. It was only meant to go to a few people."

Bridget is standing in front of her desk, her face pale as she desperately clicks through her phone. "I must have typed a name wrong and auto-correct filled in one of the lists. I can't believe this happened."

"Why are you sending explicit images to employees to begin with?" Adam says. Bridget's mouth clamps shut. "Answer me," he growls.

She lowers herself into her chair and looks away. "It's a side business."

Whoa. Suddenly the attention Bridget's been receiving from Blue's male contingent—even the shy men—makes sense. I thought it was because she's a nice person.

Boy is she nice. She's so nice she's sending them smutty images of herself.

"This is not a strip club. You understood the conduct I expected of you?"

"I did." She sounds desperate now, and she's wringing her hands. "It was a mistake, Adam. It won't happen again. The others—the managers—they were open to it. Well, as long as I kept it discreet..."

Oh, I'm sure the managers of Blue Casino were open to her side business. Dirty bastards. I feel sorry for her, but damn, this is not something we can sweep under the rug.

"Pack your things. You're fired." Adam turns and brushes past me, so angry he doesn't even look my way.

Bridget peers over pleadingly. "Can you talk to him? I don't want to lose my job. I really thought it was okay—as long as nothing like this happened." She looks down, her face pained.

I shake my head. I like Bridget, but there is no way I can get her out of this. "What you do on your own time is your business, but Adam is right. You're at work. Regardless of whether you sent the images to a select few who...wanted them, this sort of thing isn't allowed during work hours. You get that, right?"

She closes her eyes, then reaches for her purse. She looks around her desk and grabs a plastic box, removing the business cards from inside. "I'll just take these."

Tucking the cards in her bag, she glances past my shoulder. "You called security?"

I turn around to see a guard standing behind me, just past the door. "There are forms I need Bridget to sign," I tell him. "Afterward, I'd like you to escort her out."

"I'm not a threat," Bridget says.

"No, of course not." My voice is kind, sincere. "This is standard in these situations." Though, come to think of it, I doubt Blue Casino has encountered a naughty selfie breach before.

Bridget's head drops, but she follows me to my office and fills out the forms I pull together. They're basic termination documents, and even though Adam was responsible for hiring and firing her, I doubt Blackwell would want to risk her position not being properly closed. She was hired as a regular employee, after all.

The best part of my job is offering a position to an excited and worthy candidate. The worst part is letting someone go. I want to know Bridget will be okay. I want to ask her if she can go back to her old job, but that will only open a window for her to negotiate her position back, and that's not something the company can afford. Instead, I say nothing, my insides balled in knots as Bridget follows the security guard out of my office.

Maybe this is better for her. Bridget was involved somehow with the Bliss suites, and now she won't be around when all of that goes down.

I walk Bridget's termination papers over to payroll, and make my way to Adam's office. His door is always open, but not today.

I knock twice, so hard my knuckles smart with the impact.

"Come in," he calls.

His back is to me when I enter, his broad shoulders and lean legs silhouetted against the window. "Come here to gloat, Hayden?"

"You bastard."

He slowly turns. "Excuse me?"

"I hate letting people go. It's your fault I had to send that poor girl home."

His mouth twists in a wry smile. "That poor girl sent out inappropriate images to the entire management team. And you didn't let her go, I did."

"Maybe, but you didn't see her hands shaking as she filled out the termination forms, or watch her walk away with her elbows pressed to her ribs, escorted by security. I don't like what she did, Adam. Of course not. But you brought her into Blue. You were responsible for mentoring and guiding her. How could you let this happen?"

Maybe it's not fair of me, but I can't help directing my anger at him. Adam knows what's going on at Blue, and he's allowing it to happen. It sounds like some of management even supported what Bridget was doing, up until she got caught. Adam may not wear the Blue Star ring, but he's involved. He's responsible for this.

He lets out a sigh and leans against the windowsill, his fingers pressed against his forehead. "It's been a long day. Can we discuss this later?"

I'd like to know exactly what he's been up to and why he looks so drained, but I also know Adam is determined to keep everything a secret. To the point he was willing to wager with me to prevent me from discovering the truth. I have double the information on the suites that I had yesterday, and I can wait a little longer to discover the rest.

"I expect you to smooth things over with Blackwell," I finally say.

He drops his hand, his expression weary. "Already done. 'No harm, no foul,' were his words."

"How could he not... Oh, forget it," I say irritably, and turn to leave.

"I know what you're thinking," he says from behind.

I look over my shoulder.

"It's not true. Blackwell may not care about what happened today, because it didn't harm the casino, but I do." He glances out the window. "I take full responsibility for having to fire Bridget, no matter how wrong she was."

That's more than I expected from Adam. I thought he'd brush this off the way he does everything involving Blackwell.

His gaze falls on me, dark and fixed. "I'll be at your house Saturday to fulfill that bet I owe you. Be ready."

139

Chapter Seventeen

Adam

"You look like crap," Jaeger says.

I loosen my tie and walk across the pavers, meeting him at the door to his woodshop. If it weren't for his knee injury years ago, Jaeg would be a professional athlete right now. Instead, he makes dainty wood art. I give him a hard time for his choice of profession, but I gotta admit, he's a talented son of a bitch. When I feel like doing something with my hands, I head over to Jaeg's to saw shit up. It takes the edge off. But tonight I just need his tools. "Not possible. I always look good."

Jaeg snorts and moves to the saw table. He's wearing work gloves and there's sawdust in his short brown hair. I obviously caught him in the middle of a project. "What brings you here?" He blows wood dust off the table. "You need a board and saw to vent your frustrations?"

"Can't. Don't have time. I've got to go back to work." I glance around. "I came by to borrow a few things."

I have no idea what Hayden wants me to build this

weekend, but I figure I should grab tools while I can spare a minute. I've got the basics at home, but Jaeg invests in the good stuff. I play with his gear whenever I get the chance.

Working with power tools takes me out of my head and relaxes me. Which is why, despite the load of work I have at Blue, I don't mind paying off my bet to Hayden this weekend. Matter of fact, in some twisted way, I'm looking forward to it.

"I'm beginning to wonder if I should have taken the job at Blue," I say. "Maybe I should quit and cut my losses."

The pressure at work continues to build. I knew Bridget's background. I could have laid down better guidelines when I hired her, like Hayden said. But I didn't. I assumed Bridget understood that a side business selling images of herself in compromising positions to lonely coworkers was not acceptable. Ingenious, because she obviously established a nice little following, but not appropriate.

Obviously that sort of thing needs to be spelled out to some people.

I asked around. Paul confessed to knowing what Bridget was up to. He figured it wasn't hurting anyone, so he didn't say anything. I suspect he was receiving the images as well, considering I found him in her office handing over his business card along with the rest of the douchebags we work with. I wouldn't be surprised if Paul had received some sort of kickback for keeping quiet, dirty bastard that he is.

According to Paul, the guys at work were thrilled to shell out money for Bridget's naked photos, when they could have easily viewed that sort of thing for free online. Bridget in her prim and proper secretary attire by day sending them updates of her after-hours activities was too tempting to pass up.

Jaeg sets down a measuring tape, his brow furrowed.

"Cut your losses? What are you talking about? You never quit. Unless it comes to women—then all bets are off."

I drop onto the leather couch in his workshop and rest my elbows on my knees, my head in my hands. "I might need to change that philosophy. There are people at Blue who make the depraved billionaires at Club Tahoe look like upstanding citizens."

"It's casino life, what did you expect?"

"I get that, and I'm no saint." Jaeg makes a sound in the back of his throat and I shoot him a halfhearted glare. "It's more than that. I don't trust these guys, which is tough, because I want my job. My father pressured me to take it, like he normally does, but it's worked out, you know? There could actually be a future there. Especially now that there's no conflict with Club Tahoe. The old man has done a one-eighty on me. He's been calling, and has even expressed remorse for holding the trust fund over my head all these years."

"Seriously?" Jaeg turns around and stares. He's spent time with my dad. He knows what the man is like.

"Not in so many words, but he admitted to holding me back." I chuckle. "Supposedly, he's been calling my brothers too. I'd love to be a fly on the wall during those conversations. The old man must be going through some sort of midlife crisis. Admitting he was wrong to me is one thing, but *strained* doesn't begin to describe the history he has with my brothers."

Jaeg leans against the table, his head tilted down. "I remember."

My friends witnessed plenty of shouting matches between my brothers and my father when we were growing up. The fights usually led to Hunt, Bran, Wes, Levi, or some combination of the four storming out of the house and not returning for several days.

"Levi said the calls have been so awkward he actually felt sorry for the old man." I shake my head. "But all of this is beside the point. I'll figure out what to do about Blue. In the meantime, I lost a bet. I need to build something for Hayden this weekend." I glance at the wall of tools. "You mind if I grab a few things?"

Jaeg scratches his jaw, his gaze zeroing in on my face. "Why are you making bets with Hayden?"

I made the bet to protect Hayden and keep her away from the Blue bastards we work with. The irritation in Jaeg's voice doesn't sit well. "What's the deal? Are you playing big brother again? Or is there some other reason you don't like the idea of me spending time with her?"

His jaw shifts. "I don't like what you're implying. You've had a difficult day, so I'm going to let that one slide. But just in case it's not clear, Cali is my life. Hayden is a friend and someone I don't want to see get hurt."

"Sorry." I scrub my face and shake my head. "I didn't mean it that way. You're right; it's been a hell of a day. I know what Cali means to you."

Jaeger turns and picks up a rag from the table. "Forget about it. I won't ask what your intentions are toward Hayden, because I've already done that. The only thing I'm going to say is you had better not hurt her." He glances back. "And if you think I'm warning you because I'll kick the shit out of you, you're wrong. I might, but it's Cali you should be afraid of. Mira and Nessa have filled her in on all the things Hayden puts up with at Blue. Combine that with what happened to Hayden in high school, and Cali will neuter you if she thinks you hurt her."

"Duly noted." Cali is a fiery little thing, and Jaeg's right.

It's the females I need to worry about. "But I have no intention of hurting Hayden. Believe me, I'm staying far away." I stand and cross the room to the shelves of tools and other equipment.

"Doesn't seem like it," he grumbles, and glances at the tool I picked up.

I look down at the jumbo leveler in my hand. "Yeah, well, this is for the bet I lost. Otherwise, I wouldn't go near her house. You're not the only person whose shit list I'm on. I don't like getting on Hayden's bad side. Gives me a complex to have a beautiful woman hating on me."

"Never bothered you before," he says wryly.

I shoot him an annoyed look. I don't need Jaeg telling me how different I am around Hayden. I've heard it before, and I'm well aware. But it's not easy to stay away from her when we work together. What can I say? Her presence is intoxicating and it stuns my brain into stupid territory. But I've got this under control. I'll head to her house Saturday, take care of whatever the hell it is she needs me to work on, and be done with it.

Jaeg takes in the jigsaw I absently grabbed. "What are you building, anyway?"

"No idea." I rub my forehead, a bear of a headache building behind my temples.

He reaches across the table and tosses a pair of work goggles and a mask at me. "Maybe you should wear protection." He quirks a brow.

"Haha." My voice is flat. But I'm happy Jaeg's joking about my relationship—fuck, *friendship*—whatever, with Hayden. Reassures me there's nothing simmering between them. They've both said no, and I believed it, but for some reason I'm extra sensitive where Hayden is concerned.

She's a drop-dead, make-you-stupid beautiful girl, and

I'm not talking about what I see on the outside, which I could easily write an ode to. She's smart, opinionated, and she'd keep any guy on his toes. I know Jaeg loves Cali, but it's good to know he's as hooked on Cali as I am on—

No one. I'm not hooked on anyone.

Hayden is beautiful, that's all. I'm tired and hallucinating.

"Thanks for these." I hold up my loot. "I better get back. I've got more work to do."

Jaeg waves me off. "Yup. Let me know if you need anything else once Hayden gives you your honey-do list." He snickers.

"Asshole." I stumble out the door and drop the gear in the back of the XKR.

The trunk of my sports car is too small and clean to hold this crap, plus my equipment from home. I'll switch cars after I return from work. At midnight. Jesus. I can't wait for the Bliss suites to be up and running. One less thing to have to deal with.

I return to the office and the place is almost dead. Only security personnel and a skeleton crew remain on the executive floors in the evenings. I've seen Hayden here a few times, but she's not here tonight. Which is good. I don't like the idea of her working late by herself.

I send out a few messages regarding luxury features Blackwell wants complimentary in each of the Bliss suites. I've hired three out of the dozen or so people on his list of potential bodyguards. Now, because I'm handling every aspect of the hiring, I'm also working with the legal team on very dubious, if you ask me, contracts that have someone on the outside listed as the hiring company for the new employees.

And on that disturbing note, I rest my head against the

back of my chair and check the time on the wall clock. It's already past eleven.

I should set up a time to meet Hayden at her place on Saturday. I could text her tomorrow, but I'll be in meetings all day, and for some reason I feel the need to reach out now. Maybe it was my conversation with Jaeg, or maybe it's my disturbing desire to connect with her, even if it's to argue. Either way, I send her a text.

Adam: *I'll be there at 10AM Saturday.*

I set my phone down, and not one second later it buzzes.

Hayden: *Be ready to get your manicured hands dirty.*

I grin. Without thinking, I shoot off a reply.

Adam: *For you, my hands are always ready to get dirty.*

A bit suggestive, but whatever. Today was terrible, and I'd rather flirt with Hayden than fire people and feel Hayden's wrath. The banter is purely for my pleasure. Because I'm exhausted and I need Hayden's sass, which makes every day better.

Hayden: *Boundaries. Don't you think enough of them have been crossed after Bridget's illustrative text?*
Adam: *Touché. Until Saturday. Go to bed, Hayden. You have to work tomorrow.*
Hayden: *Go home, Adam. I know you're still at Blue. My spies tell me so.*

Damn.

Blackwell might alienate her, but Hayden knows more about what's going on around this place than most. Which is a problem. Blackwell is a fool not to utilize her—she's more talented than half his management crew—but I worry about the reason for his animosity. If I knew why he treats her the way he does, it would help. Since I don't, it's just better if she stays off his radar.

My heart is lighter as I pack up to leave. I try not to think about why. Jaeg was right to be worried, though I wouldn't admit it. I've got to be careful when it comes to Hayden. As argumentative as she is, I sense the attraction is mutual. I also sense her vulnerability. And I know what I'm capable of.

Caring for a woman? Sure.

Loving a woman? Not possible.

Chapter Eighteen

Hayden

I tuck the couch cushion I was using as a desk for my laptop back in place, and the sound of a car engine draws my eye to the window. Pushing the linen curtain aside, I peer at the red truck pulling up next to my seven-year-old compact SUV. The beater truck makes my used SUV look like a fine piece of machinery.

Adam said he was coming around ten, and it's about that now, but there is no way this is Adam. For one, that beater truck is not an Adam-worthy vehicle. He drove a gazillion-dollar sports car to Zach's dinner party. Nothing but the best for him. Second, the driver of this truck appears to be wearing a baseball cap.

Adam in a baseball cap? No way.

But the hairs on my arms are standing at attention, which is never a good sign if my instincts around Adam are to be trusted.

The man steps out of the truck, pulls off the baseball cap, and tosses it inside. And I have to give my body props.

It detected Adam sight unseen from dozens of feet away and through a glass barrier. And he looks...*whoa*.

I am in so much trouble.

Adam is wearing worn jeans that hug the amazing ass I normally only glimpse when he takes off his suit jacket, which is *never*. He has on a navy T-shirt that pulls taut over his shoulders and arms, and his jeans are gathered at the bottom over work boots. In short, he is mountain guy, mouth-watering hotness, and I am panting.

What the hell? How dare he come to my house looking like this? Adam in an Armani suit has my ovaries percolating—but dressed all rugged and sexy? Not acceptable.

He leans into the cab and pulls out a toolbox, his shirt riding up and exposing a swath of flat stomach and the thick muscle above his hipbone that has my jaw dropping. His hair isn't combed, but mussed and slightly wavy, flipping out in some places. Several locks tumble over his temples, and I have the urge to grab those locks in my fist and ask him what he's trying to do to me.

Goddammit. Casual, no-artifice Adam completely undoes me. And he's walking to my door.

I turn left, then right, searching—for what, I have no idea.

Get it together.

Taking a calming breath, I scramble for the door, and catch my toe on the edge of the couch. "Ahh!" My face scrunches as I hop around, mentally shouting every expletive known to man.

I drop my foot to the floor and exam my red little pinky toe. Not crooked. Pain diminishing. Just a stub.

"You okay in there?" Adam's baritone filters through the door with a tinge of humor.

Is he laughing at me?

149

I limp over and swing the door open. And suck in a breath. And look at the side of his head instead of his eyes. And take another breath.

There. That's better. *Don't look into the eye of the storm, and everything will be okay.* "Yes. It's fine. I stubbed my toe."

There's a pause, and finally I look at his face, because it's getting weird that I'm not. He's smiling, and oh my God. There's a dimple in his cheek I never noticed. It's faint, but combine it with the mussed hair, the tight T-shirt across a thick, muscled chest, and I feel lightheaded.

His brow puckers, his expression turning serious as he scans my face. "You sure you're okay? I could come back another time."

I wave him inside. "No, I'm fine." *I'm so not fine.*

He walks past me with the metal toolbox in one hand.

"Can I get you anything to drink?" I ask.

He looks around, taking the place in. "I'm good. This place yours?"

"No, it's a stranger's. I asked if I could borrow it."

His gaze slides to me, eyebrow arched, his mouth turned up. "This how it's going to be today?"

I let out a sigh. "Of course it's mine," I wobble into the living room, pinky toe feeling better, but not fully recovered.

Adam has me rattled. I can't look at him. It makes me vulnerable. And by vulnerable, I mean I want to jump him.

"So." He resumes his visual scan of the place. "What's it to be? You need a lightbulb changed?"

"Haha, you're hilarious. I believe the bet was that you would *build* me something. I see you brought your tools." I eye the large metal box.

"My *tools* are ready."

I flash him a look, and it might be filled with fear and panic. If he starts flirting with me the way he did a couple of nights ago with that naughty text, I'm dead.

"Hayden?" The humor in his eyes has disappeared. "Any chance I can convince you to stay out of my business over the next few weeks while I hire people?"

For a moment, I'm ready to give in. To tell him he can have whatever he wants. Because the look on his face is so unguarded and sincere, all my barriers come down. But I made a promise to myself to find whatever I could about Blue's underground activities. I can't back out now. "Sorry, I plan to be all up in your business. Regarding human resources, that is. Why is it such a big deal if I know about the people you hire?"

He looks away. "It just is."

I let out a sigh and try a different tactic. "What happened with Bridget could have been prevented. If you'd given me the opportunity to go over Blue's policies with her, she might have thought twice before starting her side business. Which brings up another point. Those men involved were never reprimanded. How is it that Bridget gets fired, but the guys buying dirty images during work hours were never held accountable?"

"It's been looked into. Most of them made the financial transaction after hours. And if we reprimanded all of them, it would be the entire male staff."

"Are you kidding me?"

"There were a few who didn't partake, myself included, but the rest—"

"Because you didn't know about it," I grumble.

He captures my gaze. "I wouldn't have participated even if I had known."

I wet my lips, studying his blue eyes, which appear to be

telling me something his words aren't. His presence unsettles me, makes me crazy, but the way he's looking now has my heart pounding faster.

Adam's gaze drops to my mouth, where the moisture left behind from my tongue cools. He tears his gaze away. "What's this thing you want me to build?" he says gruffly.

I clear my throat. "Over here."

I take Adam down the hallway, still rattled by whatever just passed between us, and point to the door of a closet that shares a wall with my bedroom. "I want you to close off this door in the hall and make an entrance to my bedroom. Oh, and built-ins. I would love built-ins for all of my shoes."

He stares at the door, then turns to me. "You're joking, right? You want me to build you a master closet?"

Okay, so it's more of a construction job, but hey, he agreed to it. "I'm dead serious."

He chuckles and scratches his unshaven jaw. "Hayden, this is not even close to what I had in mind. Originally, the bet was for me to fix something."

"Oh no, that's what *you* said. But I agreed to you *building* me something. And I'd love a walk-in closet using this space." I gesture proudly at the hall closet.

He cranes his head to the side, peering inside my bedroom. "What's wrong with the one you have?"

I love my bedroom. It's gray and violet with an espresso bed I bought when I moved back into the place. The furniture in the living room is old and original from when my parents and I lived here, but the bedroom furniture is new. Living room furniture will be phase two of the house remodel.

"It's too small. Doesn't fit my shoes."

He stalks inside the bedroom and opens the accordion closet doors. A single rail holds all seasons of clothing and boxes line the foot of the closet. "If you move these boxes, you'll have room for your shoes. You actually don't have very many clothes."

True, I keep my wardrobe under control, donating unused or outdated items on a regular basis. The boxes contain puffy coats and snow boots, and a few other cold-weather items.

"Actually, the shoes won't fit," I say. "Even if I put the winter boxes in the attic."

He raises his eyebrow and scans the closet. "Where *are* your shoes?"

I smile. "You see, now you're catching on. This is why I need the walk-in." I head back into the hallway and open the hall closet, turning on the inside light.

Adam peers at the shelves and slowly sets down his toolbox. He whistles. "Never knew you were a shoe hoarder."

My face warms. I hadn't thought about how personal this project might be. "I have a bit of a shoe obsession. I'm not a hoarder. I'm a *collector*."

He grabs a pair of chunky, flat Mary Janes tucked away on a top shelf. "These still fit?"

"I wore those every day of my senior year. They were my favorites. And yes, they fit."

He looks at me like I've lost my mind. "Hayden, if you get rid of some of these shoes, the rest will work in your bedroom closet."

I grab my Mary Janes and dust them off hastily with the sleeve of my shirt. "And give you nothing to do? No way. Besides, I want a walk-in closet." My voice goes dreamy. "With walls of shelving devoted to these beauties." I hug the shoes to my chest, and he covers his mouth with his hand, hiding what I detect is a smile.

I jump up and tuck the shoes back in their place on the

top shelf. "Don't you think you should get to work? It's a big project."

My hall closet is nice and deep. It's going to make an awesome walk-in.

He shakes his head and picks up the toolbox. "Sure thing, Ms. Marcos."

"Imelda Marcos? That's cute. Very funny," I say dryly.

"Isn't it?" He grins.

I purse my lips. *He's making fun of me...* I can live with that. As long as he builds a kick-ass walk-in closet for all my pretties.

Adam owes me this. Call it punishment for his arrogance these last few months, which culminated in the cherry on the top with him assuming anyone could do my job and hire good employees. Ones who *don't sell explicit photos* to other employees.

Adam would have been involved in hiring for his department regardless, but every applicant goes through a thorough human resources check. That's the part he skipped, and I'm determined to know why he and Blackwell felt it necessary.

I plop down on my bed and watch Adam remove all the items from the hall closet. And God, is it entrancing. The swell of his biceps as he pulls a box down; his muscular ass as he bends to set it on the floor. Really, all he'd have to do is move things around my house for an hour and I'd call us even. Because this view...

Should I video it?

No, that's stalkerish.

I do not stalk Adam Cade. Lust from afar—absolutely, but not stalk. Why would I want to do that when I'm forced to put up with his arrogance every day at work? But this sexy, casual Adam who uses his brawn to build me stuff? This Adam I could get used to. "Need any help?"

He sets down another box and braces his arm against the doorframe to my bedroom, the underside of his forearm and bicep bulging. "I got it. But I'll take you up on that offer of a drink now. Water would be great."

I tear my eyes away from his body to look at his face, which isn't helping because the lightly scruffed, mussy-haired Adam is equally entrancing.

It was a bad idea to invite him into my home.

"Of course." I jump up and cross the room, inching carefully past him. And okay, taking a light whiff of him. He even smells good. A just-showered, soapy boy scent.

Inside the kitchen, I suck in a breath of Adam-free air and knock my head on the fridge a couple of times to rattle some sense into it. I fill a glass of water and turn around—to Adam standing at the end of the galley kitchen.

"Your head okay?" he says, his mouth curled in a half-smile.

"No," I grumble quietly. My brain is fogged because of this *jackass*.

"What was that?" he says.

"Nothing." I hand him the water. "You need anything else?"

He shakes his head, taking in the updated kitchen. "Do you own this place?"

I glance at the space I lovingly remodeled. Before I bought the house, the kitchen was 1970s yellow. Now it features white-painted Shaker cabinets and limestone counters. "I bought it as soon as I returned to town."

Adam gulps the water, watching me. "Didn't you want to rent for a bit? Make sure you're in for the long haul? You've been gone a long time."

I fill another glass and take a sip. "It's complicated. I bought the place from my parents. They weren't able to sell it when we first left town. They rented it after we moved, but part of me always felt I owed them."

He looks around some more, as though seeing it from a different perspective. "It's small, but I don't see why your parents wouldn't have been able to sell it. Lots of people look for mountain cabins as second homes."

I set the glass on the counter and face him. "It wasn't the size, or the way it looks. You were there, Adam. You saw how people treated me—the way you treated me—"

His face tenses. "I wasn't cruel to you."

"Weren't you?"

He stretches his neck and looks away. "I told Jaeg to break up with you—"

"Yeah, I remember."

"Because," he says with emphasis, his gaze sliding back to me, "I didn't want him dating you."

Adam's eyes aren't cynical or sly. His gaze is half-lidded, and very intent.

"You didn't want me with Jaeg...and it had nothing to do with the rumor?"

He shakes his head slowly.

"Then why?"

He drops his chin, and suddenly my throat goes dry. It's not like men haven't desired me. It's that no one who consumes my thoughts ever has. And whether those thoughts are images of killing him, or kissing him, Adam has been on my mind since he started working at Blue.

What is happening? Adam flirts with me. He harasses me. But showing genuine interest? What he's talking about goes way back—eleven years. That's not simple flirting with a coworker, that's...something else.

"I was sixteen and stupid, but I shouldn't have done it," he says. "I know I already apologized, but I *am* sorry." He looks away and runs a hand through his hair, ruffling it even more. He sets the glass down and his expression lightens. "I better get back to work. It's gonna take a while to build the closet for you." His mouth twists wryly, but I'm still hung up on his admission.

I don't understand Adam. Not at all.

I lust after him. Adam flirts, because it's his nature—he's a lady-killer. But what he implied... Never in a million years would I have guessed he might have been jealous of Jaeger and me. He hinted at another reason for his actions in high school the night of the taco dinner, but I assumed he was referring to me not being good enough for Jaeger.

I was skinny, nerdy—who am I kidding, I'm still nerdy—and I wasn't popular. There could have been no other reason why he would want Jaeger to break up with me. Not with the rumor and everything else going on.

Unless he wanted Jaeger to break up with me *before* the rumor broke out. And I have no idea what to do with that.

Adam walks into the living room and glances back. "You might want to stay out here. I'll be demoing."

I'm still reeling—until I register his words.

"Wait! What do you mean?" I sweep after him into the hallway. All the shoes and boxes are out of the closet and Adam is standing inside, safety goggles on his face, a hammer poised above his head.

"Adam. Put. The. Hammer. Down. What are you doing?"

He grins mischievously. "What you asked." *Wham.* He slams the face of the hammer into the wall, then uses the claw to rip away a chunk of brittle white board.

I gape at the hole. Then him. Then the hole again. "Is this wise?"

I figured he would have backed out by now and admitted he couldn't do the work. I should have someone qualified building this, not Adam Cade.

He brushes white powder from his shirt and peers inside the wall. "You said you wanted a walk-in." He looks over and cocks his brow. "For your *shoes*." *Wham*. He slams the hammer down, knocking away more of the surface separating the closet from my bedroom. "And if that's the case, you'll need an entrance."

Insulation and white chalk float in the air, creating a cloud of dust and other crap.

"I can't watch," I murmur, and move into the living room.

I take a seat on the couch cross-legged, and flinch every time Adam bangs at my wall. He was right. This is a big project. What was I thinking?

I know what I was thinking. I wanted to punish him. Except I'm the one who will be punished when my "walk-in" comes out misshapen and nonfunctional.

It's my fault. I was prideful about work. Granted, I was right about Bridget. But still, why did I make a bet with Adam? Nothing good comes from gambling with a man who makes you mad with frustration one moment, and mad with lust the next.

After an hour of banging and ripping sounds fill my house, Adam calls me into the bedroom. And he has a power saw in his hand, tarps draped over the floor and other surfaces.

"What's that for?" My voice is high-pitched.

He raps his knuckles on the wood paneling. "Need a hole where the new closet will go. I've measured it out, but I just wanted to make sure it's a standard door you're putting in before I cut."

"Don't you dare cut up my walls."

He lowers the saw. "Hayden, how do you expect to have a walk-in closet without an opening you can walk through? You said you wanted an entrance directly into the bedroom."

I throw up my hands. "I don't know. But these are my pretty walls." I walk over and pet the wood. "What if you ruin them?"

He sighs. "Do you trust me?"

"Hell no. You're a pretty boy who shouldn't be holding power tools."

He shakes his head and steps forward, lifting my chin with the tip of one lightly callused finger that has no right being callused, according to my stereotype. "You really think that of me?" His eyes are intent. He's forcing me to admit what I've never allowed myself to.

Somewhere along the way I stopped viewing Adam as a spoiled little rich boy. He's a hard worker, whom I respect more than I like to acknowledge. He challenges me. But more important, Adam has always treated me like an equal. He's not one of the Neanderthals we work with. And I suspect there's even a sensitive side to him.

"No, I don't think that of you," I finally say.

He drops his hand, only to reach for my palm and twine our fingers. My heartbeat ratchets up a notch. He tucks our clasped hands against my belly and steps forward, pushing until I'm forced to take a step back. And another, until I'm in the hall.

He slides his fingers from mine, sending zingers of electricity up my arm, and looks at me pointedly. "Stay here, where it's safe."

Adam moves in front of the paneled wall, lowers protective glasses from the top of his head, and fires up the saw.

I cover my ears as he makes the first cut, and run for cover in the living room.

Shockingly, I do trust Adam to work on my house, which says a lot, because I put my entire savings into buying this place from my parents.

Hours pass as I try to work while not flinching every time Adam makes a loud sound. Finally, he enters the living room, carrying his toolbox.

I swing my legs off the couch and stand. "Everything okay?" I peer around him toward the hallway. "That was fast. Is it all done?"

He tucks a measuring tape in his back pocket. "Not even close. I'll return tomorrow. A little later than today, probably—around one. I have some things to take care of for work. I'll be by after that." He rubs his chin, leaving a hint of dirt behind that matches the faint dark lines beneath his eyes.

"Work on a Sunday?" I say.

He glances at my laptop and raises his eyebrow.

"Right. I guess the casino never shuts down, does it?"

"No," he says.

I hesitate for a moment. Part of me wonders why he looks so tired, with those dark shadows under his eyes, and the other part of me is eager as hell to find out what he's doing for Blue on a Sunday. "And you've been busy with...?"

He gives me a knowing smile. I guess my fishing efforts are obvious. "Stuff," he says.

"Right, stuff." Because even if I won our bet, Adam won't fill me in on what he's up to.

I walk him to the door, guilt overtaking my desire to

keep him here as my work slave, though the view would be amazing if I did. "Thank you for the closet. I know I asked a lot. We can call it even."

He glances back skeptically. "With a hole in your wall and your shoe collection homeless? You might change your tune once you take a look back there."

Awesome. Now I am worried, but I still feel like I've taken advantage of him. "I can hire someone. You've done the demo. That counts for something."

"Still don't trust me?" A small smile spreads across his face, but there's hurt behind his eyes.

"No, that's not it," I say quickly. God, why is he making this so difficult? "I'm trying to admit that it was ridiculous of me to ask you to build a closet in the first place."

"I don't mind." He turns and strides toward his truck. "I like working with my hands."

And that's the biggest shocker of all. Adam isn't as polished and uptight as I thought. He's rather handy to have around.

Or maybe it's not so shocking.

Because there's a chance I never really knew Adam.

Chapter Nineteen

Adam

Had I known Hayden intended for me to build a closet, I would have gone to Lewis's house to grab equipment instead of Jaeg's. Lewis is the contractor in the group. Jaeg is just the artsy woodworker. I demoed what I could yesterday, took measurements, and picked up drywall and wood for framing. But today I'm talking to a professional before I hack something up.

"Lewis, it's Adam. You got a minute?" I say, as I lace up my work boots.

I ask Lewis a few questions to make sure I'm building Hayden's closet correctly. Jaeg and I helped Lewis build his house a few years ago. That's how I learned about construction. I know the basics, but it can't hurt to make sure I'm doing things right.

He gives me tips on closing off the hallway, and it's toward the end of the conversation that I remember something. "Before we get off the line, I've been wanting to ask you about the remodel of Blue's penthouse suites. I was up there the other day and noticed a different company in charge. Why aren't your guys doing the work? I thought Sallee Construction filled most of Blue's bids."

"Good question," he says. "We have an informal agreement with Blue, but they claimed that even with the discount we give them, they'd found a better price. It's the first time that's happened."

"So your company wasn't too busy?"

"We're always busy, but we've got a backup crew for larger projects like Blue. Our schedule was never the problem. Why, is that what they said?"

"Something like that. You think this has anything to do with the manager who attacked Gen?" I wasn't there, but I heard it took Jaeg and Zach all night to convince Lewis not to kill the guy. "If you're not holding what Drake Peterson did against the casino, I don't see why Blackwell would have an issue with continuing the working relationship."

"Who knows why your CEO does anything?" Lewis says. "But I can tell you one thing—Gen's dad, Jeb Kendrick, didn't stop looking into Blue Casino just because Drake Peterson was convicted. From what I hear, neither has your favorite girl."

"Hayden?" Yeah, I caught what Lewis said about Hayden being my *favorite girl,* but damn, it's the truth. And I want to know what Lewis means more than I'm interested in defending myself.

"Hayden's looking for anything else to take to the police," Lewis says. "If she finds something, Jeb's men will be all over it. He's working with the police and private investigators."

No wonder Hayden's been so nosy. "Lewis, you guys need to keep Hayden out of it."

Lewis chuckles. "Nice try. You think I have any say in these things?"

"Good point," I say grudgingly. "You called Gen's dad Jeb Kendrick. He isn't the ex-football star?"

"The one and only. And he's connected."

Paul and William are shifty jackasses, but they aren't Drake Peterson. Although, considering the drugs and prostitutes Paul had delivered to my home and the way he's been throwing threats around, maybe it's time I took this seriously. "You think I can get Jeb's number? Just in case."

Lewis gives me the number for Gen's dad, and we sign off. I set the phone on the edge of the bed, and lean forward with my arms on my knees. Why wouldn't Blue use Sallee Construction for Bliss? It's strange, but I'm not jumping to conclusions just yet.

Of course Hayden wouldn't be able to walk away from putting bad guys behind bars. Because of what? A hunch? I shake my head. I don't even want to consider how I'm going to keep her away from Paul and William, and I guess Blackwell, since he's in charge, but I need to. I'm not ready to convict Blue Casino—not when the place is my livelihood— but I don't like the way Paul has put the heat on me and threatened to come after me if I say anything about Bliss. I've got a bad feeling about it, and I don't want Hayden anywhere near it.

I check my work emails one last time. Paul sent a message about the Bliss rollout. We have enough bodyguards now, and he's got a backup plan for the dancers, so I can stop hiring. Everything is on schedule for the weekend of the auction and burlesque show.

I shut down my laptop and sweep a hand through my hair, attempting to tame it. I showered hours ago when I started working from home, but combing and shaving aren't on the weekend agenda. It's Sunday, and I've only managed a few hours of sleep these last few nights. I'm running on fumes; bad hair is par for the course.

After I took care of errands for Hayden's closet yesterday afternoon, I went in to work and stayed until early morning, filling out paperwork the way I have the last couple of nights. There's no logical reason why I should pay off my debt to Hayden this weekend on top of everything else. It's bad timing, and I'm sure Hayden would agree to wait a week or two. But I don't want to wait. Spending time with her is the most fun I've had in a long time. I haven't decided if it's because I'm working on something outside of Blue, which clears my head, or if it's her. Pretty sure I don't want the answer to that. Not when I can't even refute Lewis's remark about her being my favorite girl.

I grab my keys, and head out to the Chevy I bought from the Club Tahoe groundskeeper ten years ago. My brothers and I use it to haul things around town. The beast is an eyesore, but it comes in handy and I can't bring myself to replace it.

What seems like seconds later, I pull up to Hayden's place and cut the engine. The hour may indicate early afternoon, but my ass is dragging. I stretch my neck and climb out, taking a deep breath of pine-scented air. The fresh air clears a few of the cobwebs, and I reach inside the cab for the extra items I brought today.

Hayden's house is small, but every freaking inch of it is charming, from the Z-framed front door and window boxes, to her girly purple bedroom. It's nothing like the home I grew up in, or even the house I'm renting now. Yet it's ten times more comfortable than anyplace I've lived.

I rap twice on the door. After a moment—no crashing

165

sounds this time—Hayden answers. She's in blue jeans and a T-shirt that hugs her curves, her hair in another ponytail.

My heart does an extra beat. There's something about seeing Hayden outside of work that gets my blood pumping. She gets it pumping at work too, but outside of Blue, the restraints are off. I love seeing this casual side of her.

A sandy blond wisp dangles over her cheek from the tawny bangs she's swept off to the side. "More stuff?" She eyes the buckets and other equipment I'm carrying.

"And more where this came from." I set the items on the porch and trudge back to the truck, where I grab a large sheet of drywall. Propping it against my shoulder and head, I carry it into the house and lean it against the unused portion of the hallway. "This okay?"

Hayden nods, eyeing the sheet warily.

"Don't worry," I say. "I'm only using a portion of this. Drywall comes in one size from the home improvement store. I had to buy the whole thing."

Fortunately, Hayden's hallway doesn't have the wood paneling her bedroom and living room do. I only need drywall to close it off, some tape, and matching Spackle and paint.

"I'm so paying you back for the supplies, and for your work if you'll let me," she says.

I wave her off. Like I need her money. Yeah, I lost the bet, but I'm doing this because I want to, plain and simple.

Hayden hands me a Pacifico, which I gladly accept, and sits cross-legged on the floor, watching me while I settle in to patch up the giant hole that was the hall closet. Stealthily, I glance over. She never fails to grab my eye at work, but without makeup and her hair down—or, rather, up—I can hardly keep my eyes off her. She looks like the girl she was—the one I couldn't stop tracking during high school.

I kept my distance from Hayden at work this last week because I was busy with interviews, but that's not the only reason. I'd been a hairsbreadth away from kissing her after I caught her snooping in the facility manager's office. I don't know what came over me. I blame it on exhaustion. And abstinence. And Hayden. She rubs me in a way that unleashes my most basic instincts—those of the covet and copulate variety. But other instincts as well—to protect and care for her—and where the hell did those come from?

I like things simple. Tame. And my emotions where Hayden is concerned aren't the least bit tame.

Blackwell is cutting corners to get Bliss up and running. He doesn't need to contract out employees and bypass his own human resources department, but he is, and I haven't figured out why. My long-hibernating protective instincts have me blocking Hayden from Bliss and those involved in it, but I'm not so altruistic. I need this venture just as much as Blackwell does. But I will be cautious from here on out. I'll reach out to Jeb Kendrick.

"You never finished telling me why your parents couldn't sell this place," I say, to get my mind off feelings for her I don't want to consider. And how cute she looks with her chin propped on her hand.

Her face scrunches up. "Didn't I?"

I take a moment to measure out the drywall and cut out the pieces, nailing them in place. "You said no one would buy the house," I continue. "You thought it was because of the rumor."

"It was." She leans back and stretches out her shapely legs. "People weren't interested in paying money to the family of the girl who seduced their favorite teacher and drove him out of town."

Knee to the floor, seam tape in my palm, my hands go

still. It's just so damn infuriating how judgmental and cruel people can be. "I didn't realize things spread that far into the community. You sure the house didn't sell because of the economy?"

She shakes her head, the soft swell of her cheek turned down as she carefully peels the label from her beer bottle. "The schools were the root of the problem, but once the rumor spread, it spread everywhere."

I'd heard the rumor—everyone did—but I've never heard Hayden's side. "What happened?"

She picks up a piece of red string from the floor and twists it between her thumb and forefinger, reminding me of the pine needle she played with during the bonfire at Zach and Nessa's. "It was like this ripple on the lake that first day. So subtle, you know? But that ripple grew and grew. By afternoon, one girl had shoved me into a picnic table and bruised one of my ribs. I stayed home for a couple of days, just to get away from it." She looks up. "I heard what they were saying, but I couldn't figure out why anyone would believe something so stupid. I mean, this was me, right? I wasn't a sexy minx."

I beg to differ. Hayden was a quiet, sexy nerd. She just didn't know it.

"Anyway." She takes a sip of her beer and stares back at the string. "I returned to school, thinking the rumor had died out. But it hadn't. It was worse. They were so angry, Adam." Her hand drops to her lap and she closes her eyes. "The entire school, not just the students."

The urge to hold her overwhelms me. I give in somewhat and settle for placing my hand on her knee. "I remember. You picked the wrong teacher to start an affair with," I say, trying to lighten the mood.

She lets out a long breath that ends on a nervous laugh.

Her eyes flutter to mine, moisture and pain in their golden-brown depths. "Mr. Miller was handsome, wasn't he?"

It kills me to see her like this. I shrug. "If you like the tall, athletic sort."

Her lips soften. Not quite a smile, but it's something. "Every girl had a crush on him. And the guys wanted to *be* him. Even the stoners paid attention in class, he was that inspirational. And the school made him leave because of me." Her voice quavers.

Fuck. Why did I bring this up? "It wasn't your fault."

"Everyone thought it was. *God.*" She wipes her eyes and lets out a shaky breath. "I can't believe this still bothers me. It was just so humiliating. I felt powerless. And poor Mr. Miller... The only good thing that came out of it was that he didn't get blamed. Everyone pointed the finger at me. He denied the affair, of course, and they decided not to prosecute because the only thing the police had to go on was the anonymous call that had tipped off the school. I heard Mr. Miller found a job in a different state."

I stare at the ground. "I'm sorry both of you went through that, and I'm especially sorry for causing you more pain at the time...after what I said to Jaeg."

She shakes her head. "Having my boyfriend dump me—well, I'm not going to lie, it sucked. But it wasn't my biggest issue. The rumors were so convincing, you know? A small part of me couldn't blame people for running with it. The person who'd tipped off the school said I'd met the teacher on campus after I got off work one day, and I *had* been on campus that day. The security cameras caught me there. I'd gone to grab a book I needed. No one could have known those details except—"

"Jaeg's ex," I growl, and lean back, shoving my hand

through my hair. "Jaeg finally ran her out of town, but she was a piece of work."

"The funny thing is," Hayden says, "I never suspected her, even though we worked together at the ice cream shop. She knew I was headed back to campus to pick up the book the day everything went down. I didn't put it together until it was too late. Never thought anyone would do something like that just to get to my boyfriend."

"If it makes you feel better, she put Jaeg through the wringer."

"It doesn't," Hayden says, and stares at her hands. "Makes me sad. I'm glad he found Cali."

I let out a sigh. "Jaeg survived, but what about you? Did you talk to the school?"

"After I pleaded with the principal and the superintendent that the rumors weren't true, and they didn't believe me, it felt impossible. Like I was going up against the world. And my family—my mom... She was a teacher at an elementary school." Hayden's expression turns stony. "They couldn't fire her, but everyone at the school did what they could to let her know she wasn't welcome. And the kids at our school made it *painfully* clear that I wasn't welcome."

I don't like the sound of that.

"My parents decided to make a fresh start outside of Lake Tahoe. We tried to sell this place, but no one came to the open houses. A young family from Carson finally showed interest, but they looked into the schools for their son and heard about the rumor connected to the owners and that was the end of that. My parents weren't willing to lower the price below market value. They rented it to tourists—people who didn't care about small-town gossip— and we moved to Reno."

It's amazing how easily a lie can ruin a family. If something like this had happened to a Cade, our lawyers and public relations people would have squashed it before it could take flight. But Hayden comes from a middle-class, all-American family that suffered for no good reason. Because they didn't have the power to do anything to stop it.

In some ways, I don't blame Hayden for being leery of Blue Casino and wanting to make sure nothing bad is still going on. She's trying to protect people, because that's Hayden. I also suspect it has something to do with not having others do the same for her when she needed it.

A mix of emotions washes over me. Anger, frustration, that weird need to comfort her...and guilt because I did nothing to help Hayden back then. In fact, I made it worse by convincing her boyfriend to dump her because I didn't want to see her with another guy. Especially not my best friend. Oh, that's not what I told myself at the time. I convinced myself it was the best thing for Jaeg, dumbass that I was.

Hayden was too good a person for me then, and she damn well is a better person than me now.

I blink back the realization and begin taping the wall, ignoring the tightening in my chest. "You wouldn't have a problem selling this place now."

"No," she agrees, "but that's not why I bought it." She abandons the string and peels off another piece of her beer label. "It sounds crazy, but when we left, my life was so out of control. No one but my parents believed me about the teacher. Not even my boyfriend..." Her gaze flickers over, as though she's catching herself.

A stab of guilt and something feral burns through me. "I'm sorry, Hayden. For my part. I didn't care what they were saying. I never believed it."

"You didn't?"

"Of course not. Anyone who watched you with Jaeg could tell you were hooked. You would never have cheated."

She swallows and studies me, her hand squeezing the bottle. "And you know this because you watched me?" she says carefully.

I don't look over. "Yes. I should have said something. Should have stopped it."

There'd been no doubt in my mind that the rumor about her was false. I had no reason to believe anything different than the rest of the community, except that I'd observed Hayden. She hadn't done it. I would have seen her with Mr. Miller, would have noticed her eye wandering to him... because that's how aware of her I was.

I knew she hadn't done it, and I didn't say one damn thing to defend her.

"I don't think one person speaking up would have made a difference," she says. "It was like a runaway train; there was no stopping the rumor once it was out. A seed of suspicion was all they needed."

She might be right, but it doesn't make me feel better.

Her expression grows pensive. "Adam, can I ask you something?"

I nod.

"Why didn't you recognize me when you first started working at Blue? If you knew me so well in high school..."

I shake my head. "*Know* is a strong word. I watched you. And I'm not sure why I didn't recognize you right away. You go by a different name now, so that didn't help. I also hadn't seen you in eleven years; I wasn't expecting to find you at Blue Casino. And you look...different." I peer over. "Dress different. You don't wear glasses anymore. And you've filled out." A lazy grin I can't hide spreads across my face. I allow my gaze to drop to her chest.

She frowns. "Jackass. Don't give me that. I may have changed, but not that much."

"In my defense, when I saw you for the first time at Blue, it was from behind, if you recall. I didn't get a good look at your face." I'm laughing now as an image comes to mind of Hayden crawling around on the floor, her pert little ass in the air. Not much different from the way I found her the other day in the facility manager's office.

She throws the discarded beer label at my head. "I swear, you are the only person who catches me in those unfortunate positions. For your information, I was searching for my favorite pen."

I shoot her a flirty grin. "Lucky me."

She shakes her head in exasperation, but she's smiling.

"You have to acknowledge," I say, "your face, pretty as it is, wasn't attracting my attention at that moment."

She throws up her hands. "What about later? After we'd been properly introduced."

"Yeah, that part I can't explain. You're not the quiet, hide-in-the-corner girl you used to be. You come across as an entirely new person, but I *did* notice you. There's always been something."

She shifts beside me, and I think she must sense the tension that's taken over the hallway, ratcheting up the temperature several degrees.

It's been that way from the beginning, that tension, and if I hadn't blocked my feelings for the shy girl all those years ago, I might have recognized Hayden this time around, regardless of the name change. Might have sought her out long ago.

Oddly, it feels good to admit how she affects me—has always affected me. To realize I'm not as unfeeling as I thought I was.

"I bought this place," she says, obviously changing the subject, or at least going back to our original conversation, "to prove something." She looks around.

"Which is?"

Her gaze falls on me. "That no matter what someone says or does, I can hold my own." Her expression is strong and beautiful, and for a moment, my breath locks in my lungs.

I think about kissing her.

And hold myself back with all of my strength.

This urge to kiss her has gotten out of hand.

Working at Blue Casino with Paul and William, and with Blackwell for a boss, isn't much different from working for my father, but it's also different in every way imaginable. Because my father isn't calling the shots. So I understand the need Hayden has to prove herself. She was given a raw deal when we were teenagers. This is her redemption. And I want her to have it. Just as long as she doesn't get hurt.

Her gaze drops and a small smile plays along her mouth. "It sounds stupid. Maybe I'm deranged for buying the place. I also wanted to make things up to my parents. They sacrificed everything for me."

"That's what good parents do." I think of my mother and how she died to give my youngest brother life, and the pounding behind my temples that's been teasing me these last couple of days returns. I squeeze my forehead and grab the items I'll need to prepare the mud.

Hayden is stronger than any woman I've ever met, with the exception of my mother. The light and strength that come from Hayden draw me. The more I know her, the stronger that urge to be close gets. I want all of her.

"We're the same age, right?" I ask bluntly, and out of nowhere, except that I've wondered. She's got to be my age, but her determination and decisions make her seem much older.

Her pretty, petal-colored lips compress. "It's not gentlemanly to ask a lady's age."

Never lets me get away with anything. God, I love that. "It's only ungentlemanly when you're forty or above."

"I think you mean thirty or above, but just so you know I'm confident in my womanhood, I happen to be twenty-seven."

Same age as me. "When is your birthday?"

"August thirty-first. I'll be twenty-eight in a couple of months."

I nod. "Virgo."

"How did you know?" She peers at the powder I'm pouring into a bucket.

It's messy. I should probably move it outside. "I have four brothers. Among the five of us, we take up half the zodiac."

Hayden's jaw drops. "*Four* brothers? There are five of you walking around?"

It is a scary prospect, but them's the breaks.

She continues to stare as though dazed. I point at the bucket. "This is going to get messy. Is there someplace in the yard where I can blend it? I'll need an electrical outlet."

Her eyes refocus and she stands. "Yeah, sure. This way." She smacks the back of her jeans, as if to dust them off, though there's nothing on them. Doesn't stop me from checking out her cute ass.

I follow her out and blatantly ogle her, because that's what I do, though I don't recall being this much of a dog before. Matter of fact, I can't recall the last woman I ogled. It seems I reserve that for my feisty coworker.

"When's *your* birthday?" she asks as she leads me to the

back door. We step onto a small deck. A metal table with a yellow flowering plant on top separates two lounge chairs. It's charming, just like the rest of Hayden's house.

"February fifteenth," I say. "Same age as you."

"Not quite." She pats me on the shoulder with her tiny hand. "I have a few months on you."

I chuckle at the ridiculousness of that statement. "You're only five and a half months older."

"And don't you forget it," she says, and walks down the deck steps to a fenced-in yard, shooting me a mischievous grin.

This is how things go down over the next few hours: I mud, then build the new jamb in her bedroom while the mud is drying—taking breaks with Hayden for beers and burgers she picked up from the joint a few blocks away—and we banter. The hours pass, and it's not until ten p.m. that I realize how late it is.

Hayden is in the kitchen, futzing around with something or other. I'm not really sure what, as I've been in the zone working on the bedroom wall. I put away my tools and bring in the shop vac I brought from home. Not much I can do about the dust that's collected. I brought a few drop cloths, and we covered the bedding with a sheet, but this work is messy. Dust is everywhere.

I vacuum up the debris on the floor and return my tools to the truck. I'm finished, with the exception of sanding, painting, and shelving, but that will have to wait until the mud dries.

I look around to make sure I've grabbed everything. Hayden's home is clean and orderly, the exact opposite of her office, which surprises me. The colors in her bedroom are cool tones, and calming. It's been a long week. More than once I've looked longingly at her bed. The headache that's been brewing these last couple of days in spits and spurts is going full force now, and it feels like my temples are pulsating.

I stop in the doorway of her bedroom and close my eyes, rubbing the sides of my head.

"You okay?"

The damn headache has muted my senses. I didn't hear her approach, but Hayden is standing only two feet away. At some point, she changed, because she's in sleep pants and a tank top. My head hurts like hell, but I'm coherent enough to notice she's still wearing her bra, much to my disappointment.

"Headache. I get them sometimes." I wave behind at her room. "This is all I can do for today. I'll have to return tomorrow after work. Or next weekend, if that's okay?"

She chews her lip. "Of course, but are you sure? You've put in so many hours. I said it yesterday and I'll say it again, we should call it even. You don't owe me anything."

"It's been fun and I don't mind." I attempt a smile, but it comes out as a wince. The headache has my eyes tearing.

Before I know what's happening, Hayden is dragging me by the arm toward her bed. She carefully pulls off the sheet we placed to protect it, and pushes down on my shoulders. "Sit."

I do as she says, because I'm too tired to protest. Not that I would. What sane man would refuse a beautiful woman drawing him to her bed?

She crawls up behind me, and if I weren't in so much pain, I might think of ways to take advantage of the situation. But all I can think about is that I still have to stand up, walk to my car, and drive my sorry ass home. I should have taken painkillers hours ago, but I was in the zone. Now I'm paying for it.

Warm little heatblaster hands flatten on the top of my head—and drain the pain right from my skull.

My shoulders relax, and my eyelids close. Hayden's fingers slide to my temples and she rubs in gentle circles. I rest my forearms on my knees, and my head drops. I sense her angle closer to reach me. I shouldn't lean this far forward, but it feels so good I can barely keep myself upright. One of her hands slides to my neck. She begins massaging my head with one hand and my neck with the other.

I am in heaven. Feels so good...

I should probably tell her she doesn't need to do this, but Hayden is willingly putting her hands on me. I'm no dummy; I keep my damn mouth shut. And that's when I really lose track of time, because everything melts.

The tension caused by Blue Casino.

The barriers holding Hayden and me apart.

Until I'm dreaming there's nothing standing between us...

Chapter Twenty

Hayden

I've never seen Adam this exhausted. When I went to the bedroom to check on him, he was wavering in the doorway, his hands clutched to his head. I didn't think; I simply dragged him to the bed to help relieve his obvious pain.

A gust of air escaped his mouth as soon as I placed my hands on his head. He's been quiet for several minutes now. No banter, no insults. Which isn't like him.

After another five minutes of rubbing and admiring my kick-ass walk-in closet that looks amazing and is going to make all my shoe dreams come true, I notice something peculiar. Not only is Adam not bantering with me, he isn't moving either.

I hold my fingers still. "Adam?"

Nothing.

I lean closer. His breathing is steady—really steady—and his eyes are closed. A light snore sounds.

He fell asleep?

Adam looked tired these last couple of days. He's been working late at Blue, because my coworker spies tell me so, and now I've got him working all weekend at my house. What kind of person am I? I knew I shouldn't have listened to him when he said he didn't mind building the closet.

I sit back on my hands, feeling terrible. Should I wake him? Let him sleep a little, then wake him?

I tilt my head and study his posture. He looks uncomfortable all hunched over.

Reaching out, I gently push his shoulder to the side, just to see what will happen. I fully expect him to wake.

He doesn't. Instead, he tips onto his back, one hand falling across his chest.

Adam Cade is asleep on my bed. And he looks adorable all relaxed and boyish. But still, this is weird.

Is he sick? I place the back of my hand to his forehead. He feels fine. In fact, he reaches up and covers my hand with his strong, wide palm, and my heart barrels around in my chest. His palm is warm and callused, just like it looks, and now I have Adam on my bed and my hand trapped beneath his.

And why is that such a bad thing? Adam is H.O.T., and the hero of many of my daydream fantasies, when I wish to torture myself. But I can't sit like this all night.

I could wake him. That would be the normal thing to do. But I don't want to. First of all, he's exhausted, the reason he crashed during his head massage. Seems kind of mean to force him awake. Second, and I know this is the most selfish reason of all—I don't want him to leave.

I've enjoyed having Adam over to work on the closet, shocking as it is to admit. Sometimes I would hang out with him, because it was incredibly sexy to watch him use his skilled hands—and because I enjoyed his company. We talked like we'd been friends forever. He never made me feel bad about the past. I actually felt *better* after sharing it with him. Other times, I'd get my own work done in a different room. But mostly, Adam made the space I grew up in warmer. Which makes no sense.

I gently ease my hand away, and he rolls to his side, a soft snore-breathing sound rumbling from his chest. I stand and walk around him, pulling his legs onto the bed. Instead of waking, he burrows deeper into the comforter. I carefully take off his boots. And, okay, I'm being super gentle not to rouse him at this point, but still. Most people would stir with even a light tug. Maybe he's one of those heavy sleepers?

Adam can't sleep like this forever. He'll wake in an hour and wonder what happened. Then he'll go home. Which is fine, and much more humane than shaking him awake when he's beat.

That decided, I exit the bedroom and close the door partway. I clean up the kitchen, watch the last of the late-night news, and fold a load of towels. The entire time, I'm expecting Adam to walk out, dazed, and asking me what happened.

He doesn't.

I switch out of my pajama pants and into pajama shorts that keep me cool at night, and brush my teeth. The second bedroom is an office and storage room—no bed in there—so I return to my bedroom and carefully ease under the blankets at the top of the bed. I could sleep on the couch, but the truth is, I'd rather be with Adam.

I ruffle around in the nightstand for the latest smut novel I borrowed from Mira (who gets her stash from Gen), and try to keep my eyes open.

After reading the same page three times, I give up the fight and turn off the light.

I'm cramped at the top of the bed and Adam is cramped at the bottom. One of us will shift positions and wake, and Adam will go home. No big deal. For now, I'm closing my eyes.

* * *

Adam

Remnants of my dream fade—one where I'm cruising through the mountains in the XKR with Hayden beside me, only she's wearing tiny shorts and I can't stop staring at her legs. Which would happen if this were reality. Hayden has gorgeous legs.

I rub my eyes and look around, and my back tenses.

This isn't my room. I'm not in my bed.

And then I recognize the beautiful legs from my dream inches from my face. Or really, one leg. The other is under the covers. But the leg outside the blanket is outfitted in tiny sleep shorts. The bare hint of round ass showing immediately has blood pooling to the lower half of my body.

What the hell happened last night?

I sit up on my elbow and take in the rest of the beautiful girl at the top of the bed. And then I remember. I was about to leave, but my head was pounding like a son of a bitch. Hayden gave me a head massage, and I must have conked. Considering the low golden glow streaming in through the window, it seems I slept through the night.

Jesus. I don't remember ever passing out like this, not even during my college days when I made it my business to power down cheap beer. And I'm certain it had everything to do with Hayden touching me.

When was the last time a woman touched me that way? Not for foreplay, just a gentle caress for the sake of caring for someone. Has anyone besides my mother given me that kind of attention?

I rub my forehead, certain the answer is no. And not because I haven't dated nice women. I never *wanted* to be touched in a caring way. Until last night. With Hayden. She put her pretty little hands on me, and heaven spread through my body. Everything after that is a blur.

I woke with this horrible moment of panic too. For a second I thought I was in another woman's bed. I worried I'd made the biggest mistake of my life. Because the only bed I want to find myself in is Hayden's.

This isn't an attraction to a woman I work with. It's never been that simple.

A light squeak sounds and Hayden stretches her arms above her head, her tank top straining against the most amazing breasts I've ever seen. No bra this time.

I groan. She is killing me.

Hayden glances over and sits up, confusion filling her face as she looks around in surprise. "It's morning?"

"It would seem that way." I sit up, my movements slow, and run my fingers through my hair, which I sense is standing on end. "Sorry about last night. That was... unprecedented. I don't usually fall asleep in women's beds. I'm typically too busy." I give her a lopsided grin.

She rolls her eyes and smiles shyly, and damn if she isn't stunning. I've always dated attractive women, but none of them looked like sunshine and dreams when they first woke. Oh, Hayden's hair is a hot mess, and she's got sleep marks along one cheek, but make no mistake. She. Is. Fucking. Beautiful. Her beauty beams from the inside.

We're a foot apart, and a war rages inside me. This is the same girl who fascinated me for reasons my puberty-stricken brain couldn't interpret. This is also the woman my hands want to touch and hold. But Hayden doesn't trust me, and I sense it's not all due to the past.

"I should probably go," I mumble. If I stay, I will kiss her, and I'm not sure she wants that. Being with Hayden isn't something I wish to fuck up.

"Are you thirsty?" She swings her long legs over the bed, and of course, I'm staring. Because *her legs*. "Apple juice okay?"

I nod in a trance and follow her. She's in a tiny tank top and shorts, and I can't seem to think straight.

Hayden enters the kitchen and opens the fridge. She pulls out juice and reaches up for glasses in one of the cupboards. I watch the graceful, unself-conscious move-ments that make her so utterly fascinating. And sexy. She's in pajamas with morning hair, and everything she does—the sound of her voice, the way she moves—calls to me.

She pours two glasses and hands me one. I drink half of mine in a single swallow, the ripe, fruity flavor heightening my senses, as though they weren't already on overdrive.

Hayden takes her glass and walks to the end of the kitchen where I'm standing. She hops onto a lip of the counter that's lower than the rest and supported by shelv-ing. Her legs swing back and forth, her ankles hooked together. She smiles over her juice glass. A secret, private smile. And that's it.

I set my cup down, never taking my eyes off her, and step closer.

Her smile fades and her eyes turn huge. She sets her glass to the side.

I lean in and brace my hands on the counter next to her hips. "Are we finished with this?"

"With what?" she says, her voice a touch breathless and morning-raspy. Her golden eyes are dazed and focused on my mouth, and her pulse throbs near her throat.

"The game." I plant my mouth on hers.

There's a moment when I sense her surprise, as if this wasn't the culmination of extreme sexual tension built up since the day I walked into Blue Casino and caught her with her ass in the air. Then her ankles unhook and she reaches up and grabs my shoulders, pulling me closer.

Game on.

I slide her hips flush with the edge of the counter, nestling my legs between her soft thighs—exactly where I've wanted to be for months. I'm no saint, but I am loyal, no matter what my exes say. And, apparently, hopeful. Because this is the reason for my long abstinence, even if I didn't realize it. I've been waiting for Hayden.

My arms band around her, pulling her up until she's plastered to my chest. I can feel her heart pounding. Or maybe it's mine. Either way, she fits against me perfectly.

Hayden wraps her legs around the back of mine, and my groin presses against the sweet spot between her thighs. My breath stops at the exact moment a moan sings from her throat. The sound of that siren's song snaps my control.

I pick her up and carry her back to the bedroom, her touch and taste burning through me. We reach her bed and I lay her down, immediately covering her with my body. Her arms wrap around my neck and she digs her fingers in my scalp.

I kiss the soft spot behind her ear and drop my arm over

the side of her bare leg, hugging her to my body. I skim my fingertips from her calf to the soft swell that teased me the moment my eyes opened this morning, and squeeze her round ass. She moans again and arches into the rock-hard erection beneath my jeans.

"Hayden," I say. In two seconds I could have her stripped and my body inside hers. And God, if that doesn't drive every rational thought from my head—

I blink to clear the fucking fog clouding everything except the pleasure I want to give her, and pull back. "Is this what you want?" She's already following me up, reaching for me, kissing my chin, my throat. I swallow, trying to maintain control, when all I want is to lose it. "Hayden?" This time, the question in my voice gets her attention.

She falls back and stares up at me, her breathing rough and labored like mine. But there's a split second of hesitation in her eyes—and it's enough.

I sit up and pinch the bridge of my nose. I want to be inside her more than I've ever wanted anything in my life— to own her body, and most especially her heart. And because I want that other piece of her I've never cared to own with any other, I can't make a move unless she's willing to give it all.

I stand abruptly. "I've gotta go."

She sits up and grabs my arm. "Adam?" Her eyes are searching.

I've confused her. Jesus, I've confused myself.

I reach down and slide my hand through a lock of sun-kissed hair that's fallen in her face, and cradle her jaw, bringing her close. I gently kiss her mouth and drop my forehead to hers, my breathing rough. "I'll see you at work."

Chapter Twenty-One

Hayden

I have been a jittering jumble of nerves ever since Adam left me this morning. How dare he leave me a hormone-crazed mess?

That kiss. *Kisses.* And his hands. The way he looked at me. With warmth, and also like he wanted to devour me. Had he not pulled away, I would have done whatever he wanted. Because I wanted it too. But he did pull away, and now I'm confused.

Everything felt right. The playful way we've been around each other these last two days as he worked on my house. And before then, if I think about it. When we weren't fighting, that is. My physical attraction for Adam has grown deeper and it muddles me.

I *care* about him.

I drop my head to my desk and knock it a couple of times.

"You're going to give yourself a concussion if you keep that up," Mira says, her voice ringing out.

I groan. "Don't you ever knock?"

"Why would I do that?" She walks over and takes a seat across from me.

Her eyes narrow and her chin dips. "You look rosy. And flustered. Hayden, what have you been up to? You haven't— Did you hook up with someone? I know we're work friends, but I thought you'd share that kind of juicy detail."

I roll my eyes. How does she read me so well? Oh, right, Adam said my emotions play out on my face like a book. Gotta work on that. "We are more than work friends, Mira. You're one of my best friends in town."

"Damn straight, so spill these horny details you're hiding."

I jump up and cross the room, sticking my head out the door to make sure no one overheard her. I close the door and swing around. "Keep your dang voice down," I whisper loudly. "And there's nothing to tell."

"Of course there is. For one, who is he?"

I slump into my chair. And then I lower my forehead back onto the desk. "You don't want to know."

"Oh, I think I do."

I look up to find her sitting forward. "I have a crush on someone I shouldn't."

Her eyes sparkle. "Those are the best kind."

I shake my head and let out a sigh. "No, they're really not."

Mira's warm brown gaze, a couple of shades darker than my own, drifts to the side. "Hayden, didn't Adam come by this weekend to pay off his bet?"

I don't say anything.

"It's *Adam*?" Her voice went up an octave. "I told you to get close, but I wasn't suggesting *that*."

I stand and walk around the desk, sitting in the chair next to her. I glance nervously at the door. "Keep it down already." I take in her expression and cock my head. "You know, I don't think I've ever seen you stunned before. Is this what it takes?"

"You and Adam? Um—yeah. I mean, I figured you two would go at it eventually, but I thought it would be wild monkey sex and you'd get him out of your system. I didn't think you'd fall in love."

"Lo—*What*? Why would you say that?"

Ignoring my question, she rattles on. "Adam is working for the bad guys, Hayden. What are you thinking?"

Over the weekend, I didn't think once about the Blue Stars and Adam's role in what might be going on.

I bite my bottom lip. "Is he, though? Maybe I'm wrong. I'm not sure about anything anymore."

Mira shakes her head slowly, as though she can't believe what she's hearing. I don't blame her. "Don't let your vagina speak for you."

I give her an incredulous look. "Leave my vagina out of this. She hasn't been as active as you're imagining." Not that she *wouldn't* have been active if Adam hadn't pulled the plug this morning, but Mira doesn't know that.

Mira is silent, and then she asks softly, "You really like him?"

I nod, my lips pressed together. "I really do."

* * *

Adam

PAUL IS STANDING in the middle of the third Bliss suite by the time I catch up to him late in the morning. This suite is

189

identical to the first one I visited the other day, except that it's entirely furnished. They all are now. The only workers milling around are the decorator and her assistant. The contractors have cleared out.

And the place is spectacular.

I can't say I understand why members would pay a quarter of a million plus annual dues for Bliss, but they will have access to a celebrity-worthy lounge and suite when they come.

"Decided to show up?" Paul says.

I may have arrived a little late for work after my impromptu sleepover. The best night of my life, and sex wasn't even involved.

I can't imagine a better way to wake than next to Hayden every morning, and I don't even feel a nudge of unease thinking that. Which is what I realized once I got home. I want this thing with her to work. It's why I pulled away when I sensed her hesitation. Hayden is important to me, and I don't want to screw this up.

"What was it you wanted to show me?" I ask.

"That's all you have to say?" He holds out his arms. "Well? What do you think?"

"It's fantastic. The members will love it."

"You haven't even seen the best part." Paul walks into one of the bedrooms and I follow. This room has a king-sized bed covered in red silk with a deep purple bedspread folded at the bottom. Red satin ceiling-to-floor curtains drape behind the bed. Across from it are more curtains over an oval tile stage. It's not a stripper pole, though I think the point is the same. Whoever's on the bed gets a show.

Paul sees me staring. "That's not all. Check this out." He walks across the room to the bathroom.

It's as luxurious as the one I glimpsed the other day, but

there's no hot tub. This one houses waterproof chairs and wall shower nozzles everywhere, and it piques my imagination. It's only been a couple of hours since I left Hayden and my blood is still running hot. "Nice."

"You haven't seen the pièce de résistance." Paul walks to one of two doors and opens it. And this is where my imagination screeches to a halt. "Well?" he says.

I look at him, his narrow chin that seems to take up half his face, the slick hair he combs over with a slight wave to hide his receding hairline. Paul's navy suit is on the boring side for my taste, but it gives off a certain professional air. Seeing him standing next to a BDSM room doesn't.

Or maybe it does. Maybe this is where the rich and powerful exercise their eccentric tastes without the public knowing. "I think you're catering to a certain clientele."

He chuckles. "Not even close. Our members asked for the dungeon. We provided them a taste of it with Bliss 1.0, but they wanted more. Not everyone is into it, but we've outfitted every Bliss suite with a dominatrix bedroom."

I take in the space that's the size of the luxurious bathroom. There's some kind of suspension frame and a leather bench. And dozens of whips, chains, and other forms of bindings and flagellation equipment, not to mention a sleek black chest of drawers I'm certain supplies additional sex toys. "How do you keep it all clean?"

Paul laughs. "You see the fun room, and that's the first thing you think of?"

I glance again. "I'm not a fan of STDs."

He slaps my shoulder and squeezes. I slide my gaze to the hand, then narrow it back on his face. He drops his arm and clears his throat. "Guess we know what role you'd play."

Yeah, I get what he's implying. I'm still not amused.

191

He closes the door and walks out of the suite, talking as he goes. "Our members are paying a fortune. We provide them with their own equipment, and set up the playroom to their specifications before they arrive. There's a menu of escorts and house mistresses to choose from."

"House mistresses?"

Paul stops and scratches his chin. "You really haven't been to a dominatrix?" I give him a speaking look. "Suit yourself. You don't have to like it; our clients do."

"You and William seem to be handling members," I say. "As hospitality, I assume I'm expected to make sure the high-class sex dungeon runs smoothly. What else do I need to know?" My voice is tinged with irritation.

"Bliss isn't a sex dungeon. That would be common." Paul shakes his head. "I keep forgetting you recently came into the fold." He walks to the bar, grabs a tumbler, and douses it with Gran Patrón. Must be his favorite, because he chose it the night of my promotion at Farley's as well.

He offers me some and I shake my head. Paul taps his Blue sapphire ring against the glass—an especially annoying habit of his—and stares down at the liquid as though thinking. "Bliss is meant to encompass anything and everything our clients could want." He takes a swig and studies me. "Come on. Best way to explain it is to show you the rest."

He heads for a door off to the side and opens it. "Gourmet kitchen. There will be a professional chef and staff on duty twenty-four-seven."

And from the looks of it, the kitchen is fully functional and ready to go.

Paul closes the door and strolls to what he's referred to before as the concierge area, with opaque glass for privacy. "This is the brains of the operation. Each suite will feature a

Bliss concierge, but in actuality, she's the pleasure director. You'll manage the Bliss concierges, but they will do the work of guest services. Each concierge will keep track of member preferences and supply them with whatever they need."

"Supply them?" I say.

Paul punches in a code to the glass door and crosses to a computer, where he spends several seconds typing in passwords. A new screen pops up. "Meet the Bliss database." He clicks through images of beautiful women. Dozens of them. "These are the escorts. As I mentioned a week ago, no need for you to look into more dancers. The few you hired are great, and we've taken care of the escorts. The original plan was to see if any of the dancers were willing to provide escort service, but we've come up with a better solution through Blackwell's connections. We have more women than we need, and you're going to drool when you see them in person."

I highly doubt it, but I humor Paul. "What else?"

Paul pulls up a spreadsheet. "Here is the list of equipment we supply."

Which consists of items I glimpsed in the sex dungeon, as well as condoms, lubricants, and other personal care. I point to another list. "What is that?"

"Decoy names we've come up with for the drugs our members might wish to procure during their stay," he says. "We learned from Bliss 1.0 that keeping drugs in-house could be problematic, so our escorts deliver them when they arrive."

"Which also encourages members to use escorts if they want drugs." And—Jesus—puts the criminal liability on the poor girl delivering them.

Paul smirks. "Exactly. They pay the price of two for one. Though once the escort arrives, I can't imagine they'll want her to leave." He grins licentiously. "By the way, how did you like the product I sent to your house? Haven't used it all up, I hope? That was top grade. Costs us a fortune, but we have an inside connection."

The prostitutes and cocaine Paul sent to my house were more than a test of my discretion; they were a sample. Wonderful.

I knew there had to be more to Bliss with the way Paul and William were acting, I just didn't want there to be a problem. I told myself that as long as Blackwell kept everything legal, there wasn't an issue, and he did. People bring drugs to the casino all the time. Everything else I've seen this morning isn't necessarily illegal in Nevada either. But it's enough to have my alarms sounding.

The casino is staying within legal limits, but just barely. What's stopping them from crossing that line every now and then if it brings in extra cash? That's what this venture is about for Blackwell. Revenue. In large quantities.

I was selfish because I didn't want to lose something I'd never done without. I wanted the cash as badly as Blackwell and the others, but my morals are all jumbled up now. I'm a little less lax and a lot more wary, because I have more to lose. I don't want a lifestyle that doesn't involve Hayden, and I sure as hell don't want her mixed up in whatever this is. I'm certain I'm not seeing all of it.

Discretion, Paul and William said. I figured the Bliss members didn't want anyone knowing about their sexual affairs and the drugs they brought in. But why would Paul threaten me into keeping Bliss a secret? Why wouldn't they advertise Bliss to the public?

Something isn't adding up.

Paul finishes his grand tour of Bliss and I return to my office. The hazy summer clouds paint the lake a gray-blue outside my window. Paul made it clear that to talk about Bliss would be unwise. If Blackwell is working with drug dealers, what else might he be willing to do to keep Blue Casino profitable?

I pull out my cell phone and make a couple of calls, one of them to Jeb Kendrick, Gen's father. To hell with discretion and confidentiality. I tell Jeb about Bliss, and we discuss options for looking into who's backing the drugs.

Paul has given me details about Bliss on an incremental basis. I'm not backing out, but I'm moving forward cautiously.

I wanted Hayden away from Bliss because of the secrecy and weirdness Paul and William exhibited over the venture, which is why I suggested our bet. Later, Paul's threats lent more ammunition for keeping her out of things. The more I know, the more I'd like Hayden to leave town. The escorts, the drugs, not to mention the sex dungeon—which I'm pretty sure the casino isn't licensed for—it's the kind of atmosphere that breeds trouble.

Hayden returned to Lake Tahoe to prove she deserves to be here. She wouldn't leave even if I outlined all of the above. If anything, it would spur her on. She'd want to find evidence to take to the police, just like Lewis said.

Blackwell doesn't want Hayden involved in Bliss, and I'm guessing that's because he realizes Hayden wouldn't hesitate to call him out. Smart man.

I have no idea how to manage my relationship with Hayden and my involvement in the venture. I like my job, and I think I can make it work. Bliss could well turn out to be on the up-and-up, but given the behavior of my coworkers and boss, I'll keep in touch with Jeb just in case.

I should put a halt to what's building between Hayden and me. If it turns out Bliss is more than I bargained for, I have decisions to make that could be dangerous. Associating with me right now isn't smart, if it ever was.

But I'm a selfish asshole. I let Hayden walk out of my life once. I won't do it again.

Chapter Twenty-Two

Hayden

The instructions for the new HR software are making me crazy. I check the form the database manager sent me one more time. They still make no sense. *"Grrr!"*

A second before I throw my keyboard across the room, Adam steps into my office and locks the door behind him.

I swivel toward him, my heart rate increasing. Whatever frustrations I felt are forgotten as I watch him stalk across the room. I've been thinking about him all day, wondering if I dreamt this morning and our connection over the weekend. Everything is different. I'm trying to not overthink Mira's question about being in love. I am *not* in love with Adam.

I am in *like* with him. Heavy, heavy like.

In typical Adam fashion, his hair is combed, his suit couture—and not at all like the man I glimpsed these last two days. The dark intent in his eyes, however, is exactly what I saw beneath that polished exterior. The same eyes that made me mad with lust this morning.

I stand. I don't know why, but I do. And then I'm being swept up into his arms.

"I missed you," he murmurs, and kisses me.

I wrap my arms around his shoulders and slide my fingers into his hair. I'm ruffling it, and I don't care. He is polished and beautiful, but he's also the sweet guy who fell asleep on my bed last night. And he's kissing me again, when I wasn't sure he would.

Adam backs me up against the desk and presses his body to mine. "I have a question for you."

"Um-hmm," I mumble, kissing the corner of his mouth and his neck. God, he smells good. I need to bottle it so I can sniff Adam whenever I need a pick-me-up.

"I don't want to wait until I finish your closet in order to see you again."

I smile against his neck. "Okay." My voice is breathless. And yes, I sound like a love-struck girl, but whatever. I worried that he put a stop to things this morning because he was having second thoughts. Considering the firm ridge of deliciousness pressed against my belly, the man is happy to see me.

"Come out with me tomorrow night," he says. "To a cocktail party I've committed to. Be my date."

I pull back and look in his eyes. There's a hint of nervousness there, but also excitement, if I'm not mistaken. "Are you asking me, or telling me?"

"Asking."

I lean up and kiss his chin. "Yes."

* * *

"I've NEVER BROUGHT anyone here before," Adam says as we pull down the drive to Club Tahoe. His hand is casually draped over the steering wheel, and he looks a bit mystified, as though he's surprised by his own actions.

Adam is wearing a sport coat and a crisp white button-down with a casual tie, and he looks delicious enough to eat. The speed with which this man changes from hot mountain guy to hot businessman gives me whiplash, but I'm not complaining. I like the unguarded, casual Adam best, but this Adam will do.

I glance at the entrance and see the valet running over, an eager look on his face, as though he recognizes Adam's car. "You never brought dates to your family's resort?"

"No." He puts the car in park.

The valet opens Adam's door and greets him by name. Another valet opens my door and helps me out. I'm wearing a blush-pink cocktail dress with a vee neckline and cinched waist, the skirt flowing just above my knees. There's a nip in the air, but I didn't grab a wrap before I left. I figured we wouldn't be outside long.

"Why wouldn't you bring them here?" I ask across the hood of the car as Adam makes his way around.

He rests his hand on my lower back and guides me to the entrance. "Club Tahoe isn't me," he finally says.

A doorman opens one of two massive doors made of wrought iron and logs. I should be looking ahead, but my gaze is stuck on the chandelier above us. It's a showstopper, with opaque beige glass and ornate wrought iron to match the door, the top twinkling with gemlike glass and small lights that in actuality are probably as large as my hand. I'm slack-jawed, and this is just the outdoor lighting.

Adam ushers me through, and I realize why the designer went to such great lengths on the front. Inside, Club Tahoe is like a log cabin—if a log cabin were on steroids and someone had tens of millions of dollars to spend on décor.

More wrought iron chandeliers dangle from log ceilings. The walls are dark, knotted wood paneling with rough stone arches over alcoves and walkways. Plush Persian rugs adorn the wood floors, and tufted, worn leather ottomans rest in front of velvet couches with silk throw pillows. And that's just at a glance.

I step back and take Adam in, now that I've seen the place. Between his tailored Italian suit, incredibly handsome face, and confident posture, he looks like a man you'd see advertising this place. And then I think of the guy who likes hot wings and spent his weekend building a closet for a girl because he lost a bet. And I think of the way he kisses, with utter care and passion all mixed in one.

"No," I say. "You're nothing like Club Tahoe. It's beautiful and austere, and you're so much more."

His gaze darkens. He leans down and kisses me, his breath fanning across my chin as he lingers before lifting his head. When he does, there's a naughty glint in his eyes. "Ready to play the part?"

"Of the attractive, fun-loving date to the spoiled little rich boy?" Adam rolls his eyes and reaches behind me, grabbing my ass. Hard. *"Eeep."*

"Come along, Ms. Marcos. Play the princess to your prince. Better yet, just be yourself. My father expects me to marry a society woman. I'd like him to see how much better I've done."

I glance out of the corner of my eye, because he just mentioned marriage and me in the same sentence. He's joking, but my chest is fluttering like someone unleashed a kaleidoscope of butterflies in there. Even if Adam isn't serious about the marriage part, that's the sweetest thing a guy has ever said to me.

I need to stop underestimating him. If we're dating, and based on tonight, it's safe to say we are, I have to get used to the idea that he's more than I imagined a man could be, let alone the man I once believed incapable of caring for anyone other than himself.

Adam takes me across the wide expanse of the lobby, down a beautiful corridor with antique trestle tables, glowing candle arrangements, and colorful oil paintings of mountain landscapes that hang beneath stone wall arches. We wind around a corner and he opens a wood-planked door with iron decorative detail.

Another spectacular room waits on the other side, this one holding a party. A long bar centers one wall, and there's a small dance floor in front of a tall, triangle-paned window overlooking the lake. A corner of the room contains more windows that reveal the back of the lobby and what looks to be an indoor winding pool, or river.

"This is amazing."

He looks down at me. "You've never been here? Not with your parents years ago?"

I laugh. "You do realize how expensive your father's resort is for the rest of us humans?"

He glances around, his brow puckered. To him, this place must seem like nothing special.

"Club Tahoe hosts proms from time to time," he says. "I just thought you might have been here before."

"I was only a sophomore when I left. I didn't go to proms until after I moved. Not that I would have been high on anyone's list as a prom date in this town."

He frowns and squeezes my waist. "We'll pretend this is your Lake Tahoe prom." He quirks his brow and ushers me toward the bar. "Let's get you a drink and see if I can corrupt my prom date."

"Is that how you were in high school?" I'm only half joking, because it actually *was* the impression I had of him back then.

He flashes me a grin. "Only with the girls who didn't mind being corrupted."

I feign affrontedness. "And do I look like that kind of girl?"

He places an order for us with the bartender, then looks down, his face suddenly serious. "You're not like anyone, Hayden." Adam tips up my chin and kisses me lightly, one protective arm banded around my waist.

I'm staring into his gorgeous blue eyes, reading all sorts of silent meaning behind his words—when a pair of broad shoulders squeezes in beside us.

Adam turns, his face broadening into a smile. "Levi. What are you doing here?"

The man named Levi has on a sports coat similar to Adam's, and his shirt is light blue, the same color as his eyes.

Adam's eyes are ocean blue with gray-green framing the edges. Yup, I've paid attention. Particularly since we've gotten closer and Adam's eyes have left their hypnotic mark while luring me in for a kiss. Okay, fine, there wasn't a lot of luring required.

In addition to the jacket and slacks, Levi is also wearing a cast on one leg from his knee down.

"About time you got here," Levi says.

"Me?" Adam chuckles. "I'm surprised you dragged your ass out for the occasion."

Levi releases a deep sigh and shakes his head. "The old man called a half a dozen times. Decided it would be better to show up than bear any more of his calls."

"Smart move." Adam turns to me, his arm still wrapped around my back. "Hayden, this is my older brother, Levi."

"Nice to meet you," I say, taking in the resemblance. They are of equal height, and very handsome, though Adam's hair is slightly darker and longer on top. Where Adam fits in naturally at Club Tahoe, Levi shifts his shoulders and looks uncomfortable in his sports coat, as though he'd rather be anywhere else.

"The pleasure is mine, though I am wondering why such a beautiful and sophisticated woman is wasting her time on this sorry specimen I call my brother."

"He promised to get me liquored up," I deadpan, because I get the sense that the banter Adam and I engage in is a part of the Cade charm.

Levi shakes his head at Adam, clearly enjoying my comment. "Classy, Adam. You've resorted to fraternity tactics." He looks at me again. "When you need me, I'll be at the bar. I love rescuing damsels in distress."

"She's got her hero right here," Adam says, and hands me the chardonnay he ordered.

Levi makes a sound of disbelief in the back of his throat, but he's smiling. He nods to an area across the room. "The others are over there."

Adam's eyes widen and he glances in the direction Levi indicated. "Everyone?"

"Everyone," Levi says, and slowly makes his way back to the barstool he must have been occupying when we arrived.

Adam takes a sip of his drink—a gin and tonic, by the look of it, with the lime wedge—his gaze distracted.

"Everything okay?" I ask.

He kisses my forehead. I could get used to the affection he's been dishing out now that we're on kissing terms. "Fine.

I just wasn't expecting my brothers to be here. I'm normally the only one who attends these things."

"Is it bad that they are?"

"Not at all. It's only...surprising."

I glance at Levi, sitting alone at the bar a few seats away, watching the bartender instead of the crowded room. "Why isn't Levi with them?"

Adam tucks a lock of hair behind my ear. "Levi's had a rough couple of months. And he and my youngest brother, Hunter, don't get along. At all."

"That's sad. I always thought it would be wonderful to have siblings."

He pats my shoulder. "You might change your opinion once you meet my brothers."

"I don't know, are they all as handsome as Levi?" Adam frowns, and I laugh. "Gotcha."

He sets his drink on the bar, then puts mine down too. He grabs me around the waist, bringing me to his chest. "Teasing me about my brothers?" He shakes his head. "Bad. I'll show you later why I'm the cream of the crop."

I laugh as he nibbles my neck, his smile pressing into my skin. "Knock it off. How am I supposed to look respectable with you giving me a hickey?"

"Mmm, hickies," he murmurs. "Now there's an idea."

I lean away at the threat to my pristine neck, but he's already reaching for our glasses, clearly only teasing. And thank heaven for that. I can just imagine the crap I'd receive from Mira if I walked into work with a giant hickey.

We make our way toward Adam's brothers, and even if Levi hadn't gestured in their direction, I could have picked them out in a crowd. Because holy hell. I wasn't kidding about Levi. The guy is rugged handsome, and the other three Cades are varying degrees of Levi and Adam. Tall, gorgeous, broad shoulders, and strong jawlines—each of them with jewel-toned eyes and medium to dark hair.

"Crikey," I say. "How in the world are you and your brothers single?" Not one of them appears to be with a date.

He raises his brow. "Crikey?"

I grab his arm. "I was a *Crocodile Hunter* fan. Now explain, before we get too close."

Adam tips his head toward mine, while his brothers conspicuously watch us approach. "Being single is a Cade tradition."

"Then what am I doing here?"

"You don't count," he says.

My chest constricts and my face goes still. I've dated, have even had a couple of decent boyfriends, but the past never seems to go away. Adam invited me here tonight, and he's kissed me like I've never been kissed before. That was real. I'm not sixteen anymore. Still, I can't help asking, "Why don't I count?"

He looks at me. *Really* looks. "Because you're special. And when they meet you, they'll know it too, just like Levi did."

I swallow. And swallow again. *Je*-sus. When Adam Cade charms, he does it in a spectacular fashion.

The warm press of his hand on my lower back, the intense look in his eyes, and his words—all from a man who wears a sarcastic expression like it's his second skin. Except he hasn't worn that look around me in weeks. In fact, I don't remember seeing anything on his face lately except humor and affection. Which has my head swimming.

He stops in front of his brothers, all of whom are smiling and discreetly checking me out, some more so than others. "Hayden, I'd like you to meet Wes, Bran, and Hunter," Adam says.

We exchange greetings and Hunter flashes me a mischievous grin. "Do I get to dance with the charming Hayden?"

"No," Adam responds automatically. The others laugh, but the air grows thick.

My face warms and Adam shakes his head. "Ignore him. He has no shame."

Hunter downs his drink. "Well, Hayden, when you get tired of the cheap imitation, you know where to find the real Cade."

I glance at Adam. "Is it a family tradition to steal each other's dates?" I'm kidding. But the glare Adam shoots Hunter has me wondering.

"Don't mind them." Adam pulls me close. "They wish they had a date as beautiful and intelligent as you. Jealous—the lot of them."

Wes raises his glass. "Truer words were never said."

"There you all are." Adam and I spin around at the voice from behind. An older man approaches, his rich, slightly cultured baritone much like Adam's. He glances past us. "Where's your brother?"

"Levi's at the bar," Adam says. "His leg..."

"Right." The man nods. "Well, at least the four of you are together."

Wes and Bran exchange an awkward glance.

"Father," Adam says. "This is Hayden. Hayden, meet my father, Ethan Cade."

Adam's dad studies me like I'm an insect. "And how do you know each other?"

Wow, not exactly a warm welcome.

"Through work," Adam answers, his voice laced with anger. "But Hayden is also my girlfriend."

I squeeze his hand involuntarily and shoot him a nervous glance. What's he talking about?

"Girlfriend?" his father says. "This *is* a first."

My brows pinch together. What is it with firsts tonight? Adam has had girlfriends. I've heard about his past relationships. Well, little bits, anyway. He didn't seem like much of a boyfriend, according to Mira and Cali. But the Adam they described isn't the man I've come to know.

"Hayden, do you mind if I steal Adam for a moment?" his father says. "I'd like to speak with my sons."

"No," Adam says before I can answer. He takes a sip of his drink, his hand in his pocket, though his jaw is tense. "I brought Hayden as my date. I'm not leaving her."

Adam's brothers look between Adam and their father, then at me.

"It's only for a moment," his father says. "And then you can have your...girlfriend back."

Adam stretches his neck, and I sense Wes inch between Adam and Mr. Cade. "What's that supposed to mean?"

"Excuse me?" His father's tone is filled with warning.

"Hey now," Bran says. "Can't have you two sparring. You're the only ones who get along." He smiles, but the gesture is strained.

Ethan Cade sucks in a deep breath. His eyes flicker for a moment. "I didn't ask you here to argue."

"Adam," I interrupt, "I'll be at the bar." I give his hand a quick squeeze and hurry away. When I glance back, Adam is frowning and watching me leave, his brother Wes's hand on his shoulder. I smile back and keep walking. Because something serious is going down, and I get the sense Adam needs time with his family, even if he doesn't believe it.

Chapter Twenty-Three

Adam

"You didn't say anything about private meetings," I growl at my father. "I brought Hayden tonight. I won't treat her the way you do the people in your life. She deserves my attention."

My father's face turns red and his shoulders square. "She seems like a big girl. I'm sure she can handle herself."

"That's not the point. It's rude, and I don't like it."

His eyes narrow. "Since when did you care about treating your girlfriends with such courtesy?"

I run stiff fingers through my hair and glance at my brothers, who don't seem the least bit inclined to help me out. "I've always treated them with courtesy."

"Perhaps, but not warmth."

And doesn't that rankle. The Ice King himself has called me out.

"I'm only going to say this once," I tell him. "That girl over there deserves all of your respect." I glance at my father and each of my brothers individually.

My brothers and I have always given each other a hard time, but tonight their flirting pissed me off more than usual.

I direct my next comment to my father. "If you wish to spend time with me, you had better include her." I don't know where I'm going with this, or why I called Hayden my girlfriend in front of my entire family, but it feels right. It's how I see her. And—*fucking hell*—not even since we kissed. Hayden's been special to me for a long time.

It's why I haven't been with anyone else.

Why I'm protective of her.

I shake my head and stare down, rubbing my temples. I'm in deep. Deeper than I've ever been.

"All right, Adam. I see you've grown wings since you started working at Blue." My father's tone is condescending, but I'm used to that coming from him, so I ignore it.

Hunt yawns, clearly bored now that the fireworks between our father and me are over. "Why are we here?" he says. "You know we don't like coming."

My father looks around, his gaze suddenly uncertain. "I thought it would be nice for us to get together."

My brothers are silent, staring at a man who's clearly lost his mind.

Bran speaks first. "We get together." The unspoken meaning—*we* get together, just not with the man who sired us.

"I see," my father says. "I'd hoped to smooth things over and spend more time together as a family."

Every one of my brothers glares at the brother next to him, assuming the same thing I have. Who put it in the old man's head that we wanted to spend time with Daddy?

"Why?" Levi says.

My father turns, noticing Levi, who walked up once

Hayden moved to the bar. "Because we are a family, and we are all we have."

Too stunned to say anything, I don't.

Levi downs his drink. "Speak for yourself. You should have thought about that before you made this place your priority." He spins around and storms off as best he can in a walking cast, and exits the party that's supposed to be the thirty-year anniversary of Club Tahoe. Not that any of us cares.

"I've got to be somewhere." Bran looks to Wes, who reads his silent offer of escape.

"I'll walk you out," Wes says.

"I see someone at the bar I'll be knowing by the end of the night." Hunt starts off, but I grab his shoulder, halting him. He looks back. "Not your Hayden," he barks. "I'm not as bad as you all make me out to be." He yanks his shoulder from my grasp and beelines for the bar, flagging the bartender.

My father raises his eyebrow, but says nothing. He stares off at my brothers as they leave, or take up residence at the bar in Hunt's case, his expression one of regret and longing. And I'm left standing with him. The way it's always been. Except this time, I don't want to be here either.

I glance at Hayden. She's sitting prettily at the bar, peering around the room. "Are we finished?"

My father sighs and suddenly looks ten years older than his fifty-eight. "Not quite. I'd hoped to mend the riff that exists between your brothers and myself. I'm the cause, but I don't know how to fix it."

"You're asking me for advice?" I say, stunned.

"Yes."

I shake my head. "Well, for starters, you could explain to them what you just told me. Let them know you care and that you're trying, instead of ordering us to a party and expecting us to spend happy time together after years of fighting."

He smiles, a sharp, quick twitch of his lips. "We have fought, your brothers and I. You were always the sensitive one. Until..."

He doesn't finish the thought, and I don't know what the hell he's talking about. I'm the most unfeeling of the group, which is why I can put up with this man. Because I tune him out.

"I was never good with people outside of business," he says. "Except with your mother. In any case, I don't know how to mend what I've broken. You're the only one left."

I glance at Hayden again, and catch sight of a vulture in a three-piece suit preparing to descend. "It didn't go well tonight, but you've got a lifetime to mend things. Next time, don't try so hard. It comes across as overbearing, and you know how much my brothers love to be ordered around."

My father looks down and chuckles. "About as much as I do."

"Dad, I've got to get back to my date. Are we finished here?"

He lifts his head. For the first time in—ever—there's a soft expression on his face. "Your girlfriend?"

I nod. It was a spur-of-the-moment decision, but the most efficient way to explain what she means to me. I didn't miss her questioning look, though. I'm fully prepared to pay for that slip later.

"Before you go," he says, "I need to tell you something."

I glance at the bar. Mr. Three-Piece is only one person

away from Hayden now, and he's staring at her, trying to get her attention. "Can it wait?"

"No. I think you should hear it, especially because of Hayden."

I sense my blood pressure rising. "Don't say one disparaging remark about her. She is better than you, me, and every person in this town—"

He holds up a hand. "That's not what I wanted to say." He gestures to the window overlooking the lake. "It's quieter over there. Do you mind?"

I reluctantly follow him to the window.

"Your mother was an amazing woman," he says after a moment of staring out at the lake.

My frustration grows. How long is this going to take? I should have cut out when my brothers did.

"The four of you—before Hunter came along—damn near drove her mad, but she loved you more than anything in this world."

I stare at the side of my father's face. It's difficult to hear about my mother, but I'm listening because I know this conversation will end sooner if I do. And because my father never talks about her.

"She wouldn't have changed anything, except to be there for you as you grew up. That was the one thing she couldn't come to peace with during those last few months. That she wouldn't be able to take care of you." My father's voice breaks, and my eyes grow wide.

I've never seen him cry. Not even after my mother died.

"I tried to reassure her that I would provide," he says, having cleared his throat. "But nothing I said comforted her. The only thing—" My father's throat bobs and he coughs into his fist. "The only thing that comforted her was you."

"What are you talking about?"

His gaze turns to me. And it's sincere. "I would find you lying next to her in her bed once the nurses had finished making her comfortable. She was fading, but she'd have a smile on her face as you kissed her forehead and petted her hair."

I let out a shaky breath. I knew none of this. I have no memories of my mother while she was ill, only flashes of her when she was healthy. And I remember the deep love. So fucking deep. I loved that woman more than I've loved anyone in my life.

I look up and blink back the burn, my chest tight. Why is he bringing this up now?

When I glance back, my father is staring at me. "Your mother loved all of you boys, but you had a special bond with her. I'm not sure how much you remember. You were five, six? But I wanted you to know how much you meant to her. It's okay to love a woman, Adam—"

"Whoa." I step back and shove my hands in my pockets. "That's enough. We don't need to go there."

"But we do." He glances at the bar. "I watched the walls build around you after your mother died. You didn't think I noticed those things. None of you did. But my weakness is with communication, not observation. The communication breakdown in this family is something I've never known how to overcome."

He peers at Hayden waiting. "You care for this girl?"

"I already said I do."

"Then don't allow the loss of your mother to prevent you from letting another woman in. Trust me. I speak from a lifetime of experience."

I stare at my father, thinking he really has lost his mind, but he's looking at me with such caring and understanding, I can't look away.

I shake my head. "I don't know what's gotten into you lately. I appreciate you sharing things about Mom. But yeah, I'm just not used to talking about my feelings with you." Or anyone.

"Fair enough," he says. "But I wanted to make sure the words were said."

Chapter Twenty-Four

Hayden

"Are you okay?" Adam barely said two words when he returned to the bar and told me we were leaving. He looked upset, and I didn't ask questions. But I'm asking now.

"I'm fine." He pulls down Club Tahoe's long, winding drive on the way to the main highway. "Do you mind if we go to your place?"

"Of course not. But if you're planning on blowing out some walls in your frustration, maybe we should go to your place. I don't have many left after your work on the closet, and the ones I do have I want to keep."

He shoots me a quick smile. "I thought we could grab a bite and bring it back. Hang out."

"I'd like that."

He reaches over and holds my hand. Who knew Adam was such a touchy-feely guy?

On our way to my place, we swing by a taco joint. In

cocktail wear. And it's interesting. And also the most natural thing in the world.

"Two chicken burritos." Adam glances at me. "Hot sauce?" I shake my head. "Hot sauce on one, and please label it."

"And a churro," I tell him, poking him in the rib to make sure he gets it. I'm starving. And a little buzzed after that second glass of wine I downed without food while waiting for Adam to finish talking to his dad.

"Two churros," he tells the guy.

Adam pays for our meal, and we stand off to the side, people-watching and eating churros while we wait for the rest of our order. He grabs paper napkins and hands me one, then dusts off sugar from his mouth. People come in and out of the two-table taco joint, staring blatantly, but I don't mind. Waiting inside the taco place eating churros with Adam is the most fun I've had in a long time. Come to think of it, spending any time with Adam is the most fun I've had in forever, even when he was antagonizing me and driving me crazy at work. I just didn't realize it then.

"*Sooo,* girlfriend?" I say, once we've finished our churros. There is no way I'm letting the comment he made to his father slide.

He raises an eyebrow, challenging me.

This is how he's going to play it? He's not even going to discuss it? "I take it you will be forgoing all women henceforth." I'm joking, but seriously, if he thinks he can call me his girlfriend and go around hooking up, he is crazy. I'd rather keep things casual with dates than label us before there's a commitment.

Adam walks across the room and fills small paper cups with water from the dispenser. He hands me one. "I haven't been on a date in almost a year," he says.

My eyes widen. "A formal date. But other types of...intimate relations?" My face heats. I sound like a politician. "You know what I mean."

"Nope." He finishes the water, crushes the cup, and tosses the crumpled paper at the garbage, making a perfect basket. "None of that for a long time either."

"Really?"

"Really. You?"

"I've been busy."

He wraps his arm around me, grabs my hip, and pulls me close. "Busy doing what?" There's an edge to his tone.

I laugh nervously. "Not *that* kind of busy. Busy with work."

He leans in and brushes his lips over my ear. "So you're not seeing anyone? Besides me, that is."

I lean back and stare at him. I remember our conversation at Nessa and Zach's about my dating status. He tried to fish it out of me then, and I wouldn't give him the satisfaction. Particularly since the truth wasn't very exciting. But now I don't mind him knowing. In fact, it makes sense, given all the kissing business that almost led to other business.

"No boyfriends," I say. "Can't remember the last date I went on, though I don't think it was as far back as a year. Maybe six months."

He stares at the floor a moment, as though gathering his thoughts. "I called you my girlfriend because nothing else fits." He looks up. "You're more than a friend or a coworker. More special than just about anyone. It seems fast, but not when you figure I've been...*thinking* about you since I started working at Blue. And probably subconsciously since I was sixteen and talked Jaeg into breaking up with you so I wouldn't have to watch you with another guy. It's been a long time coming."

"You know, you're kind of a bad friend," I say, humor in my voice. "I can't believe you sabotaged your best friend's love life for your own nefarious purposes."

He leans over and kisses my neck, tickling the skin with his warm breath and causing me to squirm beside him. "If he'd liked you the way he should have, he wouldn't have fallen for it. I did you a favor. And Jaeg too, because he found Cali."

I glower, even as he nuzzles my ear. "Very clever the way you've justified that."

He straightens, his expression serious. "It was a dick maneuver, but I've grown over the last eleven years. I'm not flawless, but I want this to work." A touch of vulnerability reflects in his eyes. If I didn't know him, I might have missed it. "What do you think? Do you want to be my girlfriend?"

"Oh, you're asking me now?" I say saucily.

A grin flashes across his face and he hauls me to his chest. "You're never going to back down, are you?"

I sniff his coat. "Never."

"If you're smelling me, I suppose that's a yes?"

"Yes. And I want permission to sniff you whenever I like, because you smell really good."

"I can agree to those terms, as long they work in reverse."

"Agreed." I warm up with my arms wrapped around his waist and my face plastered to his chest. "I'm not against being exclusive and finding out where this goes—take things slow."

Famous last words...

* * *

WE MANAGE to make it inside the door to my house before Adam is kissing me and I'm loosening his tie and struggling to get it off so that I can kiss his neck. Of course my fashionable Adam has to wear a tie while all his brothers skipped it with their sports coats.

"I hate this thing." Somehow, an item that should be so simple to remove has become complicated, as I've managed to triple-knot the slipknot. Adam slides the straps of my dress over my shoulders, making it even more challenging to get the dang tie off. "Arghh!"

He pulls back and glances down. He fusses with the tie for a second, then strides into the kitchen.

"Hey, where are you going?" I stand there confused, my arms bound to my sides by my dress.

I hear him shuffling around in a drawer, and then he returns, a wad of something in his hand. He passes it to me, and starts kissing my neck and the tops of my breasts again. I glance at the wad. It's his tie. Cut in two.

That's hot.

I kick off my heels and yank his coat off his shoulders. He wiggles out of it, and I start working on the buttons of his shirt. One of them shoots past my head, almost taking out an eye, but I maintain focus. Until cool air hits my back and I suck in a breath. Adam unzipped my dress, the fabric dropping to the ground.

Well, there goes that.

I'm in panties and a strapless bra that cinches like a bitch in order to keep the girls up. I'd beg Adam to remove it just to return feeling to my skin, but there's no need. With one flick, he has it off and his hands on my breasts are circulating all kinds of heated blood flow to the area.

His thumb glides over my nipple and I squeak.

He pulls back and quirks a brow. "Sensitive?"

"Maybe?"

He starts kissing me again and leans down, his palms gliding down my bare legs and up the backs of my thighs. Shivers rack my body. And then he's circling his arms around me and lifting me, his chest and arms blasting heat where our bodies connect, though I'm in far less fabric, according to my calculations. I got the shirt off, but he's wearing a damned undershirt too.

His soft, nimble mouth is seducing the hell out of mine as he carries me down the hallway. My calves hit the mattress of my bed, and then I'm half falling, half lowered as he covers me, toeing off his shoes in the process, his arms supporting his weight. But the weight that isn't fully supported feels incredible, pressing in all the right places.

I drag my mouth away from his. "Shirt. Off."

He sits back on his heels, his knees on either side of my hips, and whips the offending T-shirt over his head. He tries to cover my body again, but it's too late. I saw his chest for the very first time.

"Whoa, whoa, *whoa*. Back up, buddy." I push his shoulders until he straightens, his muscular thighs straining the dress pants he has on, a belt resting below thick ridges of abdominal muscles.

I run my hands up and down his chest, trailing a finger along the muscles above his belt.

His breathing increases, his mouth tense. "Finished?"

I don't get a chance to answer, because he's on top of me again and kissing me with an intensity that makes my head spin. "Hayden," he says, with a level of feeling I've never heard from him before. Soft fingers trail gently along my jaw as he gazes down at me. His eyes are nearly black in this light, and so warm I don't know how I could have thought him cold.

I let out a sigh and wrap my arms around his shoulders, holding him to me. When did Adam become so essential to a good day versus a bad one? It used to be the opposite, but at some point things changed. The linen and manly scent of him drugs me, his touch ignites, and his voice seduces. But his eyes—they tell me everything I've missed. Adam is not the rich opportunist I took him for. And he cares more than I knew.

I reach for his belt and fumble with it for a second, nearly shouting in triumph when I get it loose, along with the button and zipper of his pants. He kisses and licks a path to my breasts, distracting me and making my work harder, but not impossible. I push the pants down with my feet, along with an elastic waistband my hazy brain identifies as boxer briefs, and then he slides higher, kissing my neck, his thick, long erection pressing down above my panties. A jolt of pleasure rocks through me and we moan at the same time.

Seconds later my panties melt off—or he pulls them off, who knows? They're gone, that's all that matters, and he's kicking off the last offensive piece of clothing still dangling from his ankles, and then we're rolling—naked, hot, and hands everywhere.

Adam inches down, kissing my neck and cupping my breasts, the light hair on his legs scraping lightly over mine. A tongue swipes my nipple and I squeak.

Dammit that's embarrassing.

I glance to see if he noticed. He grins. "Sensitive," he says, and lightly fingers the other nipple.

I moan and wrap my legs around him. My eyes roll up in my head as his hips flex, strong muscles along his arms grazing the sides of my breasts as his erection glides up and down the other most sensitive part of me, where I've been throbbing for this man for months with or without my will.

And it must feel good to him too, because in the next moment he gasps, "Condom?"

Condom? I think dazedly. *Do I have condoms?* Where the hell are those condoms I bought?

A moment of sheer panic has my sex-drugged mind going into full alert. "The side drawer!" I say, when enough blood reaches my brain.

Adam leans up and angles over, the base of his erection —where it's most thick—rubbing in the spot that has my eyes rolling up again. I wrap my legs around his hips and arch into him.

The sound of him yanking open the drawer, fumbling around, then slamming it shut fills the room. He tears open the condom wrapper with his teeth and leans to the side. I watch him slide on the condom and my eyes go wide. I felt how much he wanted me. He's larger than average based on the proportions I sensed down below, but *Je*-sus, my mental image didn't do him justice. Reality is much better.

And then his mouth is back on mine, his palm dragging down my body, hitting my breast, my inner thigh, and then the center of me, where I'm wet and throbbing for him. His finger slides up and down that bundle of nerves, dipping where I'd like other parts of him to be. At the same time his fingers are killing me softly, he leans down and sucks my nipple.

I might come.

I bite my lip. And breathe out slowly.

And then I'm positioning him at my entrance and urging him—rubbing and lifting—for him to *get this party started*.

He gets the picture. In one swift move he thrusts

forward and my body tightens around him. But he doesn't stop. His hips flex again and again, each rock taking him deeper. And it feels incredible. I'm shaking, our lips brushing, his hand linked with one of mine beside us while the other gently cups the top of my head.

Small precursor spasms clench my inner muscles and I feel an orgasm building. Adam is inside me, loving me, and nothing has ever felt like this before. I'm shaking, adrenaline coursing through me, and before I can think another thought, I break apart, waves of pleasure and weightlessness coursing down my limbs. I moan, my head pressing back into the pillow.

Adam's pace picks up and he's peppering my face with soft kisses. And then his head lifts and his body tenses, the sexiest sound tearing from his throat.

He kisses my forehead, my eyelids, my mouth while his body moves slowly in and out, the aftershocks rippling along his spine every couple of seconds. He lowers onto me, adjusting his weight so he doesn't crush me, and nestles his face in my neck, his breathing ragged.

"I know I said we should take this relationship slow, but slow sucks," I say drowsily. "This was much better."

He reaches down and squeezes my ass. I take that for agreement. I haven't exactly given him time to recuperate.

I trail my finger over his broad shoulders. "I can't believe you hide all of this under a suit. We should initiate casual Fridays at Blue, where you wear nothing but your beat-up T-shirts, jeans, and work boots."

"That would go over well." His voice is groggy and coarse, and so darn sexy.

"It would, wouldn't it?"

He chuckles and discards the condom in the wastebasket by my bed. Then Adam shifts and tucks me closer. I sense his breathing evening out.

"Excuse me," I say, and receive a groan in response. "I realize this is prime pass-out time for you cavemen, but you have a job to do. Your woman needs food."

He props his head on his hand and grins down at me. "I like the sound of you being mine. And I thought I already did my job."

I pinch his rock-hard abs—and flatten my palm there, running it up his chest. I'm no fool. I'm not missing opportunities to feel up Adam. "That was only one of your jobs. There are many tasks on the honey-do list."

Adam rolls on his back and pulls me on top of him. "You're the second person in the last few days who's mentioned a honey-do list. Jaeg said something about one. What is this mysterious list?" His voice dips suggestively. He sizes up my ass with his palms and trails his hands down the back of my thighs, reigniting what I thought we put out.

Obviously, I know what *he* would add to the list.

"Well," I say, circling my fingertip around one of his nipples, the muscle flexing beneath. Payback is fair game, after all. "There's making sure your cavewoman is fed. You teased me with those burritos, and we haven't even eaten them yet. I hope you don't think I'm one of those girls who eats like a bird. Because I assure you, that churro wasn't enough to fill me up. And...well, that's really it. Food. And kisses. Yup, I could live on those two things."

He rolls me over until he's on top. "There's nothing else you want to add to that list?" He flexes his hips. As if I need a reminder that his mind is in the gutter.

"Well, now that you mention it, I'd love for you to finish that closet. And when you're done with that—"

Adam tickles my neck with fluttery kisses while his

fingers dig into my sides. "You are a bad girl. You know what I want on that list."

I laugh and shove his hands aside unsuccessfully. "But it's my honey-do list!"

He stops tickling me, a broad smile spreading across his face. "Then I better make my own." He quirks his eyebrows.

"You are so single-minded."

He tugs me up with him and reaches for the discarded boxer briefs. "Let that be a lesson to you. Food first, because *my* cavewoman needs it. Then we'll get back to the honey-do list I'm mentally tacking items to. Of course, it all involves being naked, or partially clothed, if we're getting imaginative."

I shake my head as if exasperated. But secretly, I love it. Love this moment and what we shared, and being here with him—all of it.

Chapter Twenty-Five

Adam

I sit across from Hayden at her small kitchen table, a jar filled with wildflowers between us, and watch her munch away on a burrito. I should be thinking about the explosive sex we just had... Who am I kidding? I am thinking about that. But I'm also thinking about how much I like this girl. Everything—the way she tastes, the feel of her pressed to my skin, her ridiculous obsession with shoes I seem to find charming. For the first time, *like* doesn't fit.

Everything about Hayden is charming or intelligent or kind, and she has so much integrity. I see her—all of her—and I can't look away. I wasn't kidding when I said I enjoyed the sound of Hayden being mine. I think of her as mine, which I've never done with anyone. I've *never* wanted more than pleasure and company. But right now, all I can think about is how great it would be to wake up to Hayden every day. To make love to her at night and fall asleep with her in my arms...

Sex with her has knocked a screw loose.

This isn't me. In a few hours, I'll be back to normal. Won't feel this pressing urge to bundle her up and never let her go.

Popping the last bite of chicken burrito in my mouth, I watch as she wraps half of hers and carries it to the fridge. She sets it inside and leans over, her forehead puckered in concentration. Her cute ass is in the air, giving me all sorts of ideas of walking up behind her and having my way with her. Before I can enact my fantasy, she closes the fridge and walks to a cupboard, reaching for something up high. I'm about to walk over and help, but that would interrupt the fascinating food scavenging she's doing and the view she's giving me. Her tank top has ridden up, exposing her panties and the most beautiful feminine form I've ever seen.

Can't interrupt. The view is too good. She *is* beautiful. Physically, but even more so inside.

Hayden has morals. She's being a pain in my ass at work, but it's because she fights for what she thinks is right. I could learn something from her.

I ball up the wrapper from my burrito and toss it in the trashcan at the end of the counter. Hayden walks over, gazing lustfully at a piece of dark chocolate she must have procured from the cupboard.

"Why did you leave?" I ask as she sits down. I'm fascinated by everything about Hayden, and I want to know the parts I missed.

Things were terrible for her when the rumor broke out during high school, but Hayden is strong. Most people would have freaked out over what happened, except Hayden isn't like most people. She's ballsy and hardheaded.

She chews the chocolate, her gaze on the table. She gives a light shrug as though coming to some sort of decision. "They stoned me."

For a moment, an image flashes in my mind of women being stoned in countries where they're not allowed to show their skin, or be seen walking with a man who isn't a relative. But that can't be what she meant. "Excuse me?"

Hayden scoops crumbs from the table with the side of her hand and brushes them into the trashcan. I still can't believe how tidy her home is compared to her office. Not that I give two shits, but it does give me pause. "My parents couldn't spare the car one day, so I walked home from school. Kids in class had been whispering about me. Someone had knocked me into a wall on my way from last period. All typical behavior since the rumor came out."

She glances up, looking slightly nervous, and I can't tell if it's because she's talking about something uncomfortable, or if it's because my face probably looks like I want to murder someone. "I was a couple of blocks from the school parking lot. I'd just turned down a side street filled with apartments. There were hardly any cars around. I remember feeling leery, but I had to get home somehow, and it seemed stupid to turn back." She lets out a heavy sigh. "A car pulled up and someone threw a soda can at my head."

What the fuck?

"I heard them laughing and I started running," she continues. "A paper bag with food came at me next. I kept running. Then I heard car doors closing and footsteps pounding behind me."

Her breathing is shaky, as though she's reliving the moment. I reach across the table and squeeze her hand so tightly I have to force myself to ease up.

"A rain of rocks came hurtling at my back," she says. "One of them was so large it bruised my shoulder blade and I stumbled, but I didn't stop. If anything, I became frantic,

228

and that stupid street was so damn long. I was gasping and crying and calling out. And then a fist-sized stone slammed into the back of my skull." The hand I'm not holding absently touches the back of her head. "I woke up on the ground. They were gone, and I was bleeding."

I lean forward. "Are you fucking kidding me?" *Furious* doesn't begin to describe what I feel right now, as the woman I...*care about*...tells me how some dicks could have killed her.

She tries for a light smile. "If it makes any difference, I don't think they planned to throw rocks at me. I was running from them—it was one of those heat-of-the-moment things. I called my parents and they found me. They took me to the hospital. I needed a couple of stitches, but otherwise I was fine. But that was it. My parents decided to move, and I supported it because I didn't want to worry them anymore."

Her expression shows a mixture of guilt and nervousness, which I don't understand. "Why does that bother you? You had no choice. It was dangerous for you to stay."

She wraps her arms over her chest and rubs the skin pebbled in gooseflesh on her upper arms. "I didn't do what the town accused me of, but I allowed them to beat me down. It pissed me off—it *still* pisses me off."

I stand and walk over. Reaching for her hand, I pull her up and take her seat, easing her onto my lap. I brush aside the hair where she touched her head. Sure enough, there's a small crescent scar beneath.

I wrap her in my arms and press her cheek to my chest where I can keep her warm and safe. I seriously want to hurt someone—preferably the dicks that attacked her. "Why didn't the police do anything?"

"They tried, but it happened so fast I never saw who did

it. I was too busy running for my life. The car I described, based on the split-second glance I got before things were being hurled at me, fit the description of half the cars in our high school parking lot. For all I knew, the kids came from another school. The rumor about me wasn't limited to ours. It spread."

Hayden and her parents didn't have the resources my family does. She wouldn't have been able to sustain a scandal like that without more bastards hurting her. "Too many people around this town think it's their moral obligation, in between living off the gambling and drinking of others, to judge," I mutter.

She settles her head on my shoulder. "I came back— that's all that matters. I'm not running anymore."

I stare down at her and lightly kiss her forehead. "You'll never need to run again."

Because as far as I'm concerned, I will do whatever it takes to protect her.

* * *

Hayden

ADAM CARRIES me back to my bed, where he divests me of what little I'm wearing and covers me with his body. It's warm and cozy, and I'm certain he means it as a comforting gesture, but our bodies can't sustain close contact before hands begin to wander and heated kisses turn desperate with need.

In the afterglow of that second bout of lovemaking, I lay my head on top of his chest, our legs entwined. He pulls up a lock of my hair and looks at it in the light of the clock.

Which reads two in the morning. I have to work tomorrow, but whatever. I never want to leave this spot.

"Why does your hair smell so good?" he says. "Like apples and cinnamon. I want to eat it."

"Please don't eat my hair. I need it to keep my head warm."

He takes a giant whiff, then carefully sets the lock back on my shoulder. "Don't get creeped out if I sniff your hair from time to time. It's your fault it smells so good."

"Don't get creeped out if I smell your neck."

He chuckles. "Why my neck?"

"Because *you* smell good."

His arms tighten around me. "You can smell me. And touch me. As a matter of fact, there's something reaching for you right now that you're welcome to touch."

I swat his chest and he chuckles. "I can't believe you have the energy for that. *Again.*"

Adam yawns. "*I* don't, but there's another part of me that perks up whenever you're near. He's on alert twenty-four-seven."

"Good to know for when I wish to take advantage of you."

"Twenty-four-seven," he repeats, his voice groggy, as though he's falling asleep.

A few seconds pass, and I'm not even sure if he's awake. My mind wanders to our conversation earlier. Being stoned by a group of kids from school was one of the most humiliating experiences of my life. I felt helpless, but for some reason, sharing it with Adam released a weight from my chest.

Secure and more comfortable than I can remember being in a long time, I ask the question that's been on my mind all night. "Adam," I say quietly.

"Mmm?"

"Where is your mother?"

His breathing stills. Then his chest deflates as he pulls me closer. "She died of cancer when I was six."

My hand flexes against his chest at the shock of his confession. "I'm sorry."

He rubs my arm. "Was a long time ago."

"What about your dad? Are you close to him?" I never found out what his dad wanted to talk to him about tonight, but his father made it clear I wasn't welcome in the conversation. I can't imagine Adam's dad knows about the teacher rumor. Whatever was bothering him, I doubt it had anything to do with me.

"I'm closer to him than my brothers are, but that's not saying much."

"How can six men who lost the woman in their life not band together?" I want to understand him. And comfort him. And if I'm going to, I need to know more about him.

He's quiet for a long moment, and then he says, "After my mother died, my father checked out. In a way, we lost both of them that day—our mother to cancer, and our father to Club Tahoe, where he put all of his energy. The only difference between my brothers and me is that I tried to stay close to our father. I lived the lifestyle he did, I worked for him—I did whatever he asked. Since stepping away to work at Blue, I've realized those choices I made never brought us closer. And they never made me happy."

His body is tense, a war of emotions playing out on his face—a handsome face that rarely reveals what he's feeling, always masked by that sexy veneer. But I don't see that Adam anymore. I see beneath the pretty exterior to the person filled with kindness, caring, intelligence, and sometimes pain. "What makes you happy?"

He shrugs lightly. "My brothers gave up their trust funds to live their lives the way they want. I thought I couldn't live without the money." He peers down and his gaze softens. "But here I am. With you. And I can't imagine a better life than one filled with jars of flowers and a beautiful girl who walks around in her underwear eating chocolate."

I grin, and he squeezes me to him. "When my father approached my brothers and me tonight, I realized it wasn't the lifestyle I craved. I wanted his time. Doing what he said meant I was close to him in some way, but it was never enough."

I crawl on top of Adam until my body is aligned with his, and tuck my face into his neck, my arms cradling his head. I don't want him to feel alone. Ever. "What did your dad say to you tonight?"

Adam flattens his hands on my lower back. "He said we should spend more time together as a family." His chest rises on a deep breath. "I can't even tell you how ridiculous that statement sounded after so long. He offered what I've wanted since my mother died, and I couldn't take him seriously."

I tilt my head to see his face. "Maybe you should. People can change."

He shakes his head. "My father—he snaps his fingers and expects us to follow orders. I get the reason why my brothers have butted heads with the old man. He doesn't know how to..."

"He doesn't know how to love you?" I say.

Adam looks down, then kisses my forehead. "I don't know what I'm trying to say. This is the first time my father has reached out to us. It's odd. *He* is odd lately." He chuckles. "My dad's suggestion had one predictable effect. Levi, Wes, Bran, and Hunter stormed out."

"Maybe in time you can give your dad a chance. If he's not used to trying, it couldn't have been easy for him to make the request, and he may not have known what to say to you and your brothers."

"Maybe." He pulls me up until our mouths are aligned. The pain in his gaze lingers, but it's quickly being overtaken by a naughty glint I'm beginning to recognize. "That's enough of that talk. We have a few hours before work. How shall we spend it?" His eyes sparkle as they skitter over my mouth to my breasts pressed against his chest. "We could tick off a few items from *my* honey-do list."

"Are you trying to avoid talking about your father?"

"Just maximizing our alone time."

"I'm going to be sore tomorrow," I say with a long-suffering sigh that's entirely insincere.

"Not if I use my mouth." He quirks his eyebrows and my heart races.

Chapter Twenty-Six

Hayden

I n the spirit of taking it slow, Adam only stayed four nights over the last week. Okay, so that's not exactly slow. I've wanted to see him, and he's been especially ardent in his attentions. Who knew we'd get along so well?

"Hayden, have you seen my tie?" he says from my bedroom.

"Which one?" I call from the hall bathroom. "You have about five hundred."

"The navy woven checked."

I walk over to where Adam is standing in front of the walk-in closet he built me, dressed in his suit pants and an unbuttoned dress shirt. I glance inside the door, and a chorus of angels sings inside my head—not really, but my closet is so beautiful I could cry. Adam finished it a couple of days ago.

Two of the three walls in the closet hold narrow shelving for maximum shoe capacity. I allowed for one wall of clothing bars with an extra shelf on top, on his insistence.

You know, for those extra shoes I might purchase. And somehow a few of Adam's clothes have made it onto a bar.

If I'm a shoe hound, the man is a clotheshorse.

"It's not here?" I ask. "You're sure you brought it last night?"

His gaze hovers on me, taking in my black silk bathrobe. He snakes an arm around my waist and pulls me close. "I can't see anything with all your shoes filling the space. Weren't you going to get rid of some?"

"I got rid of a few." Like one pair. And it hurt.

He kisses my neck and tugs at the collar of my bathrobe. I slap his hand away and wiggle out of his arms.

Dropping to the floor, I crawl on my hands and knees and reach for a piece of fabric, toward the back of the closet, that's stuck beneath a pair of suede Gucci ankle boots.

I hear him let out a tight breath. "If you don't want me to touch you while you're getting ready, this position isn't helping. You know what it does to me."

I look over my shoulder and hold out the tie with a smile, but he's staring at my ass. "You're going to be late, Adam."

He shakes his head and grabs the tie distractedly, draping it around his neck. "I know, I know." He buttons his shirt and reaches for his suit coat and wallet, his shoes in his hand.

Adam doesn't wear his shoes in the house. He says he wants to keep the place clean. I think it's sweet. I also think he's a neat freak. Except in bed. There he's a dirty, dirty boy.

He looks over and his gaze strips me bare. "Going to be a long day after that show you just gave me."

I stand and lean up, grabbing the back of his head. I kiss him, and it's not light. It's long and needy, because as nice as it is to see him at work, it also sucks. We decided to keep our relationship a secret from the employees. Mira and Nessa know, of course, but other than our friends and their significant others, we've kept things quiet.

I want to know our one-week romance is of the lasting variety. Every instinct tells me it is, which is weird and a first for me. The other part of me says, *This is Adam.*

I never thought we'd make out, let alone turn our antagonistic working association into a romantic relationship. But we have, and I need time to figure out what that means. Adam is adamant we not tell our coworkers for reasons he refuses to explain. He particularly doesn't want Blackwell knowing. I'm telling myself it has nothing to do with the fact that Blackwell hates me. It's not like Blackwell can dictate whom we see. But those Blue Stars are tight-knit, and Adam works alongside them as though he were one. He doesn't have the sapphire ring, and that's all that matters.

I could ask Adam what's really going on at Blue. That was the plan in getting close to him, but somehow that feels dirty now. Like I used him. What we have isn't about Blue Casino; it's about us. Besides, the longer I go without evidence of the illegal suite, the more I question whether it still exists.

So I found the Bliss schematics. What does it really mean if there is no proof of something illegal? I've talked to Mira about the new suites, and she thinks they could be what we're looking for, but I have my doubts. And as long as those doubts exist, I'm going to entertain the idea that Bliss is nothing more than the set of luxury suites it appears to be.

* * *

Adam

If I thought I enjoyed my job before, now that Hayden and I are together, life feels damn near perfect. With the exception of the Bliss venture.

We have three weeks until our grand opening, which coincides with the auction and burlesque event. The burlesque show gives people a reason to come to the casino, and provides the casino a chance to show off—by invitation only—its exclusive Bliss suites to the wealthy.

Inside my office, the party planner runs down a list of food for the Bliss welcome party. "Cauliflower fritters and caviar, blue cheese and pear tartlets, and Kobe beef sliders to start." She taps her pad with her pencil, her brown hair swept into a severe bun on top of her head, so tight it pulls the corners of her eyes back. "Dom Pérignon will be offered to kick-start the party after the burlesque show. Blue's specialty wines will be on offer throughout the rest of the evening and early morning, along with a fully stocked bar."

William sits forward, his distinct eyebrows winging up with enthusiasm. "We'll have three or four of the burlesque dancers who perform that night mingling with party guests."

The party planner ticks off items on her list. "And the celebrity DJ from Los Angeles?"

"I've already contracted him," I say. "The engineers are working with the DJ's assistant on setup preparations for inside the suite."

The planner checks off more items from her clipboard. "Each invited guest will be asked to wear a platinum and sapphire pin to commemorate the event and to help employees identify potential Bliss members as they work their way around the casino and hotel."

"What about rooms for the guests?" Paul asks, looking to me.

"We've booked the second half of the penthouse, and the floor beneath. All of the rooms will be stocked with premium towels and personal care products from the Bliss line."

Paul glances at his phone and nods to the party planner. "Looks like we're all set, then." He stands and the party planner does too, juggling her clipboard and huge workbag, filled with the pamphlets and brochures we've used these last couple of months to place orders for the event.

He shakes her hand. "Thank you for your hard work," he says, barely looking at her. She's not flashy or beautiful, and I get the feeling Paul doesn't give women like her much attention.

"My pleasure," she says.

Paul walks her to the door and closes it behind her. He sits next to William and crosses his legs. "We have a hundred and twenty full membership slots available, thirty-seven of which are already accounted for. Blackwell wants to offer a lesser plan for rotating members who intend to use Bliss on a short-term basis. It will cost them less overall, but more per day, and it allows us to up our membership without compromising full members. You know what that means, don't you?"

I stack the paperwork the planner handed me. "Blue will be coming into a windfall."

"As will we." He grins at William, who returns the look.

I cross the room to a safe I had installed and enter the code, ignoring their enthusiasm.

"Why are you keeping those?" Paul gestures to the files. "Blackwell wants all Bliss-related material on the cloud, or stored in the off-site safe. Security for this venture is critical. It's why we invested in that damn military-grade encryption system."

"This is a fireproof, locked safe that weighs three hundred pounds. And I'm keeping the information in here until the end of the event in case anything comes up. As hospitality director, my ass is on the line should the event suffer because subcontractors fail to deliver."

I tuck the folder in the safe and a knock sounds at the door. Hayden slips inside, a grin on her face—until she spots Paul and William.

My shoulders tense. I close the safe and move toward my desk, giving her a warning look when Paul and William aren't looking. We shouldn't be seen together outside of meetings, particularly not with these two in the room. Hayden has been ordered to stay away from the Bliss business. I don't want these guys thinking she isn't.

"Oh, excuse me," she says. "I—came to give you a list of applicants." Her gaze darts to the others as she crosses the room.

Paul scans her figure, his eyes lingering on her ass. I want to kick him in the face.

"Why are you working with her?" he says to me, ever smooth. He's gotten bolder these last few months. The power Blackwell gives him has gone to his head.

I take the folder from her and give her a courteous smile. Her eyes dart to mine, a question in them, but I look away.

"I'm working with Hayden," I say to Paul as I scan the names and backgrounds of the applicants inside the file, "because I need an assistant." I lean against my desk and cross my legs at the ankle. "Is there a problem?" I give him a pointed glare.

Paul's face colors. "Yes. You're not to work with her." He stands and hovers over Hayden, and my arms tense. "This is private," he says to her. "And I'd be happy to explain to Blackwell how you've disregarded his direct orders and butted in where you're not wanted."

Hayden doesn't back down. Her chest rises and her expression hardens. "Had I been involved in hiring from the beginning, the issue with the last assistant never would have happened. Did you know she worked for a strip club?"

Paul rubs his chin. "Did she now? I had no idea." His words are insincere. And they should be. Paul was the one who told me to hire someone from the strip club. But his boldness worries me. He's not even trying to keep it a secret. He seems to take pleasure in letting Hayden know she's been kept in the dark.

Hayden's lips press together. "I don't know what kind of outfit you're running, but unless you want the authorities coming down on your heads like they did before, I suggest you work with the department designed to help protect the company."

Paul steps closer to her. "Is that a threat?" he says, his breathing increasing.

I stand abruptly and shove him in the chest. He's lost his damn mind—probably tapping into those drugs the casino has access to.

He staggers back. "What was that for?"

"Back off." My voice is steely. "I needed someone to fill Bridget's position yesterday. I asked Hayden for help; she isn't butting in. If there's a problem, I'll speak to Blackwell."

"What about..." Paul glares at Hayden, then looks to me. "The assistant to the hospitality director plays an *important* role."

He means in relation to Bliss. "I understand, but some allowances must be made. We'll find a workaround." Paul will have to deal with the fact that my assistant can't be a coordinator for the Bliss concierges like he wanted. "In the meantime, I'll take care of the communication you're referring to."

Paul's jaw shifts and he touches his hair in a precise manner that smooths it down while covering his receding hairline. "We'll talk about this later." He walks to the door and cuts Hayden a scathing look she doesn't see, before walking out, William close on his heels.

Hayden didn't catch the threat in Paul's eyes, because she was too busy watching me. "What is going on?" she says.

I circle back to my chair and set the applicant folder on my desk. "Nothing. Paul's an ass; you know that. But he's harmless."

"Is he?" she says, a world of meaning in her voice.

I look up. "Please stay out of it, Hayden. Stay away from Paul. And William." William's too damn touchy-feely. And for that matter, I didn't like the way Paul was looking at Hayden when she first walked in. He wasn't just appreciating a beautiful woman, which Hayden is. He was staking her out—calculating. Who knows whether Paul would ever act on his desires, but I'd just as soon Hayden kept her distance.

"We'll talk later." I glance at the door, sending her a silent message that now is not the time to discuss this.

"I have plans later. I'm meeting up with Mira."

I raise my eyebrow. "Ditching me?"

Her mouth twitches, trying to hide a smile. "No, but... you just stayed the night," she says quietly. "We can't be together every night."

And for the life of me, I can't think of a reason why not. But I realize that's not rational. "Very well. We'll talk later."

She moves to the door.

I stand and follow her. "Hayden."

She turns, and I reach over her shoulder and close the door partway so that no one can see inside. "Don't miss me too much." I lean down and kiss her lightly.

Her gaze, half-lidded, focuses on my mouth. "You can break the rules, but I can't?"

"When I need to. And I needed to kiss you."

She smirks and opens the door. "I'll remember that the next time *I* need something."

Chapter Twenty-Seven

Hayden

I ended up going to a movie with Mira last night. We saw some romantic comedy guys would call a chick flick, but I call awesome. I cannot believe Paul yesterday. What the hell was his deal? He didn't put my mind at ease that everything is fine at Blue. If anything, our encounter in Adam's office ratcheted up my nerves. I may have jumped too soon in assuming Adam wasn't involved in the ugly side of Blue Casino, which worries me, given he's my new boyfriend.

Mira and Nessa sip Rum Runners next to me at the Beacon Restaurant. After the movie, Mira and I made plans to meet up with Nessa this afternoon. Work and, if I'm honest, Adam, have monopolized my time this week, and I wanted to catch up with the girls.

"So you and Adam?" Mira says. "That's all going well? You guys are getting along?"

I pray to God he isn't involved in whatever scheme Paul is up to. "You'd be surprised how well we get along." Mira glances at Nessa, who shrugs lightly. "Is it that hard to believe?"

Mira ponders her drink before answering. "It's not hard to believe you guys have chemistry. That was obvious from the beginning. But yeah, I guess I never saw Adam getting serious with anyone. Or you, for that matter. Work has always come first."

It's true, but at the same time, Adam is important to me now too. "I can't explain it," I say. "This thing with him just works."

Nessa smiles. "I understand. Sometimes lo—uh, *relationship*s take you by surprise."

"That's right." I grin.

Mira's mouth pulls back at the corner, as though she's skeptical. "What about Blue? With all the time you've been spending with Adam, have you learned anything?"

"No, but there was a situation with Paul yesterday. He got super agitated when he found out I was working with Adam to replace his assistant."

Mira's eyebrows rise. "Did you ask Adam about it?"

"We were at work."

"But after?"

"I went to the movies with you. I didn't get a chance."

She bats her long, dark lashes several times, her astute caramel-brown eyes narrowing. "Hayden, tell me you're not backing down from this because of a man."

"No, I'm just withholding judgment until I have evidence."

She sets down her Rum Runner and leans forward. "But you are looking into it, right?"

"I will, and I have. The suites I told you guys about aren't under construction anymore, but Blackwell has guards in front who won't let me in."

"And that doesn't tell you something?"

"Of course it does. But all it tells me is that Blackwell isn't letting employees into the suites. I'm walking on shaky ground where our CEO is concerned. The last thing Blackwell is going to do is make an exception for me. If you have any ideas on how I can get in there, I'm all ears."

Mira purses her bow-shaped lips and twists them to the side. She turns to Nessa. "What do you think?"

Nessa's expression is thoughtful. "Now that you mention it, I might have something. I received a phone call in marketing a couple of days ago from a vendor who lost her contact information. She was searching for someone to send her customized napkins to for a party the casino is supposedly hosting the night of the burlesque and auction. I asked her what party, and she said it was for some grand opening. When I told her I didn't know anything about a grand opening, she stammered and quickly got off the phone. If the suites are finished," she continues slowly, "and the burlesque and auction event is the same night, do you think the party is for the new rooms? I mean, if the marketing department were involved in promo for the suites —which we haven't been, and that's weird—we'd show them off to the wealthy muckety-mucks coming into town. Throwing a party for the suites during the burlesque weekend makes sense."

"Exactly," Mira says. "They're using the event to intro-duce the new dens of love."

I can put two and two together as well as the next person, but this is one coincidence I wish weren't true. I stare out at the lake. "If I can't get into the suites before then, I have to get into that party."

"One of us does," Mira says.

I shake my head. "You can't. Remember? You're going to Tyler's editor dinner that night."

Mira curses.

Nessa drums her fingers. "I'll be around, but I'm helping my boss hand out party favors inside the club. I won't be able to slip away."

"But I can," I say.

"Hayden." Mira stares at me warningly. "You just said they won't let you into the suites. As soon as Blackwell figures out you're there, he'll have you thrown out."

"Not if he doesn't know it's me. You said the last suite had drugs lying around. I just need to get in there and take a few pictures. I could dress up as a waiter, or something."

"And you'd look like yourself in a waiter's uniform. Everyone knows who you are. If Blackwell also knows you've tried to get into the suites, he's probably warned his staff."

"The staff Adam hired," I say, putting it all together. "Adam didn't want me involved in the new hires, and he has a safe in his office where he keeps his files. I saw it yesterday. Who keeps files in a safe?"

My palms go clammy. I want to trust Adam, but Mira's right. I can't stick my head in the sand because I care about him. Not over something like this.

Mira shakes her head. "Don't even think about getting into that safe. Your days of breaking and entering are over," she says, and I frown at her. "Admit it. You sucked."

"Fine. I totally got caught in the facility manager's office. And anyway, I don't want to lie to Adam. Snooping around in his office would be dishonest. And a creepy girl-friend move."

Mira's eyes widen. "You're his girlfriend now?"

I tuck a lock of hair behind my ear. "We're not seeing

anyone else, and yeah, he called me his girlfriend in front of his family."

Mira's voice goes up an octave. "You've met his family?"

"Briefly. It's not what you think."

I don't know why I'm defending myself. Being with Adam feels right.

"Hayden." Nessa smiles. "It's okay. I can tell Adam really likes you. I think it's sweet." Her brows pull together in a vee. "What if instead of going behind his back, you talk to him. Ask him about the Bliss suites."

I could have talked to Adam days ago. I didn't want to, because I was caught up in us. At that point, I had no evidence that the Bliss suites were connected to the suite Mira and Tyler found. But after walking in on the meeting between Adam, Paul, and William yesterday, and now with this revelation about a grand opening...I'm scared.

"What if I ask him," I say, "and he tells me he knows all about Bliss and it's as bad as we think? Or he tells me he isn't involved when, in fact, he is?"

Nessa reaches across the table and squeezes my hand. "He cares about you, Hayden. Give him a chance."

I drop my head into my hands. "God, you're right. We've only been together a week and I'm already screwing things up. He's done nothing to deserve my mistrust."

"Well..." Mira stands and shades her eyes with her hand, peering out at the water. "Here's your opportunity to ask him."

"What are you talking about?" I look in the same direction. At the Beacon dock. And see Adam, Zach, and Tyler getting out of a large ski boat.

"What are they doing here?" My voice cracks, and okay, I'm panicking. I'm not ready to confront Adam. I want to run and hug him, not accuse him of being in cahoots with Blue Casino.

This time it's Mira's turn to look guilty. "Well, you see, I sort of invited them. Tyler wanted to hang out today and I had plans with you girls. He may have, uh—*convinced me*—to divulge where we'd be, through clever tactics."

Nessa makes a face. "Please don't go into details on that."

Mira frowns. "He's persuasive! I mean, look at him."

And we do. We gaze across the beach at the three men crossing it, and so does everyone else in the vicinity. Because they are gorgeous. Adam's in board shorts and a fitted T-shirt, his baseball cap turned backward. He has a light golden tan and insanely sexy legs I've had the pleasure of being tangled in. He's wearing Aviator glasses and a smug grin, and I'm salivating.

When I pull my gaze away from my incredibly good-looking boyfriend, a quick scan of Tyler and Zach confirms that they, too, look pretty darn good. Not as good as Adam, but then, no one does.

The best part of this entire hot-guy-crossing-the-sand image is that Adam is staring straight at me. He doesn't seem to notice or care that every female head is turned in his direction.

Adam enters the patio where Mira, Nessa, and I are standing, and wraps me up in his arms. "Hey, beautiful. Miss me?"

My face turns the temperature of an oven. I've thought about him nonstop since I last saw him, even during that damn chick flick, and he knows it. "Maybe."

"I'll have to remind you why you like me so much. Later. In bed." He whispers that last part in my ear, sending a shiver over my tank-top-bared skin.

The funny thing is, sex with Adam isn't even the best part. Laughing over meals with him, cuddling with him in bed, or talking about humiliating life experiences and having him be outraged on my behalf—those are the best parts. The incredible sex is just a massive dose of icing on the cake, as are his handsome looks.

Adam sets me back on my feet and I look around to find everyone's gaze on us. Mira is smiling, her arm wrapped around Tyler's waist, and Tyler is looking at Adam like he's never seen the guy before, even though they've known each other for at least ten years. Zach and Nessa are sneaking glances here and there, but they have the manners not to stare.

Zach pulls out Nessa's chair for her and steals a giant gulp of her Rum Runner as she takes a moment to sit down.

Tyler flags the waitress, and the men order more drinks and food.

"So, what do you ladies think?" Adam drapes his arm over the back of my chair, his warm, muscled leg bumping into mine every now and then. I've missed this. We can't flirt at work, and Adam's flirting is about as seductive as his hands on my body. Okay, not quite.

He stares down at me. "Want to go for a ride on the boat with us?"

I cut him a look. "I didn't know you owned a boat."

He grins. "You didn't ask."

"Right, because that's a question that comes up in casual conversation."

He chuckles. "Well? You up for it?"

I look around the table, and both Mira and Nessa nod their agreement.

"Okay, then," I say. "I guess our girls' lunch just turned into a group date."

Chapter Twenty-Eight

Adam

We finish our food at the Beacon and I haul my pirate's loot—that being my beautiful girlfriend—onto my boat with the guys.

When Zach called to suggest taking out the Chaparral, I didn't need an excuse. The sky is a clear blue, the temperature in the low eighties. I welcome any reason to get out on the lake, particularly on a day like this. And when he suggested picking up the girls, I might have dropped what I was doing and hauled ass to pick up him and Tyler. Because, sorry sap that I am, I missed Hayden like crazy last night.

We've spent a few nights away from each other since I started working on her closet over a week ago, and I gotta say, I'm not a fan. I want to spend all of my free time with Hayden, but I need to chill. This is new, and I don't want to freak her out. I'm out of my depth where she's concerned.

I ended up hanging with Wes after Hayden said she had plans with Mira. We hit golf balls on the night range and drank beer. Like always, I had a great time with my brother, but when I saw Hayden from across the Beacon patio, my heart kicked in as though I were on the final sprint of a marathon.

I knew she'd be there; that's why we came today. But there's something about her face lighting up the moment she sees me that feeds a void. Because that smile is one hundred percent genuine. I was surrounded by people with shallow motives in my father's circle. There's no artifice with Hayden. She's the real deal, which is how I know I can trust her.

Mira and Tyler lounge at the front of the boat, and Zach and Nessa are sprawled on the seats in the rear. Hayden sits in the seat next to mine in shorts and a pale mint tank that's loose over her curves. She tucks her sunglasses on the top of her head and smiles as I start the motor and wave at the attendant on the Beacon dock.

"They just let you park whenever you want?" she asks.

"Sure," I say as I back up and steer the boat through the no-wake zone.

Zach laughs from behind. "Cade has a pass to any dock on the lake." I swivel my head and glower at him. "What? It's true," he says.

Hayden slips off her flip-flops and sits back in her seat. "What does that mean?"

"Nothing."

"Quit being modest," Zach says from the rear. "It means, Hayden, that because your boy is a rich son of a bitch and everyone knows his father, he can go wherever he wants."

"That's not true," I counter. "The Hyatt hates it when I dock at their north shore property."

Zach laughs. "That's because you crashed into their party yacht the summer after senior year."

"It was a slight nudge," I say, irritably. "And the driver of the other boat was high."

Nessa props her tiny legs over Zach's meaty thighs and points her face toward the sun. Zach absently places a hand on her thigh. "Rumor is," he continues, ignoring my glare, "the guy at the Hyatt said *you* were drunk."

I shake my head at Hayden. "I don't drink and boat."

She glances at the cooler Tyler is sifting through. "Never?"

"Well—I *provide it*—but no, I never drink when I'm driving the boat. My brothers and I had the fear of God put in us when we were learning water safety." I chuckle. "We were taught by a Club Tahoe groundskeeper who was an ex-Navy SEAL. He put us through boot-camp torture before allowing us to operate anything on the water. Hunt is the most fanatical about boat safety, but the rest of us are as well."

Hayden stares out at the water and smiles at a passing paddleboarder, her hands crossed in her lap. She looks relaxed and happy.

"We'll have to take the boat out sometime without the rest of the gang," I say in a low voice. She looks over. "Not that I want to change our normal setting, because I like your place."

We've never stayed at my house on the lake, and I don't miss it. But I miss the boat.

"I'd like that," she says, and my chest fills with warmth. I'm on the lake with my girl, and I've never been happier than at this moment.

* * *

Hayden

MIRA, Nessa, and I sip canned margaritas Tyler was kind enough to bring along with the beers as we bob lightly on the anchored boat inside Emerald Bay, the sun beating down on us. The guys have taken off their shirts and it's a pretty, pretty view inside Adam's boat.

Adam has one foot propped on the cooler, and he's smiling at me. How am I going to talk to him about Blue while he's looking at me like that? This relationship we're building is different. It's special, and I don't want anything to come between us.

His smile slowly drops, as though he senses my thoughts. He leans forward and opens his mouth, but before he can say anything, the sound of splashing draws our attention.

Nessa reaches over the edge of the boat and splashes Zach. He's already wet, so she must have gotten him a second ago too. They moved to the seats that face a small deck off the back of the boat, and the water is right at their feet.

Zach shakes his head like a dog, spraying water at her, and she laughs.

Nessa looks over, grinning. "Let's get in the water. What do you guys say?"

"You don't have your swimsuit," Zach points out.

"I have on sturdy underwear."

His eyes narrow. "You don't own sturdy underwear—not that I'm complaining." He grins devilishly.

"I have on my new boy-cut undies. They're like a normal bathing suit, only cotton."

He quirks his brow. "I'm game." He glances at Adam and Tyler. "You guys in?"

Tyler answers by standing and stretching his arms. He steps up onto the side of the boat and dives overboard.

"Guess we're going too." Mira starts blowing up a floatie the size of a Frisbee.

"What is that?" I say.

She closes off the end and inserts her can of margarita in the center. "Floatable beer cozy."

Mira gently sets her margarita adrift in the water, then removes her off-the-shoulder T-shirt, revealing a fitted tank beneath. She drops her shorts and dives in after Tyler.

Her damp head pops out of the water a second later. "It's effing cold." She flails around, presumably to warm up. "Tyler, get over here. I need your body heat."

Tyler swims to Mira and wraps his arms around her, grinning at her teeth chattering and histrionics. She's latched on to him like a koala bear.

Mira is Washoe, one of the indigenous tribes of Lake Tahoe, so I find it hilarious that she's a total wuss in the water. "Mira, what happened to your native roots?"

"Don't throw that in my face," she calls. "Get in here and see how warm you are!"

Adam peers at me and raises his eyebrow.

"I can't," I say quietly.

"Chicken?" His tone is low.

"No. I'm just...wearing inappropriate undergarments," I mumble. My face warms and I squirm in my seat.

He leans forward, suddenly very interested. "What do you have on under there?" His eyes dip down my body.

I shouldn't be embarrassed. He's seen what's under my shirt many times, because we've been...*active* this past week.

I flip up my loose tank top, fast, to give him a glimpse.

His smile drops and his gaze lifts to mine in a heated stare. He breathes in and rubs a hand over his mouth. "Let's get out of here. I can have them dropped off in ten, maybe fifteen minutes."

I laugh. "Adam, we can't."

He reaches across the boat and pulls me onto his lap, kissing my neck and tugging down the tank to gain access to the bra I just flashed him. "Why not? Who cares about them anyway?"

"Uh, you do? Because they're your friends?"

"If one of them was in my position, they'd dump my ass off faster than you could blink."

I laugh and swat his grabby hands. One of his palms is sliding up my leg, and the other is stealthily squeezing the side of my breast from beneath my tank top. "You're bad."

"You can't flash me like that and expect me to control myself."

"You insisted on knowing why I couldn't get in the water."

He glances at me pointedly. "And now I can't get the image out of my head."

"Hey," Mira calls. "What's going on up there? You guys coming in, or what?"

"No!" Adam yells, at the same time I say, "Maybe."

He shakes his head. "Hell. No." He leans in until his mouth brushes my ear. "Your bra is see-through."

"Well, I was thinking about you." I wiggle to dislodge his hand from under my top, which has grown more daring with each second that passes. His fingers are inside my bra and he's doing unseemly things to my nipple that have my heart racing. "I figured you'd be coming over later, and I might have dressed for the occasion."

"And I thank you for that. But there is no way I want my friends looking at your beautiful breasts." The hand I managed to dislodge from under my top tightens around my waist.

"Should I go in with my clothes on?" I ask.

His gaze drifts to the side, as though he's thinking. "Are the panties the same?" I smile, and he shakes his head with a growl. "You're killing me. You realize that, right?"

I wanted to kill him with my sexy lingerie *later*, not while our friends were around.

"I have a solution." He reaches for the T-shirt he tossed in front of my seat and throws it over my head.

I stand and Adam's shirt drapes to just above my knees.

I do the girl thing and maneuver out of the tank top with the T-shirt still on, and pull off my shorts. "Good?"

In answer, Adam picks me up and jumps overboard. "Cannonball!"

I'm gasping, choking and laughing, and slapping his chest. "Damn you!"

He grins and swims away, diving under the dark sea-glass-colored water. He pops up a few feet from me.

Mira's laughing, so I splash her, and she splashes me back. And Mira isn't nice about it, either. A damned torrent of lake water goes up my nose and into my mouth and eyes.

I dip under the water to get away. When I pop back up, Nessa is facing Zach, her arms wrapped around his shoulders, and she's kicking water with her tiny feet at Mira and grinning like a loon.

Tyler shakes his head at Nessa. "Now you've done it."

Mira's expression is all determination. I know that look, so I do what any sane person would, and back up.

Mira directs her hurricane hands at Nessa and Zach and all hell breaks loose. I'm watching it go down, congratulating myself on getting out of the fray, when something snakes under my T-shirt and grabs my ass. "Ahh!"

Adam emerges and whips his hair to the side, a huge grin on his face.

I wrap my arms around his shoulders, because Mira was right: the water is freezing. "You scared the crap out of me." He holds me up and I kiss his cheek, which is slightly chilled and a little stubbly, but I love him...

Oh my God. My smile falters.

"What's wrong?" he says.

I cut him a quick grin and blink. "Nothing." I run my fingers through his hair, close my eyes, and kiss his temple, my lips resting there a second too long, but he doesn't pull away. If anything, he holds me tighter.

This was coming. I knew this was coming, but I thought we'd break up before something like this happened, or that my first impression of Adam would turn out to be true. But I can't even see that man anymore. All I see is the one in front of me. Laughing with me, holding me, and loving me in a way no one else has. It's hot and intense, and so gentle at the same time. And I never want it to end.

I need to ask Adam about Blue. Because I love him.

Not talking about work and what's worrying me is beginning to feel like a lie. The last thing I want to do is lie to Adam.

Chapter Twenty-Nine

Adam

W e drop off our friends and swing by my place for a change of clothes.

Hayden glances around the living room. "Explain to me again why we never stay at your swank lakeside house? My place looks like a dump compared to this."

I glance at the box-beamed ceilings and large view of the lake. "It's nice, but it doesn't do it for me anymore. Your place is *you*. I want to be where you are."

She stares, and a slow smile spreads over her features. It melts me, that smile. "Okay," she says quietly.

We head to Hayden's in the XKR, and for a moment, I have déjà vu. I dreamt of this—driving through the mountains, unable to take my eyes off Hayden's incredible legs, an intense feeling of wanting something so deeply and knowing I could have it. That she wanted me too. It was the morning I accidentally fell asleep in Hayden's bed. And here we are almost two weeks later.

I grab her hand and squeeze it, peering over. She's

looking out the window, biting the corner of her lip. "Hey," I say. "Everything okay?"

She shakes her head.

This wasn't how things went in my dream. In my dream, she was happy, not worried. "What's up? You didn't have fun today?" I had one of the best days I can remember, but it's no good if she's not happy.

She glances over, that worried expression still on her face. "I had a great time. There's just something I need to talk to you about."

My mind races. *She doesn't want this. She's having second thoughts about us.* But I tell my subconscious to simmer the fuck down. "You can talk to me about anything."

She exhales and her shoulders visibly relax. "Okay. I mean, I know I can. Or I feel I can. It's just—this has to do with work. And where work is concerned, we haven't always seen eye to eye."

Fuck.

She's right.

There are things about my job I can't talk to her about. And not because I don't want to, but because it's not safe to. "Why don't you tell me what's bothering you, and we'll go from there?"

She gives me a soft smile, then looks ahead and takes a deep breath. "I have to ask you about the Blue Stars."

"Paul and the others?" I say. "Have they done something?" The thought makes the back of my neck heat.

"No—well, I don't know," she says. My eyes are on the road, but I see her studying me, out of the corner of my eye. "You never wondered what makes them special? In any other company, employees work together. But the Blue Stars are handpicked by the CEO and seem to have absolute control regardless of their position."

I pull into her driveway and cut the ignition, turning to face her. "I've never thought about it. Favoritism exists in every company." I grab her hand. "I don't like the way Blackwell treats you. Makes me crazy. But try not to let it get to you. You are extremely competent and good at what you do."

"But you're a part of them—the Blue Stars. You support the way they treat me and the others."

"I'm not considered a Blue Star. I work with them. It's a part of my job." I glance away, trying to piece together what this is about. "Do you want me to say something on your behalf? I thought you didn't want me to step in for you, but—"

She pulls her hand from mine. "I'm capable of taking care of myself. Was doing it long before you showed up."

"You started working at Blue just a few months before I did," I point out, which only seems to annoy her further. Goddamn my mouth.

"What does that have to do with anything? They hired me because they thought they could control me."

I shake my head. "Hayden, you're drawing conclusions. Paul and William and the others are jackasses. Don't let them get to you."

"What about Blackwell? You think he's just some jackass?"

I drape my wrist over the steering wheel. I'm in it now. Might as well go all the way. "No. I think he's powerful. In ways you and I can't begin to imagine."

She sighs. "I agree. That's why I'm bringing this up. Not because I need you to rescue me."

She's angry, but my own frustration is growing. "Why don't you tell me what's really bothering you?"

She crosses her arms over her chest, a subtle challenge

in her eyes. I already know I'm not going to like what comes out of her mouth next. "I believe Blackwell is using Blue to conduct illegal business."

Nope, definitely didn't like where that went.

Hayden suspects something, or she wouldn't have been snooping around the facility manager's office. *Looking for evidence,* Lewis said. Hayden is trying to find out what she's missing.

I don't know what more Blackwell is capable of, but my imagination fills in the blanks pretty quickly, considering the resources he's poured into Bliss, the lineup of ex-military at his disposal, and the mysterious source who'll be sending drugs into the casino through hired escorts. And if Hayden knew any of this, she'd try to do something to stop it. She doesn't want me to rescue her, but neither can I give her the information she seeks and put her in the line of fire.

I need to nip this in the bud and get her off the subject. "Suspicions aren't evidence."

"And that doesn't sound like denial," she says. "What have you been keeping from me?"

I let out a sigh. "I know what the rest of the managers know."

That was a vague answer, but it was truthful. I just happen to know a few extra details in addition to what the other managers know.

"Not all of the managers are aware of Bliss."

My jaw shifts. Those damn files in the facility manager's office. I knew she found them. "I'm not allowed to talk about that," I say. She shakes her head in disbelief. "This is my job, Hayden. It would be wrong for me to ask you for confidential information on employees. Please don't put me in the same position."

She gets out of the car, and I follow her to the porch.

Hayden inserts the key and opens the door, standing on the threshold. "What they're doing is illegal. Mira and Tyler know it. Lewis and Gen and the others do too. We've been trying to find evidence to take to the police."

"Goddammit, Hayden." I thrust stiff fingers through my hair. "Don't use Blue as your retaliation for the past. This isn't about you, and what you're talking about is going to get you hurt."

She lets out a shaky breath. "I'm doing what's right. Are you?"

"How do you know what I'm doing is wrong?" I shoot back.

"Are you working with them?" she asks.

"Yes."

"Then I have my answer."

She moves to shut the door and I brace my hand on the wood, halting her. "Let me come in. Let's talk about this."

"There's nothing to talk about." Her voice comes out shaky, as though she's trying not to cry.

My stomach rolls over and my chest tightens. I nudge the door open and try to pull her into my arms, but she steps away.

"Please leave," she says. "I need time to think."

"Are you kidding? I'm not the best boyfriend, Hayden. I've fucked up my share of relationships. But I know communication is important. Don't push me away." I graze my finger over the one she has on the door. "Let's talk so that we can work this out."

"I want to," she says in a light voice, her eyes studying my finger rubbing a circle over hers. "But this thing between us happened so fast. And the things I suspect about Blue are huge." Her gaze penetrates mine. "They're important, not just to me, but to our friends and anyone else who's been wronged by Blackwell and the casino. I won't ignore things the way management did when Gen filed the complaints against Drake Peterson. Maybe this *is* my redemption for allowing bullies to run me out of town all those years ago, but it's also dangerous to pretend nothing is wrong. I can't let anyone get hurt if I'm able to put a stop to it, don't you understand?" She swallows and takes in a shaky breath. "So are you going to tell me what's going on with Blue and this Bliss thing?"

I glance up and let out a growl. "I can't."

This time, her eyes gloss over and she nods. "Then I can't do us. Not right now. Not if you support Blackwell and what I suspect is happening at the casino."

"Wait, Hayden. You don't understand. And I can't give you the answers you need, but if you give me time I will."

"When?"

"I don't know."

"That sounds like evasion," she says. "You haven't exactly been forthcoming with information. Everything I've discovered, I've found out on my own."

"Which I wish you would stop doing."

I *am* evading her questions—for her own good. I don't want her involved, and I'll risk anything to keep her out of it. Even what's between us, which is the first real thing I've had since my mom died. But Hayden is worth more even than that. I won't see her hurt.

"Goodbye, Adam." She closes the door and I stand there, my hands shaking, chest sawing in and out with the adrenaline coursing through me.

I slam my fist against the doorframe and stride to my car.

Chapter Thirty

Hayden

I cried myself to sleep two nights ago and continued to cry half the day yesterday, holed away in my house. I am torn in half—in love with Adam, and so furious with him I want to rail all over his ass. But I refuse to talk to him again until I figure out what's right. Adam could easily seduce me into forgetting about Bliss. The happiness I feel when I'm with him is incredibly powerful. I let my convictions slip these last two weeks. I can't let that happen again, now that I know he truly is keeping something from me.

Mira steps into the break room, where I'm standing by the coffeemaker, overcompensating for my lack of sleep with caffeine.

"Hey." She scans my face and looks down at my hands. "You're shaking."

"Too much coffee. I'll be fine." Those damn tears that have been close to the surface reappear.

"Shit," she whispers, and pulls me out of the break room and into her office two doors down. She closes the door behind us. "What happened? I just saw you on Saturday and everything was great."

I let out a deep sigh. "I broke up with Adam."

Her eyes widen. "Why would you do that?"

My head notches back in surprise. "I thought you didn't like him?"

She sits in her chair. "Of course I like Adam. I've always liked him. I just thought he was a bit of a jerk to his past girlfriends. But he's not like that with you. The boy is in love. Like, *deep* love, Hayden."

I shake my head. "No, you don't understand. He's not in love with me; he's keeping things from me—lying through omission." I flap my hand at the door. "He's involved. With them. The Bliss suites. Blackwell and the Blue Stars. He knows all about what they're doing, and he won't tell me anything."

Her palms flatten on her desk. "What exactly did he say?"

"That he can't talk about it. He wanted me to give him time."

She blinks repeatedly. "Really? How much time?"

I stare at her. "What does it matter? He's involved."

She drums her fingers and stares off. "Maybe, or maybe he has a good reason for wanting you to give him time. I can detect a bad guy a mile away, and Adam isn't one of them."

I wince and screw my eyes closed. Mira grew up around vice and corruption. It's a testament to her strength that she didn't take the same path and die of a drug overdose like her mother. "I can't ignore what he's doing. If he's involved with them, it's not good."

She walks around her desk and sits on the armrest of the spindly metal guest chair I'm in, nearly tipping us over in the process. She rubs my shoulders. "Do you trust him?"

266

I shake my head—my level of confusion has reached epic proportions. "My heart trusts him. But my head... What reason is there to lie to your girlfriend?"

Mira stands and paces off to the side. "I don't know. I'd kill Tyler if he lied to me about something important."

"Exactly. Lying is a deal breaker, and Adam admitted he's bad at relationships." I rest my head on her desk. "I'll be okay. I just need time to get over what we had."

"Sure," comes her wry response. "You look like someone who's going to get over it real soon."

I roll my eyes at her sarcasm, but she can't see it because my head is still on the table. I take a deep breath and wipe the tears and mascara gunk from under my eyes. "I'd better get back to work."

Mira hands me a tissue. "Just consider it—giving him a chance. We've been trying for months to figure out whether or not there's still something going on. Adam knows as much as anyone about the attacks. He knows Blue has had trouble. And he's been a good friend to Jaeger. I can't see him supporting something like this."

I smile bitterly. "And yet he must be. Why else would he not tell me about the suites?"

* * *

Adam

HAYDEN WON'T TAKE my calls, and I'm about to lose my mind. I'm trying to protect her. But obviously I can't tell her that. She about bit my head off when I mentioned stepping in for her with Blackwell. I'm worried what she'd do if I told her I was keeping Bliss from her so that she wouldn't be linked to it. She has this notion it's her duty to protect the employees after the casino hurt her friends. I know it's more complicated than that—she was scarred by what happened in high school and wants to stand up for others after no one stood up for her. But I can't let her become a mark for Blackwell. Not when I'm uncertain about what he's capable of.

Paul and William walk into my office and close the door. "Ten days until the big reveal. How many are registered at the hotel?"

I stretch my neck. The last thing I want to deal with right now is Paul. He's been up my ass over every fucking detail related to the Bliss debut, even though I've laid it out for him ten times. "As I mentioned an hour ago, we have fifty prospective members registered for the weekend, and twenty of our nearly forty members will also be in town for the event. Eve is putting together a letter and gift basket for each of the rooms. Anything else?"

"And the DJ—"

"Confirmed," I say. "His assistant sent me his flight itinerary, which I forwarded to Eve, whose assistant will personally attend his arrival. The caterer is secured; the menu set. And if you want to know about the auction and burlesque show, you'll need to talk to William."

Paul shoves his hand in his pocket. "I'm sensing animosity."

"You sense wrong." He senses *right,* but it's best if Paul doesn't know everything I'm thinking at the moment.

William glances between Paul and me, an uneasy grin sliding on his face. He was always more interested in pleasing everyone. "Well now, I can tell you that the auction and our beautiful dancers are all lined up. The ladies arrive Friday for the Saturday show. Beginning at six a.m. Saturday, a crew will come in to remake the club for the evening.

I'm working with security to close off the area while the equipment is brought in."

"Looks like we're all set," I say. "If you'll excuse me." I stand to leave. I hadn't planned on leaving my office, but it's claustrophobic in here. I have the sudden need to get out.

Paul jingles the coins in his pocket. "I suppose we're nearly ready. Blackwell expects everyone to attend the midnight party after the show and to sell the Bliss experience. Plan on being there the entire night. I'll send you a list of things to tout as you mingle with potential members."

I nod, though I have no intention of reviewing his list. "Are we finished?" Not waiting for their answer, I raise my hand for them to exit first.

Paul and William walk out, but Paul turns to me once we're outside my office. He signals for William to go on ahead. "Don't forget, if everything goes according to plan on opening night, you can expect a hefty end-of-the-year bonus." His eyes narrow. "Stay the course, Adam, and all will be fine."

I watch him saunter away confidently. He ignores the gaming manager walking by, but winks at Eve as she passes. The deferential treatment toward some employees was obvious—I just never recognized how singular it was among the Blue Stars. Not until Hayden pointed it out.

I head for her office. I gave her space last night and the night before, but we need to talk. If Hayden were anyone else, I would have walked away long ago. But I can't do that. Not with her. I'll stay away, if that's what she wants, but I won't be the one to leave. Not this time.

I rap on the solid wood door, and enter at her invitation.

She raises her head and our eyes connect. Just like it did two days ago when I spotted her across the patio at the Beacon, my heart thunders in my chest.

"Adam?" She looks behind me, but I close the door. "Why are you here?"

"Because I work here?"

"You know what I mean."

"I wanted to talk to you."

She lets out a sad sigh. "Are you going to tell me what you're not saying about the Bliss suites?"

"Hayden." Exasperation fills my voice. "I love that you're strong and never back down, but for once, I need you to. I want to share everything with you, but I can't talk about this."

She squeezes her eyelids closed and shakes her head, as though fighting with herself. "If you're involved in something illegal, then you should know I'm not letting it go." An unsteady breath escapes her mouth. "I knew it would come down to this. *I knew it.* But I never thought it would hurt this badly."

I stride around her desk and pull her into my arms. "It doesn't have to. You can trust me." I plead with my eyes and her expression softens, but I can't tell if I've reached her. And God, I need to reach her.

"My heart trusts you." Her voice is light, as though the confession confuses her.

"I love your heart," I say with such feeling that I startle myself. My words were meant to encourage her to give me a chance, but it's more than that. I love Hayden. No fireworks; no sudden realization. A simple truth that's been there all along. "I haven't given you a reason to doubt me since I started at Blue, have I?"

"No," she says hesitantly, because she has no idea of the depth of what I've admitted to myself. Her mouth turns down. "Not unless you count the things you're keeping from me."

"Which is for a good reason. A reason I plan to tell you about, just as soon as I can. All I'm asking is for a little time. I may not have deserved your confidence in the past, but have faith in me now. I won't let you down."

She's quiet for a moment, studying my eyes. "I think your intentions are good, even if it pisses me off that you're keeping this from me." She lets out a long sigh. "A little time... Okay. I—I can do that."

I press her to my chest, hugging her so hard I worry I'm crushing her, but she's clinging to me, and I think she needs the connection as much as I do. We had one night—one fucking bad night that spilled into two days apart. And they've been the worst two days of my life. I thought I'd lost her.

I lift her chin. "I won't ever give you a reason to doubt me." She leans up and my heart clenches, blood warming. I want to pick her up and carry her away like the caveman she thinks I am. But we're at work, and somehow I manage to kiss the tip of her nose instead. "I'll see you tonight?"

She nods, a shy smile spreading across her face.

Hell yes, I'm thinking about spending the night with Hayden, tangled in her arms. But I also want the simple pleasure of being with her. If I'm with her, I'm happy. And I've never had anything genuine that makes me happy, until Hayden. Everything else in my life has had strings attached.

Chapter Thirty-One

Hayden

M ira pops her head in my door. "Risk management meeting in five."

"I'm on it," I say as I finish typing out an email. A weight lifted the moment I decided to listen to my heart and trust Adam. I'm still not sure where that leaves us. I won't drop this Bliss thing, but I will give him time, like he asked. He's right. He's given me no reason to doubt him, so I won't.

I thought things were over this weekend. I panicked when he said he couldn't talk to me about the Bliss suites, but I can have faith in Adam, even if I don't trust Blackwell and the others. The two are not entwined. Adam isn't one of the Blue Stars.

I make it to the risk management meeting, and not five minutes in, Eve enters the small room we use for training, her sleeveless knit blouse two sizes too small in the bust. "Hayden, there's an all-managers meeting in the conference room."

I glance at Mira. She knows the training material as well as I do, but she's still new at presenting.

"Go," she says. "I've got this."

No time like the present for Mira to take on a new leadership task. I nod and collect my things, then follow Eve out.

Eve is holding a stack of folders. Her Blue signet ring—slightly more refined than the men's version—flashes in the light of the art deco wall sconce. She is the only female Blue Star, and I've often wondered why they chose her. I think it's because she has no scruples.

In my short tenure at Blue, I've seen people fired for making the mistake of confiding in Eve. Mentioning displeasure over Blackwell, or any of the Blue Stars, is a firing offense, though a different reason is always given. Which is why I've rarely said two words to her, and say nothing now as we make our way to the conference room.

Once inside, Eve heads straight to the seat next to Blackwell, but I pause at the entrance. Everyone is present. Catering even set up a food table, which is typically only done when there's a celebration or special event.

One more thing Blackwell hasn't informed me about?

Adam is in his usual spot at the end of the conference table. He sends me a private smile, and I make my way over. The spot next to him is empty and I take it, sensing the heat of his body as soon as I sit.

"Thank you for coming today," Blackwell says, getting the meeting started, but I barely notice. Because Adam shifts, his leg pressed against mine.

All I've thought about since he left my office a few hours ago is being with him tonight. I worried that Adam would run at any small problem we encountered. He admitted he's the first to leave when a relationship gets rocky. But our disagreement over the Bliss suites *is* a big issue, and he didn't run. He came to me today to work things out. Blue is still a problem, but he's right—separating isn't the solution.

His warm hand squeezes my waist below the table and I smile.

"—proud to include Adam Cade among the Blue Stars."

My head snaps up. What did Blackwell just say?

Adam's hand freezes against my waist, then moves slowly away, taking all the warmth along with it.

I stare at Blackwell's smiling face. "Adam?" Blackwell says. "Will you stand?" He holds up a black box.

Adam rises beside me and buttons the top button of his suit jacket, his jaw stiff. He doesn't look my way before striding to the end of the table. With each step he takes, I feel our worlds growing farther apart.

Don't do it.

Adam shakes Blackwell's hand. "Thank you. It's a privilege and an honor to be considered a Blue Star. I won't take it for granted."

My jaw unhinges.

Adam removes the ring from the box and slides it on his ring finger, the cobalt of the gemstone catching the light the way Eve's did moments ago in the hallway. My stomach hitches and the room spins. I feel like I'm going to be sick.

I believed him, even if I didn't know everything going on. I believed Adam wouldn't support Blackwell all the way. But this is about as supportive as one can get. Adam has become a Blue Star.

Maybe he has no choice?

But doesn't he? Aren't we all the makers of our own destiny?

Adam is allowing this to happen. He's giving in to

Blackwell's demands, doing what the boss says to keep his job, just like he told me to do the last time we found ourselves in this conference room and I wanted to speak out after Blackwell handed off my work to William.

The noise volume in the room increases as people stand and head for food, or to congratulate Adam. *In celebration.*

I move in a daze to the door and slip out. Adam said to give him time, but he only seems to be getting closer to Blackwell. If he's with Blackwell, he can't be with me. And I don't know where that leaves us.

Because I still love him.

* * *

ADAM LEFT a note at my place last night. We had plans to get together, but after the meeting I freaked the hell out and went to Zach and Nessa's instead.

Then the entire gang showed up.

Mira was appalled on my behalf, but the guys were quiet. To them, Adam is a brother, and in some weird way, I feel like I betrayed him just by relating the story. He's my boyfriend, or he *was.* I don't know what we are anymore. These last few days have been a rollercoaster. How could something so magical in its normalcy, like churros in cocktail wear and heated kisses on the kitchen counter, go so horribly wrong?

I pull a sweatshirt over my head and pad into the kitchen in my bare feet. I called in sick today and worked from home. It's cowardly, but I can't see Adam. I need to be strong, and all my defenses disappear when I'm around him.

I didn't want Adam involved with Blackwell, but in some small way I could deal as long as he wasn't a Blue Star

—that mercurial barrier marking his transition to the dark side. If Bliss turns out to be what I think it is, I'll have to turn Adam in to the police along with the rest of the Blue Stars...

I hunch over and hold my stomach, fighting the ache. The notion of Adam getting caught physically hurts me, but I can't run from what's right. Not this time.

The front door opens and I jump, still clutching my stomach.

Adam walks in, his eyes trained on me. His eyebrows pull together and he closes the door behind him. "Are you okay? You weren't at work."

"Don't you knock?" I swallow my heart, which leapt into my throat the moment he entered the house.

"You should lock your doors." His gaze takes in my face, then drops to my body, which is layered in a sweatshirt and tank top with no bra, and sleep shorts. Yeah, I'm looking good. It doesn't stop him from walking toward me. "Are you sick?"

I step back and bump into the counter. "I needed a day off."

This is impossible. I can't be near him. Already I want to wrap my arms around his neck and pull him close. What's wrong with me?

He takes off his suit jacket, folds it, and places it over the back of the couch. He steps closer and drops his keys on the counter. "You haven't returned my calls."

"Are you going to break up with me?" I don't know why I say it. I'm pretty sure we broke up, but I honestly can't keep track with the back and forth these last few days. And I need to know where we stand. Because I can't see a happy future without the man I never thought in a million years I would fall in love with, yet I might have to.

Adam puts his hands on the counter on either side of my hips, his head just above mine. "Why would I do a stupid thing like that?"

"Because your friends say you always break up with girls before they break up with you." And I need for him to stick to that behavior. I broke up with him once. I'm not strong enough to push him away again.

"If you recall, I haven't had a girlfriend in a while. There's a reason for that."

I blink back tears, because dammit, having him close is brutal. I want to press my face to his chest and kiss him. And smell his neck. But I feel like I'm betraying people—or myself. Or him? Darn it. I don't know. "What reason?"

"I see my future with you. So, no, Hayden, I'm not breaking up with you. That's the last thing I'll do."

I glance up, and the freaking tears come back. I can't help it: I press my head to his chest and his arms come immediately around me. "I'm so mad at you."

"I know. But I need you to trust me."

I reach for his hand, the one wearing the ring, and hold it up. "How can I trust you when you're keeping this from me? What if I make a choice that tears us apart? Do you have any idea how complicated you've made everything by becoming a Blue Star?"

His arms tense around me. "Hayden, for the love of God, please don't get involved. I know you think what you're doing is right, but you don't understand the half of it." He steps back and scrubs a hand down his face. "It's dangerous. I'm not telling you about Bliss, because the more you know, the more dangerous it is for you. I don't trust Paul or Blackwell, and I worry about what Blackwell is capable of."

"Then why are you supporting him?"

He doesn't answer, head tipped down.

"Well, I'm a big girl. I can handle myself."

His head whips up. "Like you did in high school?"

I suck in a breath, my face heating.

His gaze wanders to the side, as though he can't believe he said it either. "I'm sorry. That was uncalled for." He grabs my hand. "I'm trying to make a point, not make you feel bad about the past. I will tell you everything I know as soon as it's safe."

"How can I trust you?"

He lifts the hand I'm holding—the one with the Blue Star ring—and kisses my knuckles. "You can kick my ass if I do anything to hurt you."

"I won't wait to kick your ass—I'll simply leave you."

A flash of fear crosses his eyes, and he swallows. "Come on. Let's get out of here."

"Where?"

"Someplace special." I glance at my sweatshirt and sleep shorts, and he does too. "You can wear what you have on. Well—maybe throw on pants, or sweats. Something warm. We'll be outside."

Chapter Thirty-Two

Adam drives up a long, winding road through the forest. We're on a slope of the mountain that faces the lake from a southeastern vantage point. He pulls off to the side and kills the engine. The area is pitch-dark, the only light coming from the stars and crescent moon overhead.

I step out of the car, and Adam turns on a flashlight. "Whose property is this?"

"Levi's. He lives in the house we passed."

Adam pulls a blanket from the trunk and leads the way to a tent in front of a fire pit.

I peek inside the half-dome tent. "There's an air mattress. What does your brother do out here?"

Adam sets out the blanket and grins. "Dirty girl. Not what you're thinking—or, at least, I don't think so. I don't want to know. My brothers and I come out for campfires, and Levi uses the place to mellow under the stars."

"Will it bother him that we're here?"

"Nope. I use it all the time. I texted Levi to let him know."

I sit on the edge of the air mattress cross-legged and look

up at the star-dotted sky through the wide opening of the tent and the break in the trees. "Have I mentioned how much I like Levi and his awesome piece of land? Do you think he'd mind if I lived in his tent?"

Adam drops his coat on my lap and squats in front of me. "No, but I would have an issue with it."

I hold back a smile. "As handsome as Levi is, he has nothing on you, Adam Cade. I've never met a more handsome man. Used to piss me off when you first started working at Blue. It was distracting."

His hands slide down my calves. "And now?"

"Now it's ten times worse, because I know you." My voice is sober, and I swallow the burn in my throat. Adam has asked me to trust him, and that's what I want to do, but I'm scared.

For a moment, he doesn't say or do anything. The sound of my unsteady breathing fills the tent. And then his hands come down on either side of me, dipping the air mattress as he leans forward. I drop back until I'm lying with him hovering over me.

His body slowly lowers, his hips settling between my thighs, elbows propped on either side of my head. Then his mouth covers me too. First a soft whisper along my jaw, a gentle kiss below my ear. Then his lips are on mine.

My hands flutter at my sides as Adam tilts my jaw and deepens the kiss, his tongue and lips and his palm along my jaw soothing the fear and frustration boiling inside me.

He leans on one elbow and reaches for my hand, linking our fingers above my head. He gazes down at me. He should say something, reassure me, but he doesn't. He drops his head and kisses me again. Telling me with the movement of his lips and the circular motion of his thumb against my palm how much I mean to him.

And it goes on and on like this until I feel dizzy.

A shiver racks my body.

"Cold?" he asks, and I nod. It's summer, but the temperatures drop sharply in the basin at night and I can feel the change, even with Adam's body heat above me.

He presses a soft kiss to my lips, now tender from all the kissing. "Wait here." He rises and spreads his coat over me, then rolls up his sleeves and reaches for the flashlight. Flicking it on, he walks off and disappears into the dark.

A minute passes and I don't hear him or see the flashlight. "Where did you go?" I call out.

A loud thump sounds beside me and I flinch. "Holy crap." I slap a hand to my chest.

Adam's flashlight crosses in front of me to a bunch of chopped wood. He looks inside the tent. "I'm building you a fire. Pretty sure it's on the honey-do list."

I attempt to compose myself after I nearly peed my pants over an armload of wood. "Damn straight. Get on that, will you? And please flex your muscles while you're at it."

"As my lady wishes." He unbuttons his shirt and pulls it out of his pants and off his arms, dropping it onto the mattress beside me. Then he collects the wood and swaggers to the fire pit. Adam orients the pieces in what looks like the shape of a teepee. It's really dark out, and I can hardly see anything, which pisses me off because this is as manly as it gets and I'm missing half the show. And then the glow of fire flickers, illuminating Adam's body and the wood pyramid.

Golden light touches the strong curve of Adam's jaw as he squats beside the wood, lighting it in strategic places, his thick thigh muscles straining against suit pants he never changed out of. His undershirt cuts into his biceps, accentuating the dip and swell of strong arms...

I sit back and admire. Now *this* is what I'm talking about.

Adam stands and places the extra wood off to the side, then brushes off his hands and walks over to me. He enters the tent and sits beside me, snaking his arm around my hips and pulling me closer. "Better?"

The heat of the fire is making its way to me, but it's nowhere near as heat-inducing as his presence. "Much better."

In this world, where it's just Adam and me and no one else, everything is perfect. But this isn't real life. "What happens tomorrow?" I say.

We've done a lot of kissing and not much else. Not that I'm complaining, because there were words exchanged in those kisses. I translated them as: *Hayden, I'm sorry. Hayden, I love you. Hayden, you are beautiful and I bask in your glory.* Okay, maybe that's an exaggeration, but it's how he made me feel.

He rests his elbows on his knees and stares at the fire. "We go to work, and we do our jobs. We go home"—he looks over—"to *your* place. And we make out some more."

I lower my eyes. "Just make out." I'm all for kissing, but I'm curious about why he hasn't taken things further. Adam is normally much more, uh, *assertive* in that regard. And okay, sure, things were tense there in the beginning, but we made up via heavy lip contact and silent communication.

His jaw shifts and he lets out a sigh. "Only kissing."

Whoa, what? "What do you mean?"

He shifts and faces me, a forearm propped on one knee. "There are things I can't tell you right now, but I want to be with you. As far as I'm concerned, you're my girlfriend, but you're right."

"I am?" What am I right about? Because I was just getting warmed up and looking forward to the next course. Especially after Adam's very masculine fire-building display. And I've missed him. A lot—like a *whole* lot.

"I can't tell you what you want to know about Blue and the Bliss project right now. Until I can, we shouldn't be intimate."

"Have you lost your mind?" That sounds desperate, but seriously, what's he talking about? We can barely keep our hands off each other at work, and now he wants to ban physical contact at home?

His mouth turns down in a crooked frown. "Possibly." And then he swoops in and captures my lips, stealing a kiss and my breath and whatever logic I was constructing to get him to reconsider. "I want you," he breathes, pulling back. "But I don't want you to have to question my feelings and whether or not you can trust me." He turns to the fire. "And I can tell that you do."

Well, damn. He's right.

And that makes sense. Though I don't like it. Not one bit. "So how long are we abstaining while sleeping in the same bed...and making out?"

He breathes out a frustrated sigh and glances at me out of the corner of his eye. "Hopefully not long."

Chapter Thirty-Three

Adam

Thank fucking God it's Saturday. The auction and burlesque show and the Bliss grand opening tonight need to be over before I lose my mind. I've stayed at Hayden's place every night this week. We've watched movies, eaten takeout, and made out. Lots of heavy making out. I'm about to explode. And the worst part is, I have no idea when my self-imposed abstinence will end, because for some stupid reason I've got it in my head that I can't touch her until I'm able to be open about the Bliss venture.

It seems right. I want to take a step back until we can be totally honest with each other. I'm trying to be a good guy for once. But for the love of God, this is torture.

I should quit my job. My father can keep his trust fund. I'll take up handyman work for Hayden on her ever-growing honey-do list. She likes it when I use my hands.

My hands...on her body...

I mutter a curse, just as my new assistant walks in. "Excuse me?" she says.

"Nothing, Diane." I clear my throat. "What can I do for you?"

"Oh." She brightens and walks to my desk, her plastic reading glasses dangling from a cord around her neck.

Diane came on board a few days ago, and she's lifted a load of administrative crap off my shoulders. After the Bridget disaster, Blackwell relented and allowed Hayden to find a replacement. Hayden found Diane, so of course my new assistant comes highly qualified. Whenever possible, I will happily hand off hiring good people to my girlfriend from now on.

"I confirmed that a Mr. Aldridge checked into the casino." Diane rattles off his room number.

"Thank you. I'll take it from here." I pick up the phone and dial Eve's extension while Diane exits my office.

"Hello, Adam." Eve answers on the first ring. Her sultry voice has me mentally rolling my eyes. Eve is beautiful—and I have never been attracted to her. She's sleeping with Blackwell, but that's not the reason. I've watched Eve lie her way through a meeting at another's expense, and manipulate coworkers out of bonuses for her own gain. Working with her has been a means to an end. She's one of Blackwell's top executives, and she's also heavily involved in Bliss.

"I've got one more for tonight. An ex-quarterback who's a frequent host on ESPN. He's booked in a room on the same floor as the others." I give her the room number. "Please deliver the introduction basket and agenda. He's already arrived."

"This is a surprise." I hear the light sound of a pen scraping. "Blackwell will be pleased. How did you say you know this person?"

I didn't. Eve is fishing for information because she's

been unsuccessful at bringing in new Bliss members. "A friend of a friend," I tell her.

The one thing about coming from money is that no one questions your connection to others with money.

I contacted Jeb about this evening and we came up with a small plan to ensure Bliss is on the up-and-up. Things will play out the way they will, but at least I've done all I can.

I end the call with Eve and check my phone. I've got a few more minutes before Hayden said she'd be leaving for the day. I button my coat and head down the hall. And yes, there could be extra purpose in my steps. Just knowing I'm going to see Hayden in a minute has my body temperature rising in anticipation.

Her office is open and I step inside, quietly closing and locking the door behind me.

Hayden looks up and slowly stands, her hands pressing the front of her skirt above her thighs. "This is dangerous," she says, her chest rising and falling more quickly as I stalk across the room.

"Is it?" I say lightly, my focus on her eyes, her mouth, her hair, and down.

She leans against her desk as I round it, her red skirt flaring out from her waist. She twists a strand of pearls at her throat. "You've created a powder keg," she says, her gaze dropping to my mouth.

I scan her cream knit top, which is accentuating some of my favorite curves. Well, that and the shape of her legs, the way her waist cuts in, her beautiful smile—okay, I like all the curves. I stop an inch away. "Have I?" I say, but I know damn well I have, and I'm helpless to take back what I've started.

Without further ado, I reach down and bunch the hem of her skirt, my fingers skimming over her thighs. Her hands flutter to my chest, her gaze never leaving my lips. "We can't go on like this. I give," she says, and brushes her lips against my jaw. "You can keep your secrets about Bliss. I don't need them anyway."

My hands freeze where they're kneading her ass. I pick her up and set her on the desk, inserting my hips between her legs and pulling her flush with me. I brush my mouth across her hairline. "What do you mean, you don't need my Bliss secrets?" I mumble against her smooth skin.

Her hands go still on my chest, where she's unbuttoned my coat and shirt and worked her palms against my skin. "You were right." She runs her hands over my abs. "I shouldn't have asked you to talk about something confidential."

I grab her ass and press her to me. She moans and I nip her earlobe. It's all fun and games until Hayden agrees with me. Then I know I'm in trouble.

"Hayden," I say. "What are you not telling me?"

Her body stiffens and she tries to pull away, but I wrap her arms around my neck where they stay, though I'm not holding them in place anymore. Her golden-brown eyes regain their focus and she sighs. "Nothing. Just that you have your secrets and I have mine."

"Secrets." My tone is flat. "About Bliss?"

She plays with the collar of my shirt and bites the inside of her lip, her eyes not meeting mine. "Maybe." At my frown, she hurries on. "We both have secrets when it comes to the suites, so we can forget about this no-sex rule." She slides her hand down and flattens it against my erection.

I let out a growl and step away, planting my fingers on my hips, the sides of my suit jacket pushed back. My body is on fire, but my mind is actually working for once. Because what she said has my anxiety level spiking.

Snooping around Bliss activities won't only get Hayden fired, it could get her harmed. Or worse. Blackwell put an obscene amount of money into Bliss. What would he be willing to do to silence her if she found something incriminating? What would the career criminals and ex-military he had me hire be willing to do? "I suggested we take things slow because I want something real with you, not something founded on lies."

"You're right." Hayden's gaze wanders to the side. "I can't believe you're right, but you are. We don't need more secrets between us."

Her hands drop to either side of her hips on the desk. "It's not really a secret. I'm sure you heard that Mira and Tyler found a Blue suite used to distribute illegal drugs a few months ago."

"*What?* No. Tyler never said anything."

Paul mentioned an earlier version of Bliss, which must have been the suite Mira and Tyler found.

She takes in my expression. "I'm sorry. I thought Tyler said something. I should have brought it up earlier. What do you guys talk about in your spare time if not things like this?"

Beer. Women. Sports. "Usually nothing important."

She purses her lips together, gaze thoughtful. "You know, you also weren't working at Blue then. Tyler might not have thought to mention it. We weren't sure what was going on. We sort of lost the suite. That's what I've been looking for and why I've been interested in Bliss. Your friends and I don't believe everything ended with Drake's removal. Those files you had the facility manager relocate were the first real lead I had to take to the police."

The corner of her mouth twists down, as though it were my fault that she lost the paper trail. Which it absolutely was. I had the facility manager move the files some-where Hayden wouldn't find them, because it's safer if she doesn't know any more than she already does about Bliss.

"Each of us has been touched in some way by Blackwell and his Blue Stars. I was never assaulted, but I've been used as a pawn by Blackwell while he works around the system. He's criticized me, devalued my position in front of our peers, and threatened me should I look into those you've hired. He's horrible and he's running this place and the Bliss suites. They won't let me in one of them to look around, but I'm certain that's where they've relocated the drug operation."

"Threatened you?" My tone is dark.

She waves me off. "Over your new hires. He wanted me to stay out of it—said I wouldn't like the consequences if I didn't."

I force out a sigh. "Then why would you dare go against him?"

Her face turns red. "Because he's a bully! I won't—I *refuse* to let someone do that to me again. He has no right! How can you be involved in Bliss, knowing what he's using it for?"

"I didn't know about it until they promoted me. At least, not the full extent."

"But you know now. Why aren't you doing something?"

"I never said I wasn't doing anything. I said it isn't safe for *you* to be involved."

"But it's safe for you?"

I don't answer, because she's right. It's not. But I'm in it and she isn't. As far as Blackwell is concerned, Hayden doesn't know anything. If she starts waving red flags, that won't last long. "You need to stop, Hayden. You can't go up against our CEO. I've been around men like him my entire life. He's powerful."

She hops off the desk and crosses her arms. "Finding evidence of what he's up to is the right thing to do. I'm not running from this."

I settle my hands on her shoulders. "There's nothing wrong with running if it keeps you safe."

She steps to the side and glares. "Yes, there is!"

"This isn't about some punks throwing rocks," I say, my voice rising.

She stares like she can't believe what she's hearing. "Those punks nearly killed me."

I rub my forehead. "I'm not trying to lessen what happened. It's just—This is different. If you keep pushing, you'll be hit with much worse than rocks." I gentle my voice, because I need for her to listen. "Whatever you're thinking about doing? Don't. Just give me time, Hayden. You said that you would."

"To do what? Get yourself put in prison? I care about you." Her voice quavers and her eyes grow watery. "But if I find something—even if it involves you—I'm taking it to the police."

"You think I'd willingly be a part of this?"

"Aren't you? You accepted the ring. And you're involved in the Bliss suites." She steps forward and hits my chest with the side of her fist. Not hard, but laden with frustration. "Why, Adam? Why the hell did you do it?"

I capture her fist in both of mine. "The simple answer is, because my father ordered me to work at Blue. That Blackwell brought me into his...exclusive group...was coincidental. The ring means nothing."

"It's symbolic." She shakes her head. "Do you do everything your father says?"

"Historically? Yes."

Her chin wobbles and her voice softens. "Well, maybe it's time you didn't. You *can* walk away."

I glance past her out the window, barely seeing the mountains and lake. "No. I can't." My gaze tracks back to hers. "I'm serious when I say you need to stay out of this."

She pulls away and grabs her purse.

"Where are you going?"

"Out." She doesn't look back as she heads for the door. "Don't wait up."

* * *

I RETURN TO MY HOUSE, which feels like a shell of a place. How have I lived here for so long without feeling lonely?

Right. I did. I just never knew the difference until I started seeing Hayden. I filled the void with shallow women, nice cars, and trips to Ibiza. Now I don't give a damn about any of that. I just want tonight to be over with so that I can make things up to Hayden.

I change into an evening suit and check my phone. I texted Jaeg an hour ago and told him to call me as soon as he could, but my screen shows no messages. I pull up Tyler's contact information.

"It's Adam," I say after he answers. "Have you—heard anything? Something that might be going on tonight? Hayden left work and I got the impression she was going out, or had plans."

There's a pause on the other line. "You two not talking?"

"We're talking, we're just having a slight disagreement."

Tyler lets out a loud breath. "I can't say anything or Mira will kill me."

"Jesus Christ, Morgan. You're afraid of a hundred-pound female?"

"She's a buck twenty, and hell yes, I'm afraid. She holds my balls in her tiny hands. And don't even think to respond to that. I see the way you are with Hayden. You're not one to talk."

I squeeze my forehead. "I'm worried about Hayden. I think she's getting involved in something that could make her a target for the wrong people. She's pissed at me for keeping things from her, and I'm worried she's going to do something reckless." I press my fingers against my eyebrows, pushing back the pressure that's building there. "The thought of anything happening to her is making me crazy."

"I hate to say it, Cade, but you're right. She is up to something."

My voice lowers menacingly. "You fucking asshole. If anything happens to her—"

"Hold on. First of all, I can't control Mira or Hayden. They're a vicious force when combined, and if that makes me a wuss, so be it. Second, it's my understanding that this —*thing*—Hayden is doing tonight is harmless. A bit of dress-up. Mira's convinced it's safe."

"Will Mira be there too?"

"Well—no. We have dinner plans with my editor, who flew in for the weekend."

"Then who will look after her? Jaeg? I haven't been able to reach him."

"Yeahhh, that's because he's out of town. Something about needing to talk to Cali's mom."

"What the fuck! Who is keeping an eye on Hayden?"

"Dude. That's your job."

"She won't let me! Whatever she's doing, it's behind my back. She's pissed as hell at me right now."

"For starters, try simmering down, or you're going to push that girl away."

"Son of a bitch," I mutter. "I've turned into my father." I stalk across my living room, turn, and stalk the other way.

"So your girlfriend's pissed at you, and you can't control her?" At my grunt of assent, he chuckles. "In that case, welcome to the club, buddy. The women we're with are smart and ruthless."

"Too smart. Too headstrong."

"Yep. That about sums it up. Wish I could help you, but Mira and I are about to walk out the door. Hayden left a while ago. I'll have Mira check in with her, but like I said, my understanding is that whatever she's doing, it's safe."

Why do I doubt that?

Chapter Thirty-Four

The goal of tonight's auction isn't completely philanthropic. The burlesque show seduces celebrities into the club, and the auction to raise funds for cancer gives them a legitimate excuse to be here. In the end, the casino rakes in an inordinate amount of money from wealthy patrons hitting the tables afterward, not to mention the profit earned once a select group of individuals visits the Bliss suites and signs on the dotted line.

I'm not sure how much longer I can take this. And I'm not referring to the club, though I am sick of the din of music and voices—the shuffle for attention. Hayden is the only one I want to spend time with. And if that's not evidence something important has happened to me, I don't know what is. Because I didn't want anything serious, and here I am in the most serious relationship of my life that's teetering on the edge of destruction because I can't separate my old life from my new one.

Hayden was right. I should have told my father to screw himself when he asked me to take the job at Blue. But then I might not have run into Hayden, and being with her has changed me. I was changing before I showed up on Blue's doorstep—sick of my old life—but she helped me round that corner.

Bliss wasn't what I signed up for when I first started working at Blue. Now that I've risen to management and obtained the coveted Blue Star designation, I'd like to step down. Because the stuff Blackwell is into is too much. Even for a jaded asshole like me.

I know what went down with Lewis's girlfriend and Cali when they worked here a couple of summers ago. That was one guy, and I thought it ended with him. But it didn't. Blackwell and Paul and William, and even Eve—they're taking advantage of people, rich or not. They're hiding the truth through subcontractors and escorts and encrypted clouds designed to destroy evidence. I've seen enough, and if Hayden weren't still working at Blue Casino, I'd quit, my father be damned. But Hayden is still here. In fact...

I scan a pair of shapely legs over at the bar—one of the pinup lookalikes that came in for the evening. This one has black hair. But the curve of leg into ass that swells over a handful of generous hip, pulling in at a trim waist...

I can only see her from behind. But behind is all I need. Goddammit.

I stand and smooth down my tie. "Excuse me, gentlemen," I say to Paul and the other men at the table in the club's lounge. "I see something I like."

The men laugh lewdly, which is exactly what I want. I need them to believe I'm picking up a beautiful woman, not hauling my infuriating girlfriend from the premises.

In a black wig, Hayden is standing beside a tall barstool, sipping a clear drink and stealthily looking around.

I lean against the bar beside her, and sense her stiffen.

"What are you doing?" I say casually, swirling the gin and tonic in my hand and taking a gulp.

Her head turns slightly. "How did you know it was me?" she says, her voice low, her mouth barely moving.

I take in the fake eyelashes and heavy makeup that, granted, gives her a different look. I might have missed identifying Hayden as the shy girl I went to school with when I first started at Blue, but I know her now. I could target her with my eyes closed based on the way the air shifts when she's in the room.

I flash her a look of irritation. "I know the shape of your body, the way you move your feet when you're nervous—the way you smell." Her chest rises on an intake of breath.

She turns her back to the bar and pulls her shoulders back, staring out at the sea of bodies in the club. "I'm here to enjoy myself. You?"

I level her a look that calls *bullshit*.

Her beautifully made-up face, which rivals any pinup poster I've ever seen, pulls into a sexy pout. For a second, I forget where I am.

Then I remember and my annoyance returns tenfold. "You shouldn't be here. And what the hell are you doing dressed like that? Are you trying to attract danger?"

"Danger? For dressing like the rest of the girls in this place? I think not. Paul's already grabbed my ass once. He and the others have no idea it's me." She pats her ridiculous fifties bouffant wig.

"Grabbed your ass," I say irritably. I blow out a breath of frustration through my nose. Of course Paul would try to touch her.

My gaze takes in her figure, her sun-streaked brown eyes, and I look away. "You may have fooled Paul, but not

296

everyone is oblivious. *I* knew it was you." I flash a mocking smile. "I'm attentive like that."

"You just know the size of my..."

I inch closer until the arm of my suit jacket brushes her creamy skin, bared at the shoulder by her halter top. "Do tell." I've been primed all week, and my patience is dwindling. I will not be held accountable for tossing her over my shoulder and hauling her out of this place.

She glares at me. "My assets. That's what you do, isn't it? Size up assets and decide whether something's worth your time? Which apparently Blue and the Bliss suites are, because you're here, working for the devil."

"As are you," I remind her. "And if we're talking *ass*-ets, then yes, I'm rather good at sizing up yours." I let my gaze drop to her beautiful breasts pushed up for my perusal, then lower it to her hips and round ass. She snaps her fingers in front of my face and I lift my eyes. "But you're wrong if you think I choose my friends based on their financial worth."

"Jaeger, Lewis," she rattles off. "You're telling me you don't choose rich friends?"

I stare at her for a beat, genuinely surprised. "I thought we were beyond this." Her glare falters and she blinks. "You know me, Hayden. My brothers have no money, and they are a huge part of my life. I don't give a fuck what someone's stock portfolio is worth."

"Your brothers have access to the family money, if they want it. And you don't have to work here and cater to Blackwell, but you do."

"As do you," I remind her again, growing more agitated by the minute. "You could choose to find a different job. The reason I'm staying is because I don't want to spend my life dependent on my father's money. I want to build something for myself."

"At the expense of others." She glances stubbornly away. "Go back to Paul, Adam. I wouldn't want to interfere in your fortune making. Besides, you're not the only one who's working."

My jaw shifts. "You're off duty. You have no reason to be here. Blackwell kicked you off this event." Her spine stiffens. "And you shouldn't be dressed like that. Here. Tonight."

Suspicion fills her eyes. "Why not?"

I walked into that one.

I can't tell her that Paul and William, and the rest of the Bliss-supported execs, are recruiting this evening. Not simply for new Bliss members, but for burlesque dancers too. "Trust me, okay? I need for you to go home. I'll meet you there in a couple of hours. Three tops."

She turns to me, her body pressing close, but not close enough. "Well, *I* need for you to tell me what's going on, but you won't. So I'm staying."

My jaw tightens. I might explode. No one infuriates me more than Hayden. I lean forward until my lips are inches from hers. "Stay. Out. Of. Trouble."

Her eyes dart between my mouth and my gaze, then narrow. "Don't you threaten me, Adam Cade. I have every right to be here."

"Is that why you're in disguise?" Her lips part, and then she presses them closed. "Remember what I said." I stride away before I drag her away.

I return to the exec table where my colleagues are entertaining a few athletes, plus one billionaire who owns an island—all here for Bliss. If Blackwell hadn't been so adamant we attend tonight, I wouldn't have. But it's a good thing I did, or I wouldn't have known Hayden was here too.

I ease back in my seat and tap my fingers on the table,

signaling the waitress with my other hand for another drink. *Stubborn, stubborn woman.*

Every few seconds, I glance at the bar, keeping an eye on her. Just once, I wish she'd listen to me. But I can't blame her. I'm lying by omission. I wouldn't be happy with me either.

William's attention falls on Hayden. "Beautiful girl you were talking to. I didn't see her in the show, but she should have been." He waggles his brow. "Or maybe a part of Bliss?"

"Nasty disposition, that one." I pound the last of my drink. "She wouldn't fit."

William's gaze continues to rake over Hayden. "You sure? Maybe she just needs the right touch."

I squeeze my empty glass and rest my elbow over the back of the velvet club chair I'm in. "She's a lesbian."

William's mouth twists and he glances again, as though it were possible to read that sort of thing. "Really? Still—"

Jesus, what will it take? "William, she's not interested. Her girlfriend was right next to her." He opens his mouth to say something, and I cut him off. "No, she's not interested in a threesome."

His eyes brighten. "With you, but—"

For the love of God. "You think I can't get a lady to consider it?" I smile roguishly.

He frowns. "You're a good-looking bastard. I don't suppose you get too many rejections."

Except from the woman who would prefer hanging me by my balls to sleeping with me right now.

* * *

I've kept an eye on Pinup Hayden for the last thirty minutes. Three different men have approached her. The current pair hovers like vultures, causing a frown to mar her beautiful features. I intended to remain at the club until the midnight grand opening party, but I can't sit here and watch Hayden be harassed by idiots.

"Please excuse me." I stand, and William looks up, then over at Hayden.

"I thought you said she was a lesbian." He sounds annoyed.

"I must have been mistaken. I'm about to rectify that." I nod to the others. "Gentlemen? See you upstairs in the suite."

William's mouth hooks down on one side as I turn and walk away, but I don't care what he thinks. One of the men near Hayden is touching her shoulder with his fat finger, and I'm about to rip it off his body.

I approach the bar and reach around Hayden's waist, drawing her to my side. "Ready to go?"

She glances up, her expression about the same as William's a second ago. To resist is futile. I'm not leaving her side.

She must realize this, because she plasters on a smile. "It was nice to meet you," she says to the men.

"You can't leave." The one with long hair and a ridiculous scarf glares at me. "We were just getting to know each other. I'd be happy to give you a ride home," he says to her.

"Hell no," I say, and walk away, pulling Hayden along with me.

"Was that necessary?" She skips to keep up as we make our way to the club's exit.

"Yes."

Outside the club, Hayden stops abruptly. "Adam, you're

being a caveman again. I don't need you to protect me from jackasses like that. I had it under control."

"Did you?" I turn on her. "Because it didn't seem like you were comfortable over there."

Her brow furrows. "Well, no, but I still had it under control. That wasn't the first time a man has come on too strong. I didn't need rescuing."

I look up in exasperation. "Hayden, this is more than two guys. I can't express how badly I need for you to be home safe. William's been asking about you. He doesn't know it's you, but that doesn't mean he won't figure it out. You're courting trouble by being here, dressed like that. *Please* go home."

She studies my face. "You're really worried?"

"Yes," I say emphatically.

She crosses her arms. "I'm pissed at you." She lets out a loud sigh. "I can't believe I'm considering this." She gives me a heated stare—one I wish I could say was sexual, but which I fear might be the look a black widow gives her mate before she bites his head off. "I have a good reason for being here tonight, and you're ruining it for me."

"Do I want to know what it is?"

"It doesn't have to do with picking up men, if that's what you're worried about."

I graze my thumb along her jaw. "I didn't think it did. I trust you."

"Well," she says huffily. "I wish I could say the same about you."

I grab her hands and wrap them around her back, locking them in place at the curve of her spine and pressing her chest to mine. "If you didn't trust me, you wouldn't do as I ask." I kiss her mouth gently and let go of her hands.

She wavers on her feet and grabs my arms for balance.

Her gaze goes from dazed to angry in a flash. "Don't use my attraction to you to get me to do what you want. You underestimated me back there. This is totally unnecessary. I'm not helpless, Adam."

I frown. "I don't think you're helpless. That doesn't stop me from wanting to protect you. It's a dormant instinct for me, I know, but it seems to be functioning and lively where you're concerned."

She releases a sigh and now looks really pissed. "Damn you. That was the sweetest thing you've ever said." She eases in closer and stares up. "When you get home, you're going to tell me everything that's going on."

I thought Hayden would be safer not knowing about Bliss. That keeping her off Blackwell and Paul's radar would protect her from the threats I've received. But I underestimated Hayden's ability to get into trouble. It just might be more dangerous for her to poke around in the dark.

"Agreed." I kiss her again. "You need a ride? I have a little time before I need to be somewhere."

"No," she says, reluctantly. "I brought my car. I had one drink; I'll be fine. Go back to those horrible men you work with."

She starts to pull away and I grab her hand, bringing her back into my arms. "I *will* tell you everything."

She nods, and this time when she steps away I let her go. "Oh, I know you will," she says over her shoulder. "Otherwise, you'll pay for it. Painfully." Her hips swish-swish in agitation, and I am helpless to look away. She's in a tight pencil skirt and candy-red heels, and she is killing me.

I'd like for all of this to be over so that I can go home with her, but I have a few more things to take care of. Looks like I'll be returning to the group sooner than I thought, since Hayden doesn't need a ride.

I dial the number for security. "A beautiful pinup brunette in red heels will be exiting the back entrance. Make sure she gets to her car safely."

Blue or Hayden will be the death of me. My bet's on Hayden.

Chapter Thirty-Five

William stays back to check in with a few of the dancers from the club, and the rest of us head for Bliss and the grand opening party the casino is hosting. We enter the crowded suite, and several burlesque dancers are already mingling with the crowd. There are other women there too. Considering their beauty and sophisticated but sexy attire, my guess is these other women are the professional escorts. They don't appear to be attached to any one man, and all of them are near guards I hired.

I grab a glass of champagne and talk with the CEO of a popular hotel chain. He's in his mid-fifties and wearing a wedding ring, but his gaze keeps drifting to a redheaded burlesque dancer.

"So I told the son of my business associate," the CEO says, "we don't allow prostitutes in our hotels." He glances at the redhead again and grins. "Not that there's anything wrong with paying for beauty. But our hotels have a reputation to uphold, and—"

The CEO says something else, but I stop paying attention. Because two additional bodyguards enter through the suite's elevator, along with more escorts.

I find it strange that they're entering via the emergency exit. In fact, the more I study the people inside the suite, something seems off. The escorts are sitting on love seats or standing stiffly off to the side chatting with guests, but they appear reserved...almost nervous.

I excuse myself from the CEO, and approach the escort nearest me. She's dressed like the others, very classy and pretty in a low-cut red dress, and there's a bodyguard a few feet away. I sit on the loveseat beside her, and her eyes dart around, her body tensing.

I had nothing to do with hiring escorts for Bliss. Paul said he'd found the perfect solution and no longer needed my help. I didn't find it odd at the time, particularly since I wanted no part of it. Now I'm wishing I paid more attention.

"I'm Adam," I say to the woman. "And you are?"

"Victoria," she says with a heavy Latin accent. South American, if I'm not mistaken.

"Pleasure to meet you. Are you a guest, or..."

"I work," she says shyly.

I nod, considering. "Have you been in Lake Tahoe long?"

She glances at the bodyguard a few feet away, then back at me, but not looking me in the eye. "No."

I peer at the guard I vaguely remember hiring. He was one of about ten Blackwell requested. "Do you plan to stay?"

She wrings her hands together. "Ye-yes."

That didn't come out confident. And it didn't sound like a person happy to be here either. "How old are you, Victoria?"

She hesitates. "Eighteen." This time she looks down.

It's difficult to tell, because she's dressed as a mature, seductive woman, but she doesn't come across as seductive, or secure, or eighteen.

"Have you seen much of Lake Tahoe? Taken any tours?" I'm talking to keep her engaged, because something isn't right here.

She hesitates a moment, as though translating my question in her head. "No," she says, and tucks a lock of hair behind her ear, avoiding eye contact again.

"You haven't been to the lake?" Lake Tahoe is the reason people travel from all over the world to visit.

"I not stay long," she says in broken English, then looks hesitantly to her guard. "I here for work."

"I see." But I really don't. This conversation is getting stranger by the minute. "What part of town are you living in?"

The guard steps forward. "All right, Victoria," he says, cutting off the conversation. "Give the other ladies a chance to talk to the gentlemen." He grabs her lightly by the elbow and guides her away, leading her to the elevator.

What the fuck was that?

I lean forward, elbows on my knees, and study each of the women inside the suite, including the new ones who arrived a few minutes ago. A couple of them look comfortable talking to the men in the room, and the burlesque dancers seem totally at ease, but the others appear just as uptight and nervous as Victoria. And they seem to be rotating in and out through the elevator instead of the front door.

I spot Paul across the room. He's talking to a guest—another retired athlete, by the look of him. I stand and walk over.

"Pardon the interruption," I say to the guest, and turn to Paul. "May I speak to you for a moment?"

Paul flags a waiter and grabs another drink for his guest, then waves over one of the burlesque dancers. His guest seems happy to replace him with the beautiful woman, and Paul and I move into a corner.

I lower my voice, my expression mild. "Where did you find the escorts?"

Paul nods across the room at another person who just walked in. "Gorgeous, aren't they? A little green, but that won't take long to wear off."

I keep my anger in check, but after tonight, it's a challenge. "You could say that. The one I spoke to appeared scared."

Paul's satisfied smirk drops, and his gaze slides to me. "They're trained to be friendly. Which one was it?"

"Trained? Are we discussing pets, or women?"

"Is there a difference?" At my look, Paul straightens the sleeve of his shirt beneath his jacket. "Don't be uptight, Cade. They're professional escorts. They're paid to be pleasant and friendly."

I nod toward the back of the room. "Why are they entering through the emergency elevator and not the front door?"

He chuckles. "You seem overly curious. Interested in one of them?"

"Answer the question."

This time Paul frowns. "It's more secure."

"How are beautiful women crossing the casino floor a security risk? I would think they'd be a draw for the casino."

He shrugs noncommittally. "We wouldn't want to lose one of them."

Both of us stare at the crowd for a moment, my unease growing.

I rub my jaw. "Let me ask you something. Were these women brought into the country to fill the escort positions?"

Paul grins, his gaze flicking to mine. "You're a sharp one, Cade. That's why we brought you on board. And because you've been in the business your entire life, you know how things are run."

He turns toward me and his expression shifts from charming guest greeter to cold businessman. "Our stable of escorts are"—his head tilts and he glances up unseeing, as though thinking—"exotic, from all over the world. These women wanted to come to the States, and Blackwell's connections made that possible. The ladies live a couple of blocks away—off-site, just how Blackwell wanted it. They're provided for and protected twenty-four-seven." He chuckles. "It's a damn sorority house, filled with beautiful, sexy women—can you imagine? I have it in mind to make my way over there and inspect the pillow fighting."

I ignore his attempt at humor, my gut churning with his words.

"Don't worry," Paul continues. "We have the best guards looking out for them, thanks to you and Blackwell. All we have to do is call up to the house, and an escort is sent whenever we want."

I nod slowly, as though this is fine, when it's the opposite. "Are they paid for their time?"

Paul checks his watch, and I can tell I'm about to lose him. "The guy who brought the women in supplies them with whatever they need, and they work for him. Net-net, they're ours for two years. If we like some of them, we can keep them longer." Paul's eyes narrow at the expression on my face. I might be shooting him a death glare. "Don't get your panties in a bunch. It happens all the time. These women *wanted* to get away from whatever miserable life they had. Think of it as a charity."

"To be a sex slave?"

Paul laughs outright. "Oh, come on. Let's not go that far. You know how women are. They like *things*. And these women are given designer clothing, introduced to rich, influential men. I wouldn't be surprised if we lost a few of them to powerful Bliss members who wanted exclusive access."

The heat of my anger burns the back of my neck. I look away before I hit Paul.

"Look, Cade, I've already told you. The boss's friends aren't people you want to cross. Stop asking questions." He waves around. "Just look at these women. They're ripe and stunning. They've saved this venture a ton of money—money that will go back into our pockets at the end of the year. Remember that."

"As long as the bottom line doesn't suffer."

"Exactly," Paul says, missing my sarcasm. He raises his hand as if to slap me on the shoulder, and drops it at the black look I level at him.

He glances over my shoulder. "The quarterback you brought in at the last minute just arrived. Why don't you bring him back? Give him a tour. Introduce him to some of the ladies."

Gabe Aldridge spots me and moves toward the center of the room. He's a middle-aged retired quarterback with a good reputation in the sports industry. "You're right. He'd love to meet these women."

"That's the spirit." Paul walks off, and I take a deep breath, peering around the room. I don't know how I missed it when I first arrived, but I'm seeing it now.

My hands shake with unbanked anger. This is all wrong. It has been from the moment I agreed to play a role in Bliss. Hayden was right. She mistrusted Blackwell from the beginning. Challenged him. I thought he was like my father—power hungry and disinterested, bending a few of the rules to suit himself. But Blackwell is nothing like my father. Ethan Cade would never support unscrupulous or inhumane activities. Like human trafficking.

I'm only thankful I got Hayden out of the casino when I did. I don't want to be caught up in this mess, but it would be a million times worse if she were here.

Chapter Thirty-Six

Hayden

I walk across the parking garage, my heels clicking against the concrete floor. I can't believe I'm leaving Blue. It took Mira two hours to do my hair and makeup, and I never got what I came for. But darn Adam, I couldn't say no with him looking so desperate for me to leave. He truly believed I was in danger by being there. I thought he'd burst a blood vessel if I stayed. That's the only reason I agreed to go. Doesn't mean I'm not still furious with him.

I made zero inroads into finding out about the grand opening party the vendor accidentally mentioned to Nessa, and I made sure to chat up everyone at the bar. Not a single person had heard about it. Was it canceled?

Before Adam hauled me out, I'd meant to check on the Bliss suites. I dressed so that no one would recognize me. Technically, I could still go up there. Adam didn't say anything about staying away from the hotel rooms; he wanted me to leave the club. And okay, I highly doubt he wants me near the suites, given our arguments regarding

Bliss, but he's put me in a bad position. I told Mira I'd check out the suites tonight, and it's probably the only time I can get away with it.

I stop in the middle of the parking garage and glance back. I'm in a wig and heavy makeup, and an outfit I would never wear. Not even William or Paul recognized me. Adam did, but he has a freakish sense for the shape of my ass.

I know where the Bliss suites are located; I could go there and scope things out before anyone realizes it. The guards wouldn't recognize me as the human resources director they've turned away these last few weeks. And it would put my mind at ease to have checked out the one lead I managed to find.

I turn around and head back in, speed-walking as fast as I can in my platform stilettos across the casino floor. Adam's afraid for my safety, but I've been taking care of myself since I left this town, and I'll take care of myself tonight too.

I make my way to the elevator bank before I change my mind—only I'm not alone.

The man in the dark suit standing in front of the elevator doors looks over. And it's William.

Dammit.

"Hey, beautiful!" He glances past me. "Where's Adam —the guy you left with?" he says, because he clearly hasn't figured out who I am. William thinks I'm one of the pinup girls here tonight. He doesn't realize Adam and I know each other, or that William knows me, for that matter.

"Oh, I decided to stay." I use a girlish voice I hope disguises my normal one, and it sounds ridiculous. Not that it puts off William.

"Tell me he didn't leave you?"

"Um...sort of?"

William slides his arm around my shoulders. "That idiot. Allow me to fix this. I was just heading up to an exclusive party in one of the suites. Be my guest. There will be champagne and appetizers, and plenty of stimulating conversation. I promise." He grins widely, his gaze focused in the direction of my cleavage.

William wouldn't be talking to me and checking out my boobs if he recognized me. Okay, maybe he'd be checking out my boobs, but he for sure hasn't recognized me. This could work. William is a Blue Star and he wants to bring me to a party in one of the suites. Which is exactly where I want to be. And if that suite is a part of Bliss? Even better.

"I'd love to."

* * *

The party William takes me to is, in fact, at the Bliss location. And I am blown away. This is nothing like the penthouse suites on the other side of the hotel floor. The suite we enter is huge, just as the plans from the facility manager's office indicated, and so elaborate and beautiful I'm afraid to touch anything. Or spill my champagne, which is Dom Pérignon, of course.

Sensual music plays through invisible speakers, and my heels press into plush white area rugs so soft that I sink when I walk. The sound of glasses clinking at the bar and the chatter of men fill my senses—and cause the air to crackle with an energy that leaves stinging goose bumps along my arms. It's caged and aggressive, and if I weren't here for a good reason, I'd hightail it out. But I'm here because of Blackwell and the Blue Stars, and because my instincts tell me what they're doing inside this casino is wrong.

I take in a shallow breath and spot Adam in a corner of the room talking to a huge guy who's got to be some kind of professional athlete. Adam hasn't seen me, or he'd be on his way over, riding my ass to leave. The suite is crowded, and if I don't want him catching me before I've had a chance to look around, I had better move to another room.

"How about a tour?" I say to William.

"Whatever the lady wishes." He gestures to a room on our right and I enter it, happy to be someplace Adam can't see me, though I'm not sure this room is any better.

One by one, William shows me each of the bedrooms and shares his knowledge of drugs that reduce sexual inhibition, while I attempt to appear casually interested. William also asks if I want to take one of the rooms for a test drive, but that's beside the point. Adam might kill me when he finds out I stayed after I said I would leave Blue. But not before *I* kill *him*.

Adam is involved in Bliss, which I knew, but this suite isn't your typical eccentric hotel experience. All of the rooms are elaborate and sexual in nature, with dance poles and crazy bathrooms designed for Roman orgies, but the room that really stands out is the one with the sex dungeon. I know for a fact that the casino doesn't own a license for sex-oriented business. We had to make sure the burlesque dancers didn't remove pertinent pieces of clothing during tonight's show for that reason.

Mira and Tyler called the suite they'd found several months ago the "fifty shades suite," and they weren't kidding. Only, I'm pretty sure that whatever Mira and Tyler came across, it was nothing compared to Bliss. Mira described the other suite as large, with custom cabinets filled with sex toys—not an entire room devoted to chaining someone up. What the hell?

William and I return to the living area, and I feel it. That prickle of awareness that centers in my shoulders and spreads down my chest, sending heat to my lower belly—the sense I get when Adam is near.

I scan the room and find him staring at me. The athlete is still with him, but so are Eve and Blackwell. And Blackwell doesn't look happy. In fact, he looks like he always does around me. Angry. Annoyed.

Does Blackwell recognize me?

Chapter Thirty-Seven

Adam

Gabe greets me with a handshake after Paul walks away. "So this is Bliss?" he says, and looks around.

"Where all your dreams come true," I respond dryly.

Gabe eyes the other men, then does a leisurely sweep of the women and the living space. He raises an eyebrow. "Excellent taste."

"Indeed. I'll show you the rooms, but first, I'd like to introduce you to Joseph Blackwell, the CEO. He just walked in and he doesn't typically attend casino events, preferring to remain in the background. I'd like to catch him before he leaves."

Gabe grabs a glass of champagne off a passing server, one hand tucked in his slacks, his demeanor casual and collected. He'd make a perfect fit for Bliss.

Blackwell catches sight of us as we approach, his gaze ever calculating.

"Gabe Aldridge," I say, "this is Joseph Blackwell, the mastermind behind Bliss." I rattle off Gabe's stats from when he played in the NFL, as well as his current professional accolades. "I was just about to regale Gabe with the virtues of Bliss."

Blackwell chuckles. "Bliss has many virtues. This magnificent suite, for one, and other intrinsic qualities as well." He gestures to a group of women sitting on a sofa a few feet away. "Our women are stunning, are they not?"

"Exquisite," Gabe says.

"They are unlike any you've had. They are...how shall I say this...*fresh*. In fact, a few of them have their virginity intact." Blackwell says this as though extolling the merits of a fine wine.

I choke on my champagne. "Excuse me," I mutter, attempting to collect myself.

What the fuck?

"That *is* interesting." Gabe glances over, his expression bland.

"I was unaware," I say, keeping my tone level.

Blackwell looks about the room proudly. "Bliss is elite in luxury and pleasure. It doesn't get better than this. Anything you want is at your fingertips."

"For a hefty price," Gabe says.

"But isn't that life?" Blackwell asks. "We pay for quality, do we not? And the Bliss suites—the service and women it provides—are of unparalleled quality."

Gabe swirls his champagne and swallows the last of it. "And the women? They've agreed to selling their virginity?"

Blackwell reaches out to a passing server and grabs a fresh glass of Dom, exchanging it for Gabe's old glass. "Of course. The women are well provided for, with everything they could ever want."

Except possibly their freedom.

Gabe nods and scans the room as though looking at the

women with renewed interest. His gaze stops near the door. "And the burlesque dancers?"

Blackwell and I look in the direction he indicates...and *son of a bitch,* it's Hayden. Here.

How the hell?

"The burlesque women can be bought as well," Blackwell says.

"The brunette near the door appeals to me."

My fists clench. Goddammit, what is Hayden doing? She was supposed to leave forty minutes ago.

Blackwell's brow rises. "I can see to it that you have her—"

"Not that one," I blurt, then blink back my panic. I'm not thinking clearly, and my voice sure as hell isn't level anymore. "She's not supposed to be here," I say, but it comes out tense and angry.

Blackwell's gaze takes in my features, and I wonder how much I'm giving away. "Oh? How did she end up here?"

I don't respond.

He stares for another long moment, then snaps his fingers.

Eve glides closer. "Yes?"

"Please bring over the woman in the black wig near the door."

She smiles. "My pleasure."

Gabe glances at me. I sense his concern, but I don't look, afraid I'll give away more than I already have.

Eve speaks to Hayden and she nods warily. She and William walk over, and William shakes Gabe's hand after introductions are made.

"Gabe wanted to meet the charming young woman you're with, William," Blackwell says.

William's smile falters, and he glances at Hayden. "She's my guest tonight. This is..."

"Sophia," Hayden supplies in an unnaturally high voice, and I roll my eyes.

"Sophia, you say?" Blackwell's gaze slides down her body. "Or is it Hayden?"

Hayden stiffens, her eyes darting to me.

Blackwell turns my way. "What is she doing here?"

"Leaving," I say, and grab her arm.

He holds up his hand. "Just a moment, Adam." He faces William. "Has Hayden seen the suites?"

William, a step behind the rest of us, stares. "Hayden?" His gaze rakes her body and he finally appears to clue in to what Blackwell realized the moment he set eyes on her. Our CEO may be a dick, but he is a smart bastard.

William looks back at Blackwell, chagrined. "Yes, sir. I thought she was one of the pinups here tonight."

"I'm confused," Gabe says. "I thought her name was Sophia."

Blackwell glares at Hayden menacingly. "She will be *no one* soon."

I flatten my hand on Hayden's lower back and push her forward. "I'll escort her out."

"See that you take her to the security guards," Blackwell says, a threat in his tone. "In the meantime, Eve will be happy to take care of Gabe. Won't you, Eve?"

Eve's face blanks, but she quickly replaces it with a smile. "Yes, of course."

I don't wait for Gabe's response. I head to the door with Hayden, then stop abruptly. The guards standing nearest the front are staring us down. One of them remains at the door, but the other moves in our direction.

Somehow, Blackwell signaled them. I don't know how, but he did.

"Hurry," I whisper to Hayden. "The elevator."

We cut across the living room to the emergency elevator and I press my hand against the keypad. The screen turns blue, recognizing my fingerprint, and I punch in the code I was given days ago—a second before my shoulder is yanked back. I spin around.

"Where do you think you're going?" Paul eyes Hayden maliciously.

The soft ding of the elevator chimes and I hear the doors slowly open.

I make a fist and drive an uppercut to Paul's chin. With my right hand—the one wearing the Blue Star ring.

Paul screeches and stumbles back. I tear off the ring, toss it at him, and shove Hayden in the elevator. I pound the door-close button about a hundred times, and the doors finally react. They close slowly, blocking out the party, the people staring at the commotion we've caused—and the guard still headed our way. Paul, who's bleeding from his chin and lip, talks rapidly on his phone, glaring at me as the doors finally shut.

There are only two floors this elevator goes to: the casino floor, and a regular guest floor the casino uses as a decoy for its Bliss members in case of an emergency.

I hit the decoy floor, and round on Hayden. "What in the hell are you doing here?"

"Don't talk to me like that!"

I take a deep breath. "Explain, before I lose my mind."

"Well, to be specific, you told me to leave the club, not Blue."

"You're using semantics on me now? I asked you to leave for the very reason we're running away from the suite.

Blackwell knows it's you. Do you understand what that means?"

She bites the corner of her lip. "Right. Well, I hadn't counted on that. I didn't think he'd be here, and I certainly didn't think he'd recognize me."

I growl in frustration and stare at the ceiling. "That was your plan? To go unrecognized?"

"And to gather evidence," she says. "I even brought my phone to take pictures. But, aside from kinky sex stuff the casino isn't licensed for, I didn't find much."

"Oh there's plenty of illegal stuff." Her gaze is questioning. "I'll tell you about it later," I say, as the elevator dings for our floor.

The doors open and I grab Hayden's hand. I look both ways down the hall, and catch a guard exiting one of the stairwells, his chest rising and falling on heavy breaths. "Fuck."

"Who's that?" Hayden says.

"Vido. Ex-military, petty theft—we gotta go." I pull her in the opposite direction, practically dragging her.

Between her tight skirt and five-inch heels, we'll never outrun him. "Take those things off!" I gesture at her feet.

She stares at me like I'm crazy, so I reach down, lift her foot, and pull off the damn shoe, along with its mate, shoving them in the pockets of my suit jacket. I grab the side of her skirt and tear it down the seam. "Run!"

The guard is almost on us, and this time, Hayden does as I say. We run for the opposite end, and enter the other stairwell. After flying down a flight of stairs, I pull her through the door to the next floor and we run for an elevator that's blessedly open.

I punch the button for the bottom level, and lean over once the doors close.

"Why are they after us?" she asks, her breathing heavy.

"Because you were right." I straighten and pull out my phone. I type out a quick text and tuck my phone away. "The Bliss venture is not legitimate, and the people providing Blackwell with drugs and illegal women are very bad news."

"You mean undocumented women?"

"I don't support that, Hayden. I never have."

Her beautiful face contorts in anger. "You supported it by going along with it!"

The elevator doors open and I lead Hayden away from one of the main exits and toward a back hallway. We pass through a kitchen behind a restaurant. Workers look at us, and I check over my shoulder to make sure no one is following. I open a door to the outside, and the scent of rotten meat hits us from a garbage bin the restaurants uses.

A black Escalade rounds the corner and screeches to a halt a few feet away.

Hayden tugs on my arm. "Hurry! We have to go back."

"It's okay." I guide her to the Escalade. "It's my security detail. I hired them after I decided to take Paul's warnings seriously."

Hayden climbs in the backseat barefoot, and I tuck in beside her. The driver tears out of the back alley. "You're not going home tonight," I say. "It isn't safe." She stares ahead and nods, seemingly stunned. I wrap my arm around her shoulders. "It's going to be okay."

She looks up. "How? I thought it was only Blackwell. That I'd find something at the casino I could take to the police. But the women...and from what you just said..."

"There are others working with Blackwell who are much more dangerous."

She twists to face me. "Then we need to go to the police

now. Before Blackwell and the Blue Stars get away with everything like they did last time. They know how to make it look as though the suites don't exist."

My phone vibrates, and I recognize it as an incoming call. I reach inside my pocket and check the caller ID, noting two missed calls from the same contact.

My forehead furrows. It's one in the morning. Why is the family lawyer calling? "I've got to take this," I say.

"Adam," Bill Stevens says into the phone, sounding tired. "I apologize for the late phone call." He pauses. "It's your father... You need to go to the hospital."

Chapter Thirty-Eight

Hayden

A dam answers the phone and I swear the color drains from his face. And we were high on color to begin with after running through the casino in a matter of minutes.

He rattles off directions for the driver to take us to the hospital, and I reach for his hand. "What happened?"

"I don't know." He stares out the window and swallows heavily. "That was the family lawyer. He called to tell me my father is in the hospital." He gives me a quick smile that barely moves his lips. "I'm sure he's fine."

But the entire way to the hospital, Adam stares out the window, an extremely serious look on his face. He doesn't believe his own words.

I slip on my shoes as we pull up to the emergency entrance, and tug off my wig, shaking out my hair. I wouldn't call my look respectable, because there's a hell of a lot of boob and leg in the house, but at least I'm sporting my natural color and not the giant black wig Mira put on me.

We step out of the car and I begin to shiver. It's the middle of the night and the temperature has dropped. Adam drapes his coat over my shoulders and I slip my arms through the sleeves, soaking up the warmth he left behind. He grabs my hand and we head in through the automatic sliding doors.

Adam checks in with a receptionist and she directs us to a private room. Partway down the hall, his footsteps falter. His brothers are standing outside the room.

Levi is staring at the ceiling, his fingers pressed to his forehead, and Hunter is leaning against the wall, looking stricken. The other two have their backs to us, speaking to someone.

This isn't good. Not good at all. I squeeze Adam's hand and he moves forward, his stride steady.

Levi turns and sees us. He breathes in deeply and glances away as if to compose himself. Adam stops in front of him.

"He was sick," Levi says.

Adam glances at the hospital room door. "Father was fine the last time we saw him."

Levi shakes his head. "He wasn't."

Wes and Bran move closer. "I don't understand," Adam says.

Levi squeezes the back of his neck. "He—he had pancreatic cancer. Never told us."

Adam's hand inside mine begins to shake. "Had. You said *had*."

Levi nods and presses his lips together. "He passed away about thirty minutes ago."

Adam drops my hand and grabs his older brother by the front of his shirt. "Why the fuck didn't you tell me!"

"I didn't know! I got the call just like you," Levi says

325

angrily. "And what about you? You're the one who keeps in touch with him."

Adam releases his brother and paces. "No. Not lately." He glances at me, and then looks away. "Work...I've been busy with work." He rubs his forehead. "Were you here when he..."

Levi shakes his head. "None of us were."

I walk over and put my arms around Adam. "Where is he?" he says, but Levi's back is to us now.

"In the room," Wes answers.

Adam stares at the door, then looks down at me. "I need to see him."

"Do you want me to go with you?"

"No." He pulls his fingers through his hair, ruffling what was combed and polished, even after our dash through the casino. He eases out of my arms and walks to the partially open door. Hunter nudges him lightly as he passes, and Adam glances up in acknowledgment. Then he enters the hospital room.

How could this have happened? We just saw his father a few weeks ago at the cocktail party. The man seemed fine. Thin, maybe? I don't know. I'd never met him before. Adam said he wasn't close to his father. None of them were...and the man had been trying to reconnect with them.

Oh God.

Adam exits the hospital room a few minutes later. His eyes are red and his face is completely motionless. He looks like he's in shock.

I reach for his hand, and he pulls me close—so close there's no space between us. "I'm so sorry," I say. His chest hitches, but no sound comes out of his mouth.

After a moment, he releases me, and all of his brothers

are staring. They quickly look away. "Is there anyone we should call?" Adam's voice is rough.

A woman I hadn't noticed steps forward. She looks like she's in her sixties. Very pretty, with silver hair. It's one in the morning, but she's wearing a pale skirt suit. "It's already been taken care of," she says softly.

"Thank you, Esther." Adam steps forward and gives her a hug, and she pats his back. He returns to my side. "Why didn't he tell us?"

She smiles weakly. "He didn't want to worry you. Didn't want his last months to be about the illness. He was trying to bring you together. But I think he realized he'd let things go on too long."

I sense Adam's body shaking, and based on the expressions of his brothers, they're falling apart inside too.

Levi clears his throat. "What do we do? For the services."

"It was prearranged. Right now, you should go home." She smiles at me, dabbing her watery eyes with a tissue. "I'll be in touch."

Adam hugs each of his brothers silently. Quiet words are spoken that I can't hear, and then one by one, they drift toward the exit. Alone, except for Adam, who has me. We make our way to the street. The Escalade is idling a few feet from the entrance.

"We should take you somewhere safe," he says.

Is he crazy? He just lost his father. I'm not going anywhere without him, but I don't argue. He'll figure it out when I don't leave his side.

We enter the car, and I turn to him. "I'm so sorry. What can I do?"

He shakes his head, his expression bleak. "I don't know anything right now."

327

I've seen Adam wanting and naked, angry and red-faced at something I've done, but never with this desolate look on his face. I haven't lost a parent, and he's lost both. I don't know how to comfort him, but I'm going to try.

Our phones buzz, one right after the other. It takes me a second to figure out what's going on. And then I remember.

There's an entire shitstorm of drama happening that I completely forgot about after we arrived at the hospital.

"It's from Mira." I check the text. "She says the police are at Lewis's house. They found information against Blackwell. I'll tell her they'll have to talk to the police without us."

"No. We should go." He's staring out the window, his hand limp in mine.

I shake my head. "They'll understand, Adam."

He looks over. "We're going to Lewis's. There's more you don't know, and it's time you found out."

Chapter Thirty-Nine

T wo police cars sit in the driveway of Lewis's place as we exit the Escalade. Adam and I walk up the steps to the porch and I see the entire gang through the large picture window: Lewis, Gen, Mira, Tyler, Jaeger, Cali, Nessa, and Zach. The police officers are standing in the room as well, with clipboards in their hands. They appear to be writing down information.

Mira greets us at the door, wearing a black summer dress, and ushers us to the island separating Lewis's kitchen from the living room—the only place left to sit. She hands me a glass of water and I offer some to Adam, but he shakes his head.

"It worked," Gen says to Adam after we settle. "Jeb's friend was able to record the conversation with Blackwell. They're obtaining a warrant for the house where Blackwell is keeping the escorts."

Jeb is Gen's father. "What is she talking about?" I ask Adam.

He's leaning against the counter, his head in his hands. "I spoke to Lewis a couple of weeks ago. Asked him why

Sallee Construction wasn't involved in the Bliss suite remodel. It seemed suspicious to both of us, and he put me in touch with Gen's dad, who helped with the Drake Peterson conviction."

"You organized this...without talking to me?"

"Adam was already a target," Lewis says, looking over from where he's sitting on the couch with Gen. "He didn't want you involved until we knew more and had support from the police."

Mira reaches across the island and touches my arm. "It all happened so quickly. Tyler and I were out to dinner and just found out too. So did the rest."

One of the police detectives introduces himself and closes his clipboard. "Joseph Blackwell is under arrest. As your friend mentioned, we're putting together a search warrant for the apartment building where they're keeping the women."

Gen closes her eyes and shakes her head. "I can't believe Blackwell did this." Lewis tightens his arm around her shoulders. "What happened to me was bad, but *sex trafficking?*"

"A federal offense," the policeman says, and hands each of them a card. "Contact us if you have any concerns. We'll give you updates as they come in."

The detectives leave and I rest my head on Adam's shoulder, wrapping my arm around his waist. "You should have told me," I say softly.

He breathes into my hair. "Didn't want you on Blackwell's radar."

I look into his face. "I should have trusted you to do the right thing, but you need to trust me too. We could have talked and I would have supported you."

He nods. "I didn't find out about the escorts until

tonight. There were threats by Paul before—" He shakes his head. "I just didn't want you hurt. I couldn't have stood that."

Adam was put in a tough position. I understand, but I'm not okay with him keeping things from me.

Before I can respond, Mira speaks up. "Just think, Hayden. If you hadn't sucked up your pride all those weeks ago and made nice with Adam, the police wouldn't have such good material."

Adam looks at me. "What's she talking about, *sucking up your pride?*"

Time slows. Adam lost his father tonight; he's exhausted, vulnerable, and I can read the thoughts crossing his mind. "Something silly in the beginning. It was nothing."

Mira rests her chin on her hand, leaning over the counter, and clearly not getting the tension she's causing. "Hayden was supposed to get close to you so that we could figure out if Blue was still running the suite Tyler and I found, but I never thought you guys would get *that* close." She snorts, laughing, and I glare at her. "What? You guys are cute."

"You're not helping." I turn to Adam. "Don't listen to her...Adam?"

He stands abruptly, wavering slightly on his feet. "I have to go."

"Wait." I stand beside him. "I'm going with you."

"No," he says forcefully.

I step back. "Adam, what Mira and I talked about all those weeks ago has nothing to do with you and me now."

"Doesn't it?"

My eyes widen. Anger radiates from his body.

Jaeger walks over. He's one of Adam's best friends and

he must have read the hurt on Adam's face. "What's going on?"

Adam swivels his head and sneers at Jaeger. "Protecting her again?"

"Concerned," Jaeger says. "For both of you." He peers at me, a question in his gaze.

Adam has been frustrated with me before, but never like this. He took everything Mira said the wrong way, and I know why. "Tonight's been horrible. Please just listen to me." I look at Jaeger, who's still watching us. "His father—"

"This isn't about my father!" Adam snaps. "Was it all a lie?" He waves between us. "I was a dick to you in the past, but I never thought you'd stoop to this. Well played, Hayden. Kick the jerk while he's down."

"No! It's not like that." Tears fill my eyes. Not because of his words, though I'm not too fond of those either, but because he's pushing me away—using this as an excuse. "You're doing this on purpose. I don't know why, but you are. If you'd just stop and think, you would know how I feel about you."

He shoulders past Jaeger and stalks out the door.

"Go after him," I say. "Don't leave him alone. He—His father... Just go with him. Please."

Jaeger glances at Cali, and she nods rapidly. He grabs his keys and takes off. I see him talking to Adam outside, then Adam gets in Jaeger's car and they drive off.

The next thing I know, Mira is beside me, holding me up. "Hayden, oh my gosh. I'm such an asshole. I'm so sorry. The police told us everything Jeb's friend recorded in the suite and how it all went down. I thought Adam protecting you tonight was beautiful—I didn't mean for it to come out like that."

She hands me a tissue and I wipe my nose. "It's not your fault. He's not himself."

I explain about Adam's father and the room goes silent.

"You'll stay with me and Tyler," Mira says, and I nod. I want to be with Adam, supporting him, but he has it in his head that he can't trust me.

He. Doesn't. Trust. Me. Maybe he's grieving and acting erratically, but it doesn't change the result.

All this time, I waffled over whether or not to trust Adam, believing his omissions about Blue were damning. How did things come to this?

The one guy who knew me and stood by me—and I made it so that everything we'd shared was built on a lie. My lie.

I omitted what I knew about Blue. It was unintentional —I thought Adam had talked about the original suites with Tyler—but I held back by not openly discussing it. By protecting myself and my plans for turning Blue Casino around. I don't blame Adam for thinking I lied to him.

How can *he* ever trust *me*?

* * *

Adam

JAEG and I enter Hunt's small apartment with my key. Hunt is slumped over the kitchen table, his outstretched hand gripping a quarter bottle of Jack. "Got any for the rest of us?"

Hunt lifts his head. His eyes are bloodshot, his complexion pale. "Always," he slurs.

Jaeg rests his hand on my shoulder. "You think this is wise?"

Jules Barnard

I glare at his fingers, then his face. He drops his hand. "You don't need to worry about protecting her from me. I'm done with her."

"Who?" Hunt asks at the same time Jaeg sighs and says, "It's not her fault. You don't mean that."

I collapse into the chair opposite Hunt. "She used me. It's exactly her fault. Don't know why I thought she'd be different."

"Don't be a hypocrite, Adam. You never thought about something casual with Hayden? In the beginning, before you were invested?"

I blink at Jaeg. I can't process what the hell he's trying to say to me. So I keep it simple. Everyone leaves. Hayden betrayed me. I leave her before she leaves me. "She's just like the others. They all want something."

I snort. That's exactly what Paul said about women. Great, now I'm quoting douchebags. I need a drink.

Hayden didn't want me to provide for her like the other women I dated. She wanted something altogether bigger. She wanted to use me to make her past right.

I trusted her—*cared* for her. More than I've cared for any woman. And she used me. "I was an idiot. I know when the writing is on the wall. I invented the writing."

Jaeg sighs again. "Hayden isn't like that."

"This about that girl you've been spending time with?" Hunt's voice sounds clearer by the minute. I grab the finger-marked glass on the table and reach for the bottle of Jack. "Dump her," he says. "You don't need that baggage."

I slam my fist on the table and Hunt flinches. "She's not baggage."

She's out, but that doesn't mean I'll let my brother, or anyone else, badmouth her.

Jaeg leans forward on the table. "Don't do this, man.

Your brother just gave you the advice you gave me in high school—do you remember? Things worked out for me in the end, but in this case you're wrong. Don't lose the girl."

I stare at the amber liquid in my hand. "There is no girl," I mutter, and take a swig. The liquor burns down my throat, warming the patch of ice that formed over my heart the moment I walked away from Hayden.

Chapter Forty

Hayden

I return to work Monday, and it's as if nothing happened Saturday night—no celebrity auction, no police raids. All traces of the burlesque show and the celebrities are gone, the casino floor buzzing and chiming away. Business as usual. Except on the executive floor. Up here, we're missing a few key players.

Blackwell and the Blue Stars are nowhere to be found, not that we need them to run the place. Blackwell made the big decisions, but those don't occur every day. The casino will be fine until an interim CEO takes his place. Some of the Blue Stars were managers, but somehow they mostly worked on Bliss and Blackwell's special projects—all of which have been put on hold. The only Blue Star manager who actually performed his job was Adam. Adam runs hospitality, and he hasn't shown up today. He also didn't return my calls yesterday.

I spoke to Jaeger, and he told me to give Adam time. That he'd come around. But I'm not so sure.

Without meaning to, Mira said the one thing while Adam was most vulnerable that could push him away for good. She implied I'd used him to get close to the Blue Stars. And I can't deny it, because it's true. The only difference is, somewhere along the way, I fell in love with Adam and completely forgot about my original intentions. But how do I explain it and have him believe me when I kept so much from him?

That seed of doubt about why our relationship began has burrowed in his head. Other women have used him, and I suspect that even his own father used him. Then everything happens on the day he loses his dad, a man whose love he wanted desperately? I don't know how to get through to Adam after all that.

He said that he and his brothers weren't close to their father. That Ethan Cade didn't care about them. But I've never seen a group of strong men look more stricken and vulnerable than when they learned of their father's passing.

"Hayden," Mira says, and I look up. "Go home."

I stare at the stack of papers on my desk.

I toss scissors, pencils, and about twenty notepads in my desk drawers, trying to clean it up. Then hand the pile of papers to Mira. "Will you—"

"I'll go through them," she says.

I have the sudden urge to clear all of this crap away. I was covered in filth with Blackwell in charge, tainted by dirty power and evil intentions. I wanted to make this place better. But maybe it wasn't this place. It was my past I needed to accept.

Mira looks at me nervously. "Do you want me to call anyone?"

"No. I know who I need to see."

* * *

I PULL up to Adam's house half expecting him to be away, but both of his cars are in the driveway. No security detail, I note. I imagine he doesn't need it now that Blackwell has been arrested and held without bail.

None of the documentation the police retrieved pointed to Blackwell. Had he kept to his typical practice of not attending casino events, he might have been able to blame the sex trafficking and drugs that would be brought into the casino on someone else, the way he blamed past illegal activities on Drake Peterson. But Blackwell was arrogant and proud of Bliss, so he attended the grand opening and directly implicated himself.

From what I've heard, the police have everything they need to lock Blackwell up, along with the Blue bodyguards who hid the women away in the apartment. Technically, nothing illegal occurred at the casino; there wasn't time. But between the recorded conversation from Jeb's friend and the raid on the women's home, the police had everything they needed to press charges against Blackwell and many others. The detectives said there is even evidence against De la Cruz—Blackwell's confidant and godfather—which they'd been trying to obtain for over a decade.

I'm told we don't need to worry about retaliation by De la Cruz. The only person who should be afraid is Blackwell. Apparently, Blackwell and the guards he had Adam hire possessed enough information on the drug and human-trafficking business De la Cruz ran to lock the man up for several lifetimes. Full-time guards are protecting Blackwell in prison until the trial. De la Cruz is powerful, and there's a risk to Blackwell's life even in custody.

I knock on Adam's front door. Birds chirp in the pine

trees off to the right, and the faint sound of the lake washing against the shore sounds in the distance. It's so peaceful, yet my palms are sweating.

Adam opens the door. He's in jeans and a T-shirt, his hair uncombed—and I want nothing more than for him to hold me. But his stoic expression suggests that won't be happening. "This isn't a good time."

"When would be a good time? I need to talk to you."

He leans his hand against the doorframe, glowering down at me. "So that you can use me for more information?"

I wet my lips. "You're right. I did that. But it was before I knew you."

"And that should matter? Whatever we had is based on a lie."

"That's not true," I say firmly. My gaze flickers past him into the room. "May I?"

After a heated beat, he drops his arm and opens the door. I walk no farther than the entry. No matter what I say, this has to come from him. He needs to decide. But that doesn't mean I won't try and convince him of the truth. "I know what you're doing."

He raises his eyebrows, his shoulders taut and unyielding. "Came here to yell at me? You're wasting your breath."

The cold Adam is back. The guy who wants no one to know how he truly feels.

I step closer. "Really? Because you made one miscalculation. You showed me who you are. Not the cold, unaffected rich boy, but the warm man who'd do anything for the people in his life."

He shakes his head and crosses his arms, throwing up a physical block, along with the emotional. "You don't know me."

"In the beginning, part of my reason for getting to know you was to see if what Mira and Tyler had discovered about Blue was still going on. That meant getting close to someone involved with Blackwell's Blue Stars. I didn't want to know you. I didn't like you."

"You're not making a case for yourself," he says dryly.

I let out a shaky breath. None of this is coming out right.

"Don't you see? I was wrong. And I think a part of me—the part that's all heart and no head—knew I was wrong about you. You're the son who stood beside his father, no matter how badly Ethan Cade ran the household. You're the brother who keeps the family together when the others aren't talking with one another. The clotheshorse"—my voice cracks, but I can't stop, the words pouring out of me—"who uses one-tenth of the closet so that his girlfriend can have the rest for her insane shoe collection."

Tears are streaming down my face, and I don't even care. "And you're the guy who pushes everyone away when they get too close. Because to be close is to lose them. Just like you lost your mother. Just like you lost your father. But you don't have to lose your brothers—or me."

His chest rises and falls rapidly, his face red. "Are you finished?"

"I don't know." I swallow. "Am I?"

Adam stalks toward me, stopping inches away. "All that matters is that *I* am finished. With you."

I wipe my face. "Of course you are." I take a shaky breath and walk to the door. I look over my shoulder. "But you know what? I know you. So live with that, Adam Cade. There's someone out there who's seen you, who loves you, and who knows why you pushed her away."

Chapter Forty-One

Adam

I blow sawdust off the wood I'm cutting in Jaeg's workroom, and toss back a bottle of water, feeling the cool liquid slide down my throat. I've been bent over for hours, focused on my project, where my mind won't wander. Being in town with memories of my father, Hayden—it's getting to me. I'm considering leaving. Starting fresh somewhere else. Maybe New York. I'd miss my shit-head brothers, but I don't know what else to do. I can't stay in this town.

"Hold the brace," Jaeg says to Tyler, who came over to help him put together a giant trellis he's been working on for the last several weeks. He's incorporated one of Cali's designs into it, and the end result is pretty amazing. A log across the top has a doe and buck standing together, heads touching. Shapes and spirals form down the legs of the trellis, creating a forest scene.

"What's that for?" I say.

Tyler glances at Jaeg, and Jaeg pats the base. "Engagement trellis."

I shouldn't have asked. The last thing I want to think about is someone getting married.

It's been a week since the Bliss opening. A week since my father passed and the private funeral that followed shortly after. And five days, three hours, and twenty-one minutes since I threw Hayden out of my house.

I pick up the paint for the birdhouse and focus on my project.

"So what do you think?" Jaeg asks.

I look over. He said something before that, but I was caught up in my thoughts. "About what?"

"Cali has a friend of a friend. We thought we'd set you up."

"Are you fucking kidding me? Where the hell is this coming from?"

Jaeg snorts, and Tyler hands over a fiver. "That's what I thought," Jaeg mumbles.

They're placing bets on me now? Insensitive assholes. "I'm not interested," I growl.

Jaeg balls a cloth and throws it on my table. "Before Hayden, you would have been interested in going out with someone new after a breakup." He paces closer and shakes his head. "You've turned your back on Hayden. Didn't think you'd do it. With the others—oh, every time. But not Hayden." Jaeg turns and stalks out of the workroom.

I stare after him. "What's his problem?"

Tyler shakes his head slowly, as if he can't believe me either. He leaves the same way.

I set the paint down and stare at the birdhouse I'm building. I can't look at myself in the mirror. Now my friends can't look at me either?

Moving to a new location isn't the solution, because I'll still have to live with myself. I'm no longer sure of the conclusions I drew about Hayden. I was vulnerable, scared —though I don't like to admit it. I freaked the fuck out and made a rash accusation.

Time to man up.

* * *

Hayden

I HAVEN'T SPOKEN to Adam since I went to his house. He hasn't called, and I've stopped calling him. I've wanted to, but I said everything there was to say, and if he hasn't changed his mind after that, he won't.

I told him I loved him. And he let me walk out the door. I'm beyond sad. I'm numb.

I thought... I don't know what I thought. That he'd come around? That he'd forgive me. But had I forgiven him? I was so hard on him about Bliss, and the whole time, he was just as unhappy with what was going on as I. He even sought help and put a stop to what Blackwell was doing. *Adam* did that, not me.

I put all of my energy these last few months into investigating Blackwell after I realized he'd hired me for the casino's image, and after I learned what had happened to my friends. I wasn't letting Blackwell and the others get away with that, oh no. I had to fight for the underdog.

What the hell was I thinking?

I was single-minded, stubborn—whatever you want to call it. And now I wish I could take it all back, because I lost Adam. And nothing in this world is worth that.

Adam is a total stubborn ass, but he is a good man. The best.

Tears well up behind my eyes and I growl. "Dammit." I set aside my laptop and walk into the kitchen, reaching for a tissue. A shadow on the back patio catches my eye.

"What the hell?" I swipe my cheeks and toss the tissue in the trash, my heart thundering in my chest. There's someone out there...

I reach for a knife in one of the drawers—then slowly set it back down. Wait a minute. I know the back of that head, the shape of those shoulders.

Striding to the back door, I swing it open and gape at Adam. His arm is raised and he has a hammer in his hand. "I get that you're mad at me, but don't you dare make a hole in my wall."

He cuts me a challenging look, cocks the hammer back, and slams it home—straight into a nail.

I step outside. "*Hello?* You want to tell me what you're doing?"

He ignores me, damn him, and picks up a wooden box. No. Not a wooden box. A birdhouse. A pretty one, actually. He places the birdhouse on the nail, straightens it, and tucks the hammer through one of the belt loops in his jeans. He turns to me.

And oh my God, I've missed him. His face, his rough but gentle hands. "You shouldn't come any closer," I say.

I don't know what I'll do, but I'm pretty sure it will consist of me plastering myself to him if he's not careful, and that would be humiliating. A girl can only take so much rejection. He brought me a birdhouse, but that doesn't mean he wants to get back together. It could be an apology for the way he talked to me the last time we spoke.

His jaw sets. "You're still my girlfriend."

I gape. *What the...* Is he serious? "Says who?" I mean, this is what I want, but he's lost his damn mind. We broke up. He's not making sense.

Adam scrubs his face, then steps closer. "You're not going to make this easy, are you?"

"Make what easy?"

He takes another step, until our toes are practically touching and I'm forced to look up. For a moment, he doesn't say anything. His gaze tracks my eyes, my mouth—back to my eyes again. "You were right. After my father... I couldn't lose you too."

I press my lips together and let out a slow, hopeful breath. It's not just an apology. It's more. "You won't."

"I lose everyone I care about."

So honest, and it breaks my heart. "You won't lose me."

His arms come around me. "I don't know that." I start to pull away to argue with him, but he doesn't let me. "Though I won't let it stop me from being with you. I'm going to do everything I can to make you happy, because I don't want a life without you." He pulls back just enough to look down at me. "I love you."

I'm stunned for all of two seconds, then I reach up and drag his head down until my mouth is on his, taking what I've been starving for. "I missed you," I say between kisses. "You scared the hell out of me." More kissing. "Don't ever do that to me again." More lip-lock, but this time, he tilts my head and his tongue dives inside. He picks me up with one arm under my ass and throws the door open, entering the house, moving in the direction of my bedroom.

I pull my mouth away and hold his head between my hands. "Don't you dare leave me like that again."

"Never." He drags my head back to his mouth.

Adam opens the door to my bedroom and enters. "No

more working apart," I say as he crosses the room. "We're a team from now on. Agreed?"

"Team," he says, and tosses me on the bed, following closely on top of me.

"That means trusting," I point out. "Both of us."

"Got it," he murmurs, kissing my neck and the tops of my breasts.

"Adam." I wrench his face up, my hands on either side of his face again. "Are you listening?"

He grabs one of my hands and kisses the palm. "Yes." Then the other hand and kisses it too. "I am here for you. Always. No more dick maneuvers and pushing you away. In my adolescent, hormone-stricken brain, I think I fell in love with you the first time I noticed you on the steps of our high school."

"You did?" I choke. Damn tears, clogging my throat.

"Or maybe it was the moment I saw your ass in the air inside your office that first day at Blue?"

I smack his chest. "This is a serious moment!"

Grinning, he ducks his head and kisses my mouth. "It is serious. Everything I've said is true. I'm not leaving you. Honestly, it was probably more punishment for me than it was for you. I damn near left town because I couldn't stop thinking about you. Being close and not with you was killing me. Give me another chance?"

"If you'll give me another. I was stubborn. I'm so sorry for not trusting you."

He rolls his eyes.

"What?"

"You are stubborn. I don't expect that to change. I like your stubborn side. Keeps me on my toes. Speaking of..." He reaches down and tickles my feet, sliding his hand up my leg. "You have on far too many clothes."

"Really? I was rather comfortable," I say, pretending I didn't catch his innuendo.

"Oh no. You're going to be too hot in just a moment."

His hand dips between my thighs and his mouth covers my nipple through my shirt, which he found blind through my top, homing in on it perfectly. I moan lightly. "You're right. It's too hot. You'd better take off all your clothes too."

He chuckles and starts ditching his shirt. I get distracted by his chest. "Wait. Too fast," I say with a smile, as I run my hands all over his stomach and chest and arms.

"Nope." He yanks at my pants. "Have you any idea how long it's been since we've—" He waggles his eyebrows.

"I think I have some idea. Someone decided we needed to abstain," I say pertly.

He unhooks my bra. "That man should be shot."

"Eh, I'll keep him around. He has his uses." I palm his erection, get frustrated with the jeans he's wearing—with the hammer still tucked through a belt loop, getting all up in my business—and scramble to the bottom of the bed to tug them off.

I drop the hammer on the floor. I like his tools, but that's not the one I'm interested in right now.

"While you're down there," he says, on his back now, his arms crossed beneath his head, "might as well slip off your pants too."

"Is that how it's going to be?" I grab a condom from the econo-sized stash Adam bought weeks ago.

He shrugs.

I slip off my top—because apparently that wasn't as important as unhooking my bra to him—kick off my jeans and underwear, and climb up his body.

"Shit," he breathes. "That's the sexiest image."

I rub his erection, which is straining for his belly button, and pull it back until it's upright. I slide the condom on. Adam's eyes widen and he grips my hips. I lift up and glide down, until I'm fully seated with him inside me.

Adam's head drops back. "Fuck."

I brace my hands on his shoulders and circle my hips, sliding up and down in slow movements. "This what you wanted? For me to do all the work?"

His face is strained. He flips me over. "Not today. Been too long." And then he's rocking into me, his hand on my breast, the other hand cradling the side of my face as his body hits all the places shouting their approval, having sorely missed his presence.

My orgasm doesn't roll over me; it hits me like a thunderbolt. I scream, gasping for air.

When my head finally returns to Earth, I notice beads of sweat dotting Adam's forehead, his chest glistening. He flips me over so that I'm on top again, and bucks into me, gripping my hips, stomach muscles clenched and ripped.

A groan tears from his throat. His pace slows, becomes unsteady.

He flattens his hand on my back and folds me to his chest, pressing soft kisses to my face. We roll to the side and stare into each other's eyes.

I've missed this—just this.

After a few minutes, reality sets in and I realize I need to use the bathroom. When I crawl back in bed again, Adam pulls the bedspread over me. "I'll be bunking here for a while. Hope that's okay? My house sucks without you in it."

I grin and wrap my arms around him. "My place doesn't feel like home without your suits taking up all the shoe space."

He grins and closes his eyes. "Then it's settled. I'm staying."

Chapter Forty-Two

Adam

Six Weeks Later

Hayden glances over from the passenger seat of my boat. "Are you sure it's safe to go out at night?"

"That's what boat lights are for."

"But they're so tiny."

I grin. "It's a big lake, Hayden, and it's late. I doubt we'll pass anyone."

She sits forward, scanning the dark water. "Okay, I trust you." She doesn't sound confident.

I laugh. "You sure?"

She looks over again. "What? I trust you." I wink, because I know she does. My girlfriend just has trouble not being in charge. It's a good thing I'm a strong man and can handle her.

Of course, I don't tell her that or she'd kick my ass.

I stop the boat a little way offshore and cut the engine. "Where are those blankets you carried down?"

She stands and reaches toward the bow seats, and I grab her ass. She looks back. "That was sneaky."

I shrug. "You know how I operate. You put that in my face and it gets fondled."

She shoves the blankets at me and I chuckle. "Sit in your seat for a minute."

"Why?" she asks suspiciously.

"Where's the trust, my love?" She growls, and I spread out thick blankets on the floor of the back of the boat, smiling. I grab the pillow I remembered for the makeshift bed and lie down. I pat the covers. "Join me?"

She crawls over. "What are you up to?"

"I thought we could lie under the stars in the middle of the lake."

She snuggles up and I cover her with one of the blankets. "Actually, that's kind of romantic."

We look up at the stars for a moment, my hand lazily rubbing her arm. It's all for show. I'm a nervous wreck inside. "I spoke to Levi."

"Oh?" She plasters her cold nose to my neck and nuzzles me.

"My father's will was read a while back. I didn't go. Couldn't... Well, anyway, I wasn't in any shape to see people. Levi said my father left something for me. I picked up the item a couple of weeks ago, but I wanted to wait until tonight to tell you about it."

She scoots back to look at me. "Is everything okay?"

"Yeah. Everything is perfect. Well, not perfect—we're not perfect people and we'll drive each other crazy from time to time." Now I'm rambling. *Great job, Cade.* "What I'm trying to say is that you're perfect for me and I love you. I can't imagine life without you, and I'm tired of running back and forth to pick up clothes from my place."

"So...you want to live together?"

"Yes, that, but—Hayden—" I swallow. Jesus Christ, why is this so hard? "I want to marry you. I—I love you, and I want to marry you. Will you be my wife?"

She's silent. And not moving.

"Hayden?" I lean in until our noses touch. It's fucking dark, and I can barely see her eyes, but I think she's crying. "We can wait. There's no rush—" She launches on me, squeezing the air from my lungs. "Is that a yes?"

"I love you," she says breathily, as if she's run a mile. "Yes."

I hold her tight, so grateful for my father right now. Had I not done what he said and taken that job at Blue, I might not have gotten the opportunity to know Hayden. We might have run into each other, since we have mutual friends, but it wouldn't have been the same. I wouldn't have seen her daily, had the chance to annoy the crap out of her until she was forced to succumb to my charm. Bottom line: I have a lot to be thankful for. My father, my mother, my brothers, and this woman in my arms.

I roll her to the side and dig in my pocket. "You don't have to wear it as your engagement ring. I can buy you another, but this was in the will. My father said that my mother wanted me to have it."

I hold up the ring that's set with a clear, cushion-cut diamond with smaller diamonds surrounding it. It's pretty, but I don't know much about this stuff, and I want Hayden to love whatever ring she wears.

Her lips press together, and this time I'm certain tears roll down her cheeks. I should have brought a lantern, dammit. "It's the most beautiful thing I've ever seen." Her voice catches and she slides the ring on her left ring finger. "Don't you dare try and replace it. I love it."

I pull her close and hold up her hand. And for a moment, I remember this ring. The way it sparkled on my mother's hand. She used to let me spin it around on her finger.

I look into Hayden's eyes. "I'm about to say something corny, so brace yourself." I take a deep breath and blink back the emotion threatening to steal my man card. "I've never been happier in my life than in this moment, and the last top five have featured you naked, so you can imagine the heights this one had to climb." She grins, and this one I can see, because it beams out from within. "Thank you for never letting me get away with anything, and for loving me even when I'm being a jackass. I'll always be here for you—I'll always be fighting for you."

I kiss her, and I swear the light that shines through her smile radiates into the kiss, warming my body and the heart I once thought had frozen over for good.

Epilogue

Adam

"You've got this," I tell Jaeg.

He looks like he's about to pass out. What happens when a six-foot-six, two-hundred-thirty-pound man falls in the forest? Does he make a sound?

Jaeg gulps and touches his tie. "You sure I don't look like a tool?"

"Of course you do, but that's the point. That's why it's called a grand gesture."

Jaeg's face turns white. "I think I'm going to puke."

"Don't puke. It will kill the romantic vibe. Pull it together, man."

Loud yapping sounds come from behind, and we both turn. A little brown wiener dog defies gravity and his size and launches four feet toward Jaeg's crotch. I flinch.

Jaeg catches the dog with crazy small-dog-catching agility. "Hey, Buddy," he coos in the girly voice he uses when he's talking to his and Cali's dog-child. "How's my little guy?"

"Jaeg. They'll be here soon."

Jaeger straightens and clears his throat. "Right. Here, take Buddy." He hands me the dog, and the little guy nearly squirms out of my arms. "Hold him tight. Cali will kill me if anything happens to him."

I roll my eyes. *Jaeg* would break my arm if anything happened to the dog. "They're coming. Pull it together."

Jaeg jogs in place, the light gray suit I helped him pick out straining at his he-man muscles.

"Simmer before you split a seam," I tell him.

He shakes out his arms and takes a deep breath. "I'm ready. Go hide somewhere before she sees you."

The plan is to get Cali into the middle of the forest where Jaeg had me and the other guys haul his one-thousand-pound manmade wood trellis. I might have pulled a hammy—that son of a bitch was heavy. Jaeg's been working on the trellis for months, but he only just told Tyler and me and the other guys his plans for it.

"Buddy!" I hear Cali call. I make a run for it into the woods, holding the dog like a football.

I duck behind a boulder where Hayden and the rest of the gang are waiting and spying. Hayden kisses my cheek and coos quietly at Buddy. We watch as Cali walks up the path with Gen.

Cali's jaw drops when she sees him. "Jaeger?"

Gen sneaks off toward us while Cali is distracted, taking in Jaeg and the trellis.

Jaeg gets down on one knee and Hayden squeezes the hell out of my arm, beaming beside me. "Oh my God," she mouths.

"Cali," we hear Jaeg's deep, rumbly voice say. "You are the fire, the heart, the soul in my life. I didn't know how deeply I could love someone until I met you. Will you be my wife?"

A man of few words, but it works.

Cali climbs on Jaeg's lap, straddling him, and he braces a hand on the ground before they fall over. None of us can hear anything that's being said, but I suspect it's a bunch of lip-smacking sounds anyway.

Jaeg pulls out a box and flips the top. Cali stares inside, and this time they do go down. Jaeg is flat on his back in his Gucci three-piece suit, and Cali is kissing the hell out of him.

"Maybe we should give them some alone time," I suggest.

Lewis, Tyler, Zach, and the girls all nod, and we sneak away with smiles on our faces. We head down a separate path that offers glimpses of the lake, and I pull Hayden close, Buddy in my other arm as I stare out at the water. Lake Tahoe is clear in the shallows but dark blue in the depths, and it brought all of us together. Like the lake, there is more to this town than what you see on the surface. Facets exist both good and bad, and I wouldn't change any of it, because the challenges we've faced have made us who we are.

I look down at Hayden and kiss her, thankful every day that she gave me a chance—and looked beneath the surface.

Thank you so much for reading the Never Date series! If you have a moment, I would LOVE it if you left a review for any or all of the books in the series, good or bad.

What's next?

Make the Cade Brothers your next read!

Don't miss the spin-off to the Never Date series, the Cade Brothers. First up in the Cade Brothers is ***TEMPTING LEVI*** about Adam's firefighter older brother.

Grab TEMPTING LEVI Now!

Tempting Levi

Off-limits never looked so tempting.

Levi Cade's firefighting career burned up after an accident on the job. Then is father died and left him in charge of the family's multimillion-dollar resort. Now he's forced to work with financially uptight advisors telling him what to do, and he needs someone he can trust at his side.

The perfect candidate walks through the door in a pencil skirt, fitted white blouse, and a mass of wavy blond hair she tries to contain.

The only problem?

She's his cheating ex's younger sister.

Hell no. The last thing Levi needs is another Wright female in his life.

Then again, he always liked playing with fire...

★*USA TODAY* BESTSELLER★

EXCERPT:

"My scar looks hot, does it?" he said.

She laughed as he peppered her skin with light kisses. "Very hot."

"Don't give me ideas Emily, or I won't let you go home."

Grab TEMPTING LEVI Now!

Also by Jules Barnard
USA Today Bestselling Author

All's Fair

Landlord Wars

Roommate Wars

Never Date Series

Never Date Your Brother's Best Friend (Book 1)

Never Date A Player (Book 2)

Never Date Your Ex (Book 3)

Never Date Your Best Friend (Book 4)

Never Date Your Enemy (Book 5)

Cade Brothers Series

Tempting Levi (Book 1)

Daring Wes (Book 2)

Seducing Bran (Book 3)

Reforming Hunt (Book 4)

About the Author

Jules Barnard is a *USA Today* bestselling author of romantic comedy and romantic fantasy. Her romantic comedies include the All's Fair, Never Date, and Cade Brothers series. She also writes romantic fantasy under J. Barnard in the Halven Rising series *Library Journal* calls "...an exciting new fantasy adventure." Whether she's writing about steamy men in Lake Tahoe or a Fae world embedded in a college campus, Jules spins addictive stories filled with heart and humor.

When she isn't in her sweatpants writing and rewarding herself with chocolate, Jules spends her time with her husband and two children in their small hometown in the Pacific Northwest. She credits herself with the ability to read while running on the treadmill or burning dinner.

Stay informed! Join Jules's newsletter for writing updates and bonus scenes: